FIREBIRD

Peter Morwood

A LEGEND BOOK

Arrow Books Limited
20 Vauxhall Bridge Road, London SW1V 2SA

An imprint of Random House UK Limited

London Melbourne Sydney Auckland
Johannesburg and agencies throughout
the world

This Legend Paperback Edition 1993

1 3 5 7 9 10 8 6 4 2

Printed and bound in Great Britain by
Cox & Wyman Ltd, Reading, Berkshire

ISBN 0 09 919981 5

To Terry Pratchett
for singing horses and other matters

Chapter One

The window was three times as tall as a man, and all there would have been to see beyond it was the forest of the Polish–Prussian border, shading from dark green down to black as the autumn evening shadows slid across it. But no man, not even the man standing right in front of it, could see through its glass, for each small piece was stained and patterned so that the whole huge window formed – from a distance – the picture of St Mary the Virgin, blue-robed and gently benevolent as any image in a great cathedral. Beyond that serene figure was a deep, chill moat, and open ground where the forest had been cleared for a distance of two bowshots so that no attacker could creep in without being seen by the sentries who constantly walked the ramparts. This was no cathedral, despite the presence of crucifixes, holy relics and the image of the Blessed Virgin. No cathedral ever built had walls twelve feet thick and pierced with arrow-loops, nor iron shutters that could be closed across its stained-glass windows. Nor, whatever their thickness, were the walls of cathedrals usually equipped with racks of spears and javelins alongside their fonts of holy water, with cocked and loaded crossbows forming other and more sinister cruciforms than even the many repeated images of carven Roman gallows and their tormented, spear-pierced, thorn-crowned burdens.

The man by the window stared out through cobalt-blue glass at the blue-tinged cold darkness beyond the walls and the window, and despite the warmth of open hearths and charcoal-laden braziers within, he shuddered. Albrecht von Düsberg had started out short and burly and had become stout, with the well-padded waist and cheerful round features of a man with more than a passing fondness for cup and platter. Even though such fondness had given him a somewhat florid complexion, it had at least faded from the peeling brick-red which had been his sole memento of service in Jerusalem as a knight of the Teutonic Order. His well-fed frame was topped by thinning sandy hair, cut so that the

1

advance of a lamentable early baldness might seem more like a monastic tonsure, and what with one thing and another he was entirely ordinary in both appearance and in reputation. However, it seemed that not everyone thought him so ordinary, for at the command of his overlord the Grand Master of the Order he had travelled many leagues to be here, all of them against his will – and despite the hospitality of his greeting, he could not help but wonder why.

Albrecht had been most comfortably ensconced in the palace library of His Eminence Joachim, Cardinal-Archbishop of Salzburg – a man coincidentally his cousin once-removed on the paternal side – and had for the most part forgotten the heat and the flies and the Saracens of Palestine. He had always taken care to maintain a sufficient level of work – in this instance, cataloguing and annotating the contents of the Cardinal-Archbishop's library – so that no-one could label him a slacker. At the same time, having heard nothing from the upper hierarchy of the Order in a comfortably long time, he was more than willing that they should think him dead, crippled or mad, as so many of his brethren had become during the long campaigns to wrest the Holy Land from the hands of the infidel. Certainly, correcting that assumption would neither be a kindness to them nor in his own best interests.

He had, in his own opinion, worn armour for quite long enough, and to no good purpose save that of working indelible rust-stains into some of his better clothes. Rather than mail, Albrecht had now taken to wearing the white mantle of the Cistercians over any other garment, in the quiet hope that any who might see him would presume that he had reverted entirely from military to holy orders. It had worked almost completely. But only almost. Grand Master von Salza's letter of summons had made that quite clear.

Click. The sound of a chess-piece being shifted was surprisingly loud in the echoing quiet of the great hall, but scarcely surprising since the piece itself was of polished iron almost a handspan tall, and it was being moved across a board whose alternating squares were made of appropriately coloured marble.

'Your move, Albrecht.'

Von Düsberg twitched slightly, dragging his thoughts back to the here and now. He turned from the window – which, like himself, had come originally from the Holy Land, although the

2

window had travelled by a more direct and better-escorted route – and gazed with what he hoped was nothing more obvious than a player's mild interest at the chessboard, then shrugged a shrug made more ostentatious than he had intended by the heavy robes he wore. '*Ja, danke, Herr Hochmeister*. My move. But not just yet. Allow me to consider what few options remain. A drink, perhaps?'

'Of course.' There was a soft chuckle. 'But since I think . . . Yes, I do. I have you beaten already, so there's little advantage to be gained in trying to fuddle me with wine at this late stage. Let me do the honours.'

Clink. This time the sound was of a jug's metal lid being raised and then lowered again after the blood-red wine poured with a musical chuckling into cups of horn. Those cups were the only truly simple things on the entire table, for despite the studied simplicity of everything else, chessboard, chessmen, players and all, a careful rather than a casual look would have seen that each of them bespoke a level of wealth that could only masquerade as poverty. That everything had an appearance of poorness and simplicity was more than sufficient for the two men in the hall and the others like them, and that efforts were made to preserve such an appearance was enough for their patrons and supporters alike.

The Order of Knights of the Hospital Church of St Mary the Virgin of the House of Teutons in Jerusalem had long since concluded that they could be pious or powerful, but not both, and the results of some long-dead Grand Master's decision glittered up and down the walls of *Schloss* Thorn. Sometime during the making of that decision the Grand Master had also abandoned the Order's wordy title for all except documentary use, and from that day onward the brethren of the black cross had been known to Christendom as the Teutonic Knights.

'Albrecht,' said the present *Hochmeister* gently, 'delay is pointless. Make your move.'

Albrecht von Düsberg glanced first at the Grand Master, then at the chessboard. Hermann von Salza had that effect on people, noblemen and commoners alike. Most Germans who had spent four years on crusade against the Infidel were lean and scarred, their pale Northern skins scorched beyond recovery by the desert sun. Von Salza, however, always looked as if he had never seen any climate fiercer than summer along the Rhine. Born into one of the wealthiest families of the Empire, he was everything that Albrecht was not: tall, tanned, handsome, his hair silvering elegantly at the temples rather than falling out. Even though his honey-gold skin was wrinkled at brows and eyes and mouth, the lines seemed more those of laughter than of time and long hot days of squinting against the sun of Palestine. He was as clean-shaven now as he had always appeared in the Holy Land, despite a ruling that members of the military orders serving there should at least wear unkempt pilgrim beards as an outward sign that they cared more for holiness than for appearance. Albrecht could not imagine anyone daring to enforce such a ruling on *Hochmeister* von Salza, who had probably never been unkempt in his life.

He looked even more splendid than von Düsberg remembered him. Hermann von Salza was wearing what appeared at first glance to be the white Cistercian mantle of the Order, a garment that in accordance with a knight-brother's vows of poverty and in imitation of the Shroud of Our Lord, was usually made of common, and by accepted custom, ostentatiously dirty linen. The Grand Master, as Albrecht had expected, wore nothing so plain; though it was only when he moved, and the candlelight reflected from the surface of the fabric, that his own form of ostentation became plain. *His* mantle was woven of tissue of cloth-of-silver lined with Chinese silk, light as gossamer, white as virtue, and as costly as the favour of the Pope. Von Düsberg had been surprised to see that so marvellous a garment was dirty – until he got close enough for his nose to tell him that the token dust-marks were in fact rare, sweet Persian spices that had probably cost as much as every piece of clothing that he owned.

At first he had been scandalized, wondering how the wearing of such things accorded with vows of poverty, charity and obedience; then he dismissed the rest of the thought as irreverent, dangerous, and quite possibly heretical, and instead found himself wanting to smile at the stylish way in which they had been circumvented. Despite the evidence of vows that, if they hadn't exactly been broken, had at the very least been loosely interpreted, it could not be denied that von Salza looked appropriately noble and imposing; the way, indeed, that a Grand Master *should* look. He was dressed from head to heel in unrelieved white; even the cyclas,

4

hose and boots beneath his surcoat were of that colour. *Hochmeister* Hermann had his reasons for such splendour, and those reasons could not be questioned – at least, not by anyone living within the borders of the Holy Roman Empire who hoped to continue living at all.

The token that he was more than merely the Grand Master of a military Order – if such a rank was ever 'mere' – glittered on his breast and at the shoulder of his mantle, woven in threads of precious metal: *argent a cross potent sable, in fess an inescutcheon or, an eagle displayed sable.* They had begun as arms as simple as those of most crusader knights, a plain white shield marked with the black hammer-headed cross of the Order, such as von Düsberg wore himself; but where the arms of the cross met, at what the heralds called fess-point, there was another, smaller shield, this one emblazoned with an eagle, black on gold, and that was von Salza's alone. Emperor Friedrich II himself had awarded that sign of rank to the Grand Masters of the Teutonic Order, not two years past, along with the title of *Erzherzog* – Archduke or Prince of the Empire. Appropriate enough, some had said at the time, and quite in the tradition of any ancient and far less holy Roman Emperor ensuring the support of his Praetorian Guard. That Friedrich had since been excommunicated was neither here nor there; the Papal interdiction concerned other matters altogether.

Hermann von Salza wore that sign of the Emperor's favour as lightly and carelessly as he wore his own good looks, or as he might have worn a lady's colours in a tournament, had he troubled himself to frequent tournaments, which he did not, and if the Order's vows of chastity permitted him to consort with ladies, which *they* did not. It might have appeared that cities and thrones and powers concerned him as little as they should a knight whose sword and strength were dedicated to the service of God; but since he was also Grand Master of the Teutonic Order, his Treasurer Albrecht von Düsberg was expecting every minute to hear otherwise.

He spotted an amused twinkle in von Salza's blue eyes and blushed slightly at having been caught staring. Albrecht leaned over the chessboard and moved a piece, then took a quick swallow of wine to stifle the notions that always rose in his mind when he, a very small fish in a very large pond, thought too much about the

5

politics of the Empire. Albrecht had been doing a deal of that, these past few days. He had been doing it, in fact, since the Grand Master's summons dragged him from Salzburg right across what felt like all the principalities of Germany to this grim fortress on the Vistula.

'Albrecht, sit down.' Von Salza gestured towards the empty chair on the far side of the chess table. 'You may be saddle-sore and needing to ease the kinks out of your backbone, but all this pacing is beginning to make *me* weary. After we talk, you could always soak away your aches in a hot bath.'

Von Düsberg stared, slightly appalled at the prospect of such Eastern decadence having made its way into Germany. He had bathed at Michaelmas, and intended to do so again at the Feast of the Nativity – but certainly no sooner, especially if the weather remained cold. It was widely known that too much bathing weakened a man, and too much bathing in heated water provoked lechery. It was evident that the Grand Master had spent an excessive time consorting with the Pullani, the Saracen-influenced Franks who had lived too long in Palestine, and from them had picked up such heathenish notions. He stood lost in his own thoughts for several seconds, until von Salza lifted up one of the chessmen and rapped it briskly against the board. 'Hurry up, Albrecht,' he said. 'You can sleep later. Sit, sit, sit.'

Albrecht sat quickly, obediently, and rather harder than he had intended, with the inevitable result. He stifled a most unmonastic oath and dabbed ineffectually at the spreading cranberry-coloured stain of the red Ahrwein that had jolted in an elegant parabola out of his cup, wondering in vague annoyance why it was that he never seemed to splash himself with something relatively unnoticeable, like white wine or water, when he was wearing his Cistercian robes. Not that some of the water he had had to drink in Palestine would have stained any less, but there was a difference to be observed between the pious dirtiness that showed poverty and lack of pride, and the obvious marks of wine . . .

The mopping kerchief slowed, and then stopped entirely as von Düsberg tried to convince himself that he hadn't heard what the Grand Master had just asked. Unfortunately he had heard correctly, and to emphasize the point, *Hochmeister* von Salza asked it again.

'You were our treasurer in the Holy Land,' the Grand Master said. 'But you were more recently recommended to me as a scholar who was spending his time in surroundings somewhat, ah, closer to civilization than here. So tell me, *Fra Tressler* von Düsberg – what does Christendom currently say about sorcery?'

It was much to Albrecht von Düsberg's credit that when he echoed 'Sorcery?', it came out as a proper spoken word rather than the squeak of dismay it was trying to be. He blinked three times, very fast, in what seemed an effort to keep eyes that were somewhat prominent at the best of times from popping right out of their sockets, then said 'Sorcery?' again in a voice that he hoped sounded a good deal more controlled than it felt.

Von Salza looked speculatively at the chessboard and at the disposition of the pieces, then reached out with one long index finger and toppled von Düsberg's king. 'It would have been checkmate in two moves anyway,' he said, to forestall the protest that Albrecht had no intention of making, and set his elbows on the board – a casual, apparently careless gesture that still took pains to avoid any splashes of spilled wine. Hardly surprising, since he was wearing the value of half a fief. The Grand Master made a steeple of his interlaced fingers and rested his chin on their tips, then gazed levelly at his erstwhile opponent. 'You should know the meaning of the word, *Fra* Albrecht,' he said, very drily. 'Certainly you spend enough time in other people's libraries. Unless I was misinformed?'

Pinned by the consideration of those cool blue eyes, von Düsberg thought faster than he had done in his life. The approval – or lack of it – of the Church and its clergy where sorcery was concerned seemed to depend largely on the ability – or lack of it – of that same clergy in performance of the Art Magic. A priest capable of working healing-spells for the good of his congregation would be less inclined to denounce them as tricks of the devil, not merely for the good they plainly did, but also because doing so would be to call his own holiness into question. It became that much more significant when the priest involved was someone of rank: a Bishop, a Cardinal—

Or a Pope.

Innocent III had been interested in the Art Magic and, in a small way, had been a sorcerer of note, so much so that he had been

7

awarded another title to add to the many he already held: *Factor Labori Boni*, Doer of Good Works. The vagueness of that title had not gone without comment, even though nobody had been able to point out any spell performed by the Pontiff that had been anything other than good. That he was the same man who had ordered the butchery called the Albigensian Crusade also tended to discourage close investigation.

His successor Honorius had shared the interest, but not the ability. It was as if he had been like the old Emperor Charlemagne, who could converse in Latin as easily as in his own Frankish tongue, but who could never learn to read or write because his mind made no sense of what the letters meant. Honorius had that same difficulty, not with the words themselves, but with the power that could be released by the words of a spell. He had reacted in a manner that, though wrapped in churchly phrases, was simple envy of those more talented, and had placed the practice of sorcery under interdict on pain of excommunication or worse.

Pope Gregory, possessing the ability that Honorius had lacked, rescinded the decree within a year of his election; but he also instituted a new Office of the Church. It was called the Holy Inquisition. Those two developments tended to cancel one another out, except amongst the high and the mighty. Only the Knights Templar, protected by the unspoken but widely understood knowledge that they could buy and sell any Pope yet chosen, continued with their sorceries as they had even through Honorius's reign. Albrecht von Düsberg considered in his heart of hearts that the Templars had been most unwise, and would some day suffer for that display of arrogance. Personal insults were something that even Popes learned to live with, but insults to their office was something that the Curia would never forget.

The subject of sorcery was therefore a delicate one, and still much debated in ecclesiastical circles from the Pope himself on down. That it was debated did not make it any safer. Knowing too little, and thus displaying a heretical scepticism of matters held important by the highest and the wisest in the hierarchies of the Church, could be just as dangerous as knowing too much and thus displaying . . . only God and His angels knew what. 'About what aspect of sorcery, *Herr Hochmeister*?' That was as safe a response as any; answer a question with a question, and thus buy a little more time in which to think.

Grand Master Hermann looked surprised, and then faintly disgusted. 'Aspect?' He rolled his eyes, then muttered half to himself, 'I suppose someone in the Apostolic Chancellory must have decided the subject wasn't complicated enough.' He grinned crookedly, not much amused. 'How many aspects can there be? Or more correctly, how many has the Pope decided there should be?'

'Too many for convenient dissertation, Grand Master,' Albrecht began briskly, after a pause to marshal his somewhat rattled thoughts. 'And learned authorities remain divided even as to the exact number of such aspects, never mind their deeper nature.' He held up one hand and began ticking items off on his fingers. 'Among others, then, are the actual, the mythical, the Biblical, the ecclesiastical, the heretical, the Pontifical—'

'*Verdammt und verdammt nochmals!*' The oath was made far more startling by its source than by its intensity, which was nothing much. However, knights of religious orders – never mind their Grand Masters – were not supposed to curse at all. Yet Hermann von Salza didn't seem so much to be cursing, as groaning in rather theatrical dismay as he held his head in his hands. 'The Apostolic Chancellory indeed. It can't be anyone else. Only that collection of scribbling curates are so convinced that ten words are better than one.' He picked up his wine cup and stared at it, then looked over the rim at von Düsberg. 'And I suppose you think I should give myself a penance of some sort for swearing, eh?'

Albrecht said nothing; brethren of the Order might be equal in the eyes of God, but a treasurer did not make such suggestions to his feudal lord, not even one so amiable as this one. The Grand Master, however, had made up his own mind on the subject. He nodded sagely and set down the cup again, then crossed himself and said three Paters and Aves in the fast, practised Latin of one very accustomed to either prayer or penance. When he had finished, von Salza signed another cross over the wine cup, drained it, and then refilled both from the jug. 'Now. Where were we?'

Albrecht von Düsberg hesitated, staring at his own fingers, then raised his eyes enough to look the Grand Master full in the face.

9

He didn't trouble to conceal what he thought: that no matter what question he asked, von Salza would have made sure he knew every answer already. In knowledge lay power, and it behoved the Grand Master of the Teutonic Knights to be as powerful as he could legally become. The Order was nothing like so strong in brethren or wealthy in land as the older Templars and Hospitallers, and only connections, determination – and some other, more unusual abilities – had saved them from being swallowed up.

Hermann von Salza was also more than just another knightly monk: he was also, by the Emperor's own command, a Prince of the Holy Roman Empire, and a representative of that Empire's power in a wild country not long wrested from its even wilder original inhabitants. The heathen Prusiskai still dwelt in the shadows of the forest, and their tribal shamans were wielders of a wilder, fiercer magic than any ever countenanced by Holy Mother Church. Only their lack of organization, and the mailed knights of the black cross who opposed them, kept them from reclaiming the new lands of the Order for their own once more.

'The aspects of sorcery, Grand Master.'

'A good enough place as any to begin, I suppose.' Von Salza didn't sound particularly enthusiastic. 'It would appear that everything I thought I knew is probably out of date. Popes change, opinions change, and as I've said already' – again that engaging, crooked grin creased the skin around von Salza's eyes – 'neither Palestine nor Prussia is exactly at the centre of civilized, educated discussion. Nor, for that matter, are the lands and seas between. I have made that journey four times now, and I may assure you, it does not improve with repetition. I have heard little but rumour for the past two months, while you, my dear Treasurer, have travelled directly from Salzburg, with information that I trust is fairly fresh. Among the few things that I do know for certain is that His Eminence your cousin not only journeyed to Rome for the Papal election, but has been a frequent visitor to the Holy See ever since. So,' the *Hochmeister*'s voice dropped to a conspiratorial murmur and he leaned forward across the chessboard, looking not so much like the Grand Master of a military order as a man eager to hear another man's news, 'what has been happening in the world? You may begin with the matter of Magic,' he said generously. 'But don't stop there.'

Albrecht von Düsberg smiled weakly and swallowed down a throat gone so dry that not even another hasty mouthful of wine could help. Small wonder his mouth felt dry; in any discussion that involved both the Art Magic and the Vicar of Christ, there were too many chances for a thoughtless man to talk himself into excommunication. Only the Pope himself had the power to excommunicate a knight of the military orders, but that was not much of a consolation. Gregory IX had already shown himself notoriously short of temper, patience and Christian charity; if he was capable of excommunicating an Emperor, then doing the same to a mere knightly treasurer would hardly make him pause for breath.

'The Papal attitude to sorcery at present is a form of guarded approval, *Herr Hochmeister*, referring largely to the rulings of the Fourth Lateran Council. The infallibility of His Holiness Pope Innocent the Third has not yet been called into question on any of his proclaimed edicts, whether they concern the Art Magic or more secular matters. Despite that, several have been allowed to lapse from statute during the reign of Pope Honorius, and others have been amended.'

'Yes,' said von Salza. 'I should imagine so. Especially after that stupid business when the Italian Jews were ordered to wear red hats. Or has the whole incident already been officially forgotten?'

One of von Salza's infrequent visits to Rome had enabled him to witness the embarrassing encounter between an elderly and very short-sighted abbot and a Jewish merchant wearing the red hat that marked out his race. The abbot, not seeing the hat too clearly, had made a wrong assumption about what its colour signified. In plain sight of far too many people he had mistaken the Jew for a cardinal and dropped to one knee in an attempt to ask for a blessing. Hermann von Salza had been scandalized; he had also laughed so hard that his sides hurt . . .

'Not forgotten, Grand Master. Their hats are yellow now.'

'Just as well.'

'Jews living in Germany have been commanded to identify themselves by wearing a yellow badge—'

Von Salza grunted dismissively, and made hurry-up movements with one hand. 'Never mind that. What else?'

'The interdict of the Second Lateran Council concerning the use

11

of the crossbow or arbalest was confirmed under pain of anathema except against pagans, infidels or heretics, it being a weapon hateful to God and unfit for Christians—'

'An interdict,' said the Grand Master, 'that was both passed and confirmed by fat clergymen who've never been on the wrong side of a charge of mounted knights. I don't presume to speak for God.' He crossed himself, as did Albrecht, in hasty protection against such casual heresy. 'But it's certainly a weapon hateful to the enemy you shoot with it. Given how much was spent to equip this place' – von Salza gestured at the racks of crossbows all along the castle walls – 'you as Treasurer are probably glad that the Prussians have been declared pagan. Otherwise the Order would have wasted all that money, eh?'

'Yes, Grand Master . . . Er, His Grace Otto the Bishop of Riga called for the aid of crusaders against the obduracy and recusance of the pagan Livonians in their refusal to be made Christians . . .'

At mention of the Bishop of Riga, *Hochmeister* Hermann von Salza said nothing aloud, but smiled very slightly into his wine cup. That had been a master-stroke, more masterly still for having been arranged at fourth – or was it fifth? – hand. The number of removes did not matter; von Salza had reached all the way from Starkenberg in Palestine to the shores of the Baltic, and left no-one any the wiser. Livonia had been secured by the small Order of the Knights of the Sword, led by a Crusader named Dieter Balke. It was well known that in Palestine Balke had been Hermann von Salza's principal lieutenant and most sinister henchman, and he had evidently slipped far from his Grand Master's favour to be given so severe and dangerous a penance.

Neither the Sword Knights nor indeed his Grace the Bishop were yet aware that Hermann von Salza still held the *Landmeister*'s fealty – and by extension, he now also held the Knights of the Sword and all their lands along the Baltic. The Grand Master had decided to let the Hospitallers and the Templars squabble over possession of the Holy Land, as they had been doing for so long. Von Salza had concluded that the future power and profit of the Teutonic Order lay in northern and eastern Europe, where there were heathen tribes to conquer for the glory of God and new lands to conquer for the enrichment of the Order. And the fewer who knew about it, the fewer would want a share.

'. . . His Holiness preached a crusade against the Saracens of Egypt, so that by conquering them, Jerusalem might be restored—'

'As ransom, or reparation, or part of a peace settlement, rather than by conquest.' This time von Salza did not smile, but his voice stayed quiet, its tone neutral, making it impossible to tell whether the plan behind the crusade pleased him or not. 'Well, no doubt we'll see what the Emperor can do.'

'Now that he's finally been forced to do it,' said Albrecht without thinking, then blushed bright red and clapped his hand over his own traitor mouth.

Emperor Friedrich had taken his crusading vows at the Council, in the presence of the Pope and an array of high churchmen from all over Christendom – even from England, where King John had only recently submitted to the Papal will and been welcomed back into the bosom of Mother Church. The Emperor had knelt before them all, his hands between those of Innocent III, and had promised that with God's help, he would restore the Kingdom of Jerusalem. Twelve years of vacillation and two Popes later, Gregory IX had finally lost his temper, so infuriated by the Emperor's constant postponements of his crusade that he anathemized and excommunicated him. Friedrich had immediately set about keeping his long-delayed promise, thus providing both Christendom and Islam with the peculiar spectacle of a crusade led by an excommunicate.

'Yes, *Fra* Albrecht. Quite so.' The Grand Master gave no indication that he had heard anything seditious in his Treasurer's words. 'But from the rumours that I heard, there was another reason behind the excommunication. The Emperor's own excessive interest in sorcery, and his friendship with the wizard Michael Scot. Has the Bull *Vis Natura Potentissima* received imprimatur since Gregory took the diadem, or not?'

'Yes, Grand Master. It has.'

'Good. Very good.'

Von Düsberg looked quizzically at the *Hochmeister*, noting his satisfaction with the answer. 'That was all you wanted to hear?'

'Far from it. There are other matters.' Von Salza shook his head slightly. 'There are always other matters. But that Papal Bull tells me more about what His Holiness is really thinking than any

13

number of rumours. It has a deal of bearing on my future plans for the Order—'

His words stopped short as the double doors at the far end of the hall swung silently open and two men came in. They wore the tau-crossed grey surcoats of sergeant's rank over their mail, and carried a many-branched candlestick in each hand. It was only when this new candlelight pushed back the shadows that Albrecht von Düsberg realized just how very dark the great hall had become. His eyes had been deceived by the light from the sconces along the walls, and by the rich glow from the open hearths that kept the chill at bay. Now that the illumination had been proved inadequate, the heating suddenly seemed so as well, and as the great stone mass of Castle Thorn pressed down around him, he shivered so violently that his teeth chattered. One of the sergeants glanced at him curiously from beneath the brim of his *chapel-de-fer* helmet as he set his burden of candlesticks on a table, and without being asked, walked all around the fireplaces and stoked them with fresh wood. That done, both men bowed to their Grand Master and left as silently as they had come in.

'Sergeants doing servants' work?' Albrecht wondered aloud once the doors had closed. Von Salza nodded.

'Now that,' he said, 'sounded more like a treasurer than you've done all day. Next you'll wonder if the Order can't afford to pay for servants any more.'

That was not exactly what was passing through von Düsberg's head, but it was a shot close enough to the target that he looked curiously at the Grand Master and wondered if his interest in the Art Magic had perhaps something to do with mind-reading. 'I . . .' He pulled his mantle closer around his shoulders. 'Yes, Grand Master. And unless finances are much different here than they are in the Holy Land, it would not surprise me.'

Hermann von Salza's thin eyebrows went up. 'An honest Treasurer, at that,' he said approvingly. 'Brutally honest, and not particularly diplomatic.'

'Diplomacy – and ten bezants – will buy you a camel in the marketplace at Antioch, Grand Master. If you haggle.'

'Whereas brutality can be much more effective?'

Albrecht looked at the Grand Master and remembered some of the things he had seen done in the Holy Land. Some of them had been done by knights of his own Order, men like the now-*Landmeister* Dieter Balke. 'In the proper circumstances, Grand Master. The Order needs, and has always needed, more land, more revenue, and more brethren in Palestine, but since the Hospitallers and the Templars were there first, and love us no more than they love each other—' Albrecht shrugged, a gesture that said more than words about the situation he and von Salza knew only too well, and lifted the wine-flagon.

The *Hochmeister* waved it away, sat back in his chair and sipped wine, then set the cup down in the middle of the chessboard with a small, sharp click. 'When a wise man finds one market-stall empty, he goes to another. You've been very courteous, Albrecht. You haven't once let me see you wonder what brings you here to Prussia, or why the Grand Master of the Teutonic Knights isn't where he belongs, at Castle Starkenburg in the Holy Land.' He gave von Düsberg a quick, cold smile. 'I want you to help me value the stock of that other stall. Russia . . .'

Though the Teutonic Order might have been in financially straitened circumstances, there were still enough servants in Castle Thorn to come to the rescue of a knight who had managed to spill the contents of an entire wine-flagon all over himself. Albrecht von Düsberg was quickly provided with a new surcoat and mantle, his face, hands and boots wiped with damp cloths, and the scattered chessmen were picked up and dried as each puddle on the floor was mopped up.

Hochmeister von Salza watched the whole performance without expression, uttering nothing but an occasional dry word of instruction until the servants had completed their various tasks and left the hall again. Even then he sat for long seconds in stony silence, lips pressed tightly together until all the colour went from them and his mouth became a straight, tight, bloodless line.

Treasurer von Düsberg did not expect, and thus did not see, that the Grand Master's lips were compressed not in anger but in an attempt to hide how much Hermann von Salza wanted to laugh out loud. That sort of mirth at another's misfortune would have been most discourteous to a guest – but at the same time he doubtless felt that it was much preferable to the several well-justified alternative responses.

15

By dint of great effort, von Salza brought both his face and his sense of humour back under control without hurting himself, his dignity or the laws of *courtoisie*, although there had been a time when all three had seemed likely. A certain fondness for the dramatic, which could seldom be indulged whilst dealing with notoriously humourless prelates, had deliberately dropped the word 'Russia' into von Düsberg's lap rather like a live snake, and his reaction had been – well, *appropriate* was close enough, if rather an understatement.

Von Salza considered that was just as well; a man who acted and replied in the way he thought a superior would want to see and hear was not the sort of man to give safe, accurate advice. Albrecht von Düsberg, on the other hand, had already shown a tendency to speak his mind with both mouth and body, and if he would only become confident enough to do so all the time and without twitching, von Salza was convinced that he would become an advisor well worth the time, trouble and expense of acquiring.

The Grand Master leaned his chin on one cupped hand with all the unruffled elegance of a well-dressed nobleman who has managed to stay that way by not flinging wine and chess-pieces about the place. He glanced at the shiny places on the tiled and patterned floor where the mess had been, then gazed at von Düsberg and said, in a voice so carefully modulated to neutrality that it spoke volumes, 'I presume from the enthusiasm of your reaction, Brother Treasurer, that you think the proposal is a good one. Yes. . . ?'

Von Düsberg shifted damply on his chair, and *Hochmeister* von Salza watched him ponder the ramifications of what was being suggested. He was learned, a scholar who could not only read and write, but could do so in Latin, French and High German, and von Salza knew that he was also trained in algorism, the new art of calculating with Saracen numerals. But it was certain that none of his learning helped him reach a decision, for there were too many variables and not enough certainties. There were, though, the good and the prosperity of the Order, so that finally, as the Grand Master suspected he would, Albrecht von Düsberg shrugged and said. 'Yes, Grand Master. It is good.'

Hermann von Salza relaxed, inwardly surprised to find just how tense he had become whilst awaiting Albrecht's reply. The Grand

Master was not a man given to tension; at least, not given to showing it, and not usually given even to feeling it. This, however, was different.

'*Herr Hochmeister*?' There was an edge to von Düsberg's voice that had not been there before. It drew a curious glance from von Salza, the sort of glance which, although not immediately suspicious, certainly hadn't far to go to get that way. It was the sort of glance which seemed to anticipate the word 'but'.

'Albrecht. . . ?'

'*Herr Hochmeister*, as Treasurer I understand the Order's need for lands and revenues of its own, but' – yes indeed, there was the word – 'I can't understand how such lands could be acquired from the Rus. They won't sell, and neither the Pope nor the Emperor would permit a war of conquest against another Christian nation.'

'No? I think they will.' Albrecht von Düsberg's head jerked up at the certainty in the Grand Master's voice. Von Salza regarded him calmly, and smiled. The Treasurer had been a little slow to understand, perhaps because his position required him to think overmuch in straight lines; but even as von Salza watched that plump, ruddy face, it was as if he gazed at an abacus where the beads were finally dropping into place. 'Have you forgotten what we now call the Fourth Crusade?'

Evidently Albrecht had not. He blinked, that over-obvious sign of thought, and then one hand stole to his mouth, covering it, concealing shock or disbelief. The Fourth Crusade had brought shame and, worse, embarrassment to all Christendom. Sent out like the three crusades before it, with the blessing of the Pope, to wrest the Holy Land from the grasp of the infidel, it had somehow been distracted from its course, so much so that it had ended in the sacking of Christian Constantinople by Christian knights. And the Pope . . .

. . . had said nothing.

'Of course the Crusades on that particular enterprise were mostly French,' said von Salza in a tone of voice that suggested that such a casual dismissal explained everything. 'And being French, they no longer hold possession of the lands they won. If they had been Normans, it might be a different matter. But the fact remains that Constantinople was sacked without the Pope raising his voice in protest even once. Why, Albrecht? Why?'

'I suppose because they were only Greeks,' said von Düsberg, 'and since the Greek Orthodox Church doesn't regard the Pope as its spiritual leader, His Holiness had little concern over what was done to them.' He shrugged, crookedly, with one shoulder, a gesture more characteristic of the Cardinal-Archbishop of Salzburg than he knew.

Von Salza knew it, however, and raised one eyebrow. The words his Treasurer had spoken were probably borrowed from Cardinal Joachim as well, but from the sound of it von Düsberg held that same opinion quite independently. The *Hochmeister* smiled. Converting von Düsberg to his point of view might not be quite so difficult as it had seemed at first – if indeed any conversion was needed at all.

'Think about what you've just said, Albrecht,' said von Salza quietly, 'and then think about the Rus that you called "another Christian nation".' Von Düsberg thought about it, and the comprehension that crossed his round, ruddy face was as clear as sunrise. The Grand Master nodded once, satisfied that no further prodding in that particular direction was required, and began counting points briskly on his fingers.

'First and foremost is the matter of their heresy. Since it has already been demonstrated that the Pope does not care overmuch for the Greek misinterpretation of Christianity, it stands to reason that there will be little difficulty in persuading him of the rightness of any crusade which the Order undertakes against the Rus.' Von Salza gazed thoughtfully at Albrecht von Düsberg. 'Among all the books you've read, did any of them tell you how the pagan Rus chose to become Greek Christians rather than follow the true faith?'

Albrecht shook his head. The Cardinal-Archbishop's library had contained histories, of course, but they had been histories of times and peoples comfortably long ago and far away. In them, the Greeks had been philosophers and artists, pagans through an acceptable lack of knowledge rather than heretics by deliberate choice.

The Grand Master grinned at him, a tight little stretch of the mouth that had altogether too many teeth in it. 'Then we have a book here that you should read. Remind me to show you sometime. You'll find it enlightening. This castle may be in the back of beyond, but I flatter myself that the library is as good as any in more civilized places.' He raised his hand again and counted off another point.

'Second is that matter of their refusal to accept the Pope as the head of Christ's Church on Earth.' Again the grin. 'His Holiness Pope Innocent considered this an offence against the laws of man as well as God, but at the time he was more concerned with the Albigensian heretics under his nose than with the Rus half a world away. Now that the Albigensians have been exterminated, I have long considered that drawing Pope Gregory's attention to the heathen doings of the Russians might provoke a beneficial response – beneficial for the Order, if nothing else.

'Thirdly, they have practised sorcery without asking for the Papal dispensation that is normally required by good Christians. Further, they have continued to make their spells even when Honorius banned it as devil-worship. As if they were all Templars. Dammit, man, even when they make the sign of the cross on themselves, they make it backwards!'

'But *Herr Hochmeister*, why would they ask permission to do anything whatsoever as we do it, if they don't regard His Holiness as the head of their Church?'

Hermann von Salza laughed aloud and clapped his hands. 'Exactly so!' he said, then leaned forward and stared at his Treasurer. 'But are you going to explain that small point to Pope Gregory? Because *I'm* not.'

'Ah.' This time it was von Düsberg's turn to grin. 'Damned if they do, and doubly damned and apostate if they don't.' He considered von Salza's convoluted mode of thought for a moment. 'Have the Rus been excommunicated?'

Surprised and caught momentarily off-balance, the Grand Master looked dubiously at his Treasurer. He had never considered that particular question, or its answer, since an excommunicate by the very nature of the word had once, if no longer, been a member of the Catholic Church. 'I doubt it,' he said.

Then he closed his teeth with a click as von Düsberg's question provided him with the argument that would stand even if all the others were set aside. 'They can't be excommunicates, because they were never a part of the Roman Church. That means they were never baptized, or married, or buried by the rites of the

Roman Church. Therefore . . .' Von Salza waved one hand, generously inviting Albrecht to complete the premise. '*Sic provo* . . .'

'Thus I prove that the Rus are apostate schismatics, excommunicates, and heathen infidels abhorrent in the sight of God. Just like the Saracens.'

'And just as ripe for a crusade.' Von Düsberg leaned forward to pour wine for them both, then raised his cup triumphantly. 'To the Crusade in the East,' he said. Then, with eyes piously upraised towards Heaven, 'and to the souls saved from darkness.'

Hermann von Salza eyed his sudden enthusiastic Treasurer, and was quite certain of the reasoning that prompted that enthusiasm. 'Yes indeed,' he said. 'And that, though you never asked it, is why I brought you all the way from Salzaburg.' Calmly and deliberately, the Grand Master gave the city its old, full name for the first time, and watched as von Düsberg realized the full implications behind that time-eroded vowel. 'Oh yes. Salzaburg it is, and always was, since the first of our line to bear the name of Hermann built his wood-walled fortress on the hill above the valley. My family have owned the town, and all the lands around it, since before the Romans came. We know everything, and everyone, within the walls, and we have made . . . call them accommodations . . . with Rome ever since. You are to make another. They call them *propaganda* now. So, for the sake of the Order: make a *propaganda* to set before the Pope, so that when we move against the Russians there will be none who question the purity of our motives. Do you understand me, Albrecht?'

'Perfectly, Grand Master.' The Treasurer's face was immobile. He had been given his orders, and like all within the greater Order, he would follow those lesser orders without question.

'Good.' Von Salza raised his own cup and stared at von Düsberg over its rim once more. 'And you forgot something again,' he said. 'This time in your blessing – or was it a victory toast? To the souls saved from darkness – and to their lands and gold. *Pros't!*'

Chapter Two

The birch-trees were bare and stark against a sky that had clouded to a sickly yellow-backed grey, and there was a chilly edge to the wind that swirled their dead leaves to and fro in the kremlin gardens. A promise of snow was in the air. Heavy snow. The Russian winter was coming.

The same cold nipped with sharp teeth at the nose and ears of Prince Ivan Aleksandrovich Khorlovskiy, making him shiver and mutter something questionable under a breath that came out like smoke. He was richly dressed in furs and silks and velvets, but neither his hat nor his coat nor his boots had the bright colours and embroidery that usually ornamented the clothes of a Rus nobleman; all was stark, simple black and silver. It looked like mourning, and, in an odd way, it was.

It had begun as a celebration of the year's end, its death and burial beneath the shroud of winter snow; but before long the young, the wealthy and the fashionable had seen it as a fine opportunity to parade themselves as monochrome peacocks. There was so much more challenge when choice of colour was restricted. Thus the golds and russets of autumn clothing gave way to winter fashions chosen to dramatically contrast with the crisp white of new-fallen snow and the hard-edged darkness of leafless trees.

The trees were bare enough – but as if to mock several weeks of work by the kremlin tailors, the snow had not fallen yet. Promissory nips at the nose were all very well, but they didn't compensate for looking slightly foolish and improperly dressed for the season. One might as well have stayed in autumn colours, or gone out as naked as the trees, as been seen out-of-doors in black before the snow began to fall. And of course, once the first flakes came shivering from the sky, there would be the usual mad scramble for chests and wardrobes and dressing-rooms, so that one could parade elegantly for a few minutes, black and white among the black and white, before diving indoors for mulled wine

21

or chilled vodka and another round of trivial, empty-headed chatter.

Prince Ivan stared at the empty sky for a few seconds and sniffled briefly, then hunched his shoulders so that the deep sable fur of his collar rose high enough to give at least an illusion of warmth, and kicked at the leaves rustling about his ankles.

'This has gone on for long enough,' he said. 'My ears have left for a warmer climate and my nose doesn't want to know me any more. Can't we go inside now?'

The woman who walked beside him in the garden glanced with mild interest in his direction, a look that said *so what?* as plainly as any words. There was sympathy and a sharing of discomfort in her cool blue eyes, but right now she had the same expression of tolerant amusement as anyone out for a quiet stroll might wear when their companion starts talking nonsense. Except for certain sorts of nonsense, which might not be nonsense at all. She too was wearing black, and against all that darkness her hair, fairer even than Ivan's, seemed almost silver-gilt.

She was Mar'ya Morevna, a sorceress of great power, a noted commander of armies, known to be the fairest princess in all the Russias, and above all else, she was Ivan's wife. Mar'ya Morevna glanced sidelong at her husband, and smiled. 'I suppose,' she said. 'I could provoke enough snow to make all this worthwhile, but what would be the point in that?'

'It would mean that we could go inside with snow on our boots like good winter Rus, and be seen to be foremost in fashion again. For what that's worth.'

'Poor Vanyushka.' Mar'ya Morevna cooed the endearment in a way she knew and intended to be teasing. 'His nose is cold, and his ears are frozen, and he's had to dress up like a prince again. Shame, shame.'

Ivan grinned at her, stretching the grin that little bit beyond the limits of propriety. 'Vanyushka knows a way to warm his nose and both his ears, all at once,' he said. 'But Maryushka wouldn't like it. At least, she wouldn't like it right out here in the garden. The servants would be scandalized.'

'There is a temptation, my dear husband, to call down just enough snow for a fair-sized snowball, and use it to cool your ardour right *here*.'

Parrying Mar'ya's hand, a deceptively lazy movement that he knew from past experience had all the power of a fencer's thrust behind it, Ivan laughed and pulled her close. 'Gently, gently,' he murmured, lips almost touching her ear. 'We're still trying for an heir, remember?'

'How could I forget?' Mar'ya Morevna purred like a big cat and snuggled into her husband's arms, hooding her eyes behind long lashes. 'I could wish that all our princely duties were so pleasant.'

'They could be. Just leave the unpleasant ones for Fedor Konstantinovich.'

'No!' Mar'ya Morevna pushed him away, just hard enough for her annoyance at the suggestion to be made quite plain. 'Ivan Tsarevich, you have some very charming vices, but on top of all of them, you're lazy. There are things to be done in a realm like mine that only I – or you – can do properly. Administration of law, financial conclusions . . .'

She smiled wryly, as if admitting that such subjects bored her just as much as him. But they were there, and had to be done. It was only a fool or an incurable romantic – or Prince Ivan of Khorlov in his less energetic moods – who thought that ruling a tsardom meant only wearing a crown, lolling on a throne and drinking blood-red wine out of a golden cup.

'The High Steward Fedor Konstantinovich is there to *help* us. He may be our servant, but he's *not* there to do our work for us.'

'Humph,' said Ivan, discontented and slightly frustrated as the feeling of leisurely lechery was washed away in a cold shower of duty. 'Then if I'm supposed to tell the servants what to do, I could start with' – he looked vaguely about the kremlin gardens before focusing on the ground right at his feet – 'these leaves. I thought they had been raked up and burnt last month.' He jabbed at them for emphasis with his silver-shod ebony walking-stick. 'It looks as if the gardeners have been skimping their duties.' This time he kicked at the leaves, a pointless gesture since it did no more than stir them up before they settled back around his red-heeled boots.

'Tell the servants. But don't blame them unless you're sure. And, in this instance especially, don't blame the gardeners,' said Mar'ya Morevna. 'You saw the leaves were burnt, and you know they were burnt.'

'Do *you* know,' Ivan said, poking the toe of one boot at the leaves as they came whispering back, 'it's almost as if they were following me.' A capricious gust of wind caught the leaves, picked them up and played with them, then swirled them around in a column that came almost waist-high before it collapsed back on itself.

Mar'ya Morevna's smile vanished abruptly but managed to come back after a few seconds, even though it seemed thinner and much less amused. She stared at Ivan more closely now, seeming to search for something in his face that might have been there whether he intended it or not. His father Tsar Aleksandr occasionally saw with True Sight, and perhaps the Tsar's son had inherited the gift that was no gift at all – for what kindness is it to know, among all else, the time and manner of one's own death? Whatever it was Mar'ya Morevna sought, she did not find, and shrugged the notion away with a little gesture that had rather more than a little relief about it.

'Perhaps they are,' she said quietly. 'When you cut down Koshchey the Undying, we burnt his body. The winds of the wide white world took his ashes and spread them all across Moist Mother Earth. Look at the sand on the beach, or the snow in winter – or these leaves. Watch how they swirl together, as if each has a part that wants to join with the next. Koshchey was undying. I think all the best that we could do was make him lie still for long enough to let us do . . . what we did.'

Mar'ya Morevna drew a deep breath. 'There always was a little of Koshchey in all of us. Mankind was never perfect. But now, I think there may be just a little more.' Her gentle, thin, and by now completely humourless smile went crooked. 'After all, I never gave you any promises that he was dead when we burnt him, and we've been breathing his dust for almost half a year . . .'

Ivan walked on for a few paces as if he had not heard her words, or as if instant reaction to them was beneath a Rus prince. Then he stopped short, his nose wrinkling in disgust as the full weight of her meaning seemed to strike home at once, and he crossed himself quickly. 'God between us and harm,' he said. 'That's horrible . . .'

Mar'ya Morevna was unruffled. Her experience with sorcery had inured her to things that were uglier by far than this. 'Perhaps. But would you rather have him dust in the air – or whole and

24

entire, and I his prisoner, and yourself hacked pieces in a barrel in the sea?'

Ivan stared at his wife for a moment, saying nothing. It had happened, all of it, just as she had said. He had died under Koshchey the Undying's blade, head chopped from body and body chopped to shreds, and only the skills and wisdom of his three brothers-in-law, sorcerers all, had restored him to life. Then he shook his head and reached up to touch his neck just at the spot where Koshchey had sliced it through. 'Dust is preferable,' he said. 'I would rather be alive than dead.'

'Amen to that.' Mar'ya Morevna crossed herself in turn, then reached out to touch his hand. 'I would rather have you here and now, irritable about the state of the garden and unwilling to do your work, than as the best of memories. No matter how closely you hold a memory, it won't keep you warm at night.'

Ivan quirked one corner of his mouth into a sour grimace at the reminder of work undone. The High Steward Fedor Konstanti-novich was always most grateful when his liege's husband declined to help, since Ivan's grasp of palace book-keeping was sketchy at the best of times and his methods of improvising round that ignorance a deal more trouble than they were worth, but it was not the running of the realm that made Ivan reluctant to think of work. It was the book that even now he carried in the crook of one arm. Unlike memory, it was warm. That was the problem. Even on a day as cold as this, it was always warm.

Mar'ya Morevna had long since determined to teach her husband as much of the Art Magic and the rules that governed it as his brain could contain. Like most people in the wide white world, whether Rus or Frank or Saracen, he knew some little sorcery already, but that was far from being enough to satisfy her. For one thing, Ivan had made too many mistakes in his dealings with Koshchey *Bessmyrtnyy* and with the witch Baba Yaga.

And one of those mistakes had killed him.

It was not a situation that Mar'ya Morevna intended should happen again. 'Once,' she had said, 'is unfortunate. Twice would be careless. Three times, and I might think you were trying to get away from me . . .'

Hence the slightly-too-warm book under his arm. Written on fine parchment and encased in an embossed and jewelled metal

25

cover that made it look blasphemously like a missal, it was one of the grimoires from Mar'ya's sorcerous library, and having skimmed through some of its pages, Ivan had decided that the grim part was singularly appropriate. Certainly, and not just because of the weight of its metal covers, it was not light reading. The few things he had already glanced at had caused him to lose his appetite, and very nearly his lunch. Though written in Old Slavonic, the book's title, *Enciervanul Doamnisoar*, was in a language that might have been an impossibly antique form of Hungarian – or again, might have been nothing of the sort. In Russian it would have sounded more like *Besonyat-vazavat*, *On the Summoning of Demons*, and Ivan suspected that Mar'ya Morevna had given it to him more as a warning and a demonstration of what careless talk could do than as any sort of manual of instruction. One of Ivan's most frequent errors both in sorcery and in the mundane doings of the day had been to speak without thinking, and in matters of the Art Magic, 'speak the Name and summon the Named' was more than just a proverb. There were creatures described between the covers of the grimoire that had no place being summoned even into a nightmare . . .

Mar'ya seemed almost to sense her husband's discomfort with his burden. 'Remember, I want you to read it, not just carry it about with you,' she said casually, reaching out to tap the grimoire's cover with one gloved index finger. 'I want you to understand just what can be called up by someone careless.'

Ivan thought of something described in the grimoire's dry, pedantic Old Slavonic as the Devourer in the Dark, and shivered a little. 'I can assure you, Mar'yushka, that five minutes with this book has given me a more than adequate understanding already.'

'Good. Then just think of how well you'll understand once you've spent five hours, or five days, of careful study.'

That wasn't quite what Ivan had hoped to hear, but it was more or less the sort of answer he might have expected. Mar'ya Morevna took all her responsibilities very seriously, whether they were as a sorceress, or a ruler, or a general – or, in any one of the many ways they coincided, as his wife. 'God and Archbishop Levon Popovich both know that I try to be a good Orthodox Christian,' he protested. 'But not even God knows what the Archbishop would say if he knew that I was carrying such a thing as this,

26

never mind reading it! I already know enough sorcery for my own small needs.'

Mar'ya Morevna's finger tapped again, this time against his mouth. 'Hush,' she said. 'No you don't, and I doubt you ever will. What I want you to learn is enough about sorcery for your *safety*, and that's rather a different matter. It has more to do with avoiding than understanding, but until you know what needs to be avoided . . .' She shrugged, dismissing the rest of what might have been a lengthy lecture. 'This isn't Khorlov. You don't live there any more.'

Ivan wondered a little about her last words, and about the tone in which she spoke them. It was always worth bearing in mind that Mar'ya Morevna had been a ruler of wide realms before she met him, and though they were now husband and wife and without a doubt very much in love, she was *still* the ruler of wide realms. Both in Khorlov and elsewhere throughout Moist Mother Earth, there had been plenty of kings and tsars and princes whose fiery tempers and fondness for violence matched, and often far superseded, the breadth of their domains. Ivan had not forgotten how Mar'ya Morevna had led her armies against the Tatar horde of Manguyu Temir, nor the seemingly casual way in which she had surpassed the slaughter of all who could not escape, to a total of almost five thousand men. If there was indeed any hidden meaning, warning or advice in the way she spoke, Ivan resolved to pay it all the attention that it deserved.

'Quite so,' he said, and grinned briefly. It was a hard little grin, too tightly drawn for sincerity. 'I consider myself properly chastised.'

'Idiot,' said Mar'ya Morevna. 'Vanya, unless you're feeling warmer than you look, might I suggest we both go back inside the kremlin? There's a fire in there, and that wine from Frankish Burgundy for our attention. It's come a long way just to be ignored. And you still haven't beaten me at chess.'

'Never was a truer word spoken,' said Ivan ruefully. 'I don't know that I've ever beaten *anyone* at chess. Aren't you afraid I'll give up fair play and try to cheat?'

Mar'ya Morevna leaned her head against his shoulder and laughed softly. 'No, Vanyushka mine. You're too much of a gentleman for that.'

'Then why bother playing at all?'

'Because fair or cheating, Ivan Tsarevich, when you finally lose, you always do it so very gracefully . . .'

This time it was Ivan's turn to laugh, as his momentary flicker of wariness was filed away until it should be needed again. 'That's not much a compliment, but I suppose it's the best my playing's ever likely to get. All right, *golubushka*. Chess first, wine afterwards. That way I'll at least have something besides defeat to look forward to . . .'

There were six pipes of wine in the kremlin's cellars, still on the massive wooden sledges which had borne them all the way from France, and each one was broached in turn so that its contents could be tasted. That was one of the more pleasurable duties of a ruling lord, and one not left entirely to a steward or castellan. Sooner or later the wine would be served to guests, and waiting until it was presented at table was entirely the wrong time to learn that it was bad. Only when pronounced good was it decanted from the huge pipes into smaller barrels and stored in the cool dark until needed. Otherwise there was trouble, and the writing of acrimonious letters that demonstrated – if demonstration was required – that the beautiful Tsarevna Mar'ya Morevna had not only the skills but also the raw-edged vocabulary of a soldier.

Such letters were seldom needed, but when they *were* required, there was good reason. Money had been wasted. The distances involved were such that spoiled wine could not be returned; it went instead to the kitchens, or to the peasants whose palates were quite without discrimination where free drink was concerned. Tsarevich Ivan had often suspected that when a city's fountains were made to flow with wine during a holiday, they didn't flow with anything like the finest vintages.

Certainly the fountains of Mar'ya Morevna's kremlin wouldn't flow with this wine, at least not unless there was a real cause for celebration. It was far too good to waste on peasants.

'Not the best ever,' she decided, swirling the contents of her small crystal goblet as she gazed critically at its colour. 'But not bad. Not bad at all.'

'Be reasonable,' said Ivan, unable to detect anything worthy of even that small criticism. 'It's bloody good.'

Mar'ya Morevna smiled at her husband. 'Beloved, if you used a smaller cup and emptied it less quickly . . .' She let the sentence hang and glanced instead at the chessboard. 'Then you might appreciate the subtleties a little more. And not be' – she moved a piece – 'in check again.'

'Again?'

'Or "still", if you prefer it that way.'

It was their second game since coming in from the gardens. The first had been hasty and careless, both players being more concerned with getting warm again than with the strategies of the gaming board; and by the time the second game was well under way, so was the tasting of the wine. Despite the best efforts of his father Tsar Aleksandr, who had tried to imbue his son with an awareness that thinking several moves ahead of the opposition applied in life as well as chess, Ivan's game tended to be slapdash at the best of times. There were occasional flashes of brilliance, based more often on improvisation than on skill, but for the most part Prince Ivan played chess in a style that most people tried to avoid, but with one overwhelming virtue that cancelled out most of the other faults. He never forgot that it was just a game.

'All right then, call it "still".' He studied the board with the sort of intensity that comes only with great ability or four large glasses of strong wine on an empty stomach, but saw nothing that could be changed by moving his king in any of the permitted directions. 'Check, not mate?'

'Not yet.'

'I see.' Ivan didn't actually see anything of the sort, at least not at first – which suggested that the solution was one of those blatantly obvious, painfully simple moves that tended to sit right under his nose and dare him to notice their existence. He wrinkled his nose and looked instead at his wine cup, which was empty again. 'Four glasses. That suggests there are still two pipes of untasted wine. Should we. . . ?'

'Yes, we should.' Mar'ya Morevna shot him a cool look from beneath her pale brows. 'But not until you've drunk some water and eaten something, which you haven't since you got up this morning.'

'Food sounds good.' Better, certainly, than staring at the chessboard that was openly defying him. 'What do you suggest?'

For answer, the Tsarevna picked up a small silver bell and rang it. There were two servants sitting at the other end of the room, close enough for convenience but far enough for privacy, and one of them was already getting to his feet even as his mistress reached for the bell. 'Nikolai,' said Mar'ya Morevna, 'go to the kitchens and drag Yuriy off the stove. Find out what can be made quickly, then come back and tell me.'

'At your command, Highness!'

'And bring a platter of *buterbrody* while you're at it,' said Ivan, feeling a sudden flurry of appetite that rather startled him. 'With garlic cheese. Lots of garlic.'

'Enough for two, Nikolai,' said Mar'ya Morevna. 'A woman has to defend herself somehow.'

The old servant Nikolai smiled at that as he hurried out; he had served Mar'ya Morevna and her father before her, and knew as much about her fondness for sharp and pungent flavours as Yuriy the cook. There had been jokes, crude but kindly meant, concerning the speed with which she had married Tsarevich Ivan, and those same jokes had turned to slight concern that there was still no child born to the young couple. That, however, was a dynastic affair and no concern of servants, even though their prayers often mentioned the matter privately to God.

He was not otherwise troubled overmuch by entreaties from that particular kremlin, or indeed the kremlins of Ivan's three brothers-in-law. Any sorcerer well versed in the mysteries of the Art Magic was fully aware of the greater Power from which their own lesser powers descended. God, Allah, Jehovah: the names changed, but what they attempted to describe remained much the same despite the different ways in which teachings were interpreted. At the bottom of it all was freedom of choice, that most dangerous of liberties. What religion defined as 'good' and 'evil' was no more – and no less – than the capability for any man or woman or child, sorcerer or not, to make their own decision whether to help or to hurt. It was the Gift of Fire all over again: warmth and comfort, or burning and destruction. Even though a part of the great Power, or as some believed, a good and holy man granted a clearer than usual view of its truth, had been offered up as sacrificial intercession for the stupidities of humankind, that choice remained. The uncertain bombarded their chosen form of deity with prayers or criticisms. Sorcerers like Mar'ya Morevna tried only to do what they thought was right.

Her chaplain the Kanonarch Protodeacon Sergey Strigunov had long since given up trying to reconcile Church teaching with his liege lady's magic. That she did good with it was enough; lords and princes with less power at their disposal were too often much worse rulers. He avoided the books in her private library, turned a deaf ear to her heretical declaration she needed no priest to intercede for her, and paid no attention whatsoever to more outrageous statements that he felt certain were uttered just to tease him. But when the beautiful Tsarevna discussed serious theology, Protodeacon Sergey was not deaf at all.

Tsarevich Ivan liked the chaplain. He was a wise, worldly priest, fond of food and drink, and of music besides that of his choir. Sergey Strigunov was bearded, like all Orthodox clergy, but despite his youth – the chaplain was not yet forty – both beard and hair had already turned iron-grey. Ivan idly suspected him of using that badge of premature aging as the smokescreen to conceal some distinctly unorthodox ideas. He would probably have approved, if with reservations, of Mar'ya Morevna's insistence that Ivan learn something more of magic than the little he knew already. After all, the Tsarevich had already stepped beyond the boundaries of a safe and ordinary world, simply because of the sorcerers who were his wife and his in-laws. However, those reservations would have been increased tenfold by any book whose title was *On the Summoning of Demons* . . .

Ivan considered the chessboard again, still thinking in a detached way about religion and priests, and reached out one hand tentatively towards a bishop. He paused, fingers not quite touching the piece, and glanced at Mar'ya Morevna to see if there was any hint as to the rightness of the move. It was a wasted effort; apart from mild interest that betrayed nothing useful, her face was expressionless, so that the chair she sat in might have given more away. Ivan sighed. It was as well they weren't playing for money.

Then he changed his mind abruptly, closed his fingers on the cool, carved walrus-ivory of his sole remaining knight and moved the little *bogatyr'* horseman back down and across the board, protecting his king from the threat of Mar'ya Morevna's rook by the simple and direct expedient of taking her piece. 'So!' he said, sounding just a little smug. 'Out of check and back on the offensive.'

'Oh, Vanya, you're never offensive.' His wife leaned back and grinned at him, clapping her hands in mock applause. 'And it only took you ten minutes to see that move.' She flexed her fingers and studied the board, working out multiple shifts of advantage in a way that Ivan had long envied. He had a feeling that he was about to lose that last knight, and shortly afterwards the game, for the second time that evening. Unless, unless . . .

Unless Nikolai arrived with the food, and gave him another respite.

Even though it was only a game, as Ivan had been reminding himself ever more forcefully during the past quarter-hour, he found that he was surprisingly relieved by the arrival of a platter of black bread. It wasn't just that the scent of garlicky *tvorog* cream cheese was reminding him with considerable, mouthwatering force just how empty his stomach was. More likely it was the predatory way that Mar'ya Morevna had been leaning over the board during what looked like yet another endgame. Chess was too much like the movement of troops for a warrior lady of such skill to treat it as *just* a game.

'Saved,' he said, sitting back from the board. 'At least for the time being.'

'Perhaps . . .' Mar'ya Morevna picked up an already captured piece and twiddled it between her long, slender fingers. The ivory clicked softly as it came into contact with her rings. 'And perhaps not. That's for later. Nikolai?'

'Highness?'

'What does Yuriy plan to feed us on this evening?'

'You asked for dishes that could be prepared "quickly", Highness. Not knowing how quickly "quickly" might be, Chief Cook Yuriy had me make this list.' Nikolai pulled a piece of folded parchment from his belt and handed it over, affecting not to notice that Prince Ivan was twisting his head to one side in a most unprincely way, so as to read the writing upside-down.

At least, so that he could see it. Chief Cook Yuriy might have been an acknowledged master in his own kitchen, but his handwriting, that of a man more accustomed to a cleaver than a pen, was execrable and looked more like spatters of gravy flicked from a ladle. Appropriate enough; it was unusual that he could read and write at all, when most cooks were taught by rote rather than by reading recipes. All that Ivan could distinguish from the general scratching was a small annotation beside each dish, estimating how long preparation would take. 'Why is time so important?' Ivan asked, straightening up. 'Are you expecting company?'

'In a manner of speaking,' said Mar'ya Morevna. She shot a quick look at Nikolai, and the old servant bowed low before retiring out of earshot. 'My spies came back earlier today, and I want a word with them before the evening ends.'

'Good news? Bad?'

'Neither one nor the other, or I'd have been told of it directly. At least,' and she looked speculative for a moment, 'I had *better* have been told. But then they know me better than to keep secrets back for the sake of drama or in hope of praise. I don't care much for the one, and I don't dole out the other without cause.'

Ivan knew that much already. Mar'ya Morevna's network of spies and informants – never inform*ers*, that word was considered unseemly and left a bad taste in the mouth – was quite possibly the best in all the Russias, an unrealized part of her dowry that Ivan's father had been only too glad to learn about, receive and use. Every Tsar and Prince who cherished some small hope of finding out what his neighbours, enemies and rivals were doing employed a certain number of eyes and ears, distributed throughout the various – and most suspicious – realms and city-states, who reported back what they had seen and heard. Based on those reports, the Tsar could keep his spies in place, send them elsewhere, or take whatever other action seemed appropriate. To Ivan's knowledge, only his own dear wife had pairs of eyes and pairs of ears everywhere, and every several months one half of each pair would return to her kremlin and advise her of developments, no matter how petty.

Prince Ivan had been invited, as only Mar'ya Morevna invited, to sit in on the last such session, just after the summer solstice. He had gone expecting to be bored, but had remained to be fascinated, and indeed, as some of the reports went into most intimate detail, to be much amused and mildly scandalized.

To have heard rumours concerning a politically well-married Prince's adultery with his own chief retainer's wife was interesting, but no more than gossip. To have confirmed knowledge of it, and to possess a quantity of solid evidence that backed up such knowledge, was something else again. It was to have a weapon against him, if such should be needed, far more certain and far less blameworthy than a knife to plant between his shoulders. Of course, if the chief retainer, or the Prince's own wife, or her family, should choose to do something foolish and permanent involving cutlery, that was entirely their concern and nothing whatsoever to do with the fairest Princess in all the Russias. Such information was gathered secretly; Ivan quickly learned that it could be released in the same way, its source untraceable.

'But only,' Mar'ya Morevna had said, 'if it is used as a weapon. Not as a threat. Putting pressure on your enemy may bend him to your will the first time; but that will be the only time. Afterwards, unless he's a total fool, you and your spies will have lost the advantage for good and all. He will be wary of anyone connected with you; loyal to you; who does business with you; who even knows your name. And he'll probably doubt those who deny they've ever heard of you. So use diplomacy and compromise instead of blackmail. Never apply leverage to anything that either common knowledge or common spies could tell you. That way, uncommon spies – and mine are most uncommon – remain free to come and go as they please, giving you access to the sort of information that could lift your enemy's head right off his shoulders. And if you finally need to do it . . . then take his head, and be damned to him. But *never be found out.*'

It had been a shorter lecture than many Ivan had heard, particularly from Dmitriy Vasil'yevich Strel'tsin, his father's High Steward and noted bore. But it had stuck in his mind in a way that many longer-winded perorations had not. Perhaps because Ivan himself, despite what Mar'ya Morevna frequently and gently criticized as a lack of healthy cynicism, had a fondness for the devious and the tricky that was probably a part of his ancestry. The old North people, whose chiefmost god Othinn had never been much of an example of straight dealing, had been honest traders – more or less – when they first settled on the banks of the Dnepr river; at the same time, when it suited them better, they were also the ferocious Vikings against whom prayers had been said from Germany to Spain.

Not that Ivan Tsarevich had ever considered robbing anyone to line his own pockets, several centuries of civilization and the rank of Tsar's son had seen to that. But after his experiences with Koshchey the Undying and with the witch Baba Yaga, he had taken to looking for the crooked as well as the direct routes round a problem. One tended to live longer that way.

'Whatever choice morsels they have for us,' he said, 'I'm glad you intend to eat first. They're painstaking, your spies, and I haven't forgotten how long they talked last time.'

Mar'ya Morevna laughed. 'Neither have I. Five hours, more or less. Poor Vanya! Quite a while to wait for your dinner, don't you think?' She shook her head. 'I'm going to command that they be given something to eat now, and I certainly don't intend to eat with them. My spies may be talented gatherers of information, but they're only servants after all.'

'What about eating while we hear what they have to tell us?' asked Ivan, deliberately teasing her.

Mar'ya Morevna gave him a look of shock and a slow raising of the eyebrows that was just as studied and deliberate. 'You must be joking,' she said. 'Even if the news is neither good or bad, it needs all our attention. But so does Yuriy's cooking.'

'At what you pay him, it had better.'

'Just another of life's little pleasures,' murmured Mar'ya Morevna. 'Good cooks, fortunately, can be bought. Good lovers' – she smiled gently and patted Ivan's hand, then squeezed his thumb suggestively – 'have to be found, dear heart, just the way I found you. Now' – Mar'ya Morevna flipped the little sheet of parchment around and pushed it at him across the chessboard – 'choose what you want for dinner.'

Viewed right side up, Yuriy's writing was marginally better than it was when upside-down, but not much: Ivan had to narrow his eyes almost to a squint before they were able to shape Cyrillic letters out of the general scrawl. And yes indeed, there was a sizeable blob of some sort of sauce or gravy decorating the bottom of the note, looking for all the world like sealing-wax on an important letter. It was extremely fresh gravy too; Ivan could smell the aroma of herbs and garlic mingled with good meat stock rising from the surface of the parchment in much the way love-letters were scented with perfume. 'This,' he said, waving it in the air, 'smells good enough to eat all by itself.'

'Maybe,' said Mar'ya Morevna, 'although I'd prefer something with a bit more nourishment to it. Pick something else, so that Yuriy can get to work – and so that *we* can get to work directly afterwards.' She gave Ivan a look that combined sympathy with mockery in equal measure. 'Even though I know how much you hate the prospect of that . . .'

Despite the quantity of good red wine he had on board, Tsarevich Ivan had the grace to blush. There was little point in arguing that though he did indeed find that most of the duties of a ruling Prince bored him until he wanted to scream, listening to the reports of Mar'ya Morevna's efficient spies was both salacious and highly entertaining. That was the difficulty about teasing her. She would allow each little jab to go by as if she had not even noticed it, and then return the courtesy tenfold with a single well-chosen phrase. At least she hadn't spoken loudly enough for Nikolai to hear; not that the dignified old man would have given sign of it in any case. He and Mar'ya were as happily married as any couple he could think of, including his parents and his three sisters – but every now and then there would be an unmistakable reminder that he, Ivan, was a newcomer to this kremlin, to its hierarchies and traditions. It happened rarely, and never without justification, but when it *did* happen, it never went unnoticed.

Ivan inclined his head, acknowledging the hit, but his only reply was a throat-clearing noise copied from his father Tsar Aleksandr. Some might have thought it a sound of embarrassment; others, who knew better, had likened it to the click of a crossbow brought to full cock and ready to shoot. He looked at the chessboard, then at the piece of parchment. 'Anything on this list?'

Mar'ya Morevna nodded, her mind already a little distracted by the thought of what news the spies would have brought this time. Ivan knew from past experience that news actively good or actively bad was often easier to deal with, having certain requirements of its own, than information neither one nor the other. Vague generalizations needed more work, especially if one's hand was not to be seen in the matter.

'Good,' said Ivan. He couldn't keep the grin off his face any longer. 'Then we'll start with *shchi*, very sour, with salt-pickled mushrooms, black bread and sweet butter. After that—'

'There's no after when you start with *shchi*!' said Mar'ya Morevna, coming down from her political calculations with a bump. 'Not the way that Yuriy makes it!'

'Then we'll just have a little. But I'm not missing any chance to eat Yuriy Oblomov's sour cabbage soup. Or his bread. A table with good bread on it is an altar; otherwise it's just a plank. You know what the peasants say: when you die, the Lord God' – he crossed himself – 'hangs you upside-down with your head in a barrel and then your name-saint' – he crossed himself again – 'pours in all the food and drink you spilled or refused when it was offered. How you feel after that depends entirely on what you do while you're alive. I don't intend to have more than my hair wet.'

'Have you been sneaking more of that new wine?' said Mar'ya Morevna, looking suspiciously at the jug. 'And not giving any to me?'

'No to both questions,' said Ivan cheerfully. 'You said yourself: I should eat something before we broach and taste from the other two pipes of red in the cellar. So, after the *shchi*, we'll have *ryabchik* grilled crispy, with that sharp cherry jam.' Ivan stared at his wife and smiled a long, slow smile. 'Since Yuriy has those tasty little birds on the list, I presume that they'll have been well marinated and be nice and moist by the time I get one in my mouth. I know how much you like hazel-hen with jam.'

Mar'ya Morevna looked at him, shook her head and laughed out loud. 'While you, beloved, just like food!'

'I like all sorts of things,' said Ivan, and stroked the palm of her hand with one fingertip.

Mar'ya Morevna shivered deliciously and closed her fist on his finger. 'Later for you,' she said very softly. 'But not much later.'

'After the *kasha*,' he said. 'With lots of butter. You can't spoil *kasha* with too much butter.'

'Oh, no indeed.' Mar'ya Morevna giggled a little, and looked very much as if she would have giggled a lot, and done other things as well, had the spies not had first demand on her time.

Ivan made a mental note of it. Not even his wife's most wordy informant could keep talking until past midnight, and if he tried . . . Well, there were certain privileges that went with being a

37

prince, and one of them was being able to tell almost anyone else to shut up, at least until next morning. 'And we'll finish with *smetannik*,' he said firmly. 'Though I think that should really be brought to our chambers after we're done with business for the day.'

'Otherwise we really *will* be done with business, and before it's even started.' Mar'ya Morevna knew exactly what she was talking about. *Smetannik* was a sweet pie of almost sinful richness: it was a pastry case lined with jam made from the autumn's raspberries and then filled with a mixture of soured cream, milk thickened by stewing ground almonds in it, and chopped walnuts and hazelnuts. She shook her head again, all amused disbelief. 'Vanyushechka, I've never met anyone who can be quite so – so *lascivious* about food. Probably because that's not the only thing on your mind.'

'As I said, I like all sorts of things. Shall we summon Nikolai and get this request for indulgence down to the kremlin kitchens . . . or would you like to talk some more about how lascivious I can really be?'

'I think,' began Mar'ya Morevna, then hesitated briefly as she forcibly changed her mind. 'No. I'm quite sure that we had better deal with matters in their proper order. Otherwise nothing will get done, and we'll have to start again tomorrow. Agreed?'

'Reluctantly. Except for starting again tomorrow. That part I quite like.'

'Ivan! Sometimes you're impossible! Can't you think of anything else?'

'Nothing as important as producing an heir,' said Ivan, forcing his features into an expression of prim sincerity that had long ceased to deceive anyone, his wife least of all. She snickered at him, and he grinned back and tapped the chessboard. 'But if you give me until dinner arrives, I think I might just get you into check.'

Mar'ya Morevna called over the old servant Nikolai, gave him brief instructions both for their own food and for the waiting spies' – since as she had told Ivan, she considered it unreasonable that they should wait empty during a mealtime – and despatched him towards the kitchens. Then she glanced at the positions of the pieces, laughed quietly and said, 'In one sense you've got me in check already. As for the other – until dinner arrives when? Next Easter? But it should be fun to see you try . . .'

Ivan followed Mar'ya Morevna up yet another flight of stairs, holding a candelabrum filled with white beeswax candles high overhead to light the darker corners. There were torches set in brackets along the walls, of course, but the chill in the stairwell and the way that they smoked and guttered suggested to Ivan that they had been lit only a few moments before. The tower which they climbed was the highest in the entire kremlin, *Krasivaya Bashnya*, the Red Tower, and there was a single small, comfortable and ultimately private room right at the top. Once the bolts had been shot and keys turned in the locks of every door between that room and the bottom of the tower, it was also the most secure place in the entire fortress.

'I should have put Koshchey *Bessmyrtnyy* up here,' said Mar'ya Morevna over her shoulder, 'and saved us all a lot of trouble.'

Prince Ivan smiled thinly. 'You said that before,' he pointed out. 'And I gave you the same reason why you shouldn't have done any such thing. The wasp has been swatted; I prefer that to having him still alive in a bottle. No matter how secure, a prisoner always has a chance of getting out of whatever place you put him in. Except the grave.'

'This is still Koshchey the *Undying* you're talking about, isn't it? Not some other Koshchey? And anyway, you're hardly the one to talk about death being permanent, *golubchik*.' Mar'ya Morevna unlatched yet another door and fitted a key into its lock. 'Loose that bolt and swing it around, please.'

The keyhole of each lock had sliding iron shutters on both sides of the door; when a key was put into one side and turned, the shutter on the other side was cranked down on little toothed rails and protected the entire lock from picking. The bolts, bars of forged steel two fingers thick and as long as a man's arm from elbow to palm, were much simpler. Each was held in place by a pin of the same steel that could be removed from its slot, so that the entire bolt mechanism could swivel from one side of the door to the other. Ivan wondered why at first, and whether it wouldn't have been simpler to have two bolts, one inside and one out. The reason, when he sorted it out in his head, was obvious: it prevented the awkward situation of someone shooting one of the bolts while you were on the wrong side of the door. Being held prisoner in one's own tower was bad enough, but to have actually provided an enemy with the means to do it was even worse. He listened to the clicks and rattles as Mar'ya Morevna twirled her key, then followed her again up what was the last flight of stairs.

Five people, three men and two women, were waiting for them in the little secure room at the top of the tower. All set their wine cups aside and stood to bow or make a courtesy when Ivan and Mar'ya Morevna came in, as good servants should, but Ivan noticed from the wreckage of dinner on a table in the corner that the spies had been eating quite literally like Princes. He hid a smile that itself covered a brief flicker of irritation, thinking to himself that spies and lower orders or not, much time might have been saved had everyone sat around the same table and started their discussion almost two hours ago. There was much to be said for the Frankish custom of dividing noble from commoner by the simple token of a dish of salt to mark out the partition of rank.

The difficulty was in persuading his dear wife, who as a sorcerer and commander of armies was more than usually traditional and set in her ways. It was not an undertaking for late in the evening or after a good meal; in fact, the more he thought about it, the more Ivan decided that it might be an undertaking best handled by an exchange of letters across a safe distance – or perhaps by forgetting the whole idea.

There had been no such problem last time. In the middle of summer, when the days were longer, everyone was more inclined to stay up late and make use of the daylight. It was also a deal warmer out of doors, which was where the last meeting had taken place. Instead of the lofty tower and the multitude of locked doors that were needed to provide security against eavesdroppers tonight, the bright summer evening had needed only the wide-open space of the kremlin's largest courtyard, where no-one could come close enough to listen without also being seen. Even so, the spies had worn masks against unfriendly eyes, and the chairs on which everyone sat had been placed close enough the fountain in the centre of the courtyard that the sound of splashing water would make nonsense of anything spoken rashly over-loud. That had been a trick borrowed from the antique Romans – or maybe it had been the Greeks – either of whom had known a thing or two about keeping unnecessary information from unfriendly eyes and ears.

Both Ivan and Mar'ya Morevna were in full agreement that their own kremlin had a scattering of spies among its population; any fortress with information worth gathering would have one or two, in much the same way that a well-stocked granary would have its complement of rats, and for much the same reason. A lack of spies –or by extension, rats – would be enough to have the owners of both sorts of building looking about to find the reason why. There was no point in leaving the grain of information lying about where it could easily be stolen, but at the same time excessive precautions against such theft could become self-defeating, by going too far and actually drawing attention to the fact that there might well be something even more worth stealing than the would-be thieves suspected.

If a confidential meeting was being held at the top of a lofty tower, then locking the doors behind you was entirely sensible and only to be expected. Dragging pieces of the kremlin steam-bath all the way to the top of that same tower was most definitely *not* sensible, and something to be discouraged at all costs. Mar'ya Morevna had wanted something to produce the same ear-baffling sizzle of sound as the fountains of summer; Prince Ivan had thought, said aloud and insisted that a basket of rocks, a brazier to heat them on, and a bronze canister of water to drip water on them and produce a hiss of steam was taking security precautions just a little far. The brazier was fine; it could get cold at the top of the Red Tower with winter coming on. The rest of the steam-bath equipment, however, struck him as likely to provoke excessive speculation . . .

He looked at the five spies and, out of courtesy, tried not to seem over-inquisitive even though he was bubbling with curiosity. It was only the second time in his life that he had ever encountered people whose main purpose in life was the acquisition of secrets: though he knew somewhat hazily of their existence, his father's small company of spies remained a mystery. Not even High Steward Strel'tsin got to deal with the Khorlov spies, and Ivan Tsarevich most certainly wasn't old enough. Besides, First Ministers and Tsars' sons had both been known to grow ambitious, and while he would never have believed it of his own Minister or son, Tsar Aleksandr was well aware that various now-dead rulers had also not believed it either . . . He held that only one man should have direct dealings with gatherers of information, and that one man should be the person for whom the news, gossip and other things were intended.

'These,' said Mar'ya Morevna, indicating the five with one hand, 'and their partners whom you met last season, are among my most trusted servants. They pass freely where you and I cannot go, to watch and listen on our behalf. Know them well.'

She introduced each spy in turn, and as on the previous occasion, there was much less formality involved than was customary between Rus nobility and the vassals who served them. Even so, Ivan was given only the forename, without even a patronymic; no mention was made of family, place of origin or, indeed, of the place where they had performed their most recent duties. That was the same as last time; Mar'ya Morevna took every precaution that she deemed necessary for their safety, and – unless dissuaded – a few more besides. Russian rulers, as Ivan well knew, being the son of one, had an enthusiasm for security that bordered on obsession.

'Stepan,' said Mar'ya Morevna, gesturing towards a tall, lean, dark man, his black beard heavy and bushy in the manner of an Orthodox priest rather than the more neatly trimmed whiskers worn by non-clerics. His voice was deep and musical, adding further emphasis to his priestly appearance.

'Pavel.' This one was small, slight, his hair as pale blond as Ivan's own, or that of any of the many others whose ancestry went back to Ryurik the Viking and the other old North people. Indeed, it was paler still, to the point of being almost colourless. When he spoke briefly to acknowledge his liege lady's introduction, Ivan could hear a touch of the quick, slurred accent that was typical of Novgorod the Great; but when he concentrated on that accent, it went away, no more a part of Pavel's own speech than any of the other intonations that came and went with each word and sentence.

'Nikolai.' A big man, blocky and still possessed of a remarkable breadth of shoulder even though that broadness had slipped down to his waistline. He looked as though he might once have been a man-at-arms or a city guard – but never an officer – and at the same time he gave the impression that his martial days were past, for he could as easily have been an innkeeper or a butcher, either of which was a decent trade for a retired soldier. His face was round and friendly, red-cheeked and immediately trustworthy, a useful asset for a spy – especially if he was indeed an innkeeper, for that was the sort of trade where men heard secrets, usually after too much wine and ale had been consumed.

'Natasha.' There was another who heard secrets. She was young and pretty, her hair worn in two long braids and her eyes demurely lowered in just the sort of enticing way that might prompt a man to foolishness. Her part was doubtless the oldest of the old profession of spying, that of whore – except that her clothing and demeanour suggested sufficient wealth to deserve the courtesy title of courtesan instead. Like innkeepers, courtesans always had time to listen, after business had been concluded.

'Olga.' Small and slender, her hair an unremarkable mouse-brown, Olga made Ivan glance back at the pale spy Pavel. They were two of a kind, with nothing about them to attract attention or, in a servant's post, even recognition of their presence at all. That was common enough in great houses; Ivan found himself silently applauding Mar'ya Morevna's choice. For the most part, the only time that a servant might be noticed was when something was done late, or wrongly, or not at all – and he had a feeling that these two were very, very good at whatever duties they performed. They could quite probably come into a room, light candles, turn down bed-linen, fuel a fire and dust up afterwards, and if the occupant of that room had been asked later, he or she would most likely be unable to recall when or by whom all these small tasks had been done.

Ivan blinked twice, realizing just how accurate that judgement had been. All of Mar'ya Morevna's spies fell into the same category, one side or another of the same coin: either they were ciphers, colourless to the point of transparency, or they were fully rounded characters so typical of their assumed rôles that no-one would dream of questioning them. Who notices a priest's face in church . . . or during confession? Who looks twice at the innkeeper making vague and sympathetic noises during an outpouring of drunken problems? And who, looking twice and more than twice at the handsome and clearly available young woman who is ignoring the scorn and disapproval of every matron in sight, would suspect that she might have dressed and painted her face so blatantly not to attract, but to distract. . . ?

Those were the spies. Ivan had expected more, since there had been a full dozen in attendance at the last meeting. The explanation, when it was given at last, was simple enough: only those who had something to report made the journey when winter was coming on. Travelling in summer was not only easier, but less likely to be remarked upon.

'Security again,' said Mar'ya Morevna and grinned at him, teasing gently. 'It saves all the awkward questions like "why did you go?" and "where did you go?" and "who did you see when you got there?" ' She opened the cylindrical case which she had carried from the library, and hung the chart which it contained up on the curving wall of the tower room, standing on tip-toe to secure the enormous sheet. Made of white Chinese paper, thick and heavy as linen, it was big enough that it all but filled the wall from window to window and from floor to ceiling. 'Whereas when *I* ask those questions,' she said, 'I like to see for myself.'

Prince Ivan gazed with approval at the map. It was of the Rus lands from where the River Volga flowed into the Caspian Sea in the East, to where the River Vistula ran into the Baltic Sea in the West, and its detail was superb. Mar'ya Morevna's father Koldun had been a cartographer as well as a sorcerer, and there were many examples of his work in the kremlin library – but this was better than any Ivan had yet seen. As one of the spies, Stepan, the priestly-looking one, began making his report, Ivan stood up and crossed the room to look at it more closely, wishing that he had a magnifying glass of some sort that would better allow him to appreciate the fine detail of hills and trees and cities. Certainly a glass of great power and a pen narrow as a needle had been used by whoever had originally drawn the hair-fine lines—

Then one of those same lines twitched and shifted its position, and Prince Ivan did exactly the same. He jumped a foot backwards, and swore. '*Chyort voz'mi!* It moved, dammit!'

When Ivan turned away from the map and back to the room, everyone was staring at him. The spy Stepan was still talking, but at a gesture from Mar'ya Morevna, he stopped. Nobody said anything for a few seconds, and more importantly, nobody laughed or even smiled. That was just as well: for those few seconds, Ivan Tsarevich was in no laughing mood. It took him a couple of deep breaths to regain something that passed for composure, and then he said, 'All right, so it's a map that draws itself to instruction. But you might have *told* me . . .'

Quite straight-faced, and managing to sound contrite regardless of how she felt inside, Mar'ya Morevna nodded and said, 'You're right, of course. I thought you knew already.'

It was a reasonable statement: such charts were not uncommon, though the initial ensorcellment was both sufficiently expensive and complex to deter all but the wealthiest and most determined of lords. Besides which, though she had taken the map from its case, she had produced neither pen nor ink nor paper with which to note down what her spies might have to say. A chart as large and as elaborate as this one *was* uncommon, however, and Mar'ya Morevna had only recently completed such an expenditure of power and gold on it that neither Ivan her husband nor Koldun her late father might have thought the end result justified.

Mar'ya Morevna thought otherwise and would have argued the case if Ivan had raised the subject – which, of course, not being told about it, he had not . . .

'What you see there,' she told him as he turned back to peer more closely at it, 'is no more than what I read to it from past reports. This is the first time it has heard accurate and first-hand information, and so of course everything will start to change even as you watch. Stepan, proceed.'

Ivan clasped both hands behind his back and leaned in until his nose was almost touching the surface of the chart, wishing more than ever for a strong glass – and a strong glass *of* something, too, since his heart was still pattering rather harder than he liked. Nor was he yet accustomed to the way in which his wife was referring to the map, an inanimate object, as though it had animate senses. 'Reading to it.' 'Letting it hear accurate information.' For someone who was usually so cautious about her – and anyone else's – use of sorcery, Mar'ya Morevna seemed to be enjoying this obvious and impressive piece of spell-casting just for its own sake. The spy's melodious baritone voice rumbled on

45

in the background and Ivan listened carefully even as he watched the effects of that voice take shape on the map.

'. . . marriage between Ludmyla Fedorovna, niece to Yuriy Vladimirovich, Great Prince of Kiev, and the *boyar* Oleg Vasil'yevich,' Stepan was saying. 'However, since there is small love between the Great Prince and his brother-in-law Fedor *bogatyr*', only a little land was given as bride-gift . . .' And true enough, there on the outskirts of a diminutive Kiev, a thin blue line of – was it ink or something else entirely? – whatever it was, shifted to show the change in Prince Yuriy's domain. That shift was echoed by a flickering as first tinted shading and then tiny columns of letters and figures altered themselves, presumably to show the altered values of various lordly domains: changes in alliance, indicated by colour and crest; numbers of troops capable of support on a given area of land; its tax revenues; and all the other indications of wealth, real, claimed and merely bragged-about. Ivan grinned sourly; even though the columns would have fitted in the palm of his hand, he recognized, from bitter experience with Mar'ya Morevna's high steward, diminutive pages of credit–debit accounting. This, at least, was more interesting than Fedor Konstantinovich's ledgers, and besides, he didn't have to do the arithmetic himself. Or rub out his own all-too-frequent mistakes, either . . .

'It will also,' said Mar'ya Morevna from just over his shoulder, 'answer questions.'

'I wouldn't be surprised if it liked a drink afterwards as well,' said Ivan without turning round, and was rewarded with a brief and hastily stifled titter from one or other of the two female spies. He didn't need to look back; he could imagine Mar'ya Morevna's quick glare, half annoyance and half amusement. He looked more closely at the map. 'I presume that if you asked it, say, what might happen to the balance of powers in the event of an alliance, a raid, a crop failure – or whatever took your fancy – these lines and figures would change to show the result. Yes?'

'*Yest*', *tak tochno*,' said Mar'ya Morevna, and laughed that abrupt little laugh of hers that could as easily mean trouble as good humour. 'Just so. It would do exactly that. And it seems, beloved, that you've been spending more time with your books than I thought. Well done.'

46

This time, knowing both the laugh and the tone of voice in which she spoke, Ivan did turn around, took his wife's hand and lightly kissed the back of it. To the spies – unless they knew Mar'ya Morevna far too well – it was no more than a loving and pretty gesture. For Ivan and his dear wife, however, whose marriage could be a boisterous affair when it had to be, it was a defensive movement closely related to grabbing an opponent's sword-hand . . . 'And sometimes when the facts that lead to a conclusion are set out in front of me, I just guess well,' he said, smiling. 'Dmitriy Vasil'yevich ground the rules of logic into me a long time ago. I still haven't managed to forget all of them.'

Mar'ya Morevna gave him a chilly and distinctly old-fashioned look, then retrieved her hand from just under his nose with a quick, jerky movement, as though reluctant to keep it so close to a target in case she felt inclined to do something unfortunate. Ivan grinned. 'Not in front of the servants,' he said, knowing that if he hadn't been smacked already, playfully or otherwise, then it wasn't likely to happen.

'You!' said Mar'ya Morevna, then laughed with a sound that was a deal less theatening than the look on her face. 'Have you finished, Stepan?'

'Yes, Highness,' said the spy, bowing low before resuming his seat.

'Good. Do any of you have anything to add to Stepan's report? No? Then . . . Nikolai, continue please.'

As the big innkeeper, or soldier, or whatever he was pretending to be, began to speak, Ivan set aside any further teasing of his wife, at least until later, because Nikolai began by talking about Khorlov. There was nothing uncomplimentary about Ivan's home, or his family; but he suspected that simply meant there was nothing uncomplimentary to report. Mar'ya Morevna's spies were secure enough in their liege lady's trust that they would not allow tact to cloud truth.

Most of the report had to do with the tension between Tsar Aleksandr of Khorlov and the Great Princes of Kiev and Novgorod. Ivan and Mar'ya knew a lot of it already, from other sources: that unease had been going on since before their marriage, and indeed the wedding had both eased and increased it. Whilst he had remained single, there was no chance – or risk – of

47

Ivan providing the Khorlovskiy dynasty with a legitimate heir, and thus there was always the chance that on the old Tsar's death, one or other of the Great Princes might have found a pretext on which to legally annex the little tsardom. Moreover, though Khorlov had allies, they were of its own small stature and thus no deterrent to such political and military machinations.

Mar'ya Morevna had changed the situation. Not only was she Ivan's wife, she was a great ruler in her own right, a commander of armies who had been taught all the subtle Greek Byzantine arts of war, and rumour had it that she was expecting a child. *That* remained only a rumour, kept uncorrected by diplomatic good sense even while Ivan and Mar'ya were doing their best to make it true, and for love rather than dynastic considerations. That his father Tsar Aleksandr had been prepared to make war on the Princes of Novgorod and Kiev either individually or all together, in the belief that they and not Koshchey the Undying had been behind the hurts done to his son, had not improved the situation one whit, but at least now the Princes had retired muttering into their kennels like so many mastiffs, and looked set to stay that way for a while. In Novgorod particularly, Boris and Pavel Mikhaylovich had other things to consider than frustrated ambition. They were being threatened, as they had hoped to theaten Khorlov, by the Great Prince Yaroslav of Vladimir and his son Aleksandr Nevskiy. It had all the appearance of the bad old days, and at the same time, those bad old days had been so localized that from a safe distance they weren't so bad after all.

Even the Tatars had gone away. Ivan and Mar'ya Morevna had both been concerned that there might have been some sort of revenge taken for her destruction of Manguyu Temir's half-*tuman*-strong raiding party, but it seemed that the Khakhan Ogedei regarded the loss of five thousand men as not worthy of his attention. Even more than that, since Manguyu Temir had not been acting on the Great Khan's orders, had he returned from such a venture without something to show for it, the Khakhan would have done no more and no less than Mar'ya Morevna, and probably more painfully. Ogedei, ruthless as all Tatars, probably considered the killing of so unruly and disobedient a vassal, and ninety-nine in every hundred of his supporters, to be more a favour than anything else. Besides which, the Great Khan was already busy conquering Sung China and Khwarizmid Persia, and for the time being at least, had lost interest in anything further west.

'Now *that* is a backhanded blessing from God,' said Mar'ya Morevna, and signed herself with the life-giving cross. Everyone else did likewise. They knew exactly what she meant.

'Of course, silk and porcelain and tea are going to be hard to find for the next few years,' said Ivan dryly. 'Or then again, perhaps not. More expensive though. Whoever invades wherever, the merchants always manage to reach some sort of accommodation. It's the people who buy their goods who have to pay.'

'I'd rather have high-priced silk than a Tatar horde sitting on the doorstep of my kremlin, the way they tried to do last year,' said Mar'ya Morevna, and meant it. 'There's plenty of room in China for them to run about in, and with a bit of luck, they'll all get lost.'

It was laughing from safety at the howl of the wolf, and they all knew it; but if the choice was between that mocking, insincere laughter or cowering in terror, then false mirth was easier to live with.

The spies continued to talk, and after all the reports had been delivered, some salacious, some boring, but none of them truly terrible, Ivan and Mar'ya Morevna referred back and forth to the map and for almost two hours discussed what they had heard.

'I've never had any love for the Mikhaylovichi in Novgorod,' said Ivan, 'but I'm not sure I want to see them replaced by Yaroslav's people.'

'No?' Mar'ya Morevna was surprised. 'Seeing your enemies discomfited without needing to soil your own hands always seems good to me.'

'Better the wolves you know than the bears you don't.' Ivan looked at the map and pointed at the area just beyond Prince Yaroslav's city of Vladimir. 'Manguyu Temir's Tatars came right through here, but there's no record of any plundering, any killing, any *anything*. And nothing to show why, either. What sort of . . . accommodation . . . did Great Prince Yaroslav make with the Horde of the Sky-Blue Wolves?'

Mar'ya Morevna looked thoughtful. She tapped her finger against the tiny tower that represented Yaroslav's kremlin, then ran it up the surface of the map to the city of Suzdal'. 'Close,' she said, 'but not too close. Good. Pavel?' The spy Pavel stood up and bowed at being picked out for special notice. 'I sent Yevgeny to join you in Suzdal' last summer. Is he still there?'

'Yes, Highness. When last we met he was a merchant dealing in furs.'

'Good. Very good indeed. Then his moving south to Vladimir won't seem too remarkable. Great Prince Yaroslav and his son Aleksandr Nevskiy need watching. Make it so.'

'As you command, Highness.'

Mar'ya Morevna leaned closer to her husband and lowered her voice in case the matter was too private even for her own spies to hear. 'It isn't just that you don't know the doings of the Yaroslav bear, Vanya,' she said. 'And it's more even than their immunity from the Tatars. What's troubling you?'

'This,' he said, and gestured at the map. It was blank beyond the River Vistula, except for a few patches of detail showing where the Poles and the wild Prusiskai tribes had been troublesome. 'There's no indication of the German knights we were hearing about. They ate Lithuania, Livonia and Prussia the way you or I would eat a *blin*, but nobody said anything against them.'

'It would have needed doing sooner or later, to protect the settled lands on either side of the forests,' said Mar'ya Morevna. 'The tribes have been increasingly troublesome these past years, and if the Germans hadn't done it, some poor Rus would have to. I'm glad it was the *Nyemetsi*, though. Neither you, nor I, nor anyone with a hope of coming out again, would have gone into the Prussian forests without the sort of armour that they had at their disposal. The Prusiskai use magic the way more sensible folk use fire.' She thought a moment, shook her head and corrected herself. 'No. They *used* it that way. I suspect that there aren't enough of them left to do anything of the sort.' There was another short pause, and then she looked Ivan full in the face with the sort of look that usually accompanied a gentle, loving touch on his mouth. 'And small loss. You never had to deal with them, nor did your father. *My* father did. And he, the kindest, gentlest man I ever knew before I met you, said "never again" when he came home.

'But you're right. We should keep an eye on that particular border.' She looked at the map, closely and then closer still. 'And

50

on the Teutons, the Knights of the Sword or whatever they call themselves.' There was a tiny catch of breath amongst her words, an almost missed grunt of annoyance. 'Nothing *at all*. Yes, I see.'

'And yet,' said Ivan, 'Aleksandr Yaroslavich Nevskiy has been noising his suspicions to everyone who'll listen.'

Mar'ya Morevna relaxed audibly. 'Aleksandr Nevskiy,' she said, 'would claim the wide Ocean-sea itself as a threat if he thought it might stop people thinking as they do about himself, his father –and the cosy way they seem so friendly with the Tatars.'

'But we – even *we*, with this to help us' – Ivan gestured at the map – 'can only take his word for it. Because apart from the rumours there's no information anywhere about whether he's right about the Germans or not!'

'And you were the one who teased *me* about being too wrapped up in matters of security.' She poked Ivan gently in the ribs. 'Yes, I know; so I'll send out a spy or two in the spring and have this blank space filled in with useful detail before you know it.'

'Why not now? If Yevgeny is leaving Suzdal'—'

'Yevgeny is a deal closer to where I want him to go than anyone I might send into the *Nyemetskiy* lands. And anyway, Vanyushechka, until spring there's nothing to worry about. Nobody in their right mind would attack Mother Russia with the winter coming on. Can you imagine how long an armoured German *rytsar'* knight would last before he froze, or before he and his heavy horse went through the ice on some lake or river and never came back up? No, spring is early enough to worry about them.'

Ivan looked at the map again and frowned; then shrugged and dismissed his worries. 'You're right, of course,' he said. 'Sending an army in winter would be the last mistake they'd ever make – and I doubt they'd be so stupid.' He straightened his back. 'Are we done here?'

'Until tomorrow. I have a few more questions for these good servants' – the spies all smiled and bowed at the compliment, something Mar'ya Morevna did not hand out lightly – 'before they go back about their, and your and my, affairs. But all that can wait until the morning.' She stood up, then yawned and stretched, both gestures extravagant and not particularly ladylike, but quite in keeping with a commander of armies who had been collating intelligence for almost five hours. 'I give you all my thanks, and bid you all good night.'

With one last glance at that worrying blank area over Prussia, Ivan took the magic map from the wall and folded it away into its surprisingly small bundle. He nodded courteously to the five spies, who presumably had their beds made up somewhere in the many rooms of the Red Tower, then trotted downstairs after Mar'ya Morevna.

There was someone waiting for them, lantern in hand, when they emerged from the Red Tower. The lamplight struck golden sparkles from the mail and the tall-spired helmet, and for just an instant, long enough to have him reaching for the long Circassian dagger tucked behind his belt-buckle, Ivan could not recognize the hulking silhouette. Then it moved, the lantern shifted and the droop-moustached face of Boris Petrovich Fedorov emerged from the shadows of his own making. Mar'ya Morevna's Captain-of-Guards looked at the half-drawn *kindjal* dagger, and said not a word; but it was just as well that most of his expression was concealed by the nasal bar and cheek-plates of his helmet.

'And a good evening to you too, Boris Petrovich,' said Mar'ya Morevna, nudging Ivan in the ribs to make him put the blade away. She looked at the big warrior, then frowned. 'What's the matter?'

'There is a visitor at the kremlin gates, Highness,' said the Guard-Captain, saluting. 'Given the late hour, I thought it best not to admit her without your permission, and given that' – he glanced upwards – 'there are other visitors within the walls.'

'Were you expecting another of . . . them?' asked Ivan, glancing at his wife.

'No.' Mar'ya Morevna looked at her Captain-of-Guards and said, '*Her*? A woman, alone, at this time of night? And you left her outside?'

Guard-Captain Fedorov gazed impassively at his liege lady as the flicker of her annoyance went past his ears like a sling-stone. 'At this time of night, and unannounced, yes, Highness, I did. And under guard, too.'

Mar'ya Morevna stared at him for a moment, then shook her head and made a noise that was halfway a laugh and halfway a clearing of her throat. '*Izvini*, Boris Petrovich. Excuse me. It's

been a long day. You were quite right, of course. Take us to her.'
As they walked across the darkened kremlin courtyard, she said,
'Why does this mysterious woman want to see me?'

'Not you, Highness. She asked for Ivan Tsarevich by name.'

The answer did not quite stop her dead in her tracks, but the
hesitation in her stride was too obvious to be hidden, and Ivan felt
sure that it was only the unfeigned bafflement on his face that
saved him from an interrogation more stringent than any directed
at the spies in the Tower. And then he saw the woman, dark-
haired, slim within her long black cloak, and not in the least bit
overawed by the pair of Guard-Captain Fedorov's tallest soldiers
who flanked her. She stared at him with green eyes whose colour
and brilliance was plain even at a distance and at night, and Ivan
began to smile despite himself.

'Vanya,' said Mar'ya Morevna in a tight, dignified voice, 'there
have never been any secrets between us, or so I thought. Is this
. . . person . . . someone from your past that I should have been
told about before now?'

Prince Ivan looked at her with a grin that might have eased her
mind at once, or just as easily have prompted her to knock him off
his feet. Then the grin got even wider. 'But I did tell you, though I
might have forgotten to describe the woman.'

'Forgotten? Someone like you, forget who looks like that?'

'She doesn't look like that all the time,' said Ivan. 'Or even most
of the time.' He advanced very, very slowly, stopped a short
distance from the woman, and inclined his head in a curt little bow
of welcome. 'Good night, and well met.'

The cool green eyes looked him up and down with a gaze filled
with speculation and unvoiced thoughts. '*Zdravstvuyte*, Ivan
Tsarevich,' she said.

'I'm just as pleased to meet you again,' said Ivan. 'Might I
introduce my wife, and the lord of this kremlin—'

'Mar'ya Morevna, *krasivya tsarevna*,' said the woman quietly,
and bowed low; somehow it seemed more right and proper than
the more usual courtesy. 'Who has not heard of the fairest Princess
in all the Russias, and of her fortunate husband?'

Mar'ya Morevna opened her mouth to say something, then
thought better of it and closed her teeth with a click, giving Ivan
the strange spectacle of seeing his wife at a loss for words for the

first time since they had met. 'Ivan,' she said slowly, 'just who *is* this?'

'Someone to whom I owe my life,' he said, and warily extended one hand. 'What favour can I do you, Mother Wolf?'

Chapter Three

There was no tilt-yard in *Schloss* Thorn, the castle being more a fortified monastery and not built with such frivolities as tournaments in mind. There was, however, a courtyard below the great chapel, flanked on one side by the castle's curtain wall and on the other by the lowering bulk of the barbican that led to the inner ward. Trapped and focused by those two masses of brick and worked stone, the clangorous echoes of steel on steel hammered harshly across the trodden grass, almost as harshly as the blows that brought such sounds to life.

On one side of the yard – a cleared space in the outer bailey that was much longer and wider than its name suggested – a new draft of sergeants drilled with shield and cutting-spear under the unsympathetic eye and still less sympathetic voice of one of the Teutonic Order's *Feldwebeln*. Neither they nor he were knights, and so, despite the Christian, holy and monastic nature of the Order, he was able to make use of the full heights and depths of his vocabulary of invective. It had always been sharp; senior sergeants seemed to be born that way, and this one had honed his insults to a razor edge by twelve years' service in the Holy Land, where he had kept other young men-at-arms alive by making sure they were more scared of him than of the Saracens.

And on the other side, fully clad in mail and bearing the weapons of their choice, the Teutonic Knights of Castle Thorn duelled for practice, exercise and recreation. At any rate, most of them did; one at least found the effort of wielding blunted training weapons, half again as heavy as the real thing, to be a lot more than he had bargained for.

Albrecht von Düsberg broke ground, opening the distance between himself and his opponent enough to make a salute with his long knightly broadsword that would end the bout. The other armoured man, a *Schwertbruder* from Bavaria by the look of his gear, returned the salute with a snap of the wrist that proved either he was an excellent actor or that his joints and muscles

55

weren't complaining anything like as much as von Düsberg's.

It was always the same with the confrère brethren; had it not been for the sudden burst of piety – prompted by God alone knew what sin – or by a desire to go crusading where victories were still won by valour rather than negotiation, they would have continued as mercenaries, or the sort of knight who turned a nice profit from the booty gained by winning tournaments. Either way, there was never a one of them who knew or cared about the difference between practice and a fight to the finish.

Waiting barely long enough for his opponent to walk away, Albrecht leaned his weight against notched sword and battered shield, and wheezed for breath as though his lungs were about to burst. There had been a moment or two during the mock combat when he had thought the bursting had already happened, and he knew now what *Hochmeister* von Salza had been gently hinting: that he had spent far too long in the Archbishop of Salzburg's library, and nothing like long enough encased in eighty pounds of mail. Eight hundred pounds was what it felt like, most of it dragging at his shoulders and down towards the ground. Albrecht forced those aching shoulders back; even when held more or less in place by leather thongs threaded through every fifth row of rings, a mail hauberk had the unpleasant tendency to collapse its mesh, and its weight, forward or backward – but always off balance – if its wearer gave it half a chance by leaning too much one way or the other.

The snow in the tilt-yard was ankle-deep and still falling, but Albrecht von Düsberg didn't feel in the least bit cold. That, he knew, would come later, unless he did something about it that would probably involve hot water. He was blowing grey vapour like a dragon's breath out through the slits of his helmet's demivisor, and most probably steaming like a hard-run horse through the links of his mail as well. Certainly every other knight and sergeant that he could see through his own private fog-bank were doing the same. Once the thickly quilted gambeson worn beneath armour was well soaked with hot sweat, nobody could help but steam. And stink.

Not that there was anything wrong with the smell of honest sweat. No indeed; all the armour and the padding under it, and everyone else in the castle, all reeked with that unmistakable martial aroma that came of a mingling of sweat with the sharp tang of metal and the heavy perfume of old oil. Any fortress of the military orders, Templars, Hospitallers and all, would have seemed strangely empty, cold and dead without it. And yet, despite his private reservations about such effete Eastern customs, the thought of a tub filled with hot water had grown increasingly pleasant. Not so much for the sake of cleanliness, Albrecht thought sternly to himself, for, after all, a certain pious sluttishness was something to be approved. But even so, the prospect of being warm right to the tips of his frozen toes without the uncomfortable chilly period that followed changing from armour back to indoor clothing was very appealing.

More appealing, at least, than keeping company with the three latest visitors to Thorn, who had arrived hot from the Lateran Palace in Rome only the day before. Albrecht had formed no opinion as yet about the eldest and most senior of the three, other than to wonder whether the presence of an apostolic notary was really the compliment it seemed. Father Tommaso Giacchetti was a monk of the order of St Benedict, and seemed if anything too frail to have made such a journey north across Europe. That he had done so at all, and without showing any sign of stress and strain, suggested that he was somewhat less fragile than he appeared. To learn from one of the ten men-at-arms of the escort that the trip had taken less than five weeks made Albrecht and every other knight in Castle Thorn look at Giacchetti with new respect.

If the Benedictine monk appeared a gentle – if surprisingly fit – old soul, his two companions were another matter entirely. They were white-cowled, black-robed Dominicans, and they carried an aura with them that would take as long to fade as the colour of their sombre habits. Father Willem Arnald, as had been announced on his arrival, had been appointed by Pope Gregory IX himself as joint head of the Holy, Catholic and Apostolic Office. That appointment, as was better known than his youthful secretary Brother Johann might have believed, had been confirmed on the twenty-seventh day of July in the Year of Grace 1233, no more than seventeen months past – but the reputation of Father Arnald's office was already well established.

The Dominican father was, in short, an inquisitor, responsible for enforcing the Pope's often blinkered view of the world, answerable to no one but God and his Pontiff, and by that authority permitted to use everything save mercy in the hunt for heresy. No mention had yet been made of his function here, but Albrecht von Düsberg was looking forward with queasy anticipation to finding out. He found himself hoping that Pope Gregory had remembered to instruct the Holy Office correctly concerning the Church's revised view of magic; otherwise matters in *Schloss* Thorn could become very . . . interesting.

Albrecht considered that for a moment while he fumbled with unsteady, snow-slippery hands, trying to bring swordpoint and scabbard-chape into conjunction without severing a couple of fingers. Even though his sword had started out the day as a blunt and relatively harmless practice weapon, two vigorous bouts with the Bavarian *Schwertbruder* – Josef Dietrich von Bayern or some such name – had turned its soft, untempered edge into something resembling a crude saw that would need the attention of a smith and a grindstone before it could possibly be called harmless again.

Once the long blade was out of his and everyone else's harm's way, von Düsberg slung his shield across his back on its long guige-strap, and pulled off his helmet in the hope that he would breathe more easily. With five pounds' weight of pressure lifted from the leather arming-cap beneath his hood of mail, the cap's felt-and-horsehair padding at long last stopped its constant trickling of sopped-up sweat. Apart from that, Albrecht didn't feel much better.

He wiped the last few drips from eyebrows and nose with the back of his hand, noting absently that a glove whose fabric was composed of linked metal rings made a most inadequate towel, and comforted himself with the thought that had he been wearing a fully enclosed *Kübelhelm* rather than his own, he would have felt much worse. Even though they were much safer in battle than the more open forms of protective headgear – such as the one he wore, where only an iron half-mask covered his face – the great helms always made him feel just as their name suggested, that he was wearing an upturned bucket. A bucket, moreover, whose slots for sight and breathing were always far too small and distant to be of any use. It made sure if nothing else that when he was wearing enough armour to avoid injury, he was unlikely to cause injury to anyone else.

That was just the sort of protection to gain Papal approval, thought von Düsberg: something useless. He smiled sourly without much humour, knowing himself to be the most useless warrior within the castle walls – then he shivered violently enough to make his teeth chatter. Dropping his own helmet to the snowy ground, he hugged both arms around himself and shuffled his feet in an attempt to regain some sort of illusory warmth. Now that the exertion of combat had faded, he was cooling fast, and heat in any form, even that of sinfully hot and soapy water, was rapidly becoming not so much a luxury as a necessity. He wriggled his fingers out through the open palms of his mail mittens and began to fumble with the lacings of his coif.

The point of a sword reached out from behind to tap him lightly on the shoulder. 'So weary so soon, *Fra* Albrecht?' said a muffled, sardonic voice. 'It's been plain all morning that you've spent too long out of harness.'

Weary or not, out of practice or not, the tone of that voice was not something any German *Ritter* could be expected to tolerate. Von Düsberg swung around with one bare hand already clamped on the hilt of his own sword and its blade halfway from the scabbard, heedless of the chill in the metal that burnt its way into his exposed flesh. Then he stopped, emitted a snort that in another circumstance would have been an oath worthy of several penances, and slammed the weapon back into its sheath.

One did not draw on the Grand Master.

'But that,' the voice continued, 'was almost fast enough to be convincing.' Inside his white-painted helm, crested with a stiff fore-and-aft fan of black feathers and with its reinforcing bars picked out in the black *cross potent* that was the symbol of the Order, Hermann von Salza was probably grinning. 'You really are more at home with a pen and counting-frame than with the sword, aren't you?'

Albrecht von Düsberg hated that sort of rhetorical question. Proper rhetorical questions didn't need answers; that was the whole point of asking them. But when asked by someone like the Grand Master – or indeed Albrecht's own cousin the Cardinal-Archbishop of Salzburg, who had the same unfortunate tendency

to want answers to his questions whether they needed one or not –
there was always the feeling that no matter what form the answer
took, it would always be wrong.

It was the verbal equivalent of getting fluff up your nose, a
common hazard of working in elderly libraries, as Albrecht well
knew, which if blowing into a fine linen kerchief didn't help, could
only really be relieved by the application of a finger. Except that
nobody ever believed that dust, or fluff, or a leather pouch filled
with silver coins, was anything other than a poor excuse for what
you were *really* doing with that finger . . .

'I am Treasurer for the Order, Grand Master, and you selected
me as such,' he said at last, very much on his dignity. 'I flatter
myself that being *Ordenstressler* places much more emphasis on
skill in counting and arithmetic than on any supposed ability to
chop things up.'

'Ha-ha.' It wasn't a laugh, von Salza actually spoke the sounds
aloud. 'And that's chopping people, Albrecht. People, not things.
The Knights of Christ do not make war on things – at least, not yet.
We'll have to wait until the worthy Father Arnald says his piece
before we know if that stays truth or not.'

Not troubling to sheathe his sword – it was only a practice
weapon, after all, and as such not worthy of the respect due to a
knightly sword with man-killing edges – von Salza jabbed it into
the ground and wrenched off his helm with a gesture not far
removed from a drowning man breaking the surface of the water.
'*Gottverdammt!*' he said, sketching a hasty cross over his chest
with one hand as penance for the oath even as he said it. 'I could
almost prefer those open iron hats that we wore in Palestine.
Never mind the risk of taking someone's edge in the face, at least
you could breathe easily until it happened.' He hesitated at the
beginning of what sounded like a favourite rant on a favourite
subject and cocked his head towards Albrecht in a quizzical
gesture that was strangely birdlike, almost like one of his own
hawks'. '*Was ist's, Fra Tressler?*'

Von Düsberg shook his head. 'Nothing important, Grand
Master,' he said. 'Nothing at all.' How could he say that though
Hermann von Salza was as hot and sweaty as any of the other
knights, yet he still managed to look more neat, more elegant,
more *cool* than he had any right to be. More like a Grand Master,

was the thought that had gone through Albrecht's head, and at the same time it was not the sort of thought that made enough sense for anyone to voice it aloud. There was more than a lack of sense about it; there was something almost magical about the self-contained, unflustered face that had been revealed by the removal of that helm. Knowing how the *Herr Hochmeister* valued his appearance, von Düsberg would not have been surprised to learn that there was no 'almost' about the magic involved, and that brought him right back to the Dominican inquisitor stalking the corridors of Castle Thorn, eyes narrowed for signs of heresy – or sorcery.

'We should talk,' said Hermann von Salza.

His statement made Albrecht start slightly, unseen within the carapace of his armour, at the accuracy of the Grand Master's perception. It was as if his concern had been read like letters from the expressions that had crossed his face, and maybe they had. At least there was nothing magical in that. The apparent reading of minds had as much to do with understanding how posture and expression differed from the spoken word, and it was something learned and practised by more kings and lords and powerful men than their vassals could ever know. That said and generally known, there was no reason why a spell or two – small, undetectable sorceries all – could not be added to the ploy, to make its effect that bit more . . . all right, effective.

'Where, *Herr Hochmeister*, and about what?'

Von Salza stared at Albrecht as though he had taken leave of his senses. 'About the Papal envoys, *du Blödmann*,' he snapped; then swore softly under his breath – without even sketching anything like a sign of penance, von Düsberg noticed with slight surprise – and then shook his head, hard, as though something weighty and uncomfortable was sitting on top of it. 'I'm sorry. I didn't mean that. Not even my rank permits . . .' The Grand Master didn't kneel, that would have been still more unseemly, but he crossed his hand on the pommel of his sword and bowed his head. '*Herr Ordenstressler, Ritter* von Düsberg, grant me your pardon for hard words uncalled-for.'

Albrecht looked on, startled and more than a little horrified, then gathered his wits before the stillness dragged beyond surprise and into embarrassment – and before anyone else noticed. He

61

reached out with one hand, almost laying it on von Salza's lowered head as he might have done to any other penitent, then flushed crimson with the near impropriety and pulled it back. 'Grand Master . . .' he said. 'Sir . . . *Herr Hochmeister*, I am but a knight of the Order and you are my lord, and if hard words were used they were deserved and accepted. All else is forgotten. You – you have my pardon, if pardon is needed.'

Hermann von Salza went down on one knee and made the sign of the cross, brow to belt, shoulder to shoulder, but all done so smoothly and quickly that had any in the tilt-yard glanced towards him, they would have thought only that he had dropped something in the snow. For Albrecht von Düsberg, standing upright and looking straight ahead, more embarrassed to receive the apology than to give it, that genuflection lasted an hour. He wondered, long afterwards on his simple bed in the still dark, if that had not been von Salza's intention all along.

Then the Grand Master stood up, pulled his sword from the frozen ground and reached out with it to tap the hilt at Albrecht's side in a manner that was anything but apologetic. 'I said, we should talk. And out here. Since yesterday, there have been too many ears indoors. Especially as our guests seem done with their devotions, at least for the time being.'

So they were: three figures, two of them black and white and one dead black, were standing beneath the archway of the commandery's great chapel. They were caught in a frame of its façade of moulded, decorated brick and the oak doors four times the height of a man; all of it, stone and wood, shaped to the glory of God, and all of it somehow diminished and insulted by the inquisitor who stood before its glory. Even two hundred feet away, Albrecht could sense if not see the disapproval on Father Arnald's face. It was hard to say where that look originated: from the sight of so many knights and sergeants training in the arts of killing their fellow men, or just from the sight of the steadily deepening snow in the courtyard. To a monk who wore sandals rather than boots and hose, snow on the ground meant real discomfort not just inconvenience. And maybe, just maybe, that disapproval came from another source entirely, one that might reveal itself in Father-Inquisitor Arnald's own good time.

'All his power,' said Hermann von Salza in a small, vehement voice, 'comes from hurting those who cannot strike back, those who cannot argue with him, because he knows from one minute to the next what is real in the Pope's world. Or he tells His Holiness so, at least. For the rest, *Fra* Albrecht, he knows less about a sword even than you,' and the Grand Master grinned to take the sting from his words, 'and much less about the pen that carries weight where the sword cannot reach.' He waved one hand. 'Draw blade. And pardon me again if I speak nothing but the truth: you need training with a sword as a fish needs training to ride a horse. But while this training continues, we can talk in safety. Although,' he said, glancing at Albrecht's helmet in the snow and his own encumbering one hand, 'we also need to hear.' Von Salza turned his head a little and raised his voice a lot. 'Günther, come here!' he shouted, and then more quietly to von Düsberg, 'so no helms. Of your courtesy, try not to split my skull. *Günther!*'

He glanced sidelong at the young man-at-arms who came slithering to a standstill behind him. 'If I were a secular knight and you my squire,' he said severely, 'rather than the pair of us members of an order supposedly exempt from mundane punishments, then I would warm your armoured arse with the tails of my shield-straps, as was done to me to make me prompt when summoned.' Von Salza waved one hand in a peremptory fashion at the two helmets, Albrecht's and his own. 'Take these to the armoury. Have them strip and clean the linings from both. And if they're not entirely sweet and clean the next time I put one on . . .'

Günther was gone, and both helms with him, before von Salza finished.

'Now,' said the Grand Master, and swung his shield around from his back to where he could easily run his left forearm through the enarmes, the straps on the inner side by which it was carried in combat. It was done all in a single swift, smooth shrugging movement that made Albrecht feel quite jealous. It was the same sort of jealousy that had sparked through him when he had first seen how unrumpled Hermann von Salza managed to remain inside his helm; and he wondered, just a little, whether a man who might employ magic to preserve his personal appearance might not also use it to preserve *all* appearances.

Readying his own shield for use was a somewhat clumsier

business. Riveted to padding and thus supposedly fixed in place, the enarmes had nonetheless become twisted around their buckles again, in the way that they managed seven times out of ten. As von Düsberg fought them with awkward mail-mittened fingers, he felt his already flushed features growing still redder with embarrassment.

It would have been more bearable had von Salza actually said aloud what was probably going through his mind, but a sort of misplaced courtesy kept the Grand Master's lips pressed tight shut around his comments. Only the slightest tap-tap-tap of his sword-point against one armoured foot betrayed anything of his feelings. It was probably just as well. By the time that Albrecht had successfully unravelled the cat's cradle of leather – a matter of only two or three minutes, but which seemed much longer to both knights – and rammed his arm through their loops with a force that was a fair indication of how he felt, voicing any observation whatsoever would have been enough to make him lose his temper.

Von Salza contented himself with a long, slow exhalation, a plume of grey-white vapour that trailed from his carefully unsmiling mouth. It drifted away like smoke through the snowy air and could not be interpreted as containing any words at all. 'Take guard,' he said, 'and let me see how you do it.'

Albrecht obediently drew sword as he had been taught, extending the draw until his right hand was above his head, then shifting his wrist so that the sword's blade both angled down in front of his face and pointed towards his opponent. At the same time he raised his shield level with his nose – then hesitated and peered with worried eyes at the Grand Master's critical expression.

'Passable.' Von Salza reached out a leisurely point and probed for weaknesses in the stance while Albrecht, until told not to, shifted blade and shield to block. 'Very passable indeed. Just slow . . .'

He leaned forward, not slowly at all, hooked the rim of his own shield around Albrecht's and pulled backwards, much harder than the Treasurer had been expecting. All of a sudden the triple ply of crossgrained limewood that formed his principal defence was there no longer, and Hermann von Salza's sword had flickered into the gap to poke him solidly in the guts.

64

'Very slow,' von Salza repeated. 'But with room for improvement all the same.' Moving in closer, he began to rearrange the way von Düsberg wore his shield-straps, and at the same time, in a much lower voice than before, began to talk about matters that had nothing to do with swordplay.

'The good fathers,' he said, 'took considerable pains to ensure that their escort from Rome was, shall we say, free of other allegiances. Their men-at-arms are Italian for the most part, with a couple of Frankish sergeants, an Englishman coming home from Palestine the long way.' Von Salza paused, tugged one of the straps a notch tighter, and said, 'Oh yes, and a Schwytzer.'

'Indeed, *Herr Hochmeister*? You mean, a man who claimed he was a Schwytzer,' said Albrecht and smiled briefly. The Teutonic Knights often had reason to send their brethren from place to place without advertising the fact, and the presence of just one German-speaker among the escort suggested that this man was indeed a brother-knight. 'Dangerous, though. Giacchetti the old Benedictine might not have known the difference in accent, but I would have expected better of Father Arnald and his secretary. They're both German.'

'No. Arnald's from southern Austria,' corrected von Salza, giving the face of Albrecht's shield a thump with one hand to test the new fit of the enarmes. 'The Hapsburg domains. *Fra* Gottfried knew that; he's no fool. That's why he claimed to be Swiss. He told me that he didn't expect an Austrian to have much interest in what the *Waldstätter* sound like, just so long as they do as they're told like a good conquered people should.'

'Then his secretary. . . ?'

'What makes you think that pretty young man is here because of his erudition? Brother Johann's talents seem to lie in another direction entirely. The sergeants are already calling him Little Peachbottom . . .'

Albrecht turned his head to stare at the three figures by the chapel, and opened his mouth to say something; then thought better of it and shut his teeth with a snap that stretched after only a few seconds into a wide, tight grin. 'One of the privileges of the Holy Office, I suppose,' he said. 'Nobody questions what they do, for fear of being accused of worse.' He chuckled low in his throat. 'Well, it's not exactly chastity, but it's certainly one way of

65

remaining celibate – at least in the literal sense of being unmarried, anyway.'

The Grand Master smiled crookedly and stepped backwards, raising his own shield. 'Cut to head, then to flank. No matter what they do in private life, they're both inquisitors. Let's not make them suspicious.' He took the first cut on his shield, warded the second with his sword, and said, 'Gottfried tells me that we were not the only order to be blessed with such a visitation. The Templars are also entertaining an inquisitor.'

'In God's name, why?' Albrecht rested sword on shoulder, puzzled and apprehensive both at once. 'I thought these envoys were sent in connection with . . .' He didn't say the name aloud, but jerked his head towards the East, and Russia.

'They were; at least, that's their principal function, and Father Giacchetti's only reason to be here. But it would seem from what Gottfried overheard, that His Holiness is not entirely convinced that the military orders were as obedient in the matter of magic as they claim.' The Grand Master shrugged casually. 'So far as the Templars are concerned, he may be right. They're very much a power unto themselves, and it hasn't endeared them to the Pope – or to the Emperor.'

It didn't surprise Albrecht in the slightest. Emperor Friedrich's reluctant crusade had managed to regain Jerusalem and the Holy Places by a treaty with the Saracens, something that Templar swords had so signally failed to do for many years. The Master of the Templars had been so enraged by what he perceived as an insult to himself and to his order that he had written to the Saracen Sultan Kamil, suggesting that it would be an easy matter to assassinate the Emperor as he returned from Jerusalem to Acre. Kamil, more of a gentleman than some of the Christians who opposed him, had instead warned the intended victim. The upheaval that followed, what with accusations, denials, seizures of some properties and expulsions from others, had plainly not died down yet.

'Gottfried saw a Templar knight in the Lateran Palace,' said von Salza. 'It was he who suggested that if his order was to be investigated, then so should all the others – particularly the order which was no longer interested in protecting the Holy Land from the infidel . . .'

66

'Charming,' said Albrecht between his teeth. He was glad now that the *Herr Hochmeister* had chosen weapon-practice for this conversation, because he badly wanted to hit something. 'So even though the Pope stands to benefit considerably from *what* we do, we'll need the approval of someone like Arnald as to *how* we do it.'

Hermann von Salza looked at him thoughtfully, and didn't reply. Instead he said, 'Shield higher – yes, like that. Now cut to left leg.'

Von Düsberg's sword lashed out a good deal faster than the Grand Master was expecting, and only a swift, thunderous roundhouse block – and a hasty sidestep that was almost a jump when the interposed shield proved to be nothing like enough to stop so forceful a cut – preserved Hermann von Salza from a nasty crack across the kneecap. His eyebrows shot up and he stared at his plump, perspiring treasurer with the beginnings of new respect.

'Yes. Yes indeed! The sergeants should make you angry more often, Albrecht my friend. They might have a different view of your ability.' He lifted his own sword high, its hilt behind his head and its blade straight down parallel with his spine: the posture of a knight no longer playing. Albrecht saw, and just for the moment, didn't care.

'Left flank!' von Salza barked, and took another heavy stroke on the face of his shield, so that it boomed under the blow. 'Right flank!' Albrecht's sword whirled about and slashed in again from a different angle, met this time in clangorous impact by the Grand Master's own blade. It whipped around and down, struck solidly to deflect the incoming cut, then returned to its ready position with such a lack of effort that it seemed almost weightless.

'Ward now.' As he spoke, Hermann von Salza started a crabwise move to the right and shifted the position of his own sword and shield ever so slightly. Albrecht rotated slowly on the spot, shield-rim up to the bridge of his nose, and watched that poised sword for the first warning of movement.

'Left shoulder!'

The shield kicked on Albrecht's forearm as it met the cut, but something else entirely rasped across the angle where arm met shoulder with a thump that stunned his muscles. A sword glissading over mail-rings makes a metallic rattling screech like no other sound in all the world. Albrecht heard it, far too close for comfort, and jerked away from the Grand Master, slashing his own sword in a horizontal arc through the space between them to buy himself more room.

'Hold fast,' said von Salza. 'Enough.' To Albrecht's surprise, he was breathing hard. 'You're an unusual one, *Fra Tressler*. When you lose your temper, you gain . . . I was about to say skill, but call it unexpected competence instead. With most knights, it's the other way around.'

'I dislike interference from outside, Grand Master.'

'It showed. You should try to school your expression somewhat, Albrecht. You wear what you think like a banner on your face. But so far as Father Arnald is concerned, I agree without reservation. Without his approval, nothing gets done. The problem is, he probably has less notion of what he'll be asked to consider than the average louse. Lice at least go to war, if only because some knights regard cleanliness as decadent.' He quirked one eyebrow at Albrecht, but forbore to pursue the subject. 'And one matter in particular was set in train well before the question of approval was raised. Dieter Balke has made a little foray into Russia on my behalf, looking for a sorcerer. He found one. He's on his way back to *Schloss* Thorn even as we speak.'

'Jesu!' Von Düsberg tried without success to believe that the shudder trembling on his skin was just because of the cold. He crossed himself, an awkward business with a sword in one hand and a shield in the other, but he managed it without doing himself mischief. There would be mischief enough if the *Landmeister* of Livonia was involved.

He had met Balke no more than five times in the Holy Land, and after the third time and the carnage in the marketplace at Acre when he had seen just what Dieter Balke was capable of doing, he had tried to avoid him whenever possible. The man terrified him, with a cold, gut-clenching terror that had little to do with fear in battle and a great deal to do with revulsion. When Balke was sent in presumed disgrace to the shores of the Baltic to fight against the heathen Livonians, Albrecht had said a great many prayers of gratitude to the Virgin. They had plainly not been enough. '*Herr*

Hochmeister,' he said, 'Dieter Balke is a butcher. He makes war like a savage. He—'

'—Is no gentleman?' said von Salza in a clipped voice that put a sudden end to Albrecht's protests. 'Maybe not. But he is a man who is simultaneously cunning, energetic, and brutal, the sort I need for tasks where a gentleman would refuse to soil his lily-white hands. Balke follows his orders. He does as I tell him, without question. That should be enough for you, *Fra Tressler*, because it's more than enough for me.'

'But to bring Balke – and a sorcerer – here! Why?'

The Grand Master lowered his own sword and regarded Albrecht blandly. 'Why what, *Fra* Albrecht? Be more specific.'

'Why didn't you wait?'

Von Salza appeared to think about it for a few seconds. 'Time considerations,' he said at last. 'That's as good as reason as any.'

'Time considerations?'

'The sooner this Rus sorcerer starts doing our bidding, the sooner the Rus will be at war and tearing each other apart. And the sooner the Knights of the Teutonic Order can move in to pick up the pieces and reshape them as seems best – and most profitable.'

'And if Father Arnald withholds imprimatur? Have you considered that, *Herr Hochmeister*?'

'I am sure,' said von Salza, raising his sword and swatting snowflakes with its blade, 'that the good Father-Inquisitor can be persuaded to our way of thinking. One way or another.' The sword twirled, poised, and slithered back into its scabbard. 'Enough of this. I see no reason to conjecture in the freezing outdoors when facts can be learnt in warmth and comfort. Of course,' he said idly, glancing one last time towards the three monks by the chapel, 'our guests will almost certainly consider warmth and comfort to be just one step removed from sinful luxury. Can you stand the strain of so much pious disapproval?'

Albrecht, no longer entirely certain that he still had toes to call his own, decided in short order that he could stand any amount of piety, and said so.

There was more said later, and by no means all of it came from Treasurer von Düsberg. For one thing, Grand Master von Salza had been quite right about what the Papal envoys would think of his private chambers in the *Hochschloss*. Sinful luxury was in fact the least of the things he was accused of, and none of it softened by diplomatic euphemism.

'. . . Unseemly and iniquitous,' mumbled Father Giacchetti on his third circuit of the room, poking with his staff at the mats of woven rushes which covered the floor. 'Highly improper. Such ostentation. Like the Sultan's seraglio.'

'Have you ever,' said von Salza mildly, '*seen* a sultan's seraglio?'

'Heaven preserve me from such a sight,' said Father Giacchetti, crossing himself in horror at the prospect.

'Have you, Grand Master?' asked Father Arnald, his voice oozing a disinterest that fooled neither Hermann von Salza nor any of the other knights seated with him.

'And if I have, then when, where, and under what circumstances?' von Salza said. 'That was the rest of your question, was it not?' The Dominican inquisitor shrugged. 'The answer to the first part is, no, I have not. Even for a knight sworn to chastity, the price of admission is a trifle high.' He grinned a small grin that had barely stretched his thin lips before it was gone again. 'But I can assure all of you, and the Pope himself, that rushes on the floor are not part of a seraglio's furnishings. Not even rushes sinfully woven into mats, rather than strewn loose as God intended.'

Expressionless, Arnald stared at him for several minutes. 'The intentions of God with regard to the Teutonic Order are something that might need to be discussed at a later date, *Herr Hochmeister*,' he said at last. 'For the present, we should restrain ourselves to hear what the venerable Father Giacchetti has to say. He speaks,' and the warning edge in Arnald's voice was barely veiled, 'with the voice and the authority of the Pope.'

Or at least, thought von Salza after a few minutes, in the same wearisome style as the Pontiff. He had been in audience with Pope Gregory on two occasions, and his sere, droning monotone had not been a voice invested with much authority. Giacchetti sounded just like him; looked like him, too, for the Pope had been over eighty when he was elected, and that was seven years ago. A church whose principals were well-connected antiques. Hermann von Salza heaved a gusty sigh that he hoped didn't sound too much like a yawn, and tried to pay attention.

70

'That the Knights of the Teutonic Order desire to extend their influence and that of Holy Mother Church into the pagan lands of the East is most laudable,' mumbled Father Giacchetti, still translating, in monstrously accented High German, from the scroll held up in front of his nose. 'That they should desire to do so alone and unaided is of the one part more laudable still, but of the other part a matter of sadness to Us in that it betrays the sin of pride.'

Von Salza glanced from side to side, at von Düsberg the Treasurer, at von Buxhövden the *Hauskomtur* of Castle Thorn, and at von Jülich his steward. All three knights had the same look on their faces, more or less concealed from someone who didn't know them as well as their Grand Master. It was a look that suggested accusations of pride were somewhat misplaced when coming from the incumbent of an office which claimed that Popes could never make a mistake. It was a look that betrayed heresy, since that too had been laid down: 'Whoever does not agree with the Apostolic See is without doubt a heretic.'

That made every one of the Order's officers a heretic. There wasn't a single man among them who at some time or other hadn't thought at least one of the commands and edicts emanating from Rome to be, at the very least, worthy of question by the brains that God had given his human creations. And that was before the useful art of sorcery had been added to the equation . . .

Then the Grand Master sat bolt upright, no longer finding any difficulty in giving Giacchetti's words his full attention. The envoy had reached the Papal conditions of approval for von Salza's venture into Russia, and those conditions were impossible to ignore.

'As a penance for this pridefulness,' read the old Benedictine, so buried in his scroll that he – fortunately – did not see the effect of his words, 'and as demonstration to the newly converted heathen that Christian knights have no desire to lay up treasures on Earth, We therefore desire and command our beloved son Hermann von Salza that one-third of all moveables of value seized during the first year of the crusade be transported to Rome for the benefit of Mother Church and Her servants the clergy.'

It was only the iron-bound discipline of the Order – and a swift glare from his Grand Master – that kept Kuno von Buxhövden in

71

his seat and silent. A passionate man, better suited to being a secular knight than a warrior monk, the *Hauskomtur*'s talent for ill-timed outburst had been von Salza's only worry. Albrecht von Düsberg he had trusted to keep his own council until instructed otherwise. That trust had been borne out by Albrecht's immobility, and the steward Wilhelm von Jülich was junior enough that he would do nothing without the lead of his superiors.

'One-third?' von Salza echoed, keeping his voice calm with an effort. Knowing that Father-Inquisitor Arnald's eyes were on him helped considerably. 'Instead of, or additional to, the usual tithe of goods?'

'Um.' Tommaso Giacchetti had to go looking for the answer, and that was enough to warn von Salza that whatever questions the envoys had been expecting, simple requests for information had not been among them. It was hard to be certain, but Arnald the Inquisitor looked slightly vexed. 'Here it is.' Father Giacchetti tapped at his parchment. 'Instead of the tithe, for the first year only. Thereafter, one-tenth as is customary.'

'Anything else?'

Giacchetti ran a finger down the scroll, squinting slightly as his lips shaped the words. 'The Holy, Catholic and Apostolic Office must be permitted immediate access to newly pacified areas. Nothing more.'

'Indeed?' Hermann von Salza stared deliberately at the two Dominicans and raised one eyebrow. 'I should have said that was quite enough. The well-renowned activities of the Inquisition will do little to keep pacified areas that way for long.'

'Heretics and those lapsed pagans who feigned their conversion to the Faith must be extirpated before their recusancy can spread.' Father Arnald spoke in a flat, disapassionate voice. The only emotion in it was a slight tinge of regret at what would have to be done to make the new territories safe for the Church. It was a voice that made von Salza shiver slightly, and he was not a man given to shivering.

Ferocity he understood, and used if necessary: Dieter Balke was a case in question. The stranger lusts of the flesh, those that required pain for pleasure, were also no surprise to one who had been a knight in Palestine and had seen the levels of bestiality men could visit on one another in the names of their God. But this cool

72

sadness was entirely new, and terrifying in its implications. Whatever Father Arnald did or caused to be done to suspected heretics, he would do with that serene clarity of conscience that in more normal circumstances accompanied acts of kindness – except that to Arnald and his fellow inquisitors, the hot irons and the pincers and the stake *were* acts of kindness, for the preservation of the soul if not the body.

'Thank you, Father Giacchetti,' he said, and held out his hand for the seal-heavy parchment. 'Kuno, please fetch my strongbox.'

'The strongbox? But that box is . . .'

'Now.'

'*Zu befehl, Herr Hochmeister.*' Kuno von Buxhövden struck fist to chest in salute, then did as he was told.

Heads turned to follow him, and more than one eyebrow was raised when their owners saw where he was going. The Papal envoys had evidently been expecting something as massive as they might have seen in the Lateran Palace, and if so, they were sorely disappointed. Hermann von Salza's strongbox was sitting in plain view on a cedar-wood clothes chest, and the heavy wooden chest looked ten times more secure than the metal box on top of it. Rather than the usual arrangements of riveted steel and massive, complicated padlocks, it was a handsome little casket with the dimensions and decoration of a reliquary.

Just over a foot long, it was no more than six inches deep and the same high, so that if it had once contained a holy relic, that relic couldn't have been very big. Nails from the True Cross, perhaps, or a vial of Christ's Blood, but certainly nothing as big as the thighbone of St Peter that the Emperor occasionally displayed on holy days if he was in good humour. Its decoration was Byzantine, and several centuries old: the many precious and semi-precious stones that studded its surface like grapes had been polished, but not cut into facets as was becoming the fashion, and thin straps of filigreed gold formed the frames of embossed and enamelled scenes from the Scriptures.

Von Buxhövden picked it up, and that was when disappointment became surprise in all the watchers except for Hermann von Salza – and Kuno von Buxhövden himself, who evidently knew more about the strongbox than von Salza had permitted him to say. The big *Hauskomtur* used both hands on that little box, and by the sound of the grunt that lifting it forced from his barrel chest, he needed them. He actually staggered slightly under its weight – a weight that unless the casket had been packed full of lead should not have been enough to give much trouble to someone built like Kuno. Blond beard bristling and face going as red with effort as it had earlier gone red with wrath, he heaved the strongbox across the room and set it down before the Grand Master, making the table boom like a castle door struck by a battering-ram.

'Thank you, Kuno.' As von Buxhövden sagged panting back into his seat, Hermann von Salza opened the ornamental upper lid to reveal the casket's locking mechanism. It was, in its way, just as much a work of art as the decorated exterior, being not a keyhole with a lock behind it, but a puzzle of small irregularly shaped plaques of steel that – presumably – had to be arranged in a certain way before the box would open.

'Most original,' said Father Arnald, leaning forward for a closer look. 'But surely not so secure as a key and an iron lock?'

'More so,' said von Salza. 'This does have a lock, and a keyhole. Under here.' He tapped the lid, making the steel puzzle pieces clink faintly. 'The trick lies in finding it.' His fingers began to move with astonishing rapidity, sliding bits of metal up, down and from side to side along grooves cut for that purpose into the surface of the lid. Occasionally part of a keyhole could be glimpsed between the flicker of fingers and polished steel, but never the whole thing; and strangely, never in the same place.

Arnald watched for a few moments, not troubling to conceal how he was trying to memorize the solution to the puzzle, then shrugged in defeat and sat back. 'Have you ever worked the shell game with three cups and a bean?' he asked, and just the question itself was something of an insult when addressed to the Grand Master of a military order.

Von Salza refused to be insulted. 'I use them for practice,' he said. 'There.' The keyhold sat in the middle of the lid as though it had been in plain sight all the time, not the slot that had been briefly seen while he arranged the puzzle pieces, but a deep and vaguely star-shaped depression with twelve rays of differing length and shape radiating from it. He fished inside the neck of his tunic for a moment, then extracted a thin chain from which hung a simple monastic cross and a small rod of dull, dark iron. Von Salza

74

looped the chain off over his head and began twiddling the iron rod over and over in his fingers.

'Another puzzle?' Father Arnald looked amused. 'Grand Master, all this is somewhat elaborate for so small a box. If it was big enough to actually hold something of value, I could understand, but this . . .' He made a disparaging gesture, then tucked both hands inside his black and white Dominican habit. 'It seems a waste of time.'

Father Giacchetti evidently thought otherwise, if the expression on his wrinkled face was anything to go by. Von Salza saw it and gave the old Benedictine a quick smile. 'You know better, don't you?' he said, as rheumy eyes watched his every move. More pieces of metal shifted with tiny scraping sounds as the sheaf of slivers that made up the iron rod slid and rotated into a shape that would fit the keyhold. The Grand Master moved more slowly and carefully than he had done with the lid of the box; those slivers were edged and pointed like tiny razors, and would reward a lack of caution with wicked cuts.

'So,' he said at last. The re-formed rod now resembled some strange form of marine life, all glittering sharp spikes and angles. He took the cross that hung from the chain, fitted the foot of its upright into a slot at the base of the iron starfish, and turned this strange key in its stranger lock. Then he lifted the inner lid, and, with a thin smile on thinner lips, dropped the papal parchment inside.

Father Giacchetti swallowed audibly and crossed himself. An instant later, as the realization of what they had just seen sank in, von Jülich the steward and young Brother Johann did likewise.

The parchment, even rolled into a cylinder and tied tightly with the ribbons of its many pendant seals, was more than two feet long. The box into which it had fitted, with neither bending nor folding but as smoothly as a sword returning to the sheath, was only half that. Von Salza patted the strongbox as he might have done a dog that had performed a trick, then hefted it easily on the palm of one hand. 'This is not a waste of time,' he said. 'Unless the lid and the lock and the key are all in alignment, there is nothing inside. More than that: I suspect that until the box is opened in the proper fashion, there is no *inside* at all.' With the casket still resting on his open hand, like a conjurer proving that there is no

75

deception to his trickery, he reached inside, lifted the parchment scroll into view for a moment and then let it drop again. 'And yet, once open, I have never yet found a limit to what may be put into it.'

Father Arnald did not cross himself, and though his eyes went wide, that might have been no more than a reaction to the Grand Master's impudent display of a magical artifact. They closed again in a long slow blink of satisfaction, and then he surged from his seat in righteous wrath. 'Sorcery!' he said. 'I knew it!'

'Of course you "knew" it,' said von Salza. 'Or at least you "suspected it all along". Isn't that the other thing inquisitors say? Or am I thinking of cuckolded husbands?' He gazed thoughtfully at Father Arnald for a few seconds, then shook his head. 'But then you wouldn't know about such matters. Sit down, Father-Inquisitor. Such a demonstration is scarcely necessary now that His Holiness has declared the use of the Art Magic once more permissible to Christians.'

'Permissible in certain circumstances,' said Arnald. 'So far as this Order is concerned, those circumstances have yet to be determined.'

'Only this Order?' snapped Albrecht von Düsberg, slapping the table in irritation that was either genuine or very well feigned. 'And what about the Knights Templar – or does wealth and the transfer of wealth have something to do with it?'

Von Salza glanced at him approvingly. His words were appropriate enough to the *Ordenstressler*, bringing mention of the Templars to the fore without betraying the presence of an informant either in Rome or in the retinue of the Papal envoys. 'I echo my Treasurer's concern in this matter,' he said. 'If sorcery is to be permitted or denied, then that permission or denial must be general, and if gold has changed hands to ensure the inclusion or exclusion of a specific military order, then as Grand Master of one such I should like to know about it.' He spoke softly, but there was an edge behind his voice like sharp steel contained within a fine scabbard.

Father Arnald shook his head, and the words 'I don't know what you mean' hovered on his lips. Then those lips compressed to a thin line and trapped whatever he had been about to say. When he spoke at last, it was not to make excuses. 'You will accompany me back to Rome,' he said, 'to explain yourself and your accusations before the Pope.'

'I think not,' said von Salza. 'On the eve of a hazardous venture, my place is here with the Knights of the Order.'

The contented look evaporated from the inquisitor's face, replaced by astonishment and no little amount of disbelief. 'What do you mean?' he demanded.

'I mean what I said, no more and no less. I remain here.' Von Salza tapped one finger lightly on the table and surveyed the three monks with no great approval. His voice hardened. 'And you will remain here too, all three of you, until such time as I see fit to let you go.'

Old Giacchetti and young Brother Johann stared at him in mingled disbelief and horror, but Father-Inquisitor Arnald came up out of his seat and pounded his fist on the table like a stone from a siege-engine. 'Have you no respect for the Holy Father, no respect for Rome, no respect for Mother Church?'

'A great deal – for what they represent. But very little for the Pope himself, who is after all only human and therefore subject to human failings. Such as believing only the last thing he hears to be the truth. Which is why, Father Arnald, you above all will be a guest in *Schloss* Thorn. Until matters are settled one way or the other, I think it best that . . . shall we call them distorted reports? of how I intend to conduct this war are not trickled like poison into His Holiness's ears. Rome, and the power of Rome, is a very long way away. I would advise you to remember that before you try to wield power that is no longer at your disposal. The men-at-arms who escorted you here have long since gone about their own business, on the understanding that two *Gleven* of Teutonic Knights would see you safely home again. I regret that is no longer possible. With a crusade in the offing, my knights have better things to do.'

Father Giacchetti and the two Dominican inquisitors stared at von Salza as though their own ears were playing them tricks, and Arnald spluttered something more about respect for Rome.

The Grand Master raised one hand. 'Enough of that,' he said. 'Rome's influence on Germany has always been a tenuous one. I am not the first Hermann to put Romans in their place when they step out of it. Have you ever heard of *Teutoberger Wald*?' For a moment Father Arnald looked blank. Hermann von Salza smiled wolfishly and said, in Latin: ' "Varus, Varus, bring me back my legions!" What was done to three legions could easily be done to three interfering priests.'

Arnald went red, then white. It was plain that he had indeed heard of the Teutoberg Forest, and of what had happened there during the reign of the old Emperor Claudius. There had been a certain German chieftain, Arminus to the Romans but Hermann to the Teutonic tribes he led. Three of Caesar's legions had hunted him into the depths of the dark Northern forest, and not one of those Romans had ever been seen again.

'Be advised, the Inquisition will not forget this, Grand Master,' said Arnald. He had regained control of his temper, and his voice was quieter than it had any right to be.

Von Salza was unconcerned. 'I would have been much astonished if they had. But if this venture is successful, neither I nor the Teutonic Order need have many worries over what the Inquisition think of us.' He shrugged. 'And if unsuccessful, then the Holy Office is likely to be among the least of what we have to worry us.'

Now it was Father Arnald's turn to shrug. He subsided back into his seat, drumming his fingers on the tabletop and staring at them as they danced against the polished wood. 'Very well,' he said, 'I accept your reasoning. But why, *Herr Hochmeister*, knowing that my abhorrence of heresy and witchcraft would provoke such a reaction, were you so blatant?'

'A wise man tests the water with one foot before he jumps in,' said von Salza. 'And if you think my little casket was a blatant display of magic, then I warn you, there's a deal more to follow. And unlike this strongbox, which is just an object incapable of feelings, living practitioners of sorcery can and will be insulted by your . . . abhorrence. Unlike the witches that the Inquisition burnt in Strassburg, you may find that out here on the frontiers of Christendom a witch is rather more than a bewildered old woman. So restrain your zeal. Sorcerers can take offence – and those who offend them will suffer for it.'

He turned to Wilhelm von Jülich. 'You were last into this meeting, *Herr Vogt*; had Dieter Balke returned to the castle yet?'

The steward shook his head. Youngest and most junior of all the

78

castle's officers, he had been keeping very small and quiet throughout this discussion. Having seen the Grand Master and his entire Order make enemies of the Holy Inquisition, he now seemed slightly appalled to be asked anything at all that might bring him to notice. 'Er, not yet, Grand Master. The messenger he sent ahead said that his arrival was—' The thin, high scream of a trumpet from the courtyard cut across his words, and von Jülich looked relieved. 'His arrival was imminent,' he finished, and went back to being inconspicuous.

Hermann von Salza laughed aloud and slapped the table with his open hand. 'The *Landmeister* of Livonia's attendance on his cues are sometimes so perfect that I think he should have been an actor!' He glanced towards the tall, narrow windows that overlooked the castle courtyard, torn between wanting to go and look, and a very reasonable desire to maintain his dignity. 'Assuming that *is* Dieter Balke, and not someone else entirely.'

'If it is,' said Kuno von Buxhövden, 'we'll know soon enough.'

He was right. Within a few minutes, mail-clad feet came hammering along the wooden floor of the corridor outside. There was a brief, thunderous knocking on the great double doors that was plainly only for courtesy's sake, since before anyone could invite the knocker to come in, he had done so all by himself.

The man who entered was as massively built as von Buxhövden, made more massive yet since he was clad in full armour, and carried his crested helm in the crook of one arm. He stalked from doorway to table without looking either to the right or to the left, plainly convinced that after the Grand Master, he alone was the most important man in the room. It was true enough, but as he watched the mailed figure stamp towards him, von Salza thought, as he always did when confronted with his lieutenant, that he had never seen rank and position displayed with such arrogant lack of subtlety. Certainly Balke ignored everyone else, sparing not even a glance for the Papal envoys though he must have known that the presence of Dominican friars meant like as not the presence of the Holy Inquisition.

He bowed his head, then saluted noisily with armoured fist to armoured chest. 'Grand Master, I found you a sorcerer,' he said without further preamble. Then he grinned a big, sloppy grin like a retriever dog that hasn't brought back the bird but is trying to make do by fetching the arrow instead. It was an odd expression for a man so powerful in both rank and physique, and served to dilute both his arrogance and his stature to more manageable proportions. Otherwise, Hermann von Salza had decided long ago, Dieter Balke would be intolerable.

The *Landmeister* flipped the fingers of his right hand free of their mail mitten, and ran them through his cropped blond hair. 'Or rather,' he corrected himself ruefully, 'the sorcerer found me.'

'There was no resistance? None at all?'

'Quite the reverse. As I say, she came looking for us.'

Von Salza blinked three times in rapid succession before he managed to get his facial muscles back under control. This was an unexpected random factor in the equation, so unexpected that he had never considered it at all. For the first time in a very long while, the Grand Master was at a loss. Talking about witches in the abstract was one thing, while this was quite another. 'She. . . ?' he echoed, just for something to say, and shot a wary glance towards the monks.

Father Giacchetti, disgusted with the whole business, was hunched up inside his black habit and had apparently decided he wanted nothing further to do with these proceedings; after his first shock, Brother Johann was scribbling busily in his ledger like a good secretary; and Father Arnald met the Grand Master's eyes for only an instant before his own gaze wandered off elsewhere. It was impossible to tell what the inquisitor was thinking, but Hermann von Salza found himself wishing that Dieter Balke had not arrived at this most inopportune of moments – or, failing that, had had the sense to keep his mouth shut and himself out of the way until briefed on what he should or shouldn't say. But that was an idle dream. Balke and sense were like oil and water: they didn't mix without a severe shaking, and they separated out soon after.

'Very well.' Von Salza brushed at his robes, tidying himself both physically and mentally. 'Show us this volunteer, this flower of virtue that needed no persuasion.'

'Volunteer yes, Grand Master,' said Balke with another of those grins. 'But scarcely a flower. A weed, perhaps. Or a fungus. Certainly something poisonous.' He raised his free hand and snapped his fingers at the two sergeants standing to either side of the door. They moved with a flinching rapidity that suggested they were glad to do so, and someone came past them from the corridor outside.

She was little and white-haired and wrinkled, and the heavy cloak she wore did little to disguise her cadaverous scrawniness; but it was her face that provoked a sudden flurry as everyone in the room – except for Dieter Balke, familiar by now with her appearance – signed themselves fervently with the cross. That face was not just ugly, with hair-sprouting warts on chin and cheek and hatchet-blade nose; her eyes glittered with such wickedness that their direct gaze was a startling, frightening thing.

'This is Baba Yaga,' said Dieter Balke, waving his hand towards her; and if that gesture was less an introduction than a warning for the ancient hag to keep her distance, von Salza could not blame him. 'She claims,' the *Landmeister* continued, 'that the sorceries she can work on our behalf have already begun.'

'All well and good – if it's true.' The Grand Master looked her up and down, a quirk of disgust tugging at the corner of his mouth. 'You are Rus, old witch-mother,' he said, granting her the title as all the ingrained courtesy of knighthood surfaced almost against his will. 'You must know our intentions. Why did you volunteer to help?'

Baba Yaga returned his stare, and her mouth twisted into what, on a less hideous face, might have been an ingratiating smile. 'Dear Lord and Master,' she said, her voice a beggar's whine, 'are you and your knights of the black cross so pure that none of you can understand revenge?'

'Revenge?' Von Salza was immediately on his guard, and his hand, like the hands of everyone except the unarmed monks, was immediately on the hilt of his dagger. 'Against whom, and for what cause?'

'On every Russian, rich or poor, alive or dead, who ever slighted me because I am old and weak and ugly,' said Baba Yaga. The fawning self-pity in her voice was like poisoned honey. 'But on one, most especially. Prince Ivan of Khorlov. The man who killed my lovely daughter . . .'

Chapter Four

'Mother *Wolf*?' said Mar'ya Morevna in a way that conveyed much more than just those two words suggested. She stared at the dark woman swaddled in her darker cloak, and then at her husband, and there was just a trace of bitterly amused suspicion, a cold hardness like crushed diamonds, beginning to glitter in her eyes. 'I remember you told me about the wolf, Ivan – but you appear to have left out some very important details.'

'As I said, just now, she saved my life.' Then he realized what he was hearing in Mar'ya Morevna's voice: jealousy, mixed with a little outrage. He felt a spike of annoyance twist in his guts; annoyance with Mar'ya Morevna that she should be so ready to think that he would parade an ex-lover in front of her like this, and with himself for the forgetfulness that had made such an error possible.

He had indeed told Mar'ya Morevna all about the mother wolf who had aided him against Koshchey the Undying, but if he had just thought to explain a little more about her – most particularly, that when she took on human form, that form was astonishingly beautiful. Except that his mind had been filled first with terror of Koshchey the Undying and then by his victory over that old necromancer, and a little forgetfulness could be forgiven. It could have been forgiven then, at least; trying to give such an explanation now would only serve to make things worse.

It was the cloaked woman herself who saved the situation from descending through its present level of a silly mistake into something more serious, for which Ivan was thankful – though he would also have thanked her to stop grinning in the knowing way that hadn't improved matters from the start.

'Highness,' she said, stalking queenly proud past the two sentries and into the pool of lamplight within the kremlin's gatehouse, 'wolf you named me; wolf I am.'

She spoke no other words, and made no dramatic gestures with her hands except to draw the cloak more comfortably in around her shoulders. A cloak, Ivan noticed as if for the first time though he had known it all along, that was made all of dense black fur. For an instant the light silently collapsed in on itself, dragging a vortex of shadows in from the night beyond the gateway so that the black cloak and the black shadows and the black night all became a single swirl of darkness. The wolf-change was not as tale-tellers described it in their stories: there were no cries of anguish at the reluctant twisting of joint and bone and muscle, no sprouting of coarse fur from unwilling skin. There was just that flicker of light and shadow, a warping of reality instead of a warping of flesh. It lasted whilst a bird's wing might beat thrice before the light flowed back as if it had never gone. Only the woman in the cloak had gone.

In her place was the biggest wolf that anyone had ever seen.

Guard-Captain Fedorov, that taciturn and imperturbable man, crossed himself three times and swore several new and quite original oaths. His two soldiers were less inventive, but made up for that with vehement repetition. Mar'ya Morevna, more accustomed to sorcery than her guards, slowly lifted both her spun-gold eyebrows. 'Well now,' she said. 'A wolf indeed.'

Prince Ivan stared hard at Mother Wolf, now that she had returned to the shape that he knew best, and put his head on one side. 'You've put on weight, *Volk-matushka*,' he said at last.

The wolf twitched her ears back just a bit, and made a low rumbling in her throat. 'Better manners would just have said "you've grown".' Her voice, though deeper and growling now where the other had been merely somewhat husky, was still that of the woman in the black cloak, and Ivan grinned as he heard Boris Petrovich add another few earnest words to the monologue with his personal deity. One of those words was *oboroten'*.

Mother Wolf turned her head to look thoughtfully at him. 'No, not a werewolf,' she said. 'They make such a performance out of becoming a beast. So much pointless uproar.' The shaggy mane of fur across her shoulders moved in what could only be a shrug, and it was a gesture both like and yet peculiarly unlike that same shrug when she was in human form. 'But then, they have little choice in the matter. Once a month, as unavoidable as the tides that ebb and flow on the Ocean-Sea or in a woman's body. Whereas we, mere beasts already, can become human whenever the fancy takes us.'

'I think,' said Mar'ya Morevna, 'that I owe someone an apology.'

Ivan's grin diluted down to a smile, but stayed where it was. 'It was an understandable misunderstanding,' he said softly. 'And I'll collect that apology in private, please.' Then he blushed to the tips of his ears as the wolf wrinkled her long muzzle and emitted an unmistakable snigger. His voice might have been low enough for privacy from other human ears, but Mother Wolf had heard him quite plainly, and been much amused by the whole thing. *Bitch*, he thought, then laughed inside at just how accurate the insult was – if indeed it was an insult at all.

Darkness whirled like a fog beneath the lanterns, and the woman in the cloak came back. 'From what they were saying to God,' she said, 'I think your guards feel much more comfortable with this shape.'

'Mm. Thank you for the consideration,' said Mar'ya Morevna. From her tone, it seemed to Ivan that she would have preferred the wolf-form as being, if nothing else, less likely to provoke unseemly gossip – as if the appearance of a talking wolf in the courtyard of the kremlin after midnight was not a source of gossip all by itself. Or maybe he was doing his wife the same injustice that she had done him.

'There was some talk of favours,' he said. 'You didn't give me a reply. What brings you here?'

'A favour indeed,' said Mother Wolf. She made a dismissive gesture with one hand. 'Nothing that you can do for me. But for my son – now that is another matter.'

'Your son?'

'Yes indeed. He owes you his life, as I'm sure you recall.'

'How could I forget, when you were breathing down the back of my neck at the time?'

Mar'ya Morevna jabbed him in the back with one finger. 'Easily,' she said. 'Quite easily.'

'Quite so.' The wolf-woman smiled thinly, but didn't specify which statement she was agreeing with. 'Now I, his mother, who asked you for his life, consider that by my various advices and assistances freely given, the debt has been repaid. My son, however, being a son and greatly taken with thoughts of his own honour, is of another turn of mind.'

Prince Ivan was puzzled by that, and Mar'ya Morevna so mystified that for once she withheld her own opinions on the matter and merely listened. And perhaps she merely kept silent so as to better keep an eye on the astonishingly handsome woman who was talking to her husband. Whatever the reason, *Volk-matushka* glanced from one to the other and then back again, then said 'My son has decided that he should go into your service.'

'My service?' echoed Ivan.

'Yes,' said Mother Wolf. 'For the usual: a year and a day, no more and no less.'

Shape-shifting may be easy enough in a furred cloak worn for the purpose, but doing the same thing in armour might be rather a problem . . .

That, at least, was what Ivan was about to say, and for all he knew, similar sentiments were poised on the tip of Mar'ya Morevna's tongue as well. Good manners and good sense prevailed. The question might well be entirely reasonable, but at the same time he had seen Mother Wolf in her true form, and insults, even unintentional insults, were not something safely directed at a grim grey Russian wolf. '*Volk-matushka*,' he asked, choosing his words with care, 'just what exactly would your son the wolf *do* in my service? I take it that he has no military training, no experience of sword or shield or spear?'

'Just as I had no experience in sorcery and politics,' said Mother Wolf. 'Yet it seemed to me that I was of some small use to you in your dealings with Baba Yaga and Koshchey *Bessmyrtnyy*. Certainly, Ivan Tsarevich, you appear to have your head still solidly attached to your shoulders.'

Ivan cleared his throat, grateful to be able to do so. That she had saved his neck – and the rest of him – from Baba Yaga's cooking-pot, was undeniable, although he wondered whether the wolf-woman knew how that same head had been cut off. '*Bol'shoii spasibo, Volk-matushka*,' he said. 'Thank you again for that. And thank your son on my behalf, since I don't see him here.' He peered into the darkness beyond the kremlin's torchlit gateway, but saw nothing. 'Where is he, by the way?'

'You tell me!' Mother Wolf sounded just a little peeved. 'Because I can tell you no more than I know, and that is little enough. This is – what? – twelve hundred years after the birth of

85

the White Christ, and children still wander off without asking and tell their parents no more than they think their parents need to know. If I remember my reading of the Scriptures, your Christ child was no more obedient.'

'Mother Wolf, please. Can we leave religion out of this? Just tell me: where is your son, what is he doing, and why can he not be here himself to ask for entry to my service?'

'And,' said Mar'ya Morevna rather sharply, 'why is he asking now, through you, rather than a year ago with his own voice when he first met my husband?' She came down heavily on the word 'husband'.

Volk-matushka glanced from one to the other and back again. 'A year ago,' she said, 'he was no more than a cub. Did your *husband* not tell you as much – or has he told you anything at all besides the most basic information?' She sounded more disappointed than annoyed by the thought of being left out of whatever story Ivan had told. 'At any rate, my son is grown now, and he has heard – and read – too many legends and folk stories for his own good. Since he cannot be a prince himself, he has decided that he would like to be in the service of a prince, and I can see no real harm in it. Certainly some few hours of guard duty will get such foolishness out of his system.' Mother Wolf grinned crookedly, and her teeth glinted. 'As for the rest of it,' she shrugged, 'what mother knows where her son might be, especially when that son has passed the age when mothers still retain the right to ask their children where they go at night. Even you, Mar'ya Morevna, fairest Princess in all the Russias, must know something of the tribulations of a mother with young children?'

'Ivan Tsarevich and I do not have any children,' said Mar'ya Morevna with an air of great dignity that covered what she truly felt. 'Not yet, at least.'

The dark wolf-woman blushed darker yet, and made another bow; not just an inclination of the head this time, but the deep obeisance with right hand extended of Rus nobility before a superior. 'My apologies, Highness,' she said, and seemed to mean it. 'But from what I had been told – and from what is said by common gossip—' She stopped abruptly in the way of one who realizes that whatever they might say is going to be taken in ways other than intended.

'That Prince Ivan and I would have had several children by now?' Mar'ya Morevna put out one booted foot and kicked Ivan lightly but firmly on the ankle-bone, to keep him quiet. 'So far as common gossip is concerned, Mother Wolf, we try. Oh, how we try. But so far' – now it was her turn to shrug, a gesture made expansive by the heavy fur of her robe – 'without success. Never mind a son, politically useful though that might be; we would thank the good God for a daughter.'

'Who when she grows could be married to a powerful prince,' said Ivan. He saw Mar'ya Morevna's boot-toe twitch, and added, 'if she wanted to, of course.'

'So then,' said Mother Wolf, 'until such time as God gives you a son of your own, I give you mine to take his place.'

Mar'ya Morevna and Prince Ivan exchanged brief glances and briefer nods. Then she looked at Mother Wolf. 'In such a case, duty and obligation would work both ways. And in my place as liege lady – and mother – I would be happier if I knew where your son was right now.'

'You speak for both of us, Highness. I tell myself that he is old enough to take care of himself, so that I worry less than I might.'

'Do you perhaps worry less than you should?' said Mar'ya Morevna softly. 'You told us that less than a year ago, he was only a cub.'

The wolf-woman snuggled deeper into the hood of her heavy cloak and smiled, shaking her head. 'I think not. As many of humankind, even the wisest, are prone to do when they see us only in this assumed shape, you forget that we are wolves. Cub he may have been last year, but wolves grow swiftly or not at all.'

Ivan shivered a little; not at anything that had been said, but because he was growing cold, and he had grown tired long before. 'Mother Wolf,' he said, 'it's becoming so late that soon it will start to get early. We have both had a long and wearying day . . .'

'So ruling a realm requires as much work as I have heard?' said the wolf-woman with interest.

Ivan grinned, but it was Mar'ya Morevna who said, 'More even than that. Much, much more.'

'And so,' said Ivan, 'we'd like to get some sleep.' He looked thoughtfully at Mother Wolf, and if he was admiring what she had dismissed as her assumed shape, Mar'ya Morevna would not really have found it in her heart to blame him. Even muffled by the folds of the ankle-length fur cloak, that shape was much to be admired. 'You're in human form,' he said. 'Does that mean you sleep by day, or by night?'

'I sleep whenever the opportunity presents itself.'

'Then might we offer you guest-right in this kremlin?'

'My son has said this long time that he wanted to serve a noble prince and his fine lady, and named you. It is pleasing to learn that my son's choice was a wise one. I thank you both, and yes, I would sleep – if you could give me a private place to sleep in, with a door between me and the rest of the world. Humans sometimes walk in their sleep; wolves change their shape, and I would not want to scare your other servants.'

Ivan looked quickly from side to side. The guards had returned to their posts in the kremlin's gatehouse, so that they were unattended except for Captain Fedorov – and Fedorov, like most of the guard-captains of most of the kremlins of Russia, was the soul of discretion. 'Boris Petrovich,' he said, 'it's late and I have no desire to waken anyone. Can you tell me if there is a room anywhere already prepared for unexpected guests?'

Fedorov saluted. 'Yes, Highness, there is: in the Armoury Tower.' He permitted himself a quick grin. 'Your Highness's sisters and their husbands have a positive talent for arriving without any prior warning. As a consequence, High Steward Fedor Konstantinovich has made sure to maintain the lordly suite in the tower at all times.'

'Then have those chambers made ready for this guest,' said Mar'ya Morevna. 'Candles and lamps, a fire, a flagon of wine, meat and a fresh-baked loaf under a fair white cloth.'

'When the baking for the day has begun, of course,' said Mother Wolf. 'Right now, meat would be quite sufficient. A length of sausage, perhaps? After all, I am a wolf. Food is food, and bread is food – but sausage is meat, and meat is better food by far.'

She grinned more widely still, and Ivan saw just how very white her teeth were in that darkly tanned face. Human teeth of course, in a human face; but teeth that were not only white but strong and sharp and apparently in quite excellent condition.

Mar'ya Morevna showed her own teeth, but in a yawn-and-stretch as luxurious and extravagant as the one which had demonstrated her tiredness to the spies. 'Your pardon,' she said, 'but if I don't get to bed myself, I fear that I'll insult one and all by falling asleep right here.'

Ivan kissed her hand. 'Later,' he said.

'Not too much later,' said Mar'ya Morevna, and strode away.

Whether that was warning or invitation, Ivan Tsarevich was not quite sure. If warning, it was unnecessary. *Volk-matushka* in human form was a pretty enough lady, but she was not by any means the fairest Princess in all the Russias, in comparison to whom any other woman could only strive for second best. And having seen her change to her true shape and back, right here on his own front doorstep, it was impossible to forget just what that true shape was.

'I did not know when last we met that you were seeking a wife,' said Mother Wolf, 'although I soon heard mention of her beauty. Permit me to congratulate you,' and she bowed again.

'*Volk-matushka*,' said Ivan, 'no matter what your son may think, neither you nor he owe me anything – while I will always owe you my thanks, for my wife and for my life.'

'As I said before, Prince Ivan: you know what children are. Once they get hold of an idea, it cannot be shaken. And if you do not know it yet, or remember it from your own childhood – it was not so very long ago, surely? – you will, soon enough.'

When Ivan rolled his eyes at that, she leaned forward and smacked him sharply on the hand. 'Now stop that nonsense,' she said in that tone of voice perfected by mothers all across the wide white world. 'I do not prophesy; I do not foresee; I do not promise. But I think that I speak the truth when I say that you and your wife will indeed have children, in God's own good time. A son, to preserve your line and keep your father's mind at rest, and a daughter to fill your heart with joy. After that' – she shook her head, – 'I do not look so far. Other sons, other daughters, other joys. But trust my sight in this at least.'

Ivan looked at her long and hard. Harder perhaps and closer than he might have done had Mar'ya Morevna still been there. 'I trust you,' he said. 'And I believe you. If that trust should be misplaced, I think that it will be through accident and nothing more.' He shivered again; it was really very cold, even in the lee of the gatehouse and so out of the worst of the night wind, although

89

Mother Wolf showed no sign of feeling it. 'Let me show you to your room. But not, for honour's sake, any further than the doorway of the tower.'

'You are concerned for the honour of a wolf?'

'For the honour of a lady; and if that lady should be a wolf, then say I show respect to what I and the world can see, rather than what I alone might know.' Ivan stared into the darkness for a moment, then shook his head. 'No. Regardless of the shape, I show honour where honour is due.'

They walked together in companionable silence across the shadowed courtyard, and when they reached the Armoury Tower, Prince Ivan opened the door and held it for her. 'The third floor,' he said, 'all of it, is at your disposal.'

Volk-matushka nodded abstractedly, looking at him with an expression of slight puzzlement on her face as though trying to think of something else entirely. Then she brightened, and one hand dipped into the pouch that hung from her belt. 'My memory can sometimes be as elusive as yours,' she said, producing a small flat packet. 'Your father gave me this. A letter to you.'

Ivan took it and turned it over in his hand. 'Sealed?' he said, looking at the criss-cross of cords and the two blobs of gold-sifted wax that held it shut. The seal, apparently untouched, was indeed his father's, as was the handwriting.

'As I received it. I have no interest in the correspondence between father and son, and even less in that of Tsar and Tsarevich. So here it is; do with it what you will.'

'If you had this from Tsar Aleksandr,' he said, and looked curiously at Mother Wolf, 'just what brought you to Khorlov in the first place?'

She grinned at him. 'Trying to find you,' she said. 'If the child is hard to find, then ask the parents. Especially in a case where the in-laws move from place to place with no warning whatso-ever.'

That Ivan knew well enough, from trying to find them himself. 'So my father told you where to find me.'

'As I said. He regarded me with a deal less suspicion than your wife first did.'

Ivan laughed quietly. 'As well he might: he's not married to her. But my thanks for this, and a good night to you.'

She glanced up at the sky, and at the few stars that blinked through the high, ragged clouds. 'You mean, a good morning.'

'You know what I mean.'

'Yes. Later . . .'

Once the door of the Armoury Tower had closed behind her, Ivan cracked the seals on his father's letter. Regardless now of the chill, he found a stone mounting-block convenient to one of the torches that cast a guttering light across the courtyard, sat down and began to read. It was such a letter as a father and mother might send to their son now married and living far from home: inquisitive as to his doings, gossipy as to theirs – and yet, ordinary though it seemed, between the lines there was something more. Ivan read it again, and then a third time, and with every reading the small frown that had indented itself between his brows grew deeper. Slowly he folded the sheets of parchment back into their original packet, staring not at what he was doing but at the ground while his brain sorted through the various meanings of what it had detected.

Then he stood up and went to bed, not now so much to sleep as to find somewhere warmer than the courtyard in which to lie and think and stare up at the unhelpful ceiling. This latest letter seemed just like all the others that he and Mar'ya Morevna had received; and yet somehow it felt different. It was unlike Tsar Aleksandr – or even his mother the Tsaritsa, from whom such sentiments might have seemed more reasonable – to mention not once but four times that he was much missed and should come home to visit more often. Unlike, and unlikely, because despite the distances involved, Ivan and his wife returned to Khorlov frequently enough to keep any parent happy. Yet here, in brown ink on good cream parchment, was a request – no, a demand – that they not let so many months go by between visits as they had done the last time.

Ivan had no need to light a lamp to read the letter again; it was as if its words were engraved inside his skull, and what all those words meant was *Come home. Now. We need you. Both of you.*

The pallid light of dawn found Ivan just as wide awake as when he went to bed. Courtesy – and simple caution born of past experience – prevented him from shaking Mar'ya Morevna

91

awake, but once she began to stir he stroked her face lightly with his fingertips, both to speed the waking process and to make sure that she would not just roll over and go back to sleep. Never at her best first thing in the morning, she regarded him a little blearily; but when he showed her the letter and explained just a little of his suspicions, she sat bolt upright in the bed and stared at it.

Mar'ya Morevna drank cold water, splashed a little in her face and scrubbed the knuckles of both fists into her eyesockets. After that, certain that she and her eyes and her brain were all as wide awake as they were likely to become, she took the letter from him and held it up in front of her nose. At first she did not read it, despite what Ivan had told her; instead, taking his suggestion to read between the lines quite literally, she studied the structure of paper, cords and seals to discover if there were other words than just the obvious and visible ones. 'Nothing under the wax,' she said, 'or mixed in with it. Nothing between the braiding of the cords. No smell of lemon or onion juice from the paper, and no pattern of pinpricks on view when it's held up to the light. But then, Tsar Aleksandr – or more likely Dmitriy Vasil'yevich – knows all of those methods well enough to employ something more subtle. Sorcery, perhaps. . . ?'

'Or words, dammit!' said Ivan, his patience finally giving way. 'There's no secret writing. Do the one thing you haven't done yet, Mar'yushka, and read the words. That's where the message lies; a message that I didn't even notice first time round.' Mar'ya Morevna read it three times, as Ivan had done, and on the third reading slapped the letter down against the bed. Ivan glanced at it, then looked at his wife. 'You see what I mean.'

'Yes. Your father – grant me pardon for this, beloved – is a garrulous old gentleman, worse even than your dear mother. They both love to gossip, whether face to face or in their letters. This, however' – she tapped the sheets of parchment with one finger – 'when compared to their other letters, is terse to the point of rudeness. And of all the things your parents have been, are and will be, rude is not one of them. We go to Khorlov, just as quickly as we can.'

'How?'

'Do you really need to ask?' said Mar'ya Morevna. 'The quickest method is down in the stables.' Ivan groaned softly, as though remembering past discomforts or anticipating those yet to come. 'I know, I know; but those horses cover in one day as much distance as would take a week mounted on anything else.'

'Yes indeed. And that one day of travel gives you all the aches and pains of being in the saddle for a week.'

'You didn't object last time,' said Mar'ya Morevna, more primly perhaps than she intended.

'Last time,' said Ivan, 'we were being chased by Koshchey the Undying. Or have you forgotten?'

'Of course not. But until we find out what's troubling your father, can either of us put hand on heart and say that it's any less urgent?'

Ivan looked and felt slightly ashamed. 'I was thinking of myself . . .'

'No. You were thinking of your backside. At least you weren't thinking with it.'

'And I was thinking of a Gate.'

Mar'ya Morevna looked at Ivan and grinned. 'You really have been keeping up with your studies, haven't you? Exceeding them, in fact, because they're not mentioned anywhere in the grimoire I gave you. So where did you read about Gates?'

'I found a book – one of your father's, I think – in the library. It was mostly maps, but there was a sheaf of handwritten notes bound into the front.' Ivan went on the defensive. 'If I wasn't supposed to see things like that, they shouldn't have been on the shelf in plain view.'

'That's one of the oldest excuses,' said Mar'ya Morevna disapprovingly. 'You should be able to do better. And you should know well enough by now that what's mine is yours.' She grinned again. 'The last time I didn't trust you enough to leave something in plain view, or at least tell you about it, we both had no end of trouble.'

'Koshchey *Bessmyrtnyy*.'

'Who else. We'd have just as much trouble with a Gate. They're just as dangerous as Old Rattlebones. My father, God give him rest' – she crossed herself – 'found the Gate spells during his travels in the Prusiskai country, and being a wary as well as a wise man, researched them before he tried to use them. It was just as well, because—'

'But I thought you just constructed the Gate where you were, and stepped out at the other end . . .' Ivan's interruption trailed off at the amused look on Mar'ya Morevna's face. 'Ah. Apparently not.'

'Definitely not. Tell me: how would you work out where the other end was going to be?'

Prince Ivan opened his mouth, hesitated for an instant while he thought about what he was going to say, decided not to, and closed it again.

'Exactly. You would just make a wish, eh?' Mar'ya Morevna shook her head regretfully and punched one fist into the palm of the other hand. 'And that's what would happen. Unless you were very lucky indeed, and Koldun my father didn't believe in luck, you'd step out of the other side of the gate and find yourself—'

'Halfway up a tree?' said Ivan, and might have laughed – except that his wife poked him hard in the chest and turned the unborn laughter into a coughing fit.

'Stop interrupting, and pay attention! Halfway *through* a tree, more likely, or standing, though not for long, on thin air two feet to the wrong side of the tower-top you'd planned to land on, or six feet under the ground without the benefit of a funeral, or sharing the same space as a kremlin wall.' Mar'ya Morevna quirked an eyebrow at him. 'The wall and the tree and the ground were all there first. The place in the world is theirs. They would win. I should think that compared to any of those prospects, an aching rump from too much time on horseback is much to be preferred. My father suspected that just wishing to be in a place wasn't enough, that you had to go there the long way and prepare what he called somewhere soft to land. Afterwards, of course, there shouldn't be any problem. It would be like knowing the safe route.'

'We both know Khorlov—'

'But neither of us know just how necessary that soft landing-place might be in such a circumstance. Nor the protocols of the spell, for that matter. And I for one don't plan to jump into the dark without being certain that there's a nice thick mattress waiting at the bottom. You'd better concede defeat, Vanyushechka. The only bottom involved here is the one that fits the saddle.'

94

The rest of the morning was taken up in arranging the running of the realm during its ruler's absence. Those arrangements had been made before, many times; but never with as much urgency as now. Normally when Mar'ya Morevna took leave of her kremlin, for whatever reason, there were several days of preparation; today, however, she grudged even that necessary several hours.

Her High Steward was the only person in the whole kremlin – with the exception of Mother Wolf, who had received the news with total equanimity and then gone back to sleep – who seemed unruffled by the Tsarevna's abrupt departure. Fedor Konstantinovich at least had the advantage of not needing to be told his duties, since they remained the same whether Mar'ya Morevna was in the kremlin or halfway across the wide white world, and he eased matters considerably by spending a quarter-hour in discussion with her, and then proceeding to do half, and more than half, of the giving of instructions.

Of all the things that a ruler should bear in mind when selecting a High Steward, she had once told Ivan, three were most important of all: that he should be loyal, capable – and totally without a trace of ambition. Otherwise, the first time that ruler went away, it would probably be a waste of time returning home again . . .

Ivan thought about that more than once, knowing that what he felt – it wasn't anything as fully formed as a suspicion – had more to do with his own personal dislike of Dmitriy Vasil'yevich Strel'tsin than anything the man had said or done in all the years Ivan had known him. He was *khitriyy*, a word meaning both shrewd and subtle; very right and proper for a Tsar's High Steward, and as much a part of his position at court as his staff of office and his long grey beard. But the word also had less flattering interpretations: a person considered *khitriyy* could also be crafty, sly and cunning, and even though there were certain Great Princes of the Rus who encouraged such attitudes among the wise men in their service, Ivan was not happy with the thought of such a one standing behind his father's throne.

It was all nonsense, of course. Probably. Strel'tsin had been High Steward to the Khorlovskiy Tsars for more years than most people in Khorlov had lived, never mind remember, and in all those years he had never betrayed their trust. It seemed unlikely that he would pick now to do it. Even so, Ivan found it easier to focus his mind on something he could understand, no matter how unlikely it might be; otherwise his brain filled with wild imaginings that were far more unpleasant than an old family servant turning traitor.

Despite his tutoring in the running of a tsardom, first from Dmitriy Vasil'yevich and then from Mar'ya Morevna, Ivan still found himself sitting in the idle eye of an industrious hurricane. It was all very well being instructed in what to do, but after that someone had to ask you to help do it, and they seemed to be getting on quite well without his assistance. Finally he shrugged, made his excuses, and escaped gratefully to the stables. Having been set into his first saddle, and watched fall out of it immediately afterwards, by the Don Cossack who commanded his father's guards, Ivan understood horses rather better than the tangled logistics of politics.

He understood his own great coal-black stallion even better than Captain Akimov had taught him and, in fact, better than he sometimes understood Akimov himself. Even after so many years in Khorlov, when he spoke Rus the Guard-Captain still had a heavy Cherkassk accent.

The horse Sivka had no accent at all.

Instead he had a voice like the great pipe-organ of Khorlov's cathedral, and Ivan, long since accustomed to the fact that he could carry on a conversation with his horse and more to the point get a sensible reply, had once tried teaching Sivka to sing. Granted, that had been after his saint's-day dinner and rather more vodka than was good for him, but it still said a great deal about Sivka's love for his master that the big black horse had restrained himself like a gentleman, merely observing mildly that horses did not sing, and it was probably just as well they didn't drink vodka either. It was a pity, Ivan had thought through the pounding of his head the next day. Sivka would have provided a fine deep bass in any close harmony you cared to name.

'Good morning to you, little master,' said that same voice as Ivan came into the stable. Straw rustled as something huge and heavy shifted its position and peered through the shadows that lay thick in the winter's dawn. 'There seems a deal of bustle in the kremlin today.'

'Too much for me, old friend.' Ivan glanced into the tack-room to make sure everything was in place. It was: saddles arranged on padded bars, reins and bridles and headstalls all hanging from their proper hooks. 'I felt like you must when the blacksmith puts on your shoes: standing in one place and looking like a piece of furniture, while everything else goes on behind your back.'

'You never felt tempted to kick, the way I do, just to let them know once in a while that you're still there?' said Sivka, and snorted to himself. Prince Ivan grinned; coming as it did from a trained war-horse who was at the same time the calmest animal during a shoeing that Ivan had ever seen, that was a piece of arrant nonsense.

'I kicked my way out, but very quietly,' he said. 'That seemed the best thing to do at the time.' His eyes were growing accustomed to the gloom, which was a necessary part of seeing a black horse in an unlit stable. 'We have to go to Khorlov.'

Sivka stood up and shook straw from himself, then stamped. Even standing six feet away, Ivan felt the concussion of that hoof slamming against the stable floor. It was just such a hoof that had hammered Koshchey the Undying back into oblivion, smashing him so dead that being immortal didn't seem to matter any more. Everything about the black horse was magical in one way or another; truly magical, as in his speech and his speed and the way he had grown from a dirty colt rolling in the mire to a full-grown horse in seven days, but also magical to one who, knowing the good and bad points of horseflesh, had encountered animals that have brought a whole new meaning to the term 'dumb brute'. Sivka had no faults: he neither kicked nor bit without good reason, such as the direction of his rider; he did not throw his head up unnecessarily, the cause of more broken noses than falling out of the saddle; and most wonderful of all, he didn't plant those iron-shod platters of hoofs on other people's tender toes.

'How quickly do you want to be there?' the horse asked, looking at his manger. It was not an idle question, since the faster Sivka ran, the hungrier he was at the end of it and the more food he needed to eat beforehand. Ivan glanced about, saw what he was looking for, and rather than summon a servant, lifted the grain-bag with his own hand and balanced it on the other side with a new bale of fresh, sweet hay. Sivka watched him, and

97

blinked his long-lashed eyes. 'Ah,' he said. '*That* quickly.' Then he fell to.

Chyornyy was Mar'ya Morevna's horse, and brother to Sivka. Named for his colour, he had once belonged to Koshchey the Undying – if belonging could begin to describe the cruel, abject slavery which that dark sorcerer laid on the brave beast. He could speak too, just as well as Sivka, but not often, and for a very simple reason: whenever Chyornyy had spoken to his old master, and no matter how useful that speech might have been, the horse was beaten for it. Koshchey *Bessmyrtnyy* had been one who could always find an excuse to beat his servants, whether they were human or animal. The horse had either been too slow in speaking, or he had spoken insolently, or he had said something that Koshchey had not liked to hear. As a result, now that he was under no obligation to speak unless he had something worthwhile to say, Chyornyy was usually as quiet as an ordinary horse; though Prince Ivan would have been the first to admit that, like Sivka, his stable-brother's behaviour was far too good for either horse to be anything other than magic.

Chyornyy stirred a little, then scrambled up from his bed as Ivan peered into the stall and wished him a good morning. The horse trusted Ivan as he trusted no other human on the face of Moist-Mother-Earth. The Tsarevich had been the first person in the black horse's life to utter a kind word of any sort. Born into Baba Yaga's horse-herd in the desolate land beyond the burning river and considered useless because he would not learn to eat the flesh of men as all the other horses did, he had become Koshchey's steed and faithful servant, a servitude and a faithfulness enforced by fear. There had been no soft words from either of them, only curses, threats and hard blows for no good reason.

'I smelt a wolf's smell on the wind last night, Prince Ivan,' said Chyornyy in a small, scared voice, nuzzling against Ivan's outstretched hand. 'I still smell it now, by the light of day.' He was a stallion almost as big as Sivka, and a year of grooming and good food had banished the wretched, whip-scarred animal that he had been; but Ivan was aware that having spent most of his life afraid of something or other, this horse found it very easy to be afraid again. Especially of wolves.

In the next stall the steady munching of hay ceased for a

moment, and Sivka snorted in a reassuring way. 'No need for fear, brother,' he said. 'I know that smell. It is a wolf indeed, but the mother wolf who saved my little master from Baba Yaga's cauldron. You could call her a friend.'

'A *wolf*?'

'Then call her not an enemy.'

'But a wolf for all that.' Chyornyy put his ears flat back against his skull, stamping and grumbling and swishing his tail during the whole time that Ivan saw to his feed and made sure there was plenty of clean water for them both to drink.

As he untied hay and poured out oats, Ivan wondered all that time how he would explain to both horses that, in the not-too-distant future, the wolf-son of that wolf-mother would be entering his service as only the good God knew what. It was plain that despite her human form, Mother Wolf still carried the scent of her true shape, and confident declarations of friendship might not last beyond the first time that either son or mother came too close. And that was only Sivka. From the sound of it, Chyornyy would be far worse. A horse's definition of safe distance, even from an ordinary two-legged would-be rider that it knew and trusted, was an area the length and width of whatever field they happened to be paddocked in. If a far-from-ordinary thing that looked like a human but smelt like a wolf stepped inside that perimeter, at least one of the sorcerous steeds would be halfway across Russia before pausing to think that such a reaction was perhaps excessive.

Then he dismissed the problem, if it was really a problem at all and not just one more of those pointless niggles his mind was manufacturing so that he had something other than unexplained fears to worry about. The wolf could be a problem when the time came; when it became that problem, rather than just the possibility of one, that would be the time when he would start to be concerned. There were other things to deal with long before that.

Such as feeding himself, for instance, and putting provisions for the ride to Khorlov into his saddlebags. There wouldn't be much, since a journey that took one day instead of seven required food and water only for that one day. Bread, wine, some cheese, some sausage if Mother Wolf had left any in the kitchens; not much, but enough for when they broke for a midday meal, and he and Mar'ya Morevna tried to work the cramps out of their muscles. He was less concerned about what they would eat come nightfall, for if black Sivka moved as fast as he was able, they would eat dinner at his father's table.

Call it five hours instead of five days, he thought as he left the stable. Then he looked up at the sky, frowned slightly, and revised both figures upwards. The lowering clouds were leaden grey, heavy with more snow. The ground crunched beneath his booted feet, frozen hard by the overnight frost, and that at least would provide firm going for the horses. Not too firm, Ivan hoped; riding across the iron ground of deep winter without fresh, soft snow to cushion their hoofs could do a horse's legs as much damage as galloping the beast on cobblestones.

Even this pair, at least until they got into their stride. After that, the state of the ground – or even whether there was any ground at all – seemed not to matter. Mar'ya Morevna, better educated in such matters than her husband, had speculated that once they had attained their full speed, the horses from Baba Yaga's herd no longer ran across the face of the wide white world as ordinary mortal creatures had to do. Instead they seemed to set their hoofs on some other earth where the ground was flat and free of potholes, and where they always knew the swiftest route to take; the straightest line between two points, whether they were points on a map – or points in time. Ivan had never dared to test the theory: putting Sivka at an unbridged river and watching to see if the black stallion jumped or ran across it seemed to be tempting Fate. It was enough for him that his mount ran with an even gait and had no vices except for a certain tendency to make bad jokes.

Ivan thought of his ongoing tuition in the Art Magic, and wondered when Mar'ya Morevna would start teaching him something like this, something that had at least a semblance of logic and order to it. It would make a pleasant change from lists of hard-to-pronounce names, and lists of grisly creatures that such names would call up from the Pit if he ever succeeded in forcing the jarring conglomeration of letters out of his throat. *Say the name, summon the Named*. Names, as a result, that could not be spoken aloud even if he ever did learn how. Now that, if asked, was what Prince Ivan called a truly pointless education. It was just as well that no one ever asked . . .

Then someone called his name. Wrapped in a heavy fur coat

with sleeves that reached beyond her gloved fingertips and a hem hanging almost to her booted heels, Mar'ya Morevna strode across the courtyard towards her husband. As she swirled the coat across her body to close it with an arrangement of loops and toggles that ran down its right side, it billowed out despite its weight and Ivan could see the furred Cossack kaftan and the baggy, quilted trousers that she wore beneath. A scarf hung around her neck, and a fur hat with earflaps was on her head, and garments of similar material and generous cut were being carried by the servants who hurried in her wake.

'Here,' she said briskly, 'put these on. Close them up as tightly as you can. The air would cut you this morning, even standing still – and we won't be standing still for long. How are the horses; ready to go?'

'Just as soon as they've finished eating.'

'That's always the way with horses,' said Mar'ya Morevna. 'Everything is after they've finished eating.'

'It's the way with husbands, too.' He extended his arms to let the servants dress him, then staggered slightly, almost losing his balance, as they failed to pull on his outer kaftan with the proper swift, smooth, single movement. Its fur-lined sleeves clung to his inner coat and were most reluctant to let go. Ivan shook the servants aside and, by dint of much wriggling, succeeded where they had failed. 'The lie of the pelt is wrong,' he said, and realized just what that meant. The kaftan's sleeves had been stitched on upside down, and because they still looked right on the outside, it meant that whoever had done so had been too lax to correct the error by taking the coat apart again. Instead they had just cut and reshaped the cuffs, and presumed that no one would notice. That last petty irritation was enough. Suddenly all the real and imagined fretting of the past eight hours came boiling up like the abrupt sour spew that follows too much vodka.

'Oleg Pavlovich, to me!' snapped Ivan, and his principal body-servant was at his side in an instant, bowing in the quick, wary manner of one who knows and is rightly cautious of that tone in a Prince's voice. 'Find the tailor of this kaftan,' said Ivan Tsarevich. 'Give him five – no, ten strokes of the knout. To help him remember what he's doing next time he makes me a coat.'

Ivan wrapped the kaftan around himself and buckled its belt, then shrugged into the big fur riding-coat that went on top of all. There was more to that shrug than simply settling the heavy garment on top of his other clothing, but Mar'ya Morevna looked at him and only raised her eyebrows slightly, saying not a word.

'Another thing,' he said. 'How was it that your man Nikolai – or Stepan, or whichever name it was – mentioned nothing in his report from Khorlov of whatever is troubling my father?'

Mar'ya Morevna clapped her hands and waved the servants away. 'That, my dear, is something he will answer. To me. I do not pay my people just to admire the scenery and pass on gossip. But right now, they can wait. You should eat – something to sweeten your temper would not come amiss, I think. And I should eat, and then we should be on our way.'

Ivan let the shot go by with only the briefest of nods to acknowledge it. That spasm of annoyance was fading already, and he was beginning to regret his hasty words. 'Before that,' he said, 'I should call Oleg back.'

'No. The punishment is deserved, the tailor made a mistake, and he'll be careful not to make it again. It's not as though you make a habit of ordering your servants beaten, Vanyushka, whether your temper's bad or not. The fact that you're capable of doing so will not go unnoticed. Let it go.'

They ate, they drank, and then they collected the weapons and necessary accoutrements for travelling even briefly in the hard lands beyond the kremlin walls. Servants carried most of them ahead, to be hung in the proper places from their horses' saddles, but Mar'ya Morevna insisted that Ivan should also take the book *Enciervanul Doamnisoar* to Khorlov with them.

'Why?' he said, emboldened with mulled wine and hot honey-cakes to feel just a little bit rebellious.

'Because I ask you,' said Mar'ya Morevna in a voice every bit as sweet as the little cakes. 'And because you should continue your studies when you can. And because it might be useful.'

It was not a reason that Ivan Tsarevich had wanted to hear, but he shrugged in what he hoped was an unconcerned manner and thrust the book deep into his saddlebags, wondering privately if the fresh shirts also in the bag would still be fresh, and still indeed be shirts, after keeping such unpleasant company.

The horses were waiting in the courtyard, saddled, bridled and –

from the set of Sivka's ears at least – eager to go. Or perhaps the black horse was just amused at how his little master looked, this grey and chilly morning. Ivan and Mar'ya Morevna were both so well wrapped in furs that they resembled the bears who had originally owned those pelts, and they moved with the same fubsy clumsiness, forced by their thick, well-padded and extraordinarily awkward limbs to stand on mounting-blocks before they reached the saddle.

Ivan, already pink to the ears from overheating, blushed redder still as he clambered on to Sivka's back. He had not needed to use such a block since he was six years old and granted permission for the first time to mount Guard-Captain Akimov's great charger. 'If you laugh,' he hissed in the black horse's ear, 'if you so much as snigger . . .' Then he laughed himself, and let the unfinished sentence die as he settled his boots in the high Cossack-style stirrups. He could think of no threat sufficiently horrible, and anyway, by now Sivka knew him well enough to believe none of it. He saw Mar'ya Morevna nod an amiable farewell to Fedor Konstantinovich, but as Ivan looked at the High Steward and his staff of office, his laughter faltered and went silent as he wondered whether he would be so glad to see the other High Steward who would be waiting for them when they came at last to Khorlov.

They set heels to their horses, and amid a clamour of hoofs that rolled like thunder, lightnings billowed out of nowhere to enfold them, and borne up by the wings of that enchanted storm, Ivan and Mar'ya Morevna went away.

It was a quiet journey, in both senses of the word; without event, and for the most part, without words. Ivan and Mar'ya Morevna spoke only when they stopped to rest the horses and let them eat, and by wordless mutual consent, the conversation avoided touching matters of significance. It was enough that Ivan's stomach rebelled after more than a couple of mouthfuls of the bread and sausage; that told Mar'ya Morevna all she could have needed to know about her husband's state of mind.

Ivan saw the way she was looking at him, and shook his head. 'I'm just not hungry,' he said. That was a lie, and they both knew it. There was all the world of difference between having no hunger and having no appetite, but standing in the blasted white desolation that lay between their and their father's kremlins was neither the time nor the place to argue over it. No snow fell from the sky now; it had become too cold for snow. Instead, driven by that unremitting wind, ice-spicules slid rustling across the frozen drifts and struck into exposed flesh like handfuls of needles. It was not long before they were back in the saddle again.

Travel was less painful than standing still, for at least it was less achingly cold between the worlds. Despite the speed with which the landscape rolled by, there was no wind when the horses ran, and that was a mercy. Ivan did not like to think about riding at such a speed into the flaying gusts of ice-laden wind. Regardless of whether they seemed to strike against snow or ice or wind-scoured naked ground, or even, once, a river still unfrozen so that the black water passed beneath them like a naked blade, the sound of hoofbeats did not vary from a solid thudding that more usually went with running on the open plain.

Sivka and Chyornyy did their riders proud. Leaving Mar'ya Morevna's kremlin in mid-morning, later than intended because of one thing and another, they still came to the gates of Khorlov before the last light of the short winter day had faded from the sky. They were unexpected, and thus no-one greeted them as they blurred through the kremlin's walls, but there was no disguising the sight or sound of their arrival. The horses broke through the barriers that separated place from place and world from world in a coruscation of jewelled fragments and a great rending boom as empty air was hammered from their path, slackening their headlong sorcerous gallop to come dropping back into the reality that was Mother Russia with a skid and a clatter of hoofs on the chill flagstones of the courtyard. The noise came reverberating back from the towers of Khorlov's kremlin with a sound that was thunder indeed, and within minutes the empty courtyard began to fill with people.

Among the first to arrive was Dmitriy Vasil'yevich Strel'tsin, and at a pace that suggested he had flung his close-garnered dignity to the four winds of the world and run. He slowed immediately to the stately stride that was his more usual gait, stalking along in time to the measured taps of his tall staff of office, and when he reached the customary five paces from the son of his Tsar and the heir to the realm, he bowed low.

Ivan lifted one eyebrow in the old coolly disdainful look and responded with no more than a slight inclination of his head. He gave the haughty old man a close, hard look when he straightened up again, but Strel'tsin's face betrayed nothing save honest concern for the realm and what seemed sincere pleasure at seeing the Tsarevich returned to his old home. *What did you expect to see?* Prince Ivan thought to himself. *The word guilt printed in big letters on his forehead?* Nonetheless he was relieved, certain that he would have sensed something out of place had Strel'tsin genuinely had something to hide, even though as High Steward, First Minister, Tutor to the Tsarevich and Tsarevnas, Chancellor, Castellan and Court Sorcerer, besides other, lesser posts, Dmitriy Vasil'yevich almost certainly had an appropriate expression to go with each.

Strel'tsin snapped his fingers and gestured to one of the servants, and the man came forward with a plate on which was a round loaf of black rye bread with a wooden dish of white sea-salt set into a recess in its centre, the traditional offerings of hospitality to a guest. Ivan felt the tautness of control and concealed emotions go out of his face at that. Surely there could be nothing wrong; neither fire nor foe nor storm would keep the High Steward from his duties. If that trust was foolish, then so be it; but he had known Dmitriy Vasil'yevich since he was old enough to know anyone and anything, and trust was more wholesome by far than cuddling an unproven suspicion. Ivan took his knife and cut two slices from the bread, dipped them in the salt, and gave one to Mar'ya Morevna. When those were eaten, token that even this simplest of foods was gladly received, they scrambled awkwardly from their saddles and dropped to the snow-powdered stone of the courtyard.

The kremlin palace looked unchanged from the last time that they had seen it – except for one thing. Hands innocently busy with removing the outermost layer of her clumsy travelling clothes, Mar'ya Morevna jerked with her chin towards the walls, where three times the usual number of sentries patrolled the battlements. Most of them carried heavy recurved Tatar bows in cases at their belts. 'More guards,' she said softly. 'Far too many for a peaceful place like this.'

'Too many indeed.' Ivan kept the scowl from his face with an effort, and more for something to do than any other purpose, he began tugging at his own heavy fur coat. 'They wouldn't be there unless they were needed.'

'So do we ask, or wait to be told. . . ?'

'Wait.' He said it reluctantly, confused by the conflict of information between what he saw here and now and the worries that had gathered like black crows in his own head. 'Apart from the presence of the guards, there's nothing – well, nothing *wrong*. Nobody looks afraid. I don't want to say something aloud to change that. My father—'

'—Is here.' Mar'ya Morevna touched Ivan's arm and turned him towards the great stairway that led up and into the kremlin palace.

Flanked to either side by guards, and with Captain Akimov in full armour at his back, the Tsar of Khorlov stood in the doorway. He looked down into the courtyard and began to smile. 'Ivan!' cried Tsar Aleksandr Andreyevich, and had it not been for the respect with which he held his royal station and the many eyes who would have seen him put it aside, he would have run at once down the stairs to embrace his son. Instead he remained quite still until Ivan and Mar'ya Morevna had done him courtesy and then, no longer a Tsar but still very much a father, only then did he begin to run.

'You got my letter,' said the Tsar when all the hugging and kissing and back-slapping was done. 'When? Three days, four days ago?'

Ivan grinned. 'You forget about the horses that we ride, *batyushka*. If just after midnight counts for something in your calculations, then the letter was put into my hands this morning. And here we are tonight.' His face became more serious and he lowered his voice. 'What was wrong, to make you write such a cryptic thing and send it by such a messenger?'

'I have come to doubt the security of my letters this past few weeks, and as for the wolf-woman, that was an opportune crossing of paths and purposes, no more. I would have asked the Devil himself to be my messenger, had he been going the right way.'

Shocked, Mar'ya Morevna crossed herself, and after a moment's pause when his mouth opened and then shut with a click of teeth, Ivan did likewise. Unlike his wife, he knew that the Tsar had meant exactly what he said.

106

'Have either of you eaten yet?' There was an odd sound to the way that Tsar Aleksandr asked his question that made it unlike his usual invitation to the table.

'Not since a little after noon,' said Mar'ya Morevna. 'I thank Dmitriy Vasil'yevich for his bread and salt, but that was greeting, not dinner.'

'Just as well,' said the Tsar grimly. 'It would have been wasted. Strel'tsin, Akimov and the guards who can be trusted to keep their mouths shut know about this matter, but not the rest, and certainly not the other servants. Both of you, follow me.'

Ivan's mouth quirked as though he had tasted something sour, and he glanced sidelong at his wife. Neither of them spoke a word, but if his own expression was like hers, then their faces said all that was needed. Both of them could form at least a rough idea of what this oblique preamble meant; and both of them were too experienced in the more brutal forms of death to have other than a vague idea of what they were about to see.

They followed the Tsar into the kremlin and up the spiral stair leading into one of the towers. The sullen rhythmic tramp of the soldiers' boots and the oppressive shadows thrown by the lanterns they carried threw a brooding presence over everyone, and the sweat on Prince Ivan's hands and forehead did not come from the heat of the furs that he still wore. They came to a door, an ordinary enough door, locked and bolted, the key still in the lock and guards standing at either side. But they were standing as far away from that ordinary door as their orders would allow.

Prince Ivan Aleksandrovich hesitated, staring, scared, and not overmuch concerned about who knew it. The last time he had opened a locked door, his death had been waiting inside it. And there were worse things even than death. He recognized this door, and the room beyond it. Dmitriy Vasil'yevich Strel'tsin had tutored three generations of royal children in there, teaching them in his dry voice how to rule a kingdom or a husband. If any of the Princesses were bold enough to point out that he was of the wrong sex to know anything about being a wife, he in turn would point out without a change of tone or inflection that sex had nothing to do with ruling, and rather the reverse. Had Ivan not already seen the old man down in the courtyard, he might have begun to worry about him; as it was, there were worries enough. 'Father,' he said at last, reluctant to ask but needing to know, 'did something dreadful happen? And was – was it – someone that I knew?'

The Tsar looked at him, laid one heavy, kindly hand on his son's shoulder, and smiled a solemn, reassuring smile. 'No,' he said. 'No-one that you knew.' Then the smile died and his lips compressed in recollection until they resembled a bloodless scar across his silver beard. 'But something dreadful did happen. Yes. Something very dreadful.' Then he opened the door.

Inside was a room with bookshelves along the walls, like a library. It was a small place, not so much a room where books were kept in great numbers as a small, comfortable, private chamber where one could bring things from the great library in the kremlin's main building, and read or teach from them in quiet comfort. Some few volumes were shelved against the walls; there were cushioned chairs instead of benches; a wine-flagon rested in the centre of a small table, and there was a faint smell of cooking.

And a blanket lay in the middle of the floor; a stained horse-blanket, made lumpy and irregular by whatever was beneath it.

'Show me,' said Mar'ya Morevna, her voice held steady only by the same effort that had driven her nails into the palms of her hands. One of the guards who flanked the Tsar stepped forward and carefully, with a terrible, useless gentleness, drew back the blanket.

It was too generous a shroud. Far too big for the shrivelled, flaking charcoal doll that it had covered. It had been a man, once. A man, clad in armour that had been of no protection. He had been wearing mail and plate and studded leather, and now the bronze plates of his arm-defences had slumped and run like wax, and the brass studs of his leather tunic rested at the bottoms of the burrows they had seared down into his body, and only the iron mesh of the mail held the crisped and blackened corpse together. Of cloth and leather, there was no trace left.

Ivan looked, and flinched, and thought that it would have been far better to have eaten something after all, and to have been honestly sick at the sight and smell of what lay before his appalled gaze, than to have felt as he did now. The corpse was like nothing human, and that was just as well. Ivan was able to recover some semblance of control more easily. Otherwise, empty or not, he would have spewed his guts up on the floor. But worse was to follow. His eyes were blasted by what they saw, and his brain was shocked, but when that shock made him drag in a long, convulsive breath, what happened after made him feel more ashamed than any vomiting. Knowing nothing about horror but everything about hunger and the savoury aroma that he had inhaled, his mouth began to water.

The rich scent of roasting meat that had permeated the room emanated from the sad and ghastly thing beneath the blanket. Ivan's mouth went crooked with disgust and he scrubbed at his lips with the back of one gauntleted hand, wiping away the chance that someone might see a drop of saliva with a force almost hard enough to bruise. He stood back, well back, staring at nothing, feeling both emptily nauseated and utterly betrayed by his own reflexes.

Candles burned in sconces set around the room, their flames almost immobile in the still air, golden spears pointing the way to Heaven through the miasma of burning and corruption, and the wax wept hot tears. Mar'ya Morevna gestured for the dead man to be covered, and stared at the candles. Her brows came together in a frown. 'Father, we must talk,' she said to the Tsar. 'First Minister Strel'tsin and Guard-Captain Akimov as well.'

'But for the love of God,' said Prince Ivan behind her, 'can we please do it somewhere else. . . ?'

Mar'ya Morevna glanced sympathetically at him. 'Commanding armies in the field inures you to certain things,' she said. 'I forgot I have that . . . advantage over you.' She took a flask from where it hung from the belt of her travelling clothes, gestured quickly at it with one hand, and held it out to Ivan. 'Here, beloved, drink this.'

Ivan took it gratefully, pulled out the stopper, and drank as though the contents were water and he had been long lost in a desert. The flask contained vodka; having seen it filled, he knew that already. But then it had been *pschenichnaya*, Tsar's vodka, the clear, herbal-flavoured or near-tasteless spirit suitable for the drink-flask of a Princess. Now, changed by that small movement of Mar'ya Morevna's hand, it had become the raw, harsh, oily stuff that the peasants drank, especially those peasants whose lords were less than kind. They called it *forgetfulness in a bottle*.

And forgetfulness was exactly what Prince Ivan needed.

Chapter Five

'You, witch! I have been looking for you. What are you doing in here?' demanded Hermann von Salza from the doorway of Castle Thorn's library.

Baba Yaga was curled up on one of the seats beside the windows, hunched over a massive leather-bound book half-hidden in her lap. When she finally deigned to notice his angry presence and turned to look at him, she waved the volume in the air as though greeting a friend – although, from the size and weight of the book, she might as easily have been threatening an enemy. 'Reading, if it please your fine worthiness,' she said in that familiar whining voice which had begun to grate raw on the Grand Master's nerves. 'What else would a poor old woman be doing in a library?'

Von Salza leaned against the lintel of the door and grunted dubiously. 'An ordinary woman could do little enough that would concern me,' he said, 'save only to set me wondering what any woman would be doing in the fortress of a monastic order sworn to chastity.'

'As those two magpie friars are sworn, eh?' sneered Baba Yaga. 'Or do pretty boys not count?'

The Grand Master felt his face grow hot. Whether it was with embarrassment that Baba Yaga had seen what he had taken such pains to ignore and thus also seen his own studied omission of censure, or whether this foul creature was daring to tell him his duties, von Salza did not know. What he did know was that he disliked either possibility. 'The Dominicans are not of our Order,' he said in a warning tone, 'and what they do is between themselves and God.'

Baba Yaga tittered. 'Does your god take part in their unnatural embraces as well?'

The heat in Hermann von Salza's face flooded his eyes, so that for an instant before he regained control of himself, the old witch shimmered red, as though she had been dipped in burning blood.

'*Gerechter Herr Gott!*' he growled, low in his throat, and then his voice rose to a parade-ground bellow that slapped across the room. '*Halt's schweinisches Maul!* Shut your filthy mouth!'

The Grand Master strode towards her, flanked by the two mailed sergeants who had accompanied him since Baba Yaga and the inquisitors made their separate ways to Castle Thorn. Both soldiers had laid hands to their sword-hilts, and von Salza would take only a word from their commander to cover Baba Yaga in blood that was very real; her own.

She watched them approach without concern, smiling an unpleasant smile, plainly confident either in her own powers or in her importance to von Salza's plan for Russia. One at least was correct. Hermann von Salza stopped in his tracks and waved the sergeants back as a huntsman might leash in his dogs. 'You task me, witch-woman,' he said. 'You test my limits of endurance.' One finger jabbed at her as though it was a spear-blade. 'Believe me, when you push me too far you will not live to benefit from the knowledge!'

'Threatening a defenceless grandmother with armed guards, *Herr Hochmeister*? So this is how the Knights of the Teutonic Order prove their courage. I had often wondered.'

Von Salza dismissed his guards back to the doorway with a curt gesture, out of earshot – and out of reach of the temptation to use them to wipe that mocking sneer from Baba Yaga's face with a hard-swung blade of God's good steel. The witch-hag watched them go, then stared coolly at von Salza. 'No need for those two apes anyway,' she said, 'since I see that you carry a blade yourself, and wear armour underneath your fine robes. You never did that before. Do I frighten you so much?'

'I am a knight and a Grand Master of knights,' said von Salza. 'The wearing of mail should come as no surprise.' His excuse was a feeble one, he knew, but he would lose all hope of Heaven and be damned to Hell before he would admit to this wrinkled, unwashed and louse-ridden hag that yes indeed, she frightened him, as Salah eh-Din Yusuf and all the hosts of Islam ranked in battle array had never done. He looked more carefully at the book in Baba Yaga's lap and frowned.

'What *is* that?' he said, staring at its tooled-leather binding. The leather had been gouged in many places, and scorched along the gouges as though the entire book had been raked with spikes of red-hot metal. 'It didn't come from any shelf in this library.' Of that, von Salza was certain; this was not a book such as he would forget, once seen.

'No indeed,' said Baba Yaga, and cuddled the heavy volume to her shrivelled breasts as though it was a child. 'It's mine. *Liber Tenebrae*. I found it. One of the other things I gain from this enterprise besides my revenge on the Khorlovtsy.'

'*The Book of Shadows*. A book of sorcery, then. I should have realized. Stolen, no doubt, and kept from me. That was no part of the bargain that you made.'

'Not made with you at least, Grand Master Hermann von Salza. With a man more flexible and practical about getting what he wants. Have your *Landmeister* of Livonia tell you all about the rest of it.'

Von Salza glowered at her. 'Dieter Balke has returned to Russia,' he said. 'As you well know. And he told me nothing before he left.' Balke had indeed said nothing, which was entirely in keeping with his habit of obsessive secrecy. He was one of the few knights of the Order who had mastered the Slavonic language enough to pass himself off in Russia – at least if not closely scrutinized – as coming from a different city where they spoke with a different accent.

'As I well know,' said Baba Yaga smugly. 'You should have asked him. Some of the arrangements made on your behalf, dear *Hochmeister*, are not confessed as freely as you might think. And all because what you do not know, you can deny knowing. There now. The sins your loyal friends commit for you, just so that you can keep your innocence, what there is of it.' She opened the book again and began to leaf through its pages, then paused to glance up at von Salza with an arch, sly lifting of her straggly white eyebrows. 'Although to an untutored and ignorant old peasant woman—'

'—Who has somehow learned to speak perfect German!'

'—Who can do a great deal more than you can begin to imagine, Hermann von Salza, including see further than these weak and ancient eyes might suggest. And what they see, Holy Grand Master of the Holy Teutonic Order, is a man who might well want this little sweetmeat for himself.' She patted the book, then picked a bit of charred leather from its cover with a crooked, dirty fingernail.

Von Salza stared at her, his own eyes narrowing. Then he walked to the window and looked out at the cracked winter landscape and the snow, falling, falling from the dead grey sky. He walked to the charcoal brazier that kept chill from the room and pulled off his white leather gloves to warm his hands. Then he dismissed the two sergeants of his guard beyond the library door – dismissed them twice, when they hesitated the first time and gazed uneasily at Baba Yaga – and waited until it had been closed behind them before sauntering back to where the ancient hag was watching him, with an expression of amusement on her face among the warts and the dirt and the wrinkles. 'I might consider it, witch-woman,' he said slowly. 'What sort of price had you in mind – gold? Power, perhaps?'

'I have small need of gold, von Salza, and as for power of the kind I desire, I already have that in plenty. What else can you offer?' Baba Yaga shifted her scrawny legs under her dirty peasant skirt and apron in so blatant an attempt to seem seductive that Hermann von Salza would have laughed in her face, had he not found both the proposal and the prospect totally revolting.

'There are some things with prices higher than any sane or self-respecting person would care even to consider,' he said, and managed to keep the twist of abhorrence from his mouth and voice. His fingers tightened on the hilt of his long dagger against the chance that Baba Yaga would take offence, but instead she sniggered at him.

'Although you'd order Dieter Balke to pay that price in your stead if you weren't so wary of how he would react, eh?' She cracked two errant lice with her thumbnail, then tugged her skirt back down over the expanse of bony, flea-pocked skin that passed for her shins, straightening its dingy fabric with as much care as if it had been the finest Moorish satin. 'Evidently you Germans have never heard of the stories where if a brave man dares to sleep with an ugly hag, he awakes beside the beautiful maiden who was under an enchantment to cheat her of high rank and a rich inheritance.'

Hermann von Salza put his head on one side and eyed Baba Yaga in much the same way as he might have studied a loathsome insect from underneath a stone. 'That must be a strong enchantment indeed,' he said, eyes and nose both assailed by the signs of slovenly poverty. Even the Lazar Knights of Jerusalem, afflicted by God with the grim disease of leprosy, did not look and smell so vile. And then, scarcely believing the possibility in one so hideous: 'Not you, surely?'

'Of course not.' Baba Yaga fluttered her gummy eyelids at the Grand Master and cackled, and in that grating laughter von Salza heard for the first time what real wickedness could sound like. 'But you were beginning to wonder, were you not? And there have been the greedy or the goatish ones who did more than wonder . . . They were disappointed, poor boys.' She grinned at him and ran the tip of her tongue in a mock-erotic lick across the ragged spikes of iron that did duty as her teeth. 'But not disappointing. Very toothsome lads they were, one and all.'

Von Salza clutched with both hands at the collar of the hauberk he wore beneath his gardcorps mantle, as though it was suddenly too tight and throttling him – or to keep those same hands from reaching out to throttle the insolent old witch. His fingers flexed against the leather jerkin that made a soft lining for the shirt of hard iron rings, squeezing until the bones of his knuckles showed white through the tightly drawn tanned skin, and his breathing was shallow and rapid by the time he trusted himself to speak. 'You are defying me,' he said. 'And trying to defile me!'

Baba Yaga looked him up and down, and all of the evil amusement went from her face, leaving it as emotionlessly ugly as a stone gargoyle. 'Oh no, *Herr Hochmeister*,' she said. There was no smugness in her voice now, no satisfaction; just the flat statement of fact. 'Not trying. Not even I can do something that has been done already. You call me evil and yourself good, but you use me to gain your ends just as I use you. Where does the difference lie, Grand Master? Perhaps you might tell me, from the store of your great wisdom, because this poor stupid old peasant woman can't see it for herself . . .'

For all his faults, Hermann von Salza was a just and fair-minded man; even though justice could be ignored when it had to be. The old witch spoke nothing but the truth as she saw it, and if it was seen and spoken in coarse terms, what else could a knight and nobleman expect from a dirty foreign vassal who probably couldn't even spell 'manners', never mind know what the word

114

meant. Such reasoning, at least, was what kept his hands and his dagger from Baba Yaga's throat until he had fought himself calm again, and that fight was one of the hardest things that he had done all day.

'*Kommen Sie hier, marsch! marsch!*' the Grand Master said sharply, not a shout but loud enough. In the corridor outside the library, his two sergeants had been waiting for just such an order. They flung both doors wide open and came through at a dead run with their swords already drawn in expectation of immediate use. Von Salza was rewarded by a gratifying expression of stark fear on Baba Yaga's face in the instant before he brought them to a skidding halt with one upraised hand. It suggested to him that for all her bravado and all her vaunted skill at sorcery, if she was taken suddenly and without time to prepare, then she might well prove as vulnerable as anyone else to a blade delivered unawares or from behind.

'Have no fear,' he said, leaning as close into her stench as his fastidious nostrils would allow, his voice deceptively gentle and formal. 'They are here to protect you, not me. All you need to do is try my patience again like that last time, and all my plans would have to be wasted. Because if I didn't kill you outright with my own hands, I would give what was left to the Holy Office.'

Von Salza straightened up, walked a little distance away from Baba Yaga and breathed deeply of the clean air again. With his composure restored, he glanced at her over his shoulder. The witch seemed appropriately chastened; at least there were no more word-games or misplaced coquettish looks. 'Good. It seems I have made myself quite clear. Now what about the other details of the bargain? The attention of your sending has been concentrated solely on Khorlov. It's high time you turned your attention to the others. The Princes of Novgorod, Kiev, Pskov and the rest.'

'Why?' The question sounded more surprised than insolent.

'Because I command it. That should be enough.'

'More than enough; far too much.' Baba Yaga uncurled herself from the seat and waved one dismissive hand at the very idea. 'None of the Princes of the Rus have any great love for the rest, *Herr Hochmeister*, but they do occasionally talk to one another, even if only through ambassadors sent between the cities to avoid unnecessary little wars. A better arrangement than your military orders of chivalry – oh yes, I know enough about the Templars and the Hospitallers for that.'

'And so. . . ?'

'So if all the Princes that you name can complain that they have been troubled by some sorcerous occurrence, who can they blame? Whereas if only one has suffered, who will they *not* blame? Those accused will deny all knowledge, of course; but such denials are only to be expected from the guilty. Thus the Tsar of Khorlov will lash out blindly and be punished for it with the conquest of his lands and the extirpation of his line; the remaining Princes will squabble over such a conquest and fall upon each other, giving you your war to weaken them before you send your knights across the border; and I have my revenge.' Baba Yaga gave the Grand Master another of her snaggle-toothed grins, and he struck his hands together in sardonic applause.

'Very pretty,' said von Salsa. 'And what happens if something goes wrong?'

'Ask Dieter Balke. He is already taking steps to prevent it. You see, Grand Master, the *Landmeister* and I understand one another in a way that you do not. He told me where he was going, and what he intended to do when he got there. Aleksandr Khorlovskiy and Yuriy of Kiev have never been friendly. They are about to become something much worse.' The witch sat down again and tucked her legs beneath her, then pointedly opened her book and began to study it. 'Now go away. I want to read in peace.'

'Are you giving me an order, hag?' Hermann von Salza was also amused by an impudence he knew now to be over-confident. 'I warned you not to do that.'

Baba Yaga looked at the book again, her lips moving silently. Then she made a quick grasping movement with each hand, fingers spread wide so that the untrimmed nails extended like claws, and the sergeants to either side of von Salza made startled little grunts as their armoured chests exploded in a spray of blood and ribs and burst mail-rings. Baba Yaga watched complacently as both ruined bodies slumped to the floor, and grinned raggedly at their Grand Master when he stared at her in horror.

'Yes, Hermann von Salza,' she said, 'I was giving you an order indeed. And a warning. Don't let your sergeants threaten me with swords unless you no longer need them.' Baba Yaga looked at the

116

still-throbbing organ meat that filled her open hands, and leisurely licked her lips. 'Not that such heartless brutes are much of a loss . . .'

'He was burnt, that much is clear. But before or after he died?'

Whether it was the fierce vodka that Mar'ya Morevna had given him, or just being away from the blackened horror that had so turned his stomach, Prince Ivan had become all cold business in a way that would have gratified his wife's High Steward. He glanced at her, then at his father the Tsar, seated in state at the head of the table and flanked by Dmitriy Vasil'yevich Strel'tsin the First Minister of the realm, and Petr Mikhailovich Akimov its Captain of Guards. Ivan was standing, as was the custom for one making a first statement in any court business, and he was the focus of attention. Indeed, the faces of all four were attentive enough to make him feel just a little shy about having opened the proceedings so bluntly, but it seemed better to reach the point of discussion than to merely circle it. 'We should also try to learn why,' he finished, feeling rather awkward, and gratefully resumed his seat. 'And by what.'

Mar'ya Morevna stood up, then remembered that she was not the lord of this kremlin and looked to the Tsar for the right to speak out of turn. Aleksandr Andreyevich nodded once, granting permission and approval of the courtesy with a single inclination of his silver-maned head. 'Even though this is not a crime that should involve the constables of the City Watch,' she said, 'murder has been done. Regardless of the manner of that murder, it should be handled from the first as just another crime; at least until we have learned enough to treat it otherwise.'

'This is the only murder, Mar'ya Tsarevna,' said Dmitriy Vasil'yevich, 'but it is not the only crime. Some thief has dared to visit his depredations on the Tsar's own kremlin palace.'

'A thief, *here*?' Mar'ya Morevna's eyebrows shot up in disbelief. She turned her head to stare at Prince Ivan, and he shook his head in silent astonishment that any criminal should be so bold. The rewards of stealing from any lord's palace were matched only by the savagery of the punishments when the thief was inevitably caught. It was one thing to make away with coins and common goods from some merchant's house, where the one could be spent

117

and the other sold unnoticed at any market stall. It was another thing entirely to dispose of the jewelled, precious-metal trinkets that would tempt light fingers in a palace. A thief with sense would never dare to steal such things, but then why enter the kremlin in the first place? The very fact that he or she or they had done so argued against them having any sense at all. The stupidity of it was almost funny, at least until Ivan thought to ask what had gone missing. After Strel'tsin's reply, it didn't seem quite so stupid, or so funny, after all.

'Magical things, Highness,' he said. The words came from him slowly, reluctantly, like an embarrassing confession drawn out by a persistent priest. 'At first they were only the small things that anyone might misplace, or set down and forget.'

'Such as?' said Ivan, mentally stamping down hard on a tendency to smile. There had been enough times in his youth when Strel'tsin had pried a lesson from him just like this, or worse, the admission that it had not been learned. It was only that the occasion was most incorrect that prevented him from getting what little enjoyment he could from this reversal of rôles.

'A spelling wand, five charm-stones in a box, some candles of Arabian gums and spices mingled with rare wax.' Mar'ya Morevna, listening to the recital with arms folded and head lowered, looked up sharply at that as it reminded her of something else. 'As I say, Highness,' the First Minister continued, 'they were the sort of little items only missed when looked for and not found. Until the night when the guard was killed. That was when the book was taken.'

'Book?' echoed Mar'ya Morevna. 'You mean a book of spells, a grimoire? Is there no safe place in the library for such things?'

Dmitriy Vasil'yevich looked truly miserable, for though she had taken care not to say so aloud, there was the implication in Mar'ya Morevna's words that if he had put his toys away after playing with them, they would not have gone missing. At least, not so easily as when they were apparently left lying around for anyone to find. 'Yes, *gospozha*,' he said, 'there is an iron book-chest with an iron lock. But I had been reading it only that evening, late into the night, and . . .'

'And the library is a long way away for an elderly gentlemen who would rather go to bed,' said Ivan kindly. 'Especially when

118

the book is large and heavy, and he hasn't finished with it yet. Do I guess right?'

First Minister Strel'tsin gazed at Prince Ivan for a moment, and there was gratitude in his eyes such as Ivan had never expected to see there. The softer emotions were not strangers to the old man; but in his long life he had buried two wives and seven children, and gentleness had rusted after that for lack of use.

Mar'ya Morevna took that cue from her husband, and the edge of irritation left her voice. 'Never mind the book for now,' she said. 'We can come back to it later, when other things begin to make some sort of sense. But tell me this, Dmitriy Vasil'yevich; how long have these thefts been going on?'

'Perhaps a week, Lady; ten days at the most. That was when I first noticed that certain things were gone from where I had left them – and not just because I had been looking in the wrong place.'

'Highness, Lady, the guards were reinforced five days ago,' said Captain Akimov. 'I had hopes that they might see something, or even catch the thief red-handed; at the very least they should have deterred whoever it was from coming back.'

'Or whatever it was,' said Ivan. 'Petr Mikhailovich, the dead man must have seen the *something* you were hoping for.'

'And little good that did him, Highness, or us. He died without a sound. Whoever – or as you say, whatever – killed him made certain that he would say nothing more about it.'

'In that, the murderer was mistaken.' Mar'ya Morevna steepled her fingers and tapped their tips against her chin. 'As murderers so often are. But my concerns are deeper than mere murder. Yours too?' She looked from Strel'tsin to the Tsar and back again. Faces sombre, they both nodded.

Ivan looked at them, not understanding. 'Worse than murder?' he said at last. 'Worse than *that* murder? What the hell are you talking about?'

Tsar Aleksandr gazed at his son and smiled grimly at Ivan's outrage. 'More deaths than that of a single guard,' he said. 'The destruction of the realm. If this thief and murderer was stealing jewels alone, it wouldn't be so worrying. But since he – it – is taking only magical items, we have to start wondering about the security of the most magical thing in any kingdom: the Great Crown itself.'

'*Izbavi Bog!*' Comprehension and the memory of words spoken long ago hit Ivan both together, with the force of a hammerblow. Like kings and tsars and princes all across Moist-Mother-Earth, his father had several crowns and caps of state, worn each for its appropriate ceremony. But there was only one Great Crown in any realm, and it was worn on only one occasion: the coronation.

Even in the lands to the west, people spoke of 'the Crown' as they might speak of 'the power of the king'; as though the two were one. They were. It was small wonder that, rather than the debased circlets of European monarchs, all the Great Crowns of the Russias kept their old form. Once the trimmings of rich fur, the inlaid precious metals and the jewels were all stripped away, what remained was the conical shape of a helmet. It represented the power and protection by the Tsar of his lands and his people, and if *that* was stolen away, the land and the people would perish.

There were few thieves who would be so bold as to contemplate such a crime; but there were creatures beyond the edges of the wide white world to whom it would be no more a calculated theft than a magpie stealing trinkets. Such creatures could bring a tsardom to ruin, not knowing that they had done anything wrong. But they could also be sent, with that very purpose in mind . . .

The discussion rambled on for a quarter-hour more; or rather, everyone else talked while Mar'ya Morevna gently prompted them with questions that they had never considered before. Finally she looked up and down the bare expanse of table-top and frowned a little. 'I thought I asked for pen, ink and parchment.'

'Here when required, *gospozha* Mar'ya Tsarevna,' said Strel'tsin, producing them from the pouch at his belt like a conjurer performing a trick. The parchment was his own tablet of cut sheets clipped into a notebook by two metal rings; the pen, ink and sandcaster came all together in a single travelling case of carved, age-darkened wood that he opened out and assembled with the ease of long, long practice.

Ivan picked up the pen and twiddled it in his fingers, watching while Mar'ya Morevna stared into space and organized her thoughts. Once she was ready to speak them aloud, Ivan – whose writing had always been reasonably swift, as if to make up for its untidiness – would scribble them down for future study. It was a sharing of labour to which he had grown accustomed in the running of their own realm, since it had given him a way in which he could be of some use during his many weeks of learning how to be a Prince in more than title.

'Item,' she said at length, 'that the unfortunate guard was killed by burning, or burnt during his killing, but in either instance, so swiftly that there was no outcry.

'Item, that the heat by which he died was great enough to melt his arm-guards, made of bronze, yet the candles on the wall remained undamaged. Even if they had been replenished since the murder – were they, First Minister? Yes? But only in the normal way, when they had burnt down to stubs? Good, very good. Had the original candles taken harm from such heat as we are considering, they would have dissolved into the air so fast that they would have sprayed boiling wax and black smoke all over the walls. Yet there was no trace of any such thing. Therefore this heat was extremely localized.

'Item, First Minister Strel'tsin spoke of other candles, candles that were stolen – but not melted. Nor were there signs of scorching in any of the other places where thefts have taken place, at least not obvious ones or someone would have mentioned them before now. Therefore this heat is a selective and voluntary phenomenon rather than a constant one.

'And item, though the bronze plate armour was melted, the iron mail remained unharmed, loose and flexible. Iron needs a greater heat than bronze before it melts, or so my father and my armourer have told me in the past. However, I speculate from the other items that there is another reason besides this difference to explain the survival of the mail, and that is the metal itself. Cold iron is not affected by sorcery. Therefore this fire is not of nature, and I surmise' – Mar'ya Morevna paused briefly to massage her forehead with the tips of her fingers, and Ivan took the opportunity to shake an attempt at cramp out of his writing hand – 'that my book *Enciervanul Doamnisoar* may well give us the name or at least the species of the murderer.'

Only the First Minister gasped and crossed himself at the book's title; the Tsar and Captain Akimov looked blank until Ivan, done at last with sanding ink-damp letters, looked up at them and smiled sadly at such comfortable innocence. 'It means "On the Summoning of Demons", in what seems to be some dialect of old

Wallachian,' he said. 'And though I don't know what Dmitriy Vasil'yevich was reading late into the night, I would heartily recommend that no-one tries to do the same with *this*.'

His hand moved and a book thudded onto the table, skidded slightly on the polished surface, and lay there, seeming almost to squat like something alive. It had come apparently out of thin air, but in actuality from where he had been carrying it inside the cross-wrapped front of his furred travelling tunic, a garment already so well padded that the bulge made by the book had gone mostly unnoticed. *Enciervanul Doamnisoar* was not the sort of thing one left unattended for the servants to find and talk about; Ivan had the nasty feeling that even in uneducated hands it was capable of creating far more unpleasant things than just gossip.

Mar'ya Morevna reached out for it, but Ivan's hand was already flat against the grimoire's gem-encrusted metal cover, pressing down and holding it shut. She shot him a look that was more curious than annoyed, and he shook his head. 'No, Mar'yushka. Not even you, so late at night in a place where ugliness has happened. This goes into the library's iron chest until tomorrow, because whatever has been visiting Khorlov would find such a thing a tasty morsel indeed.'

'What are you thinking, my son?' said Tsar Aleksandr.

'Two things,' said Ivan. 'Either the thief has been sent to look for objects of magic, and takes what it can find – or magic simply attracts it, like wasps to a honey pot. And if that's the case, then I'll wager this book smells most damnably sweet.'

'Sent?' said the Tsar, and there was sudden menace in his voice. 'Who would dare send such a thing to Khorlov?' There was no need to list the possible suspects, since first in any such list would be the rival lords of Novgorod and Kiev. Ivan twitched inwardly and bit his tongue at using so loaded a word, remembering too late the shortness of his father's temper where interference with the Tsardom was concerned. It was bad enough that there might be something lurking in the shadows of the kremlin, stealing magical baubles with as little motive as a rat might steal grain. To discover that the malice of an enemy might be guiding its depredations was far worse. That way lay accusation, reprisal and ultimately, war.

'Until we know just what it is, Little Father,' Mar'ya Morevna said quickly, 'guessing at its source would be no more than that: a guess, and a poorly informed one. Vanya's suggestion is a better one by far.' Ivan glanced sideways, wondering what words she was going to put in his mouth this time. 'We should put the book in a safe place, get whatever sleep the good God sends us, and continue this debate in the clean light of morning.'

Ivan Aleksandrovich picked up the grimoire, disliking as always the way it seemed too warm in his hand. 'I suggested all that?' he muttered in a voice that only Mar'ya Morevna could hear.

'You suggested locking the book up for the night, and I agree. You merely implied that we should leave all this until tomorrow; but Vanya, dear one, when did you ever *not* suggest that we should go to bed. . . ?'

Strel'tsin's room in the tower was a more pleasant place by daylight than it had been the night before. It was icy cold, because the narrow windows that overlooked the kremlin palace had been flung wide open; but the air smelt sweet and clean again, and there was no longer any ghastly bundle underneath a blanket in the middle of the floor. Prince Ivan acknowledged the salute of the guard at the door, then held it open for Mar'ya Morevna to go inside.

She was carrying the book *Enciervanul Doamnisoar* under one arm, and Ivan's scrawled notes from last night's meeting in the fingers of that hand. Ivan carried nothing; but the Circassian dagger was back in its customary place behind the buckle of his belt, his favourite silver-mounted *shashka* sabre was hanging at his hip, and his tongue was well-equipped with reasons – for those ignorant of the truth – as to why the Tsar's son might need to bear weapons within the walls of his father's kremlin. So far no-one had given the blades a second glance; Mar'ya Morevna's reputation as a warrior lady was well enough established that it seemed only proper her husband should go armed. The shirt of light mail that he wore beneath his kaftan, and the iron skullcap under his furred hat, might have caused more comment had they been on view, but Ivan had made certain that the armour was well covered before he and Mar'ya Morevna left their chambers.

They examined the room more closely than Ivan would have believed possible, even to crawling on hands and knees with their noses bare inches from the Khazan rugs scattered over the tiled floor. Finally he straightened up, grunting slightly when the muscles of the small of his back registered their complaint with a sharp twinge of pain, and sat on the floor with his shoulders braced against the wall and his legs stuck straight out in front of him. It looked most unprincely, but at least it felt comfortable.

Mar'ya Morevna looked at him and sat back on her heels. 'Five minutes,' she said. 'Just five minutes more and we'll be done. Then you can rest.'

'Observe,' said Ivan, waving one hand at his outstretched legs but not otherwise troubling to move. 'I'm resting already. You should do the same, and take some time to' – he leaned over and dabbed at her nose, – 'wipe the smuts from your face. This floor isn't as clean as it might be.'

Mar'ya Morevna muttered something she had probably overheard on campaign and rubbed vigorously with her sleeve until Ivan nodded approval of her renewed cleanliness. Then she too sat back, grinning. 'All right. Make that five minutes' rest. After that, we'll finish.'

'Mar'yushka, would I sound very stupid if I asked you what the hell we were looking for?' He sounded so plaintive that she laughed out loud.

'I thought I told you last night, before you went to sleep.' Mar'ya Morevna stared at her husband for an instant, then shook her head and laughed again. 'I must have mistimed. There was no "before" about it, was there? And you didn't even have the decency to snore, so that I could wake you up again or save my breath.'

'I was too tired to snore,' said Ivan grumpily. 'And anyway, I don't.'

'You should stay awake and listen to yourself sometime, loved. Or listen to the opinions of those who know. Once more: since Dmitriy Vasil'yevich's study is the only room where we can be certain the thief was seen by that poor young man, God give him rest . . .' They signed themselves with the life-giving cross. 'Then it's the only room where we'll be likely to find some trace of what that thief is; size, shape, that sort of thing. Only when I know what to look for will I start looking through *Enciervanul Doamnisoar*. As you said yourself, it's not a book for idle browsing.'

Ivan gave her a crooked smile. 'And what was I doing with it, if not browsing?' he wanted to know.

'Learning,' said Mar'ya Morevna simply. 'A different state of mind altogether. With one, you're busy; with the other . . . well, demons can find work for idle brains as easily as idle hands. If I was to open that book now, wanting to find something but with no more than an unformed notion of what it was, then rest assured I'd certainly find some *thing*, but there's no saying what it might be. Anything at all could be summoned into being by a simple desire for knowledge.'

Glancing sidelong at the grimoire's ornate covers, Ivan suppressed a little shiver. 'And yet you want me to go on reading that thing. . . ?'

'Later.'

'Much later, if at all. I don't much like the notion of claws reaching up out of the page and pulling my face off. And that seems the least of . . . Are you listening?'

'You said claws,' said Mar'ya Morevna. 'And I'm looking at them.'

Going from sitting flat on the floor to standing upright in a fighting stance with a drawn blade in each hand is never easy, but Ivan managed it without seeming to move his legs. Mar'ya Morevna gazed up at him and slowly began to clap her hands. 'That was very dramatic, Vanya,' she said, not mocking him more than a very little. There was too much concern on her face for that. 'And you're more nervous about all this than you've told me, even in bed, where we're supposed to have no secrets.'

Ivan Aleksandrovich relaxed, and rather sheepishly returned the sword and dagger to their scabbards. 'I thought you had already guessed. And when you said you could see claws, well, what was I to do except . . .'

'Except protect me.' She reached out and held his hand between her own. '*Spasibo, lyubovnik.* Even though there was no need, thank you, beloved.' Then she tightened her grip and, ever the practical one, used that gesture of affection as a means to haul herself upright. 'I should have said I could see claw *marks*, but I didn't think that you – well, never mind.' She pointed at the back of an intricately carved wooden chair. 'Look there.'

Ivan looked, and saw, and drew in his breath with a sharp little gasp. The two sets of incised parallel lines were almost part of the chair's elaborate decorative pattern, and could have passed for such unless someone chanced to look at that particular part of the chair-back from behind – and simultaneously from below. Someone who was sitting on the floor, which was not a usual practice for anyone likely to use the First Minister's private study, and especially not a Tsar's son or the fairest Princess in all the Russias. Warily putting out one finger, Ivan traced the lines; and when he looked, his fingertip was charcoal black.

'Does this help?' he asked, holding the blackened finger out for Mar'ya Morevna's inspection.

'It does more than help, Vanya,' she said, her face almost merry as she lifted the book *Enciervanul Doamnisoar*. 'It makes me nearly sure. And I think we can leave out that "nearly" in just a moment. Elements, elements, elements,' she muttered to herself as the pages flipped over, filling the air with a faint and deceptively pleasant aroma of some sort of spice. 'Elements, good. Void, no, earth and air, no, water – perhaps later. But fire; ah yes, here we are. Ah-*hah!*'

'Ah-hah?' echoed Ivan dubiously, manoeuvring to get a better view of the page. It was mostly text, which he didn't mind; the text of this particular book was nothing like as horrible, at least to a first and casual glance, as some of the illustrations, but even the few drawings that he could see represented ordinary enough creatures. Although he was looking at them upside-down, Ivan could distinguish a boar from a horse, and a farmyard cockerel from an Oriental pheasant. Birds and beasts all had a little touch of gold about them, real gold leaf and thus both expensive and eye-catchingly unusual in what was, after all, not a coloured illumination but a simple pen-and-ink line-sketch. The boar's bristles were gold, as was the horse's mane; the cockerel had a golden comb, and the pheasant had golden spurs. It all looked very handsome and not at all in keeping with the nastiness portrayed elsewhere in that particular grimoire, so much so that Ivan at once became suspicious of what the text said that the pictures did not – or dared not.

'These are the forms of the *zhar'yanoi*,' said Mar'ya Morevna, tapping each drawing in turn.

'Fire-sprites?'

126

'Call them fire elementals; it's more accurate, as well as more respectful.'

'Respectful . . .' That gave Ivan Aleksandrovich a sinking feeling in the pit of his stomach; or rather, it accelerated the rate of sink already there. 'And is it disrespectful not to like the sound of that?'

'Far from it.' Mar'ya Morevna smiled gently and patted Ivan on the arm. 'Not liking something engenders caution, and you can never be too cautious when dealing with elemental forces.'

'But these *zhar'yanoi* aren't demons.' Ivan turned the book so that he could see a little better, and stared hard at the little pictures. Upright or inverted, the animals and the birds remained what they appeared: quite normal, except for that touch of gold. Probably far too normal to be trusted. 'I think,' he added, and then, since that sounded a little lame: 'At least they don't look like demons.'

'Of course they aren't demons,' said Mar'ya Morevna, and if it came out sounding ever so slightly testy, that was only to be expected from someone who had been trying for six months to teach her husband enough about the Art Magic that he wouldn't come out with just that sort of idiotic observation. 'I told you not half a minute ago: they're elementals.'

'But,' said Ivan, and grinned briefly at Mar'ya Morevna's exasperated groan, 'but you and I know perfectly well that fire isn't an element. Why aren't there any, uh, iron elementals?'

'Because the blacksmiths keep hitting them with hammers,' snapped Mar'ya Morevna in a tone of voice that suggested she was exactly balanced between amusement and genuine annoyance. 'Vanya, the alchemical elements of sorcery are not the chemical elements of science. Aristotle the Greek knew that well enough, just as he knew well enough to say nothing else about the matter.'

'I had Aristotle and Pliny and all their fellow philosophers rammed down my throat until I choked on them,' said Ivan. 'In this very room. And I know that their philosophy allowed of only four elements; so what about the fifth, the Void? Not Greek, surely?'

'Now that's a sensible question at last. And about time, too. The principal of Void, of nothing as a balance to everything, comes from the lands of the East. It seemed sensible enough; so it was adopted by sorcerers.'

'Why? If void is nothingness, then how do they know that it exists at all?'

'How does a good Christian know that God exists? Faith, and trust in the writings of those who seem to know more about it than we do. Understand this, Vanyushka: those who work with the Art Magic are a cautious lot. Until someone disproves the existence of the element we call Void – which is likely to be a difficult proposition since, as you point out, its very nature makes that sort of conclusion awkward to pin down one way or another – then we'll behave as though it really does exist. Safer that way.' She put her head on one side and studied Ivan quizzically. 'Now what are you smirking about?'

'I asked you a simple question, and you gave me a lecture on the meaning of preternatural philosophy. Just like Dmitriy Vasil'yevich. There must be some aura about this room of his—'

'Other than whatever it was that burns unsuspecting guardsmen to cinders, you mean?'

Ivan stopped smiling and looked shocked. 'That was uncalled-for.'

'On the contrary, loved, it was very called-for. You would rather think of anything, even that tutoring in the doings of the old Greeks which you found so boring, than what we're doing here. Because it frightens you? That's nothing to be ashamed of.' Mar'ya Morevna took Ivan's hand, gently at first and then gripping hard enough that it was almost painful; certainly enough that the pressure and the words that went with it could not be ignored. 'I told you before, I tell you again, and I'll keep telling you until you understand all of what I'm saying. If you're afraid, you'll be careful. But if you're careless, you'll be dead. And I don't want to be a widow again.'

Ivan digested that in silence, feeling . . . feeling all the emotions and sensations that he should have felt, and a few more besides. Certainly his ears were hot, and there was that unmistakable fluttering like a moth's wings, one of the big, blundering, furry ones, in the pit of his stomach. Everything, in fact, that accompanied saying or doing something stupid – at which he had had plenty of practice, one way or another – and even though all those feelings came and went in the space of a few breaths, it didn't make Prince Ivan Aleksandrovich Khorlovskiy feel any less of a fool.

'Point taken,' he said at last, looking a little shamefaced. There was another uncomfortable moment which he felt certain Mar'ya Morevna was expecting him to fill with some sort of intelligent remark, and that low-level tension dragged out to a jangling extent when it became equally certain that she wasn't going to speak first.

'So why are you studying a page about elementals in a book that's so obviously concerned with demons?' said Ivan. He spoke slowly, picking his words and doing his best not to watch his wife's face so as to make sure that those words were right. Fortunately, they were.

Mar'ya Morevna pulled out one of the chairs at the table – taking care not to use the one which had the claw marks scored into it – and gestured Ivan to another. 'Because what happened here was nothing to *do* with demons,' she said, and then, because it was too easy a target to ignore and also an entirely justifiable comment, 'as you would know by now if you read the damned grimoire, instead of just carrying it about with you and complaining that you don't like the subject matter.'

'Forgive me now, or criticize me later,' said Ivan, using the old formal phrase for courtesy's sake. 'But tell me what you mean.'

'*Slava Bogu!*' said Mar'ya Morevna fervently, crossing herself and casting a grateful glance towards Heaven. 'The light begins to dawn, and we'll make an enchanter of you yet.'

'Heaven forbid!' said Ivan, though he was relieved that Mar'ya Morevna's quicksilver mood had gone back to being merry again. He loved her very dearly, but there were times when she could be a hard woman to live with. Much of that, he supposed, came as a result of his knowing so little of what played so large a part in her life: the three powers of sorcery, soldiery and politics. He had been trained to some of the second and third factors, and trained well; Guard-Captain Akimov and High Steward Strel'tsin knew their special subjects as well as any man. But as for the first, Ivan had known only the small magics that any Rus with the ability to learn them was taught when first learning to speak. The rest, the High Magic, was quite literally a closed book.

'What I mean is quite simple, if you know what I mean,' said Mar'ya Morevna, and smiled at her own crooked speech. 'If a spell of fire had been used here, or a demon of fire summoned into this room' – she swept one arm out in a gesture that took in the oak door and the pine-panelled walls and the cedarwood ceiling – 'there would be nothing left in it except for bare stone. Even though there would always be enough splashover to ignite such furnishings as these, spells are at least selective. Demons never are.'

' "Elementals, on the other hand, can control the substance that is their very nature," ' quoted Ivan, and drew a look of pleased surprise from his wife. He basked in her regard for a second or two before honesty got the better of him and he pointed at the open grimoire. 'And Princes with a certain education can learn to read book-hand – even when it's upside-down.'

Mar'ya Morevna stared, then smiled, then grinned. Finally she laughed out loud and spun the book around so that Ivan could see better. 'You should have kept that part quiet, and impressed me some more,' she said.

Ivan shook his head. 'It would only have lasted a while, and once you found out the truth, you wouldn't have been impressed at all.' He read quickly through what *Enciervanul Doamnisoar* had to say on the subject of fire-elementals, and found the text to be mercifully less offensive and explicit than what it had to say on virtually every other subject. 'These, at least, we can eliminate.' He put out one finger and tapped the illustrations of horse and boar, moving quickly and warily because, seen properly for the first time, those bright highlights of gold leaf were not merely decorative but represented flames – and Ivan would have been pained but not surprised to discover that the flames were hot. They were merely warm, in the same unsettling way that the entire book was warm, but if that was meant to be a comfort, Prince Ivan didn't find it so.

'Why those two?' asked Mar'ya Morevna.

'Beloved, the average kremlin guard isn't blessed with brains or he'd be doing something that paid better for shorter hours of work. That said, I don't think he'd be stupid enough to get too close to either a horse or a boar that he found in a tower room after midnight. And neither animal could leave the claw marks I found.'

130

'A reasonable theory. And therefore. . . ?'

'A bird of some sort, obviously.'

'Oh, of course obviously.'

'And a bird capable of carrying away a book big enough and heavy enough that even a careful old man like Strel'tsin didn't want to take it back to where it belonged.'

'A copy of *Liber Tenebrae*,' said Mar'ya Morevna. 'That's the old Roman language. *The Book of Shadows*. I asked Dmitriy Vasil'yevich earlier today. It measured three-quarters by one-half *arshiniy*, and weighed almost half a *pood*.'

'More than a foot by almost two, and nearly twenty pounds,' said Ivan. 'In the Western measure.'

'Very impressive,' said Mar'ya Morevna dryly, not much impressed at all. 'And it tells us what?'

'A big book?'

'And a big bird. I think you can ignore the golden-combed cockerel. Magical or not, all these elementals have their limitations. One of them is size. They have to appear in a size proper to their chosen form, and there isn't a cockerel hatched that could lift so heavy a book.'

'So how big is this golden pheasant?'

'Tsk!' Mar'ya Morevna poked at the grimoire in another of those tiny teacherly flickers of impatience that made Ivan doubt if they would ever need tutors for their children – assuming, of course, that they ever did have children. 'Where did it say "pheasant"?'

Ivan looked again, twice, and then, in exactly the tone of voice he had been forced to perfect during Dmitriy Vasil'yevich Strel'tsin's lessons on logic, he said, 'Ah.'

'Ah indeed. That, Vanyushka, is a Firebird. It says so. Here.'

'So how big is this golden Firebird?' Ivan's voice had not altered its tone by one iota since the last and incorrect attempt at that question, and Mar'ya Morevna gave him a sharp look. Then she shrugged.

'Big enough to fly away with the lost grimoire. Other than that, who knows?'

'If it's big enough to fly away with Strel'tsin's book, then it's big enough to fly away with my father's crown, to the ruin of the realm. We need to find out what we can, before we do anything else. I could find out.'

Mar'ya Morevna turned slowly, first her head and then her whole body, until all of her attention was focused on her husband. 'I'd be grateful,' she said, 'if you would explain that.'

'This is a matter of duty, Mar'yushka. The crown will be mine one day. I should do *something* to defend it.'

'We don't even know there's any threat.'

'And never will, until it's too late. Let me do this thing. Use our own grimoire as bait. For all we know, the Firebird – if it *is* a Firebird, and we aren't even sure of that yet! – is sent here every night, and it leaves again at once if it can't . . . smell anything magical, perhaps?'

'Good enough until we know better. Go on.'

'All right, if there's nothing to attract it, then it goes back to wherever it came from. But, and I don't know how discriminating they are as a breed, if this Firebird can be tempted by something as insignificant as the candles Dmitriy Vasil'yevich used for his little spells, then a book like *Enciervanul Doamnisoar* would be like a beacon. We could leave it somewhere accessible: here would be good enough. I'd wait to see what appeared, and—'

'And you would be roasted, just like the guard!'

'And I would not permit it,' said a quiet voice from the doorway. As Ivan and Mar'ya Morevna scrambled hastily to their feet, Tsar Aleksandr stepped into the little room and closed the door behind him. Neither of them had heard it open, but then the old Tsar, despite the weight of his sixty-seven years and his regal portliness, could still move like a cat when the mood was on him. 'Apart from anything else, what could I tell your mother?'

Strel'tsin could probably think of something meaningless and heroic, given time, thought Ivan, and then dismissed the thought unspoken as being unfair and unworthy. 'I don't intend to put myself at any risk, Father,' he said aloud.

'I'm sure Guardsman Pavel Il'ich had the same intention,' said Tsar Aleksandr grimly. 'Intention seems not to be much of a defence against this . . . this Firebird.'

'But iron armour is!'

'How can you be sure?'

'I . . . That is, we – oh damn. Mar'yushka, you know more about the whys and wherefores than I do.'

'Little Father,' said Mar'ya Morevna as the Tsar's regard swung onto her like a siege-catapult taking aim, 'from what I know of this creature and from what I saw last night, it is unable to harm cold iron. This is one of the most ancient laws of sorcery, and—'

'And there are enough harnesses in the Armoury Tower so that I could put together something to cover me from head to foot with cold iron. If I used any of the full hoods of mail, all but my eyes would be . . .' Ivan faltered; if he had hoped to carry his father on the wave of his own enthusiasm, that hope was dashed.

'All but your eyes would be protected,' the Tsar finished for him. 'So the you could live, but go through life without your sight. My son, your reasoning is somewhat at fault.'

'My father, all your children have married sorcerers, but only one of those sorcerers, my wife, is already in Khorlov. If you don't intend to use her wisdom, the only alternative is to wait until whatever correspondence you sent out succeeds in finding one or another of your sons-in-law. However long that might take. And if you intend to wait, then why did you ask for our help at all?'

'Not only your reasoning is at fault, but your manners. Ivan Tsarevich, I have three daughters, but you are my only son, and I forbid this foolishness.'

'Less foolish than risking the death of another guard. Would you have it said that you gave the life of some other father's son to protect the life of your own?'

'Yes, when that son is the sole heir to my Tsardom,' said his father tranquilly. 'That is why tsars and princes employ soldiers. To die on their behalf.'

Ivan closed his eyes for an interval too long to be called an ordinary blink, and his voice dropped until he was talking almost to himself. 'And if I disobeyed you anyway?'

'You would not,' the Tsar began to say. Then he hesitated, staring for a long time at his truculent son, and at last he began to smile. Although he was bearded and Ivan was clean-shaven, what was visible of their smiles was each a mirror-image of the other. 'Or perhaps you would. You have grown, Vanya my son. Grown considerably. And other than locking you in this room until you come to your senses, which would be lacking in any kind of dignity, or asking your good wife to change your mind on my behalf—'

'Which with respect, Little Father, is also lacking in dignity and which I would not do,' said Mar'ya Morevna.

'Then I am forced into changing my mind, and giving you my blessing.'

Ivan did not cheer at his small victory, even though it was greater than it seemed. His palms and forehead were both chilly damp, and there was a knot in the pit of his stomach that made breathing difficult. For all he knew, he had just successfully condemned himself to an unpleasant death, and the half-proud, half-shocked look on Mar'ya Morevna's face did little to reassure him.

'There are conditions, of course,' said Tsar Aleksandr Andreyevich, sitting back in his chair in exactly the same posture that Ivan had seen him adopt during trade and treaty wrangling. The Prince tensed inwardly; this was where so many who thought they had beaten the Tsar of Khorlov found that the victory could become hollow indeed.

'At your command,' he said, and waited.

'First this: I am proud, very proud, of your courage – and I am aghast beyond measure at your rashness. Every father wants his son to be brave, but when he has no other son and will have no other son to inherit his domain, that father could almost wish his brave son was a coward. No, not a coward. A more practical young man. So my conditions are this: do nothing except watch; do not stay near this book of yours if you are threatened; lose the book rather than take hurt; and if you must, run. Understand me, Vanya. Nothing you can do during this enterprise can detract from your valour in undertaking it at all. So survive it.'

'Little Father,' said Mar'ya Morevna, 'there are spells of warding that I can lay over—'

'Do it.' Tsar Aleksandr heaved himself out of his seat, and for just an instant, he looked far older than his years, and afraid. 'Do whatever is required. And if any of the priests object, even the Metropolitan Archbishop himself – refer them to me. Not even God' – he crossed himself – 'can object to a father trying to protect his son. By whatever means he can . . .'

It was cold in the study, despite the charcoal brazier, and darker than seemed reasonable in a room lit by so many candles. The grimoire *Enciervanul Doamnisoar* lay at the geometrical centre of the table, and seemed to soak up more than its fair share of what light there was. Prince Ivan Aleksandrovich stared at it for the hundredth time; then his gaze flinched away and he shifted uncomfortably in his chair near the door. He felt chilly and itchy; itchy inside his armour, and itchy inside his skin. Mar'ya Morevna had cautioned him about this side-effect of her shield-spell, but advance warnings of discomfort seldom did much to alleviate that discomfort when it arrived. Ivan smiled thinly; it was like the time he had over-drawn an arrow so that its point had spiked him through the web of the thumb. The hole had needed stitching shut, and one of the kremlin's chirurgeons had told him, in all kindness, that what was about to happen would hurt. Ivan had already known that needles hurt, and being reminded of it had never stopped him yelping yet. But at least the discomfort of ordinary pins and needles went away eventually. The ones pricking at him now seemed only to be getting worse.

He resisted the desire to scratch, as he had resisted the desire to stamp his feet or slap his arms around himself or blow on his fingers in an attempt to drive away the cold, and for much the same reason: to do any of those things effectively, he would need to take his armour off, and to do them with it still in place would be noisy enough to scare away all but the deafest thief. Ivan greatly doubted that the Firebird could be that much hard of hearing.

Quite apart from that, getting into the bastard suit of pieces borrowed from half a dozen other harnesses, mail and scale, lamellar and plate, had taken him a good ten minutes even with assistance from Petr Mikhailovich Akimov, and without the Guard-Captain's help that same operation might take twice as long. Ivan had no great desire to be halfway in or out of his armour when the Firebird finally deigned to put in an appearance. He stretched out to where a jug of mulled wine sat steaming above the charcoal, poured and drank some, and tried to convince himself that he felt warmer.

It had been Dmitriy Vasil'yevich Strel'tsin's idea to leave the window of his study open, and even though Ivan had pointed out that the Firebird had needed no such convenient access the last time it had entered the kremlin, Strel'tsin refused to be swayed. 'You will be sitting by the door, Highness,' the old man had said. 'If it should come in that way, then you might come to some harm.'

Like a roast left too long on the fire comes to some harm, Ivan had thought at the time, but in his mother and father's presence, had kept his mouth shut so as not to worry them any more than they were already. The Tsaritsa Ludmyla had seen him go from the kremlin on the great adventure that had won him a wife, but never waved him farewell as he rode to a battle that she knew might take him away from her. Now, watching him embark on a dangerous venture within the walls of that same kremlin – the kremlin that had been and still was his home – the threat of such a loss plainly struck her to the heart. After her attempt to dissuade him had failed, she had said nothing further, and only stared at him with her dark eyes as though fixing his face in her memory in case that was all some misfortune might leave her.

Mar'ya Morevna had fastened the gauntlet on his right hand, but Ludmyla Tsaritsa had claimed a mother's privilege and helped him to put on the left. They were not a pair, and so while Mar'ya Morevna simply secured the buckled strap that ran around his wrist between hand and cuff, the Tsaritsa had to lace a heavy leather thong in place though loops linked for that purpose between the smaller rings of mail. She had tied it in a bow, and neither Ivan nor Mar'ya Morevna, though they both knew full well that such a knot was far too easily loosed, had the heart to tell her of the mistake or to correct it.

There was little point, since in Ivan's opinion the whole harness was a mistake. Apart from anything else, he was accustomed to his armour – when he wore it at all – being a great deal lighter: a helmet, vambraces for his forearms, and a shirt of mail, perhaps one fitted with handsomely engraved or embossed plates that not only reinforced the ringmail but made it look much finer than those worn by the common soldiers. What he was wearing now made him look as clumsy in its own way as the bulky travelling furs, and with much less style.

Mar'ya Morevna had spent a quarter-hour talking to Guard-Captain Akimov, explaining – probably with diagrams, if he knew his dear wife – what it was that Ivan was to be protected against, and then the pair of them had gone off to the kremlin's Armoury

Tower and ransacked it. They had come back at the head of a train of servants, all carrying some form of armour or other, and had instructed Ivan without so much as a pause for his own opinion or a by-your-leave that he was to put it on.

After that, Ivan's memory of things became rather confused. Since none of the harnesses had been made specifically for him, some were too large and some, more awkwardly, were too small, and unlike overly tight cloth garments which at least had a degree of stretch in them, these ill-fitting metal garments pinched abominably. Abdominally as well, if it came to hard fact, and suggesting with every hard-won breath that since his marriage Ivan Tsarevich had been devoting himself rather too well to the pleasures of the table and the couch. There was uncomfortably more of him than previously, and the armour nipped without mercy at every bit of surplus Prince that it could find.

Sections of rejected harness were strewn all over the floor by the time he had been armed to everyone's satisfaction, hammer-formed plates for chest and head and arms and legs like the pieces of a broken metal man, and small, deceptively heavy grey lumps where discarded mail had collapsed together and lay in wait to stub unwary toes. Finally they were done, walking around him with their arms folded, studying what they had built from disparate parts with all the satisfaction of sculptors eyeing their latest statue. Even though they fitted together more or less correctly, those parts bore no more relation to one another than the iron of which they all were made. Mar'ya Morevna had told Ivan the origin and provenance of each piece of armour as it was fitted into place, and now he stood encased in half a thousand years of history. The hauberk that reached below his knees had come to the Rus lands long ago with a Viking, one of the old North people who were Ivan's ancestors. The *chausses*, stockings of mail, were those of a Frankish crusader knight; the iron shoes and the vambraces and greaves, long splints of iron riveted to fine mail, had once belonged to a *kataphractos* of Byzantium; and the helmet with its visor hammered into the shape of a moustached face had been looted from a Kipchaq warrior by Captain Akimov himself.

The only other thing that Ivan could remember clearly from that part was the heat. Heat that he could appreciate right now, up here in the cold dark. At first it had stemmed from the gentle teasing he had suffered as one hauberk after another had been rejected when it failed to fit, but by the end of it the weight of metal, and the padding such a weight needed to protect its wearer from itself, was more than enough to make him sweat without embarrassment to fuel the flames. If the German knights were so ponderous, then small wonder they would never dare to invade Russia in the winter months. A single wrong move, a single over-heavy step on the ice of lake or river, and they would be through it and heading for the bottom.

He drank a little more of the hot wine and stared at the candle-carved shadows across the room. Even though he was encased in just as much metal now as he had been before, all of the warmth was gone, leached away by the chill of the night and by the chill of his own apprehensions. Brave words in the full light of day seemed more like foolish bravado in the lonely middle of the night. Ivan stood up – or rather, hauled himself to his feet against the downward drag of all that iron – and took a turn around the study. Metal scraped against itself, or tapped and rustled softly if it was mail. There was no other sound anywhere in the kremlin; even the expensive Switzer-built clock in the Bell Tower had been stopped, by the Tsar's command. If his son cried out for help, Aleksandr Andreyevich did not want that cry drowned out by the sound of an hour being struck. It was reassuring; and yet, at the same time, the thought of what might prompt him to cry out sent a shiver down Ivan's spine. Looking down from the window, he could see the pools of amber light as guards with torches moved to and fro; how quickly could those distant figures get up to a small room in a tall tower if his life should suddenly depend on them?

He wondered if it was midnight yet, and wished the clock had not been stopped after all. If nothing had happened by midnight, that most appropriate hour for sorcery, then he could leave the oppressive little room with his honour intact – except that it might have been midnight long ago, for all that he knew of the passage of time. Ivan circled the table again, looked at the grimoire again, drank wine again, and as he had done so many times before, wished it was vodka.

'When the candles burn down again,' he said aloud, but not very loud, 'I'll have waited long enough.' There was a supply of fresh

138

candles in a basket by his chair, and he had been using them one by one as the old candles were consumed. If nothing else, the honey scent of beeswax was better than the smell with which his memory kept filling the room. But not now. When they burnt out, and there was nothing to see but the darkness that was there all the time, rather than some magical bird that plainly was not there at all, then he could leave.

Ivan rubbed at his jaw through the mail hood that covered his face to the brows, relieving the sorcery-born itch a little and smearing the sweat on the hood's leather lining into a clammy film on his skin. That was unfair; if he was going to sweat, then he might at least do it through being warm, rather than just because the thin, oily leather kept sticking to him. It was no more than a casual grumble; like any other man whose rank or career required the wearing of armour now and again, the alternative to that leather lining was to have the mail in direct contact with his tender flesh. Leather was more forgiving, certainly, than a mesh of interlocked iron rings so abrasive that when it was no longer of any use as armour, it was chopped into sheets and sent to the kremlin kitchens to scrub pots with.

One of the candles drowned in molten wax, and another guttered, its flame fluttering between a dirty yellow bead and a golden spear-point before it too died in a spiral of black smoke. The darkness began to close in at last. Ivan sat down again, reaching for the wine-jug one last time, to drain its contents into his cup and then the cup's contents into himself.

Then with shocking suddenness the darkness became light, and he spilled all of the wine onto the floor instead.

Ivan had seen the heat-borne dust devils of summer, and the rustling columns of leaves that the wind made sport with in the dry days of autumn. What he saw now was like the wind and dust and leaves, but all made of motes of golden fire. It was a spindle of sparks, and it danced silently in mid-air, needing no floor to rest on nor ceiling to hang from. Remembering his own dear sorcerous brothers-in-law and their preferred method of entry, Ivan glanced once at the ceiling to see if it had split apart, but the polished cedar planks were unharmed. There was no distant rumbling of thunder in the heavens, no gust of storm, nothing save that noiseless firefly glitter.

Easing himself out of his seat with equal silence, he reached out without taking his eyes from the whirl of glowing specks, and opened the door behind him just as wide as it would go. He was too fascinated to consider leaving right now, but if hasty departure did become an option, Ivan had no desire to waste valuable running time in wrestling with inconveniently closed doors.

For the first time, he began to hear something; and even though his mind insisted that the sound was a familiar one, it took Ivan several seconds to identify it. The reason was simple enough: he knew the faint, high hissing of an armourer's smelting-furnace with its bellows working hard well enough, but it was not the sort of sound his ears were expecting to hear in a tower room eighty feet above the ground.

And then the Firebird appeared.

Ivan's first thought was that whoever had sketched it in the grimoire had neither seen it first-hand nor heard it described by anyone who had; and his second thought, as the elemental took shape, was that he didn't blame either the artist or his informant for wanting to keep their distance. Had he known even slightly what to expect – besides that lying portrait of a pheasant with golden tail-feathers – he would never have volunteered to wait for the creature.

This was no pheasant, golden or otherwise. With its cruel curved beak and hooked talons and maniacal sparrowhawk's eyes, it looked far too predatory for that. The wings that bated like an angry falcon's were wider from tip to tip than Ivan stood tall, even in his best red-heeled boots; far wider, eight feet or more, plumaged not in gold but in the shimmering yellow-white of a midsummer sun and just as hard to look at. As the Firebird settled onto its previous perch – the carved chair-back spurted grey smoke as those great talons dug into the wood – Prince Ivan could feel the heat washing off it. He had been cold before; he was cold no longer.

With his mailed back pressed closed against the wall and the open doorway conveniently to hand, he stared, squinting and dazzled, filled with a wonder that was well-mingled with dread. His armour seemed meagre protection against something like this, for if the Firebird's wings burnt like the sun, then its head and body burnt hotter still, the intolerable blue-white that might dwell

140

at the heart of a star. The shadows that it threw splashed all across the study, so black against the glare that they seemed almost solid, as sharply defined as though they had been cut out of the air with a razor. Let Mar'ya Morevna say what she pleased about the ancient laws of sorcery; there was heat enough there to melt any metal, be it bronze or silver or the coldest iron in all the world. With the stench of burning in his nostrils and the greedy yammering of flames in his ears, Ivan began to edge towards the door.

Directly he moved, the Firebird's head snapped round and it stared at him over one blazing feathered shoulder. It was a bird-of-prey stare, both eyes at once sighting down the scimitar beak as though down the stock of a crossbow. Ivan met the glare of those crazy killer's eyes, and knew in one fearful instant what a mouse must feel when a shadow slides across it in the meadow and it looks up at the plummeting kestrel-hawk. Like the mouse, Ivan froze; but unlike the kestrel, the Firebird did not strike. Instead the wicked beak parted in what looked uncomfortably like a laugh, and it opened its wings wide, mantling its prey.

The grimoire.

Sickle claws flashed out and struck, driving into the book's metal cover and then through it as the talons flexed and closed their grip. Uncut jewels popped from their settings with the pressure and spun rattling across the table-top, and the silver-inlaid bronze sheet that clad *Enciervanul Doamnisoar* lost its embossing as it softened and flowed sluggishly like honey in winter. As its wings struck downward and the grimoire lifted free of the charring table, the Firebird's beak gaped wide, but if it uttered some triumphant cry as it hovered and began to fade away, Prince Ivan could not hear it.

Nor could he hear the warnings inside his own head, otherwise he would have stood still and watched the elemental return whence it came, and afterwards thanked God for the adventure and his own surviving of it. Instead, as the Firebird became no more than a sketch outlined in fiery ink, Ivan lunged forward and grabbed at the streaming feathers of its tail. The bird screeched, its first and only uttered sound and one which drove needles of anguish through his ears, and then the darkness came back with a rush as the Firebird vanished; but not completely. It was kept at bay by the tail-feather gripped in his left hand, a feather that though it was by no means as bright as the Firebird itself, still glowed with the fierce light thrown off by molten gold.

Pain struck into Ivan's hand an instant later. The cold iron of his gauntlet was undamaged by the sorcerous heat of the Firebird, but it was *cold* iron no longer, transmitting that heat as easily as any common poker left too long in the fire. Smoke was already billowing from the bullhide glove within the gauntlet's plates and rings by the time that Ivan wrenched free the simple bow-knot tied by his mother – with a small prayer of gratitude that she had not known the proper way to tie such things. He felt the armoured glove go slack on his wrist, but those same plates and rings were starting to glow red-hot when he snapped his whole arm sideways and the loosened glove flew off across the room like a shooting star. It struck the wall in a spray of incandescent sparks, leaving gouges and char in the white pine panel, then clattered onto the floor and lay there, cooling.

The Firebird's feather cooled more slowly. It lay where he had dropped it on the patterned tiles, no longer as noonday bright as once it was, but still glaring enough to pain the eye that stared at it too long and hard. Beneath its sullen sunset glow, the tile's coloured glaze melted and reformed into strange new patterns, and the ceramic tile itself blackened, baked and cracked across. A thin wisp of smoke drifted out of the crack, evidence that even the floorboard beneath had not survived unscathed.

Ivan pushed the door almost shut and sat down again, unsure whether he wanted to cheer, or be sick from the reaction of delayed fright and the stupidity that from the look of it could well have cost him his left hand. Smoke from the burnt gauntlet rolled out into the corridor, and he felt the itching inside his skin stop abruptly as Mar'ya Morevna cancelled her warding-spells. She had constructed the patterns for the magic in another of the tower rooms; it was far enough away for safety, but also far enough that Ivan wondered vaguely how it was she knew that the spells were no longer needed. He was still in the chair and his frantically beating heart had slowed almost to normal again when she came bursting white-faced through the doorway. She threw both arms around him and held him tight, and when Ivan could see her face again, two great tears were glistening in her eyes. He brushed

142

them away gently, not knowing what had made her weep until he took in a breath to replace what she had hugged from his lungs – and then, with the stench of scorched leather clogging his throat, he understood everything. Why she was crying, why she had cancelled the spells, why she had come running in, pale with a terror that she had not dared to speak aloud.

She had smelt the smoke.

'It didn't burn me, loved,' he said, cuddling her close. 'Only the gauntlet lining. Only the gauntlet.'

Drawing in a long breath that brought back something of her composure, Mar'ya Morevna put out one hand and touched his cheek. 'Are you hurt?' she said.

'Grievously,' said Ivan, holding up his left hand for inspection. Between easing himself bit by bit out of the armour – and regretting the spilt wine – he had been soothing his fingers with a wad of snow scraped off the outside windowsill, so that the rising blisters were much less impressive than they might have been. 'I've done worse pinching out a candle. Hush now. . . .'

Mar'ya Morevna ignored the blisters. She looked instead at the Firebird's feather sizzling gently on the floor, and realized what he had done. She snuggled her head against his neck, heedless of the rough coldness of the armour he still wore, then released herself carefully from his embrace and stood up. Ivan watched her; not the sorceress, not the commander of armies, not the fairest Princess in all the Russias, but just the wife who loved him and had been terrified beyond all measure that through his own courage she had lost him. 'Never again,' she said. 'Not alone. Whatever happens, whatever needs to happen, we go or stay together.'

'But you don't have the grimoire any more.'

'I don't need a book about demons when what we're hunting is no demon. *Enciervanul Doamnisoar* was bait, and it worked. You, my bold, brave, foolish one, you confirmed what I needed to know: that it was indeed a Firebird. This' – she dabbed at the feather with the toe of her boot – 'is even more proof than I expected. Now I know which books to study.' Then to Ivan's shock she bent down, dabbed at the feather with outstretched fingers, cautiously as a cat – and then picked it up. 'Cool,' she said, bouncing the plume lightly on the palm of her hand while light and shadow played tag with one another across the walls and ceiling. 'Quite cool. I wonder if the light will fade eventually, or not. . . ?'

Ivan stared at it with his head cocked on one side like a sparrow; then he reached out and touched it with his bare hand, the same hand that this same feather had blistered through a layer of iron and a layer of leather not three minutes past. It felt . . . strange. Mar'ya Morevna had said that it was cool, and he had expected something like a strip of silk; something at least with some weight to it. Instead it had more of a sensation of coolness, the sleek and pleasant promise of fresh linen sheets on a hot summer night. If one could touch smoke, Ivan thought, it would be like this. But smoke that shone like burnished brass. 'It's beautiful,' he said softly, and then, his terror all but forgotten since he had taken no harm from the experience, 'all of it was beautiful. So beautiful—'

'And so dangerous. Whether it was the spells, or the iron, or just your own good luck, you got off lightly. You might not be so fortunate next time.'

'I'd rather there wasn't a next time,' Ivan began, then saw the expression on his wife's face and raised one eyebrow. 'But there might be. Or should I say, there *will* be?'

'That depends. Someone is summoning the Firebird and sending it to steal things from your father's kremlin.'

'Then summon it yourself and make inquiries.'

'No. That would show our hand.' She smiled briefly. 'Blisters and all. And I'd as soon keep what we know a secret from . . .' Mar'ya Morevna shrugged in annoyance at not having a name. 'Whoever it is.'

'Then where do we go? Your library?'

'There first. And after that, beloved, further than you think. East of the Sun, and West of the Moon, to the land where the Firebirds live. Then maybe we'll find out who's been sending it here, and why. And maybe, just maybe, get all that stolen property returned to its rightful owners.'

Ivan swung an iron Byzantine shoe by its straps, then let the piece of armour drop noisily to the floor. 'Wonderful,' he said. 'After Koshchey the Undying, I thought we deserved some peace and quiet. Apparently not.'

'Peace and quiet means helping Fedor Konstantinovich with

collating my vassals' tax returns for last year,' said Mar'ya Morevna with a wicked smile. 'Your choice. What do you think?'

'I think hunting the Firebird is preferable,' said Ivan. Freed of most of the armour, he threw out his arms and stretched; and it was as if all that weight of metal was suddenly replaced by an equal weight of weariness. 'In fact, almost *anything* is preferable. Including getting some sleep, if there's enough left of the night to make it worthwhile.'

'There's enough. It lacks a few minutes of the first hour of morning, and I think you could be justified in rising late.'

Then the door opened again and Guard-Captain Akimov came in, and one look at his face told them both that whatever had happened tonight was not yet over. He bowed to Mar'ya Morevna and saluted Ivan, and when his eyes fell on the Firebird's feather they went wide, driving the rest of his message momentarily from his head. 'You did it,' the Cossack breathed in delight – for Ivan's success could not but reflect well on the man who had taught him how to be brave, or at least how to conceal fear so that nobody knew it was there – before he remembered abruptly who he was speaking to and saluted again. After that Akimov reached out and gripped Ivan's hand in both of his own big paws, beaming all over his bushy-bearded face. 'Well done, Highness.' The Cherkassy accent was very thick. 'Well done indeed!' Then his pleasure faded as the duty which had brought him here reasserted itself. 'Highness, I apologize, but if you and the *gospozha* Mar'ya Tsarevna could follow me at once? The Tsar's Majesty awaits you both.' Akimov saluted a third time, then swung about and stalked from the room, not doubting that they would do as he requested.

Ivan and Mar'ya Morevna exchanged glances and at least one shrug, then fell into step behind the Captain. 'Petr Mikhailovich, I thought my father would have been in his bed by now,' said Ivan. 'At least, he told me as much earlier tonight.'

'That is as he intended you to believe, Highness,' said Akimov, not slackening his pace either for the conversation or the spiral stairs of the tower. 'He and the Tsaritsa your mother have been at prayers in the Great Basilica since you entered that room. Prayers for your safety.'

'Ah.' Ivan crossed himself, and from the corner of his eye saw

Mar'ya Morevna do likewise. 'Either they were heeded, or they weren't needed.'

'Whichever pleases you, Highness.'

'But I'm glad of them all the same.'

'Captain Akimov,' said Mar'ya Morevna, 'just where are we going? The Basilica? The Tsar's chambers?'

'Neither, *gospozha* Tsarevna. He awaits you at the main gate of the kremlin. There has been' – and for the first time Akimov faltered slightly – 'a messenger. Of sorts.' Then he accelerated again, so that Ivan and Mar'ya Morevna were forced to scurry in order to keep up with his long stride.

The stairwell was not as brightly lit as it might have been, but there were still enough lanterns and torches for Ivan to see his wife's mouth shape a single, silent word. It was *volkovich*.

Wolf's son.

The scene by the gate was a familiar one to them both, so much so that Ivan almost expected to see the dark-haired woman in the long black cloak standing haughtily in the midst of the knot of guards. Instead they saw his father the Tsar, and Levon Popovich the Metropolitan Archbishop of Khorlov, and instead of Mother Wolf's husky, sardonic voice, they heard the prayers for the dead.

Tsar Aleksandr turned, saw his son approaching, and gathered him into an embrace like that of an affectionate bear. 'Forgive an old man's fears, my son,' he said in a voice lowered for privacy. 'I should never have doubted you.'

'There's nothing to forgive, *batyushka*,' said Ivan as he returned the powerful hug, burying his face in the heavy fur of his father's collar as he remembered how scared he had been. He realized how much worse it must have been for those who loved him and had perforce to stand on the sidelines while he lived or died. 'It would have been worse if nobody had cared.'

'Success?' said the Tsar, bracing his son at arm's length while he looked for damage.

'Success, my lord.' Mar'ya Morevna held up the Firebird's feather triumphantly, and a bloom of light brighter than ten thousand candles pushed the snow-shot darkness back. 'More than we could ever have dreamed possible. And all thanks to your son. My husband.' The pride in her voice was worth more to Ivan in that moment than all the gold of Greek Byzantium.

Then he saw the head.

Time and cold had relaxed its features from whatever twist of terror had come with impending death, so that now, freed from the handsome box of carven cherry-wood and the packing of tamped snow that had kept it fresh, its only expression was one of dull-eyed, slack-lipped surpise. Ivan stared at it, gazing into dead eyes that were like wet and milky pebbles, and for a single instant saw not just this head but thousands, piled up in dreadful crow-haunted pyramids to mark the passage of their slayers. Whether he saw with the True Sight that was his father's occasional curse, or whether he saw only through the colouring of his own imagination, Prince Ivan Aleksandrovich looked upon this solitary dead face and saw instead the face of War.

A fuming of incense drifted across his vision as Archbishop Levon continued with the sonorous requiem prayers, and Ivan shivered as though awakened from an ugly dream. '. . . It was flung at the gate by a rider whose horse never even slowed,' Akimov was saying to Mar'ya Morevna. 'I can't blame the guards, *gospozha* Tsarevna. They turned out as fast as they were able – I was there, I saw them – but no man can catch hoofbeats on the wind, and that was all was left. Except for that.'

'Who and where?' Ivan cloaked his own shuddering with the sort of terse, forceful façade he had seen employed by his own father. Such short sentences were a mercy; they never lasted long enough to betray a tremor in the voice.

It was the Tsar himself who answered, but not before he had gazed thoughtfully at his son as though recognizing and approving one of his own tricks of speech. 'He was one of Khorlov's spies in Kiev,' he said. 'One of the very best. And until now, I would have sworn on the life-giving cross that no-one in Kiev suspected him.'

The Archbishop finished his prayers and pronounced a general absolution, and all present signed themselves and said Amen. Then Ivan said, 'Is this Great Prince Yuriy's way of declaring war on Khorlov?'

'Hardly.' Mar'ya Morevna shook her head, denying the possi-bility. 'He would not have been so blatant. As I read Yuriy Vladimirovich, he would only declare war when his armies were encamped around this kremlin and he had it already under siege. It was meant to look like his work, and meant to provoke – but Kiev did *not* do this. It's both too obvious, and not obvious enough.'

'The Princes of Novgorod have their own troubles,' said Captain Akimov thoughtfully. 'But might they have done this thing, trying to gain advantage while shifting the blame for it elsewhere?'

'Maybe. Or maybe not.' Mar'ya Morevna shrugged the question aside. 'Captain, Little Father, we are merely snatching at whatever straws the wind blows by. Ivan Tsarevich and I already have the problem of the Firebird to contend with. Let us deal with that one first.'

'Who knows,' said Ivan, and forced a humourless laugh at his own ridiculous notion, 'perhaps all these matters are connected, somehow and somewhere.' He averted his eyes as the spy's severed head was gathered up and taken away, and looked instead at Mar'ya Morevna. 'But I take it that the possibility of sleep has gone away?'

'It has. We need to get to the library in my kremlin by morning. Have someone roust out the horses.'

'And explain the rude awakening to them.' Ivan grimaced at the thought of the complaints. A talking horse was a magical, marvellous thing, but a horse that never shut up was a bloody nuisance; and depending on Sivka's mood, he had both. He traded a look and a sour, crooked smile with his father the Tsar, who had watched the exchange with grim good humour. 'When we come back from wherever we're going, *batyushka*,' said Ivan, 'we'll somehow contrive to stay with you a while longer. Just don't declare war on Prince Yuriy till then . . .'

Chapter Six

The kremlin of Kiev was at the centre of the city, and today it was also at the centre of an uproarious celebration. When the Great Prince Yuriy Vladimirovich made merry on his naming-day, he was known not to restrict that merriment to within the walls of the palace. There was a consort of musicians playing a lively dance-tune in one corner of the kremlin courtyard, and playing it well even though their efforts were almost drowned out by the dancers themselves, leaping and whirling and hammering their boot-heels against the wooden boards laid over the pavement for just that purpose. In the other corner was an old storyteller, surrounded by people who listened quietly – although they cheered the exciting parts – as he strummed on a *gusla* psaltery of fine maple-wood and recited the old tale of 'Il'ya Muromets and the Dragon'.

In between the two were acrobats, jugglers, conjurers whose tricks were plainly nothing to do with the true Art Magic, and every variation between respectful silence and disrespectful uproar. Great Prince Yuriy had caused the kremlin's fountains, usually frozen solid by this time of year, to be melted clear – by cunning placement of the same fires that had cooked a large variety of livestock to tasty perfection; Yuriy Vladimirovich was no miser, but he didn't burn two lots of firewood if one would do two jobs – and now the fountains that weren't running with wine were running with beer instead. Except of course for the one which had been allowed to freeze again, and now sprayed a plume of icy vodka into the air.

Even without the play of the fountains, there would have been a fair amount of alcohol hanging in the air around the kremlin of Kiev. The Great Prince's nephew-in-law, Oleg Vasil'yevich, had just become the father of a fine son, and though Prince Yuriy had little time for most of the lesser members of his family, seeing them rightly or wrongly as hangers-on out for what his rank and position could gain them, he had been quite happy to add Oleg's celebration to his own. Apart from anything else, it stopped people counting back from the birth to the marriage and coming up with an unfortunate six-week discrepancy.

The man in the heavy bearskin cloak drifted gently through the crowd, looking about him with a benevolent smile for any who met his inquisitive gaze. He carried a roasted rib of beef in his left hand, and a knife in the right with which he cut off small slivers of meat to nibble on. Now and again he stopped, his attention drawn by a pretty girl or a particularly agile acrobat, but for the most part he simply ambled about, enjoying the festival atmosphere. If he had a tendency to stare and gape, that was hardly unusual, since there were plenty of people in from the country who had never seen the magnificence of Kiev's great kremlin before – although his staring was less at its magnificence, and more at the defences of towers, walls and moat.

Dieter Balke sliced himself another strip of beef, his edge gliding through the meat with an ease that indicated it was a great deal sharper than the average eating-knife, and chewed it thoughtfully. It would be best, he decided, if he left Kiev in the next day or so. His guise as a seller of poultry, with a good supply of chickens, geese, ducks and squab, had been more than adequate until this damned party was announced without any prior warning. It had literally eaten up almost his entire stock, because after a week in which he had become known as a man who drove a hard but fair bargain, a sudden refusal to sell would have seemed highly suspicious. It meant, however, that instead of a poultry butcher who had made a killing from the Great Prince's kitchens – well, the butcher part was accurate enough and the killing would come later – Balke was now very obviously a man who kept pigeons.

He thought about it again, and cursed himself again; the excuse had occurred ten minutes after the Prince's servants had left, and by then it was too late. If he had thought to keep a couple of pairs of each type of fowl as what he could claim were breeding stock, then the pigeons would have been far less obvious. As it was, once today was over, people in a position to ask their questions in a most stringent and painful manner would start to wonder why he had kept only the pigeons, and what other uses could be made of such birds besides good eating.

Yes, leaving Kiev would be sensible, and maybe not even

waiting for that next day or so would be more sensible still. But not just yet. He sheathed the knife and, gnawing at the savoury crisp shreds on the back curve of the beef bone, began easing his way through the crowds towards the kremlin steps, where Great Prince Yuriy would publicly accept the homage of his vassals and the gifts of his retainers. There was one gift in particular that Dieter Balke wanted to see opened before he took leave of Kiev. He had arranged it by means of a cryptic small note sent by pigeon, on the same day as he had prepared a similar gift and sent it by messenger. Both pigeon and messenger had gone to the same place.

Khorlov . . .

Even though sending severed heads about the place was likely to encourage the dislike each Rus Prince held for all the others, especially if the current least favourite of those others seemed to be the source of the latest head, Balke did not expect immediate success. Baba Yaga had warned him about that. The Rus had drawn too much of their culture from Greek Byzantium for any precipitate action. There would be talking first, vehement protestations of ignorance and innocence; but those would seem no more than lies when the next lopped head arrived in its packing of snow. Or the next head; or the one after that. Dieter Balke had his orders, and he was ready to obey them for as long as necessary.

If those Princes and little Tsars had been French or English, it would have been another matter. He had had dealings with Frankish knights during his time in the Holy Land, and whether they belonged to the other military orders or owed their allegiance to the Kingdom of Outremer, they had been all one in their pride and in the impatient hot temper that would send them riding over their own foot-soldiers and headlong into whatever trap had been laid for them, if only they could be provoked enough. As for the English, even though that maniac King Richard *Löwenherz* was long in his grave, his barons remained just as passionate and foolhardy as he had ever been, while his brother and successor John, though a cold fish and not given to open battle, would doubtless find some means of revenging himself by stealth on a supposed enemy – a means that would be ultimately as effective in provoking war as what Balke himself was doing.

There were two other men in Kiev that he wanted to meet

151

before he left the city. Neither of them knew him as the *Landmeister* of Livonia and Hermann von Salza's right-hand man, or as a seller of poultry for the table; instead, after meetings that Balke had kept carefully separate and concealed from each other, they had been led to believe he had been sent from their respective cities as an additional pair of eyes and ears.

Such persons had indeed been sent, from Novgorod and from Aleksandr Nevskiy's domain of Vladimir – but with the aid of spells taught him by Baba Yaga, Balke had met them both. There had been no spells involved in the way he had taken their secrets from them, only the ancient, cunning use of blade and fire that he had learned from a Saracen master of the art. Dieter Balke gained no pleasure from such unknightly actions. He had extracted the information from each spy as carefully and as dispassionately as he would have crushed juice from an orange, and afterwards, though their useless pulp had been left in the snow to nourish wolves and bears, he had first made sure to say the appropriate prayers for the dead.

Trumpets blew, their shrill notes cutting through the babble in the courtyard and beyond the gates of the kremlin, so that a sort of murmurous stillness had fallen by the time Great Prince Yuriy came out onto the steps. As the cheering began, as much to thank him for free food and drink as because anyone truly liked the man – which few did – Yuriy acknowledged the outcry with one hand waved regally in the air. Dieter Balke cheered just as hard as those surrounding him, enjoying the hazards of this potentially lethal situation as much as he had enjoyed anything since leading the Teutonic Knights on their holy crusade into the forests of Prussia. He had not been expected to succeed, or even to survive; how could he, commanding only the twenty knights and two hundred sergeants that were all the Order could spare?

Balke had survived, succeeded and ultimately prospered, learning in that long and bloody process the value of real rather than token ruthlessness in war. His force had built fortresses as they advanced, simple ramparts and ditches topped with timber palisades cut from the over-abundant forest. They were primitive, true, but the heathen Prusiskai had nothing to match them, and striking from the safety of their wooden walls, the knights had burnt every village they encountered and exterminated every man, woman and child who refused conversion to the True Faith. Pacification of the pagans had taken two years, with the constant risk if captured of having your living guts reeled from a hole cut in your belly and wound round a holy tree to gratify the gods of the forest. In that wilderness of bog and heathland, forest and wind-torn dunes, death came quickly to the weak and the wounded even without the tender ministrations of the heathen. It had been an exciting time, a time when every knight and sergeant not dead already knew what it was to be strong and whole and truly alive, and Dieter Balke had found nothing in the rank of *Landmeister* that could match it.

Until now.

The trumpets sounded again, and the cheers faded to an expectant silence; then to the relief of all concerned, Grand Prince Yuriy chose not to waste a speech on the common people assembled in the kremlin courtyard. Instead he waved once more, a gesture that this time was plainly a dismissal, and turned his attention to the richly dressed nobility who had been standing off to one side.

Merchants, townsfolk and peasants returned their attention to the more important business of the holiday: selling and buying, eating and drinking, entertaining and being entertained. While there was still beer and wine running in the fountains and meat still waiting to be cut from the slowly turning joints of beef, pork and mutton, very few of them were interested in the gifts their Prince was receiving. Those gifts were in any case so expensive that the simpler people could not relate what such value meant to terms that they might understand, the size of a field or the number of a flock. The solidity of a leg of chicken and a pot of *kvas* was much more easily grasped, and more easily absorbed as well.

Dieter Balke knew the value of one gift with absolute certainty: it was both the cheapest and the most expensive thing that the Great Prince would receive today, for it had cost Balke nothing to provide except a little effort, but it had cost its original owner his life. Ensuring that the head in its fine wooden casket would be presented not only today but in public had required the spending of some gold; but it had been only a temporary expense, and he had recovered it later, before adding his late helper's corpse to the other holiday flotsam bumping under the ice of the River Dnepr.

Baba Yaga had taught him words to speak aloud and a symbol to draw in the air, and being an inquisitive man, Balke had kept his knife sheathed and tried out the spell. He had been somewhat surprised by the consequence: the man's head had exploded like an egg hit with a hammer, to such effect that Balke privately resolved not to use the spell indoors again, and certainly not on either of the spies he was meeting.

It was a pity, because he was rather taken with his new-found skill at sorcery and would have liked to use it again, but quite apart from the mess – which didn't concern him over-much, since a good solid mace-blow did much the same thing to a pagan if its skull was small enough – it left what remained of the head quite unrecognizable. Since his plan required knowing who the head had been, where it had come from and therefore presumably who had sent it, the spell was regrettably useless.

That was why he had made a point of buying the beef rib. If the spy, or rather, the late spy from Khorlov, was a typical example of the breed, then Balke might expect to be searched, and to hand over the knife that looked just like an ordinary eating-knife so long as nobody tested the edge. But nobody could be suspected of meaning mischief with part of their dinner; right up to the moment when it was swung with killing force at the brow or the temple or the nape of the neck. If only Samson had known, thought Balke; a beef rib was so well shaped for a focused strike, and much handier than the jawbone of an ass.

He nibbled at it some more, his teeth scraping slightly against the almost-stripped bone. Unless he cracked it for the marrow – which he had no intention of doing – there was little to be gained in working at it any more; but that small and pointless activity served to cover his intense interest in the doings of his betters, up there at the top of the steps. Yuriy Vladimirovich Kievskiy was admiring a handsome robe, gold-figured blue velvet lined with Siberian sable.

Balke admired it too, but rather critically, finding it just that bit ostentatious for a knight in an austere and holy Christian order. In any case, he was more interested in the gift borne by the young servant standing next in line of presentation. It was a rosewood chest, nicely inlaid with mother-of-pearl and just the right size to keep a furred winter hat in.

Prince Yuriy evidently thought so, for after a few seconds spent

154

fruitlessly looking about for the donor of this fine present, he said something that made everyone laugh, then took off his own hat and opened the box. The laughter stopped as though cut off with a knife, but of all the commoners milling about in the kremlin courtyard, only the most uncommon of them noticed. Dieter Balke snorted, turned it into an aborted sneeze, then clamped his teeth on the beef-bone to hide his grin. From the look on Yuriy's abruptly salt-white face, it was plain he did not appreciate the kind thought that had not only given him a box to put his hat in, but also provided something inside to put it on. . . .

Prince Ivan and Mar'ya Morevna returned to their own kremlin with even greater speed than they had left it, arriving in the courtyard at the core of a thunderous blast of light and sound and displaced air that shattered several of the kremlin's expensive glass windows. Reining Chornyy back almost onto his haunches when he skidded on the ice-crusted snow, Mar'ya Morevna cocked her head to listen to the distant, almost musical clash of falling shards, and gave Ivan a tight smile. 'Oops!' she said, although with no evidence of feeling any guilt. 'Fedor Konstantinovich is going to have words with me about that. He warned me before: I can make a dramatic entrance, or I can have glass in my palace windows, but not both at once.'

The High Steward, although he arrived at a scamper that looked most peculiar on one of his venerable appearance, did not in fact mention the broken windows. Nor indeed did he pass any comment on the suddenness of their return from Khorlov. Having served Mar'ya Morevna for twelve years, and her father Koldun the enchanter for the fifty years before that, Fedor Konstantinovich had long since learned when to speak and when to keep silent. He merely bowed low as his liege lady and her husband hurried past him into the kremlin palace, and watched them long enough to make sure that they were not only heading – as he had suspected – for the library, but that once there they would be consulting books rather than doing any of the married-couple things that were better not interrupted. Once certain of both, he clapped his hands and set about the business of having food and drink prepared and sent up to them.

'. . . All that, without a word being spoken to him?' said Prince

Ivan, marvelling. He had paused at the head of the stairs to glance back down at the High Steward, and Mar'ya Morevna had given him a terse explanation of what the old gentleman was staring at. Unfortunately she had not paused at all, so that when he turned to follow her, Ivan found himself forced into a less than dignified trot in order to keep up with her raking stride. Mar'ya Morevna was, in the opinion of many, the most beautiful Princess in all the Russias; in her husband's opinion, she had also the longest legs, and when she was in a hurry they could propel her along at a startling rate. His trotting perforce got faster and faster, until finally he gave up, and ran.

He was out of breath by the time he reached the kremlin library and flopped down into one of its heavily padded reading chairs. Ivan, like the chair, was heavily padded; neither he nor Mar'ya Morevna had paused to take off their thick travelling furs when they dismounted in the courtyard, and while such garments were ideally suited to their proper function of keeping the cold out while riding on horseback through the Rus winter, they were much less appropriate for running along a kremlin's corridors and up and down its stairs.

'You look as if you're melting,' said Mar'ya Morevna as she tugged off her gloves and dropped them onto the table before starting off along the stacked shelves, muttering under her breath as she pulled books to and fro so that they would be easier to find. Even though she had not spared the time to remove her furs, she had at least opened the ankle-length outermost coat. It flapped dramatically around those long legs, threatening to trip her up at every stride though never quite succeeding, but at least it kept her cool.

Ivan muttered a few choice phrases himself, wiped a drip of sweat from the end of his nose, and hurriedly stripped until the furs were a large heap on the floor like some sort of sleeping animal. Since the library had not been heated prior to their arrival, as was usually the case, the rapidity of that undressing was a mistake. Clad only in a slightly sweat-dampened shirt and the light riding-breeches customarily worn underneath the travel-furs, he stood steaming like a hard-ridden horse for a few seconds and then, starting a rapid slide from one uncomfortable extreme of temperature to the other, his teeth clattered together with a noise like a stick drawn fast across a paling fence and he began to shiver.

Mar'ya Morevna looked up at him from the stack of scrolls and parchments which were starting to hide the library table from view, and raised her eyebrows in surprise. 'They'll be along with braziers in a moment, Vanya,' she said. 'Keep yourself warm in the meanwhile. You know the spell.'

'I thought you might want me to stay awake for a little longer,' said Ivan. He bent down to lift his outermost fur coat from the untidy pile on the floor, and pulled it around his shoulders. 'If I use what energy I have left on working any spells, I may end up warm, but I'll also be fast asleep.'

'Sleep, then.' Taking her fur hat off as though just then remembering its presence on her head, Mar'ya Morevna shook her hair free of its loose braid and combed at it a little with her fingers. 'You need it more than I do.'

That was true enough. She didn't look in the least bit tired, which Ivan thought was rather unfair. Just bright-eyed, eager and very, very beautiful. 'What about you?' he asked.

'Excitement and strong tea for now,' she said, grinning. 'The tea at least when Nikolai or one of the others gets a samovar in here. Maybe a weak enchantment later, if I think I need one. But I wasn't up all last night playing catch-as-catch-can with a Firebird.'

'No, you were up all last night making sure you weren't married to a scorched roast by morning.'

'Of course. What would the servants say?' Leaving her books for a moment, Mar'ya Morevna kissed him lightly on the lips – then laughed and fended off his hands. 'I thought you were tired!'

'For some things, yes – for others, never.' Ivan gave her a leering grin, then rather spoiled the effect with an enormous yawn that sneaked up on him out of nowhere and all but dislocated his jaw.

'You really, truly are a most marvellous lover, my dear one,' said Mar'ya Morevna. 'But even you have to be awake first.' Ivan shivered again, despite the coat across his shoulders, and she frowned as she reached out to press her right hand flat against his chest. He could feel the warmth of it through the fine lawn shirt, just as she could almost certainly feel the clammy chill of his skin. 'Idiot. Well, all right, if you won't, I will. *Tyeplyosh'!* Be warm!'

It felt like another shiver, but this time there were waves of comfortable heat that spread out like ripples from her hand; not hot enough to make him start sweating again, nor enough to dry out the fabric of his shirt, but more than enough that his teeth stopped chattering almost at once. Mar'ya Morevna eyed him critically, rubbing her right hand against her left and flexing her fingers to bring back the feeling that the transmitted spell had stunned from bone and sinew.

'A bite to eat when High Steward Fedor gets that part organized,' she said at last, pronouncing the words as though they were a sentence at law, 'then strong steam with some oil-of-rosemary on the stones, and finally either an invigorating roll in deep snow or two, no, three buckets of cold water over your head and at least four hours of sleep. The one to keep you from catching a cold, rather than just feeling that way, and the other so that you'll be alert enough to be of some use when I finally do need to call on you for help.'

'Dear God! Do I look so bad?'

'Dear heart, if I said that the only thing holding you up was your being too stubborn to lie down. . . ?'

Ivan flung the back of one arm across his brow in the theatrical swoon of a second-rate actor. 'O lay me down that I might die!' he declaimed, and fell backwards into the overstuffed chair again.

'That,' said Mar'ya Morevna pointedly, 'is more or less what we're trying to avoid, remember?' She was grinning all the same, even if it was a much smaller grin than usual. 'Just no more pulling out of feathers, please.'

She picked up one of the cased scrolls and slapped it thoughtfully against her open hand. 'I'll know better when I read this through, but I already suspect what must have happened. Whoever sent the Firebird to Khorlov was using one of the simplest Gating spells: it creates two Gates, one to enter by and the other to leave from. Neither Gate lets whatever passes through it return by the same route, and from what you tell me, the Firebird had already begun to fade when you grabbed it by the tail. It was already partway through the Gate, and so couldn't come back. Otherwise my wardspells couldn't have saved you, and that suit of cold iron would only have served to hold your cinders together.'

'But cold iron protects against magic,' Ivan protested. 'You said so yourself.'

'Within reason,' said Mar'ya Morevna. 'Remember what happened to the gauntlet. The fault for that, Vanya, was yours. You came to no harm until you laid hands on the Firebird, and after that the iron of the armour had to obey natural law. It conducted heat from the contact like a poker left in the fire. The rest you know.'

'*Sokhrani Bog!*' said Ivan softly, feeling a shudder run down his spine on icy little mouse feet. This time the charm of warmth was no protection. 'I hadn't realized I was so lucky.'

Mar'ya Morevna looked at him long and hard, with no expression on her tanned, high-cheekboned face. Certainly there was not even a suggestion of a smile. 'Luck, my loved one, had nothing to do with it, and certainly doesn't begin to describe it.' There was a glitter in her eyes now; they were a blending of light blue and dark, flecked with grey, wonderful to gaze into in the hot, breathless moments when loving was over and resting had not begun. It was a glitter born of terror, but terror so strong that it could only be expressed by a sound that was indistinguishable from anger. 'For the love of God and Jesus and Mary, Ivan! And for the love of *me*, if it matters at all! Just for me, be more bloody careful!'

Perhaps because of the sound of raised voices from inside, even though they were plainly raised in concern rather than anger, the knocking on the library door was timid and faint enough to go unnoticed at first.

Prince Ivan Aleksandrovich stared at his wife with high colour bleeding into his face, angered by being shouted at, more angry still because it was entirely justified and he was in the wrong because he had broken his promise to be careful and been stupid instead. Mar'ya Morevna returned that stare, angry at herself for having shouted, even though shouting was needed, and because, though she was in the right, it was hardly fair to yell at her own loved husband as though he was a peasant just because he had been brave. If he had been a coward, it would have been far worse.

Both of them were breathing hard and each was ready, but neither was willing or able, to say all the things that would have gone beyond worrying and into wounding. The knocking at the door, repeated three times without effect and now much louder, was a welcome distraction for them both.

'Food,' said Mar'ya Morevna.

'Drink.' said Prince Ivan. Then he softened all the unspoken meanings of that single word with a single smile. 'But not tea. That would keep me awake.'

'A drink is perhaps just what you need,' said Mar'ya Morevna in a tone of voice that was capable of several interpretations. 'And certainly some sleep.' She glanced at the door, being tapped on yet again by someone too highly placed to worry about, or too stupid to realize, the reaction he might provoke. 'I think we can continue this later.'

'If you think we need to, later.'

'Later, then.' Mar'ya Morevna slapped her own face lightly a few times, to even out the raging spots of colour that burnt on her magnificent cheekbones, and turned toward the door again.

But it was Ivan who barked, 'Come in!'

Half a dozen servants filed in, deposited the food and drink they carried on whatever clear spaces they could find on the library table, and then disappeared just as quickly and quietly as they had arrived. Only Nikolai the chief servant and Fedor Konstantinovich the High Steward lingered beyond the bounds of courtesy, and if Ivan had been expecting a glare from both or either of them, he was not disappointed. It came as more of a surprise to see the same annoyance directed at Mar'ya Morevna. As the senior servants and more especially as the friends – as they had become – of her late father, it was within their right to disapprove of matters as he might have done, but it came as something of a shock for Ivan to be a witness as it happened. In Khorlov, since his own father was still alive, not even Dmitriy Vasil'yevich would have dared usurp the Tsar's position of chiding or chastising. This was very different. As servants, they could say nothing aloud to their liege lady; but in that unique position as friend, advisor and surrogate father – even though Mar'ya Morevna was old enough to survive without a surrogate anything – the set of their features said a great deal more than words. It lasted for perhaps twenty seconds before they clanked down the silver and crystalware they carried, and stalked out of the library, leaving the room a good deal colder even than it had been before they entered.

Two cats had come scampering in with them, tails held high with the unmistakable hook of good cheer at the end. They were mute friends about the kremlin, falling somewhere between the hunting-dogs in the kennel, who were noisy and slobbery but had nothing to say, and the horses in the stable, who frequently had too damned much to say and no inclination to shut up until they had said it. Lylit' the black cat, so named because she was female and a little devil, spoke only in purrs and trills; Kasha – whose coloration was so close to a plate of buckwheat that she lacked only a lump of melting butter between her shoulderblades – was less vocal but conveyed her wants and needs quite adequately with head-bumps and arching back and tiny little mews. From the enthusiastic activity at knee-level, what they both wanted was everything that had just been brought in.

The presence of these two cats, and especially the name of the black one, had caused a fit of near-apoplexy in the Graubundener pastry-cook who was the most recently acquired member of the kitchen staff, and both cats had spent an afternoon huddled near the stove in dripping fury after being doused with holy water. It had been reported to both Ivan and Mar'ya Morevna and dismissed as unimportant, although Mar'ya Morevna had let it be known that if she was good enough to employ people from other countries because they were good at their work, then she would thank one and all of them to remember what *she* did, and that a sorcerer's little joke in the naming of a poor dumb beast did not necessarily suggest affiliations beyond the humorous, and that the cats should each be given cream to make it clear that there were no hard feelings, and that if Gottfried Kuchmann or any other of her servants didn't like it they could find employment somewhere else. After that, and breathing rather hard, she had put the matter from her mind and turned to more important business.

The servants had evidently taken her warning to heart, at least those of them who had needed warning in the first place. There had been no further incidents involving cats and holy water. At least, none that had been reported.

The meal was typical of something prepared in a forenoon hurry by the well-stocked kitchen of a kremlin whose lord and lady both enjoyed their table. There was a lot of smoked fish, herring and salmon and sturgeon, together with various pickled things, beetroots and marinated onions sliced wafer thin, slimy-wet salted mushrooms that felt like raw oysters in the mouth, and brine-preserved cream cheese with cucumbers and basil. Because of all the saltiness there was a lot to drink, and perhaps because of other reasons entirely, much of it was alcoholic. High Steward Fedor had left a porcelain pot containing *zavarka*, the brutally strong tea concentrate to be diluted with water from a samovar whose little chimney was already emitting smuts and charcoal fumes, and there was a jug of honey *sbiten'* simmering on its lid, but the rest was beer and wine and crystal flasks of fragrant herbal vodkas packed in snow.

Ivan Tsarevich tripped over enthusiastic cats, examined plates and lifted lids for another twenty seconds before he dared meet Mar'ya Morevna's eyes. There was still a coolness about them, but the glacial chill had gone and there was even the beginnings of a smile around the corners of her compressed mouth.

'All right,' she said, 'confess. When was the last time you had *your* wrist slapped like that?'

'Longer than I care to remember. And even then it wasn't done as well.'

'And later?'

'Later can take care of itself.' Ivan poured tea for Mar'ya Morevna, and wine for them both, and silently toasted her health. They ate in companionable silence for a while, and then he ran up a flag of truce, if not quite surrender. 'Certainly when this business of later comes around, I feel sure that I'll have other things to talk about than what was said before.'

'It's a strange thing, given that we got so over-wrought about it all' – she sipped her tea and then spooned heavy, sweet and fragrant raspberry jam into it – 'but I've come to the conclusion that so will I. But first' – she put down the eggshell-fine porcelain teacup, the tea within it plainly visible as a shadow through its sides, and stared hard at Prince Ivan – 'I think you should rest a while.'

The enchantment, quietly constructed in her head and delivered without dramatic hand-gestures, was applied with enough delicacy that Ivan had time to finish his mouthful, then empty and set down his wine-goblet, before slumping limply into the padded chair. It was also applied with enough force and focus

162

that by the time Mar'ya Morevna came round the table to arrange his loose-limbed body and tuck the heavy riding-coat around it as a makeshift quilt, Ivan's breathing had slowed right down to the rhythmic pattern of deep sleep.

'That's better,' she said, and kissed him on the cheek. 'Now I can do some work. And afterwards . . .' She kissed him again, on the mouth this time and with enough interesting pressures that though he didn't stir, his lips twitched sideways after she was finished in a slow smile. If he had been a cat he would have purred and stretched so that his toes wiggled. 'Afterwards, we can talk about it somewhere much more comfortable than here. And you two' – she looked down sternly at the cats begging shamelessly for the fish that Ivan plainly wasn't going to be eating now – 'can just shut up.'

'If even half of this is true, *Herr Hochmeister*,' said Albrecht von Düsberg, waving the sheet of parchment almost wildly in the air, 'then the Order has no need of the witch Baba Yaga. Dieter Balke is an act of war all by himself!'

Hermann von Salza allowed himself a little more red wine, and a thin smile. 'Albrecht, the *Landmeister* of Livonia has a maxim that he coined in Palestine: "There can never be too much confusion or too much hatred among your enemies." ' He raised the wine cup in a silent toast, and sipped at it with satisfaction. 'I happen to agree with him.'

'But the witch!'

'Is a necessary part of this whole plan.'

'And four Rus spies with their heads cut off. . . ?'

'Are another necessary part. Before God, von Düsberg, you're a delicate one.' The Grand Master of the Teutonic Order gazed thoughtfully at his treasurer and concluded – not for the first time – that had Albrecht von Düsberg not been so skilled with numbers and calculation, it would also have been necessary that he meet with an accident, most unfortunate, *requiescat in pace*. On the other side of the equation, as von Düsberg might have put it himself in that Greekish logic he was so fond of bandying about, the Treasurer's apparent spasms of conscience were nothing more significant than the adoption of the other side of the argument in order to achieve a rounded picture of the whole. Von Salza had no objection to fair-minded argument, just so long as whichever rounded picture it created came out well-balanced in favour of the Order.

He smiled thinly to himself, wondering when the other quarrel-some parties in *Schloss* Thorn would accept the notion of a fair argument. Father Giacchetti hardly counted for anything at all; the old man, who had grown visibly older since he reached the Prussian fortress, should never have left the warmth of Rome. Father Arnald and his secretary, being Dominican friars of the Holy Inquisition, presumably felt nothing so worldly as dis-comfort. For his own interest, and afterwards to appal von Düsberg, the Grand Master had acquired, if only briefly, the Father-Inquisitor's own copy of the *Libro Nero*. This, the Black Book sanctioned by the Pope himself, was their guide and instruction for the treatment of heretics, witches – and as he read between the lines with the eye of a power-politician tempered in the hard school of the Holy Land – anybody else of whom the accredited inquisitor might disapprove. If Dieter Balke had various stern little mottoes that he was prone to quote when they seemed appropriate, the Inquisition had refined their mottoes down to one, more grim than any Balke might utter.

The prisoner is assumed guilty until proven so.

And then he is burnt. Hermann von Salza let that thought roll about inside his head again, and it still felt like iron dice shaken in a cup carved from a human skull. Probably the easiest way to avoid all future problems, once this business was concluded and the Rus lands had been secured like Prussia, Latvia, Livonia and the rest, was to let Baba Yaga and the inquisitors fight it out amongst themselves, and devil take the hindmost.

Of course, in this instance the devil would be deputized by Dieter Balke and that spiked Turkish mace he was so fond of, but one could not maintain strict accuracy in everything. So long as the mace was accurately swung, that was quite sufficient.

'If it's all so necessary,' said von Düsberg, his plump features not quite managing to hide an expression that mingled craftiness and realization in equal measure, 'then why is it also so secret?'

Von Salza groaned inwardly. It was comments like that one which had to be balanced so carefully against Albrecht von Düsberg's usefulness to the Order, and more to the point, kept from the ears of brethren like Dieter Balke, who would not have troubled to balance anything against anything when a long hard swing with a long sharp sword was so much simpler.

'It is secret, dear *Tressler*,' said von Salza wearily, 'so that the Rus Princes hear nothing that would make them suspicious of anything except each other.'

'Suspicious?' said a voice from the doorway. 'Who is suspicious?' A muscle in the Grand Master's face twitched slightly. He knew the voice and knew the speaker, and he had grown very tired of the sound of the one and the presence of the other.

'Come in, Father Arnald,' he said. 'No need to knock or ask permission; just come right in and make yourself at home.'

The Father-Inquisitor stalked in, lean, ascetic, and plainly unmoved by von Salza's poorly veiled insult. The coarse black-and-white cloth of his Dominican habit made a stark contrast to the rich tapestries and the banners both Christian and Moslem which hung from the walls of the castle, softening the harshness of its bare stone and brick. He looked from side to side, examining them and all the other small aspects of luxury that offset the dreariness of a grim grey fortress on the far northern edge of Christendom, and then he snorted in studied disdain.

'All alone today?' Hermann von Salza's enquiry was just that little bit too honey-sweet for sincerity, but he made sure that it was not so obviously undiluted sarcasm that the inquisitor could make an issue of it.

'Father Giacchetti is resting,' Arnald said in his most colourless voice, 'and Brother Johann has work to do.'

'Ah. A report for Rome, no doubt.'

'Of course.' Father Arnald sat down, pointedly selecting a plain and rather uncomfortable bench rather than the cushioned chairs in which the two knights were sitting. He tucked his hands into the capacious sleeves of his habit and gazed at von Salza with what on a more charitable face might have been an expression of mild amusement. 'Did you perhaps think that he was writing poetry?'

'Where you and he are concerned,' von Düsberg began angrily, and then caught himself before anything rash could be said. 'Or indeed any members of the Holy Office, the thoughts of ordinary people seem irrelevant.'

'Just so long as those thoughts are neither irreverent nor heretical,' said Arnald softly, 'their relevance is indeed no concern of ours.' He looked from Grand Master to Treasurer and then back again. 'I ask again: who is suspicious?'

Von Salza sighed. 'You are very persistent, Father-Inquisitor. To the point of being stubborn.'

'It is no more than one of the accepted ways of getting answers to a question,' said Father Arnald.

The Grand Master flicked a single glance at that bland face and thought for a moment about the other accepted ways: the lash, the hook, the hot irons, the knotted cords. And behind them all, the fire. Hermann von Salza, Dieter Balke, even Albrecht von Düsberg in his own quiet way, were all violent men, their violence proclaimed by the armour they wore, and by the swords they carried to cut down the infidel in the name of God. But that violence and those swords were cleaner by far than what Father Arnald and his kind would do, still in the name of God. The company of Baba Yaga was preferable. Almost; at least Arnald and the other friars washed once in a while.

'Then the answer that you want is simple enough. Those whose suspicions we fear are the Russian lords and Princes we are trying to deceive. The Order wants them to fight amongst themselves, so that when the time comes for the knights of Christ to ride against the schismatics, they will already be weakened and thus many of our lives will be spared.'

'You are planning a crusade, and yet you talk of hoarding the lives of your knights as a miser holds tight fists around his gold.' If the outrage on the inquisitor's face was simulated, then it was skilfully done. 'Do you, Grand Master, perhaps not believe in what the Pope himself has said, that those slain on crusade shall go straightway to Heaven with all their earthly sins forgiven by their great sacrifice?'

'I had heard something of the sort,' said von Salza. 'If I remember aright, it was from a Saracen mullah calling the faithful to prayer from the top of a mound of Christian corpses. Except of course that he said "*jihad*", not "crusade" and "Paradise" instead of "Heaven".' He smiled at Arnald, a bleak stretching of lips that was as much a threat as anything he might have said aloud, but was a great deal harder to describe in whatever report young Brother Peachbottom was compiling.

'It is as well for you, *Herr Hochmeister*, that this conversation is not taking place in Rome.'

'And it is as well for you, Father-Inquisitor,' snarled Albrecht von Düsberg, 'that what word of it might eventually reach Rome will be of no concern to the Teutonic Order after its victory in the East. Otherwise steps would be taken to ensure that no such word ever went beyond the walls of this fortress.' Von Düsberg glowered at the Dominican friar for several seconds, then drained his cup. He managed to do even that with a ferocity that was totally unlike his usual easy-going manner.

Von Salza glanced in well-concealed astonishment at his Treasurer and concealed a smile with the back of his hand. He remembered how Albrecht had lost his temper in the exercise yard with a sword in his hand, and found it entertaining to watch the same thing happen now, when fortunately there was nothing more dangerous to hand than the wine-jug. Whether von Düsberg's dislike was of the Inquisition in general or this inquisitor in particular, the Grand Master neither knew nor cared. But it was a useful trait, if it could be harnessed and properly directed. Hermann von Salza had broken horses to his will, and trained the fiercest of falcons to take meat from his fist; tutoring the ill-tempered whims of one fat, choleric knight was not likely to cause him many problems.

And had it not been an impolitic thing to do, he would have given von Düsberg a sack of gold just to reward him for the expression that his outburst created on Father Arnald's face.

The inquisitor recovered himself quickly, though von Salza guessed that it was proving an interesting experience for the Dominican to be the subject rather than the source of threats, in circumstances where those threats could be made a bloody reality. The terrified bravado of a suspected heretic strapped to the rack was vastly different to the looming presence of the black-crossed knights in Castle Thorn, especially when those knights plainly owed their first and best allegiance to someone other than the Pope.

'Enough of this,' he said. 'Father Arnald, I presume that something besides a desire to make cryptic comments from the doorway brought you here. What was it?'

The inquisitor looked at the Grand Master for a few seconds, then pushed his hands – clenched into fists, from the bulky outline plainly visible through the cloth – further up inside each sleeve in the nearest thing to an inverted shrug that von Salza had ever seen. 'I have been examining ledgers, chronicles and records,' said Arnald. 'They contain the history of this Order virtually since it was granted official recognition by Pope Innocent. Thirty-five years of information.'

'And?'

'And what is it doing here, when it should be at the head-quarters commandery in Montfort?'

'Starkenberg.'

'What?'

'Montfort was a Frankish castle. We are a German order. We call that castle Starkenberg now.'

'What does a name or the language of a name matter? Has the Order of Teutonic Knights decided – without reference to the wishes of the Pope and the rest of Christendom – to abandon the defence of the Holy Land?' Arnald's voice had grown shrill during the recitation, and von Salza waited while the tension-laden seconds stretched to minutes before delivering his reply.

'Yes,' he said.

Father Arnald looked for just a moment as though he had been struck in the face, and for just that moment Hermann von Salza felt almost sorry for him. It was only ever an almost, and the moment was soon gone, washed away by the glowing flash of anger that anyone, and especially this creature, should have dared rummage through the Order's private papers without so much as a request for permission.

'But . . .' For once, the Holy Inquisitor was plainly at a loss for what question to ask next, and von Salza had to frown an impending smile off Albrecht von Düsberg's face. 'But *why?*'

'Why not? The principal officers of the Order, from myself and *Fra Tressler* von Düsberg down, have concluded that the defence of Palestine is a losing battle, and a waste of time, effort and lives that could be better employed elsewhere. Our castles will remain manned, of course – we are not cowards – and Acre will at least continue with its appearance as our headquarters. But the Holy Land will be lost, and when that happens, the Pope and the rest of Christendom – without reference to those who have given their lives in its defence' – he flung Arnald's own words back at him with a deliberate, savage relish, – 'will turn on the survivors and try to find a scapegoat. Let them find the Templars. Let them ask the Hospitallers for excuses. Those worthy orders have been so determined to exclude all rivals, even those who were willing to help them. They wanted to keep the land, the influence, the glory. Then let them keep the blame for losing all of it.'

Von Salza poured himself more wine, to refresh a mouth gone very dry and to rinse away the foul taste of that long betrayal. If the other orders, and especially the Templars, had been more concerned with their sworn duty and less interested in amassing a fortune through their banking activities, then perhaps he would not have had to say such things. And if the Holy Land was to have been lost despite all, then at least it would have been lost cleanly, by fighting men beaten in a fair battle rather than by petty rivalries and pointless negotiations.

'Then the accusations will begin to fly,' he said, his voice bleak and his eyes unfocused as though they looked beyond *Schloss* Thorn to another time and another place. 'We are envied, Father Arnald, we of the military orders, but some, the richest, the most powerful, the most arrogant, are hated and feared as well. Almost as much as the Holy Inquisition.'

Arnald said nothing; he sat quite still, and listened with all the patient intensity of a cat outside a mousehole. Von Salza looked at him and smiled. 'No heresy, Father-Inquisitor. Just truth, that most unpalatable dish. I speak nothing but the truth as I see it, even if some of that truth will be years in the making. But once the Holy Land is gone, the purpose for the continued existence of the orders who chose to remain there will also be gone. There will be those who see their chance to profit by plundering treasure no longer needed to finance a war already lost. The wily ones will allege such crimes – treason, heresy, and why should sorcery be ignored? – that if, no, *when* the guilty verdict is pronounced, then all lands and goods fall forfeit.'

'To the crown of whichever country hosts the trial, Grand Master,' said von Düsberg, pedantic as always. 'No private citizen could bring such charges.'

'No private citizen would dare. Am I not right, Father Arnald? Well?'

'You are,' said the inquisitor. He spoke reluctantly, unwilling to tolerate such thoughts against a Christian monarch and yet driven by some need to appear fair-minded and reasonable even when his own judgements had already been formed and carved in immutable stone. 'Only a king would dare to make such monstrous accusations.'

'Because only a king would dare to covet wealth on such a scale. Who then? England? Spain? France? The Holy Roman Emperor? Or the Pope of Rome himself?'

'You are drunk,' Arnald said icily. 'That can be your only excuse for, for . . .'

'For telling the truth? But that's what your people always ask, before they start the cutting and the crushing and the tearing. Tell the truth.' He stared hard at Father Arnald, and saw perhaps for the first time on that emotionless scholarly visage a flicker of something other than zeal and pious wrath. Von Salza saw instead an anger that was defensive, embarrassed because of it, and maybe, just maybe, ashamed.

'Are you claiming that you have never used torture?' the inquisitor snapped. His hands were out of the sleeves now, and only an iron control that the Grand Master hadn't expected to see in a mere priest was keeping Arnald from banging his fists on the table to drive home the point that he was trying desperately to make. 'Because if you are, *Herr Hochmeister*, then you are lying!'

Von Salza did not answer the question. 'And have you ever *not* used torture?' he said, very quietly. 'Your own Black Book of instruction states that a confession given freely before the Extreme Question – oh, how circumspect a term – must be presumed to be no more than an attempt to avoid suffering the pangs of the Question, and therefore no sincere confession at all. We torture, yes. But when we wring the secrets from some poor wretch, we do it for necessity. Not in an attempt to save his soul.'

That, Hermann von Salza knew, was more than enough to confirm his own rendezvous with the spiked machinery of supposed salvation, if Arnald had anything to do with it. The inquisitor was sitting upright on his plain chair, and for once he was not troubling to hide the little smile of satisfaction that von Salza's words had brought to his mouth. Albrecht von Düsberg, on the other hand, looked appalled. That might have been out of

170

concern for the Grand Master; or because accusations of heresy were like flung mud and tended to spatter bystanders as thoroughly as their target.

'And what about Baba Yaga, Grand Master?' Father-Inquisitor Arnald leaned forward slightly, cool and predatory and patient once more, all trace of shame and embarrassment forgotten. His patience had already been fully rewarded; this had to be mere curiosity. 'Why does she continue to squat in your library, if,' and he slapped down an exact copy of the parchment in front of von Düsberg, 'your *Landmeister* Balke has done all that he claims. Excessive, surely – unless you have other reasons, affinity perhaps, for employing witchcraft. An art which, need I remind you, was never a form of sorcery approved by any Pope.'

Von Salza shrugged and smiled. 'Harsh times, harsh places, harsh measures,' he said. 'Surely an inquisitor of all people can see that. . . ?'

'Feeling better?'

'Nguhnf.'

Prince Ivan stirred, stretched and then yawned until his jaw went click. 'Much better,' he said after considering the question, then spent a moment taking inventory to make sure the statement was more or less true. There was a crick in his neck, the way there always was after he had slept in a chair rather than stretched out in a proper bed, and one of his feet hadn't properly woken up yet and was playing host to a conventicle of pins and needles. His mouth tasted as though it had been used for a barrow during the mucking-out of the kremlin stables after a long winter, and he suspected that Mar'ya Morevna had best kiss him only at her own risk. Other than that, he felt fine.

Mar'ya Morevna herself looked disgustingly fit and cheerful. For someone who had been awake since – Ivan glanced out of the window at the sun, already westering past its zenith – since just after dawn of the previous day, she showed no trace of the weariness that might have been expected from such an effort. In fact, she even looked as though she had taken enough time to bathe; certainly she had changed her clothing from bulky furs to the more comfortable blouse and boots tucked into baggy Cossack trews that she preferred when she was just a liege lady with no

171

need to present herself as A Princess. The Russian language lent itself rather well to that sort of emphasis, and like Dmitriy Vasil'yevich Strel'tsin in full prolix flow, who seemed to be paying for each of them in gold, Mar'ya Morevna always liked to get full value from her Capital Letters. It simplified matters; at least, that was what they had both told Ivan.

He, being a practical young man, believed one-eighth of talk like that, even when it came from his own dear wife. The other seven-eighths of it, he took with salt. And whichever other condiments seemed appropriate, since all sorcerers, whether insignificant political ones like Dmitriy Vasil'yevich or much-loved ones like Mar'ya Morevna, were well-known as notorious liars.

'Did you sleep?' he asked.

'Yes. Enough that I needed,' said Mar'ya Morevna.

Ivan looked at her and raised an eyebrow, then gazed at the sky outside which, being clear, told the time as plain as any clock. 'And just when did you take the time to do that?' he said.

'While you were sleeping. You didn't notice.'

'If you slept while I slept, then who did this.' Ivan gestured at the table; instead of the serried ranks of books and scrolls and parchments that had been there when he had been *told* to go to sleep – the realization of truth struck him with somewhat annoying force – there was instead a neat and tidy pile of carefully copied manuscript, secured with a ribbon tied crosswise. He had no need to go closer to it, nor indeed to try to read it upside-down. Mar'ya Morevna's distinctive hand was quite clear, and more to the point it was new. These were not pages extracted from notebooks, a straightforward task which might, just might, have given her enough time at the end of it to catch a brief nap. Everything in that all-too-thick bundle had been painstakingly copied out, after the original had been hunted down in whichever of the many, many books in this library had hidden it. 'All right,' he said, 'when did you do it?'

'When you slept,' Mar'ya Morevna repeated.

'But that was when you said *you* had been sleeping,' said Ivan stubbornly. 'There is enough work here to have kept you busy from the time we came back from Khorlov, never mind the few hours I was asleep. So. . . ?'

Mar'ya Morevna looked at him and smiled slowly. 'All right,' she said. 'I would have told you eventually, I suppose. Or you would have found out for yourself. Even though I don't trust the Gate sorceries for travelling – at least, not yet – I trust them well enough for privacy within the walls of my own kremlin.'

Ivan cleared his throat. 'I think,' he said, 'that I missed something there. You'd better explain some more.'

Mar'ya Morevna smiled ruefully. 'I've been anticipating that for months now, so much so that I had my explanation prepared and rehearsed like an actor's speech. All the questions that you might have asked, all the answers I would need to give, so that you would understand what was happening. And now I've forgotten all of it. The words are still there, but the sense has gone. All I can think of is the Firebird.'

'Then,' said Ivan, 'try guessing.'

'All right,' said Mar'ya Morevna. She sat down at the table, pushed the manuscript to one side, and gestured to Ivan that he should sit opposite. After a moment of doubt, not liking the secrecy of all this, he did so.

'The way the Gates work, more or less, is like this: when you step through a Gate that you've created in one location, you step out of the Gate you have already prepared – and concealed, if you were wise – in another place entirely.'

'I follow you so far,' said Ivan. 'But what if you created more than one Gate? How do you, er, know where you're going?'

'There are protocols in every Gating spell that determine your destination. Otherwise . . . Well, remember the last time this subject came up, and I told you all the things that could go wrong?'

'Yes.'

'This is another one.' Mar'ya Morevna's words were flippant enough, but there was nothing flippant about the expression on her face. It was grim, with that stony set that comes from recalling an unpleasantly personal experience.

'And this is when it starts to get complicated?'

'If by complicated you really mean dangerous but don't want to say the word aloud, yes. More complicated than you can imagine, more dangerous than your worst nightmare. And as for *when* it starts to get complicated, is the time between the stepping in and the stepping out soon enough for you?'

173

'*Kristos*, as quickly as that?'

'Yes, just as quickly as that. Now you understand my caution. There are so many refinements involved in the spell that there are an equal number of ways for them to twist and become a trap. If something seemingly insignificant is forgotten, then instead of the spell simply failing – you've seen that happen – it can warp the most innocent intended use into something horrible. Like passing through a Gate without another by which to leave.'

'Oh, dear God! Is that what happened to your father?' Ivan was only guessing, but her father's death was something that Mar'ya Morevna seldom mentioned, and from her haunted look he suddenly suspected the reason why.

'*Izbavi Bog!* God forbid, no,' she said, shaking her head violently and making the sign of the life-giving cross over her breast. 'Koldun my father is only dead, God send him rest. This was worse.'

'Worse than being dead?'

'In certain circumstances, death can be turned back on itself. You of all people should know that. But as for between the Gates, it can't exist because by its very nature there must be more than one Gate for it to *be* between! And if there isn't . . . Nothing can be done about that.'

'Was he a friend? said Ivan gently.

'Of my father. Another sorcerer. I had spoken to him once or twice, but otherwise I hardly knew the man. I would have forgotten him by now, like the others who came and went in this kremlin, if I hadn't been there when he went through and – and never came back. The Gate he used was the most simple. One way. He couldn't return through it, and there was nowhere else to go . . .'

'And you still play with this? I'd rather give a child an open razor.'

'I do not play, loved, nor am I a child. I use it, carefully, and try to learn how to manipulate the enchantments so that no-one else has to live with my memories.'

Ivan backed down with diplomatic speed. Mar'ya Morevna made use of the images of anger to lend emphasis to what she said, or simply to offset the immediate reaction of those who didn't know her, who saw 'only a woman' and in consequence proceeded

174

from that most dangerously incorrect assumption. Her husband *did* know her, and the difference between feigned and real anger. She was approaching the real thing now, just as much as if she had laid hand to sword-hilt, and Ivan realized that she felt a great deal more strongly about the magic of the Gates than he had suspected. *Finishing what her father started*, he thought with a sudden flash of clarity. *And I was making fun of it.* Play *was not a clever choice of words.*

Like all her displays of fury, whether real and simulated, this gathering of stormclouds faded rapidly. Unlike some people Ivan knew, including one of his own sisters, Mar'ya Morevna did not cuddle her rages close as though she liked the heat of them. They normally lasted only long enough to achieve the desired effect, whatever that might be: anything from a killing to a simple apology. And once they were gone, they were gone.

'I learned things my father, Koldun the enchanter, never knew,' she said, looking beyond Ivan, the library, even the kremlin. Ivan could see the pride in her achievement, and the sorrow that her father had died before he could witness it and say 'well done'; and quietly, without saying anything, he found something to do with the manuscript until Mar'ya Morevna came back from her past.

'What was there to learn,' he asked eventually, 'apart from the dangers and how to avoid them?'

'I learned about the empty void that took Gregor,' she said. 'And I learned that it was not empty after all. There are places between the Gates, empty places, still places. Private places. And it's possible, if you understand the subtleties of the spell, to stop there, to pause a while, quite alone and undisturbed in all that emptiness; even to sleep.'

'Ah,' said Ivan. 'I begin to understand. I think. And because this still and private place between the Gates is neither one thing nor another, neither *here* nor *there*, time runs differently. Yes?'

'My,' said Mar'ya Morevna. 'You really have been studying hard after all.'

'It helps that I also guess well,' said Ivan. 'And now another question. How much does the passage of time differ from, from—'

'From the passage of time in the real world?' said Mar'ya Morevna helpfully. 'That's not quite the proper terminology, but it has the saving grace of a clear meaning. And the answer is that

175

the difference is as much or as little as you want. Don't forget that it's a place with no time of its own. I think that time as we know it doesn't exist. At the very least it runs slowly.'

'The way it does beneath the Elf-Hills,' said Ivan, and was given an odd look for his trouble.

'They called such places *Alfheim*, half a thousand years ago,' said Mar'ya Morevna. 'Is this family history?'

'Something like it. When I was very little, there was an old *babushka* who told stories to the children of the court. She didn't restrict her stories to the lands of the Rus. And anyway, if you go back far enough, past Rurik the Norseman, past when there were any Rus dwellings in the wide white world—'

'Half a thousand years, perhaps?'

'You would find that the fathers of my line were among the old North people, the ones who came viking down the rivers in their longships.'

'With your colouring,' said Mar'ya Morevna, very dry, 'I would never have guessed.'

'Hah,' said Ivan. With his blue eyes, and fair hair that went flaxen-pale in summer, there was no arguing with such an observation. 'There were some of their stories that said how, if a mortal man went willingly into the halls of Elfland, then there would be no knowing how long he might truly spend there. He might think that it was just overnight, but it would be ten years – or a lifetime, all his friends and family long dead and in their graves, and himself forgotten. Whatever tricks might have been played with time, they were never to his benefit. Those are the stories, anyway.'

'Close enough,' said Mar'ya Morevna. 'Except for the unpleasantness. Or rather . . . let me say instead, that such unpleasantness exists – I've seen that for myself – but only if you don't know what you're doing. I know exactly what I'm doing; and last night I was getting a good night's sleep, after having done a good day's work. I created that still place for myself, and the cares of the world have no part of it.'

Ivan gazed at her for a long time, then smiled a little and shook his head. 'I can't help but think that it sounds like you're cheating, somehow. Not that I mind, you understand. From what you've tried to instruct me about magic, the effort is often out of all proportion to the reward. It's very pleasant to find that there's at least one spell which works the other way. And now I start to see why you never seemed tired when you were working hard. But why at other times?'

'It's hardly proper to use the extraordinary when the commonplace is good enough.'

'Just so. But, loved, I keep remembering how many times you've told me that all the Gating spells are dangerous. I would never dare command you to stop doing this—'

'Good.'

'In fact, I'll ask you to teach it to me. But please be careful.'

'Oh, I will be. Just because I haven't yet dared use those spells for getting quickly and quietly from one place to another doesn't mean that every other sorcerer is as cautious. Because of that, the Gates worry me. They can't be seen except by whoever created them – at least, not without vast trouble. Of course, they can be Seen.' She gave the word an odd twist, a definite emphasis that confirmed the presence of the capital letter. 'But maintaining that particular enchantment is an exhausting process. It can kill.'

'It seems to me that too much about sorcery can kill, or maim, or cripple.'

'But that, my own dear love,' said Mar'ya Morevna, 'is what makes the Art so interesting.' She smiled, and Ivan returned it weakly. He had long since given up trying to work out how a woman who looked so beautiful could also look so wolfish, and suspected long hours of practice in a mirror. Mother Wolf could do it even better, but then Mother Wolf had what one might call a natural advantage. Prince Ivan smiled inwardly at the thought of what comments she would make about such a cumbersome attempt at humour. Then, much less amused, he found himself wondering how, with all the frantic galloping to and fro across Moist-Mother-Earth, the Wolf's son was supposed to present himself and offer service.

'He'll doubtless have his own way of doing things,' said Mar'ya Morevna in answer to the question. 'Just like his mother. But if he's hoping to find either of us in this kremlin, he had best move quickly.'

'Oh God, not again,' said Ivan, sagging slightly as all the

pleasant relaxation he was feeling went away. 'I had thought we might at least have had a few hours more of sitting still.'

'That wasn't really a thought.' Mar'ya Morevna squared the edges of the stack of manuscripts and gave its securing web of ribbon a tug to tighten it. 'You were dreaming. So dream on. But be ready to leave in an hour.'

'I would like at least to take a bath.'

'I know the way you take a bath, my loved. Two hours, no more.'

'Are we perhaps trying to match some fortunate conjunction of the stars?' That at least would make some sense from all the haste, even though Ivan might have expected to be warned in advance. That was one great advantage of stellar conjunctions: they didn't happen suddenly. Unlike Mar'ya Morevna's notions.

'Conjunction? No. I'm just in a hurry.' She dropped the manuscript into a slim metal case whose lock was almost as bulky as the lid it closed, then slapped the case cheerfully. 'I spent all night, whichever night it was, copying out every spell that I thought we might possibly need.'

'All?'

'Well, most. More importantly, I found the spell we need to go between the worlds, *slowly*. It isn't a Gate spell exactly, and it doesn't rely on the horses, at least not quite. We will be able to go East of the Sun and West of the Moon almost as easily as your brother-in-law the Raven, and probably more quietly.'

Ivan compared the thunderous arrival of Mikhail Voronov in Raven's shape with the thunderous arrival of Mar'ya Morevna and himself on the two horses out in the stable, and found very little difference between them. Saying so, however, was something that he deemed unwise, and he kept his mouth shut on the subject. 'How do we do it?' was all he said.

Mar'ya Morevna stood up and tucked the case of copied spells under one arm. 'More easily shown than told,' she said. 'Go take your bath, and meet me in the courtyard. And Vanya, dress for summer.'

There was more than a foot of snow on the sills of the library windows, and the glass – those panes of it that had survived their arrival and had not been replaced with sheets of oiled parchment – was fern-patterned with frost. Ivan looked at the raging depths of

winter just outside and said: 'Dress for summer,' in a chilly tone
that could have meant almost anything, then went quickly off in
search of soap, hot water and lots and lots of steam.

When Ivan eventually reached the courtyard, he was still glowing
from the effects of a steam-bath taken as leisurely as he reasonably
could. It was just as well: the winter wind was slashing around the
kremlin towers, and the snow it carried struck exposed skin like a
handful of dagger blades. Even the heavy cloak that someone
wrapped around him was of little help against such a cold, and it
bit through the summer clothes he was wearing as though the
garments weren't even there.

Mar'ya Morevna had been busy, although Ivan was quite willing
to believe that she had been wearing something a damn sight
heavier than silk and velvet while she was doing it. The snow in the
open courtyard was deep, nearly three feet in the drifted places by
the walls where there had been no need to brush it away, and
already four inches or so had sifted over where the servants'
brooms had cleared less than an hour before. It had stayed there,
by Mar'ya Morevna's instruction, and she had used its clean white
surface as the page on which to draw her patterns of force. The
lines of the diagram were incised right down to the flagstones, and
where those lines had been drawn, with spellstave and with stylus
and with naked hand, they remained unmarred by the freshly
fallen snow. Some of them looked familiar, awakening memories
of the simple circles Ivan had been taught to draw, but others were
so convoluted that even trying to follow them with an eye and a
pointing finger was impossible. Some of the sweeping curves
appeared to descend not merely through the snow but through the
stones beneath, and there were angles that seemed to fade from
sight not merely from a delicacy of touch when they were drawn,
but because they ran beyond the boundaries of the world and
simply ceased to exist.

'East of the Sun and West of the Moon,' said Mar'ya Morevna
cheerfully, smacking powdered snow off her sleeves and seeming
not to feel the weather on a day when, for all the sign there was of
it through the scudding layers of grey cloud, the sun might have
been no more than a happy dream from some warmer world. 'As
far away as yesterday, as close as the other side of your own

shadow.' She flung out one hand towards the complicated pattern covering the courtyard, and at half a dozen sections of it that were much more than just lines drawn in snow. 'And as the conjurers like to say, all done with mirrors.'

They were mirrors indeed, almost as tall as a man and half as wide, and Ivan didn't even trouble himself with wondering how it was the wind had not already blown them down. If keeping blizzard-driven snow out of a line drawn on a drift had not troubled Mar'ya Morevna, then making sure that six times sixty pounds or so of silvered glass stayed in its place was not likely to be a problem. Ivan looked at one of the mirrors, and his reflection looked back out of it. Neither the real Prince nor the reflected one looked very happy, and the glow of bathing had all but been extinguished by the wind.

'Whose clever idea was this?' rumbled a basso voice at Ivan's elbow, so suddenly that he jumped. Apparently the snow was already deep enough to muffle the sound of hoofs, even those of a horse as big as Sivka. Under his horse-blanket the black stallion was already saddled and bridled, tricked out with saddlebags, bowcase and quiver, a mace hung at the pommel and a bedroll strapped across the cantle. He looked from Prince Ivan to the swirling lines of the spell-pattern, and put his ears flat back in silent comment.

'Guess,' said Ivan, jerking his head towards where Mar'ya Morevna was giving final instructions to her steward.

Sivka glanced that way, scraped at the frozen ground with one fore-hoof and stamped. 'That's all right then. If it had been you, dear little master' – his great eyes glittered with wicked amusement – 'then I might have been more concerned. The lady your wife knows her business.'

'Very droll,' said Ivan. 'Very humorous. And what do *you* know about this world beyond the world?'

'A little. It is a pleasant place. Warm. Green. Soft underfoot. Some people call it *Lyetnaya-Strana*, the Summer Country, even though that's an old name for where the dead go, before the White Christ invented Heaven. This place' – the horse tossed his mane to dislodge a build-up of snow – 'is East of the Sun and West of the Moon. If it really is the Summer Country, or if it has another name, no-one has told me. I know these places better to travel through than to visit, if you take my meaning.'

180

'Yes, I do. But this time, we're visiting.'

'Then be honest while you're there, little master. Always tell the truth.'

'I try to do that anyway. Why more so this time?'

'Because what you say will *be* the truth,' said Mar'ya Morevna as she walked over. 'The good horse is right. If, for whatever reason, you were to say that you were not Ivan Aleksandrovich the Prince of Khorlov, then you would cease to be so. Ivan Tsarevich would not exist, because you had denied that you were he.'

'Then what would I be?'

'Alive, dead, someone else . . . Who knows? You would have to try it before you could say for sure.'

'Thank you, no.'

'Lady and little master, if I may venture an opinion – could not this discussion be continued somewhere warmer?' There was a crust of frost beginning to form over the polished steel that decorated Sivka's harness, and the big horse contrived to look as miserable as he could despite the heavy blanket that he wore.

Mar'ya Morevna laughed shortly and beckoned Chyornyy closer, then swung up into the saddle. 'Told my business by a horse,' she said.

'Not by me, mistress,' said Chyornyy, and if Sivka's stable-brother sounded rather pious, it was probably only by comparison.

Ivan mounted up, settled into the saddle and then gasped and stood up in his stirrups as its leather struck chill right through his summer-weight riding breeches. Mar'ya Morevna looked at him and laughed at his rueful expression, then signalled to the servants standing beside each of the mirrors.

One by one the heavy sheets of glass were shifted into alignment with marks made in the snow, and the reflections of the snow-laden courtyard became reflections of themselves. As the images bounced to and fro between the mirrors, each became smaller and smaller, diminishing out towards infinity; until the final mirror slid into its proper place in the spell-pattern, and the courtyard and the horses and the snow all went away. Instead, caught within the frame of that last mirror as though it was a suddenly opened window set in an unseen wall, Ivan could see a land of green rolling hills and blue sky, of birch trees and silent rivers.

'Stay close by me,' said Mar'ya Morevna, sidling Chyornyy in so that they were knee to knee, as though preparing for a close-order cavalry charge. 'Now ride slowly, into the reflection. Slowly, and close. Slowly, and close . . .'

Even though Ivan wasn't quite sure how he, Sivka, Chyornyy and Mar'ya Morevna were supposed to fit all together and all at once through a space that looked barely enough for himself on foot, the black horse beneath him knew. Advancing at a stately pace, Sivka walked straight towards the mirror – or the window, or the Gate, or the gilt-framed hole that had just been torn into the fabric of this reality and out on the other side.

And through it.

The snow-laden wind blew through where they had been, in a kremlin courtyard that was suddenly much colder after that brief glimpse of summer. The servants stared for a few seconds at the empty glass of the last mirror, even though there was nothing to see, and then as High Steward Fedor Konstantinovich clapped his hands, they set about tidying up.

All except one. He had watched unseen from the shadows within the kitchen doorway, and was now in the furthest and most deserted pantry, drawing a pattern of his own in flour on the flagged stone floor. Gottfried Kuchmann, a German knight who had in his time been a Schwyzer mercenary and was now a Graubundener pastry-cook – and who had pretended in his time to be many other things – laid a letter at the centre of it once the spell was primed, watching as the sealed parchment faded to translucence, and for an instant before the letter disappeared entirely, he could see his own words as though written on glass. Three layers deep, they ran together and made no sense, but the letter's salutation was quite plain and clear.

It was addressed to Dieter Balke.

Chapter Seven

A blackbird burst from underneath a flower-laden tangle of wild raspberry bushes, screaming his alarm call as he fled in a streak of sable. A few minutes later, his panic forgotten, the blackbird was digging his yellow bill into the ground near where two huge black horses had appeared from nowhere almost on top of him, watching them warily from one gold-rimmed eye even as he reaped the benefit of their heavy hoofs in the shape of startled bugs. Two butterflies fluttered in their usual haphazard way through shafts of dusty sunlight that struck down between the gnarled branches of the trees, and one of them settled for a moment between the larger horse's ears.

Prince Ivan looked at the butterfly, at the blackbird, and most of all at the sunlight. A moment ago, barely a heartbeat in his past, a wind that had come screaming down all the way from Siberia had been slicing the meat from his bones, and now the warmth of high summer in the deep forest soaked through his clothing to drive the chill away. Like all the people of the Rus, Ivan endured but did not enjoy the winter, and to have left the midst of it, and especially the storm that had been sweeping across the kremlin, was a luxury beyond price. He shook his head, and laughed aloud, and somehow in those surroundings, the sound seemed very right and proper. '*Lyetnaya-Strana*,' he said to nobody in particular. 'So this is the Summer Country. I *like* it!'

The forests of the Summer Country were alive with birdsong, more even than the noisiest springs and summers that Ivan had heard. Whatever birds might sing for in the real world, finding a mate, proclaiming a territory, warning of enemies, the birds here seemed also to sing for the pure joy of it.

'A man could spent his winters here quite happily,' Ivan said, 'and return to the Rus lands only for the summer there.'

Mar'ya Morevna grinned, and the grin seemed to suggest that she had been expecting such a comment as that. 'I think not,' she said. 'When we go home again, I'll go back to the kremlin library and—'

'I know,' said Ivan, and leaned over to pat her hand. 'You'll show me books explaining in exhaustive detail why not. And what are the books going to tell me that you can't? That the Summer Country is a place prohibited to Christians? Or that mortal men of whatever faith are not permitted to spend more than a certain time in it?'

'Almost right on both counts,' said Mar'ya Morevna. 'But almost wrong as well. You were trying to be too subtle. Spend any longer than the waxing and the waning of a moon here, and by the dark of that moon it won't matter. You, or I, or anyone else for that matter, could no more spend the rest of our lives here than we could spend it under water.'

'Is it so dangerous, then?'

'Not so much dangerous as alien. We don't belong here; just as fish don't belong on dry land. Like water, we can use it, drink it, wash in it, even swim in it if the mood moves us, and you know how pleasant a deep hot bath can be. But as soon as we try to breathe it . . .' Mar'ya Morevna drew an eloquent finger across her throat.

'But what about all the stories – or even though this place exists, are the stories about it just stories and nothing more?'

'What stories?'

'The stories about men, or women, who spent years in what sounds very like this Summer Country, and when they returned as shrivelled ancients to their own land, found that no time had passed at all. Or the other stories, where they spent what seemed only a night and found when they came back that it had been a hundred years, and died of old age almost at once. I thought it was just what happened when people tampered with the Gating spells, but the stories always mentioned a country of some sort.'

'Ivan, think again. Take away all of the embroidery, and what did those stories say?'

He looked at her for a moment, then quirked his mouth in annoyance at himself for not seeing it sooner. 'They went to a place that was not their world, and when they came home, they died of it.' Ivan grimaced as the thought extended itself further. 'Or they would not leave voluntarily, but being in that place killed them, and only then did their bodies return to where they really belonged.'

'Safe to visit,' said Mar'ya Morevna softly, 'safe to admire. Just don't think that you can live here. Any more than the biggest, strongest and most noble king sturgeon could drag himself out of the moat around your father's kremlin and expect to live long enough to be Tsar of Khorlov.'

Ivan stood up in his stirrups, the better to see over the undergrowth and between the crowding tree-trunks of silver birch and gnarly oak, of lime and beech, and here and there of dark yew. There was a fine sweeping range of hills just visible beyond the forest, glowing under the sun, and he shook his head sadly. 'A pity,' he said, flopping back into the saddle. 'There's nowhere in the world like this. Whenever it *does* look like this in summer, there's always the thought of winter to follow, and if you ride far enough south to be sure of the sun, it's too hot and dry and it never stays green.'

'And that's the melancholy that makes the Rus reach for their vodka-flask,' said Mar'ya Morevna with just a touch of disapproval. 'Always looking for the dark side of things.' She snorted a little laugh. 'I think it's just a fine romantic excuse to have another drink or two. Or three.'

Ivan raised his hat politely, then grinned and made such play with his eyebrows that it completely spoiled his grandeur. 'Maybe,' he said. 'But then who needs excuses? Certainly not such a noble commander of armies as you . . .'

Mar'ya Morevna looked at him, raised one of her own eyebrows a mere fraction, then flicked playfully but with considerable accuracy at the hat with her riding-whip. After that she sat smiling indulgently for several minutes and made helpful comments as he fished for it among the tangle of elder, raspberry and bramble that grew so profusely between the trees. 'And of course,' she said as he eventually succeeded in retrieving the hat, both it and he slightly the worse for wear as a result, 'such weather encourages vigorous growth throughout the year.'

Ivan picked bramble-hooks from fur and figured velvet, yelped slightly, and put a well-thorned finger in his mouth. 'So I notice,' he said in a somewhat muffled voice, then clapped the hat back on his head after a despairing look at its egret-feather plume. 'Is there truly never winter here?'

'If there is, I've never seen it,' said Mar'ya Morevna. 'And I've visited *Lyetnaya-Strana* eight, maybe ten times, for one reason and another. It might have been named the Summer Country because of that, or, and I can't say with anything like certainty—'

'Or put more simply, it isn't confirmed by any of the books in the kremlin library—'

'Perhaps it's because you find what your mind expects from a name. I could call this place the Winter Country, and perform exactly the same spell as I did in the courtyard not ten minutes ago, and we would have ridden into a place where the sun never shone and the snow would never melt away. Which would you prefer?'

Ivan cupped his hands and blew on them dramatically, not needing to say more than that. 'And what about the Firebird? Where does it live?'

'The particular Firebird we're looking for, or the whole breed? Both live wherever they please.'

Ivan took the wrong meaning from that, and laughed. 'I shouldn't think anyone would try shooing them away!' he said.

Now it was Mar'ya Morevna's turn to grin. 'It wouldn't be very clever, no – but they come and go as they please, and in passing they visit the kremlins and the mansions of this place.'

'Why would they do that – to steal things?'

'Hardly! The folk of the Summer Country take a dim view of thieves. They hate them almost as much as those who fail to speak the truth. The Firebirds are gentle creatures' – Ivan thought of the incinerated guard and snorted derisively – 'whose principal joy in life is gossip.'

'Gossip? You must be . . . No. You're not joking, are you?'

'No, I'm not. Call them newsbearers, if it makes you feel better about it, but *boltun'ya*, gossips, are what they are.' Mar'ya Morevna slapped the saddlebag containing her manuscript of spells and the transcribed pieces of potentially useful information from her library, and smiled wryly. 'At least, that's how they're described here.'

'But the Firebird has been stealing from my father's kremlin. How can that be justified, if the world from which it comes is so set on honesty and truth?'

'Anything can be forced to act against its nature,' said Mar'ya

Morevna. 'What we have to discover is who has been doing that forcing, and for what purpose.'

'If it can be forced to steal, it can be forced to tell us why.'

Mar'ya Morevna reined in and turned a cold blue stare on her husband. 'I hope,' she said, 'that you meant that to sound other than the way I heard it. There will be no more forcing. That, among other reasons, is why we came to the Summer Country instead of merely summoning up the Firebird as any common sorcerer might do.' She managed to make the words 'common sorcerer' sound like the worst sort of insult, then made a *click-click* with her tongue and shook Chyornyy's reins. 'Walk on. And anyway, I lack the proper tokens for a summoning, even if I wanted to perform one. Which I don't. And won't.'

'So you keep saying. What do we do, then? Invite it to drop in for a chat?'

'Yes, actually.'

This time it was Ivan's turn to saw back on the reins, so abruptly that if there had not been a bit in the way, his black stallion would have had words to say on the matter. As it was, Sivka kept quiet, for the expression on his little master's face was fit to curdle milk. Teasing he could take, but being actively mocked, even by his own dear wife, was another matter altogether. 'We would offer it wine, I suppose?' he said, the sarcastic rasp in his voice very close to the surface. 'And a dish of fresh honey-cakes?'

Mar'ya Morevna laughed softly at him, quite unruffled by the flash of petulance that was caused more by the worries he was holding in check than by any real bad temper. Ivan felt the tips of his ears burn as he blushed. He was always like this when he was out of his depth in any of the subjects that Mar'ya Morevna handled with such competence, whether politics or finance or especially sorcery, and he would have been the first to admit it – if that same lack of ability had not been usually his own fault.

'Your problem with any book of sorcery, *golubchik*, is that you go looking for the interesting bits. Or the horrific bits, so that you can be so properly scandalized at them. Try to look at the means to an end, rather than just the end itself. Because you're so often nearly right that I think you've got real talent.' Mar'ya Morevna rode a little closer, close enough to lean across and kiss him. 'At least, where magic is concerned. Where some of your other talents are concerned, I already know.'

Prince Ivan made a grab at her, just an instant too late as she swayed back and heeled Chyornyy around. 'Ride on,' she said, still grinning. 'And next time, read everything.'

'Not honey-cakes and wine, then?'

'Not quite. Try vodka set aflame in a silver cup, and a golden platter of hot coals,' said Mar'ya Morevna. 'From a fire of applewood or cedar. Something fragrant, and preferably expensive.' Ivan whistled through his teeth. 'That's the way to gain a Firebird's attention. Oh yes, and a place of honour for it to perch.'

'A golden birdcage?' hazarded Ivan. 'Jewelled, maybe?'

'Not a cage, a falconer's perching block made of gold and iron. The one for respect, the other so that everything won't melt. But no cage, jewelled or otherwise; the Firebird is a guest, not a prisoner.'

'The one we're dealing with is a servant.'

'A pressed servant, no better than a slave. I plan to offer it a chance at freedom, if I can. After that we can maybe come to some sort of arrangement, you and I. But we have to find it first.'

They rode where the undergrowth was thinner than elsewhere, and after a while it became obvious that it was a path of some sorts running through the woods. Who had made it was rather less obvious. If it was someone's hunting trail, then it was either poorly maintained or little used, while if it was a track made by the routine passage of some forest animal, that animal had evidently developed a habit of using its track for a certain distance up between the trees and then no further.

For their part, Ivan and Mar'ya Morevna could see plainly that they were riding towards the area of most use. The bushes and the brambles opened out around them as they rode, and Ivan for one was not particularly surprised when the surface of the path changed eventually from the softness of rotted leaves and crushed vegetation to a firm paving made of great wooden discs sawn from logs and rammed into the earth. That at least proved the path had been constructed not by accident but by human agency, unless – an unsettling thought that was not beyond the bounds of possibility – the wood-beavers of the Summer Country were much more advanced than their counterparts in mortal Russia.

The trail continued to lead through the forest, meandering here and there like a sluggish river, until it reached a clearing. Ivan reined in, and loosened his sabre in its scabbard. The clearing was perfectly circular, and Ivan had seen such a place before. That last time, Baba Yaga's sinister hut had stood there on its hen's legs, ringed by her ghastly fence of bones and the staked heads of all those who had gone there before him. There was no such unpleasantness here: the clearing was empty except for a slim column of stone set exactly at the centre. As Ivan rode cautiously into the clearing, he could see even from horseback how trees and brush had been cleared away, the ground rolled flat, and the grass cut as short and neat as any Tsar's formal garden. Behind him, Mar'ya Morevna glanced warily from side to side, then pulled her bow from its case and set an arrow to the string. Her caution was not based on any horrid memory, but a simple military awareness that this open space was dangerously exposed after the deep cover of the forest.

Three other pathways ran from the clearing, paved like the first with slices of tree-trunk and each one pointing like an arrow toward a cardinal point of the compass. Neither Ivan nor Mar'ya Morevna had any way of confirming their guess, but it seemed unlikely that someone should go to so much trouble to make this strange place and then lay down the roads with anything less than care and significance.

The standing stone, when they reached it, was four-sided, as tall as a man, and had been set here by only the good God knew what hands. There were letters carved into each face, and carved deep. Out of curiosity he leaned from Sivka's saddle and thrust his index finger into one of the letters. Those letters and the words they made were plainly meant to last a long time, because they were almost that finger deep. Only his knuckle remained visible by the time his fingertip reached the bottom of the incised line. Ivan sat up again and frowned. 'Here's a mystery,' he said. 'Carving lettering so deep but so precisely takes a long time, and the stonemasons change accordingly. There must be something more behind its meaning than just a warning. All right, so maybe it is no more than an elaborate way of saying go no further. But look at the way the letters are shaped, and the way they make up sentences. It's like something you would see in church. This is *old*.'

'A small mystery only, Vanya,' said Mar'ya Morevna. 'Here's a bigger one.' Dismounting, she jabbed an arrow into the ground to mark the side from which they had approached the stone, and then dropped Chyornyy's reins to the ground beside it. That was a signal trained into any horse, never mind one that could talk and understand the speech of men, and the meaning was quite simple: he was to stay where he was, as though tethered, but the advantage of such training was that there was no fumbling with knots if a hasty departure suddenly became necessary. She walked around the stone, studying each face in turn and reading its inscription until she came back to where she had started. 'Yes, a mystery indeed. Because no matter what direction you come from, the wording is exactly the same. One might expect it to change . . .'

Ivan swung one leg over the pommel and slid gently to the ground, taking care to move quietly even though nobody had yet suggested it as a sensible thing to do. Where threats were concerned, no matter how obscure they might be, Ivan Tsarevich had long since stopped treating them as a joke. He walked around the standing stone as Mar'ya Morevna had done, then walked back in the opposite direction. If he had been half-expecting the letters on the stone to shift and change like the words on Mar'ya Morevna's map, he was disappointed.

'Handsomely done,' he said. 'Expensively done. And three out of the four are surplus to requirements, even without the odd business of the directions. Why repeat the same threat four times? Once is usually enough, if you mean what you say.'

Even though Chyornyy had been 'tethered' in place, Sivka had not, and Prince Ivan rather doubted that the horse would have stayed in one place anyway. He followed Ivan on a third circuit of the stone, then nosed at the pillar and put his ears back. 'It smells bad,' he said. 'Not foul; ominous. I have a bad feeling about this.'

Ivan glanced sidelong at the horse. 'So you should,' he said, then realized, even as he spoke, something that he had not considered before. Just because Sivka, like all the horses of Baba Yaga's herd, could understand human speech, it did not necessarily follow that the horse could also read. What the horse was feeling was not related to the words cut into the stone pillar, and

Ivan wondered just what was troubling his steed. 'Well,' said Sivka, just a little bit impatiently, 'what does it say?'

'*The man who goes left will lose his life*,' Ivan read, aloud this time and tracing along each word with his open hand as he did so. '*The man who goes right will lose his horse.*' Sivka blew and stamped at that, and both horses laid their ears flat back. '*The man who goes straight on will lose his way; and the man who goes back will lose all the time that he has wasted here.*'

The black horses looked at their riders and then at each other, and it was Sivka who first summoned up enough boldness to speak. 'I think,' he said, 'that we will not be going right.'

'And I think,' said Ivan, 'that we may have to.'

'In that case, little master,' said Sivka, baring his teeth ever so slightly, 'you will walk on your own legs and not on mine.'

His stable-brother said nothing, but poor Chyornyy was looking so frightened that Ivan pitied him at once. He glanced quickly at Mar'ya Morevna, who nodded. 'In that case, my lady and I will both walk.' And then a memory of his lessons in the Art Magic, half-buried by other concerns and the thought of the Firebird, came back to him with rather a jolt. 'Just how specific is a spell,' he asked, 'where gender is mentioned in its written form?'

'Very,' said Mar'ya Morevna absently, her mind on other things. Then she turned to look at him and at the wording of the warning on the standing stone, snapped her fingers and said, 'Of course! Chyornyy, can you find your own way home?'

The black horse perked up at once. 'Across thrice nine Tsardoms, mistress,' he said.

'I thought so,' said Mar'ya Morevna. She picked up the dangling reins and knotted them securely across the high pommel of the saddle, pulled various useful items off it – including the saddlebag containing her carefully copied manuscript of spells – and patted Chyornyy on the nose. 'Then I command you: go home, be safe, wait for me there.'

Chyornyy turned and began to trot back along the path in the direction from which they had come; but even before he reached the edge of the clearing he began to fade, like smoke. There was a momentary gust of freezing wind, and a handful of snowflakes came whirling out of nowhere to melt in the warm air of the Summer Country and patter like rain onto the clipped grass. By the time they were gone, Chyornyy was gone too, back to Khorlov and the safety of his own stable.

Sivka remained. The big stallion looked from Ivan to Mar'ya Morevna and then back again. 'I promised, little master, that I would serve you faithfully,' he said. 'But even the most faithful of servants is entitled to ask why he has been chosen to die.' There was no fear in the great bass voice; nor anger, nor accusation, nor condemnation. All that Ivan could hear was simple curiosity.

'You will not die,' said Mar'ya Morevna.

'I would not permit it,' said Ivan. 'But Chyornyy has suffered enough fear in his time with Koshchey *Bessmyrtnyy*. He was suffering needless fear again, and I will not permit that either. You, black Sivka, have never been truly afraid of anything in your life. Not even me. I will not let you die.'

Sivka stared at them both for a moment, then turned his head to gaze at the standing stone, and at the carving which he could not read but whose meaning clearly needed no reminders. 'There seems no way to avoid it, if you are determined to take the right-hand road.'

'There is.' Ivan cuffed gently at where the horse's sleek black neck became a sleek black shoulder. 'If I give you as a gift to my wife. You are now Mar'ya Morevna's horse.'

One of Sivka's flattened ears went forward, but the other stayed back as the horse swished his tail thoughtfully.

'The nature of spells is this,' said Mar'ya Morevna. 'They are words, but words that give a certain shape and form to intention and to power. So at all times they must be clear and accurate.'

'As if I was to say to you not merely "go", but "go to such-and-such a place and do such-and-such a thing when you get there",' said Ivan. 'Otherwise who knows what might happen.'

'With an imprecise spell,' said Mar'ya Morevna, 'much worse than a hoof planted on someone's foot. And this' – she waved one hand at the carving on the stone – 'refers most specifically to "a man" suffering all of these promised difficulties. "A woman" is nowhere mentioned. Whoever carved it plainly didn't expect women to be so bold.' She winked at Ivan. 'Or maybe, so foolish.'

'But I am still Prince Ivan's horse, regardless of who might be

192

sitting in my saddle,' Sivka persisted, as well he might considering that his life was under threat if Mar'ya Morevna was wrong. 'All the Tsardom of Khorlov knows that. It cannot be changed.'

'It can,' said Ivan. 'You call me a Prince; I am, and so my words have as much power and weight in their own small way as any spell. And I say now, where I stand under the blue sky, that you are Mar'ya Morevna's horse; I grant her your strength for her service, your speed for her help, and your faithfulness for her trust, if she accepts the gift.'

'Where I stand under the blue sky,' said Mar'ya Morevna, 'I accept all these things, if you, black horse, black Sivka, are willing in your turn.'

Sivka looked at the standing stone, then at Ivan, and finally at Mar'ya Morevna, and then lowered his head almost to the ground so that she could lay her hand easily between his ears. 'I will bear my little mistress the Tsarevna wherever she is pleased to go across the wide white world,' he said, 'and for as long as she is pleased to have me do so. But I would hope that when my task is done that she would think it fair to return my service to Ivan Tsarevich.'

Ivan drew his long *kindjal* dagger and with it cut a piece of turf from the ground in front of the standing stone. It took him only a few moments to gather enough dry twigs for a little fire, built on the square of bare black earth where he had cut the grass away and lit with the tinderbox from his belt. Mar'ya Morevna was watching these preparations with an expression that suggested she knew what he was doing, but not why.

Ivan caught the quizzical look, and smiled. 'The writing on the stone is old,' he said. 'I just thought that it might be safer to confirm our . . . arrangement . . . with an oath made in the old way. It can't do any harm, and it might well do some extra good.' He turned to face the standing stone and bowed low to it, right arm extended until the fingers of his open hand almost touched the ground, as he might have done to show respect to his father or any other important personage honoured by the dignity of age. Then he took the water-bottle that hung from Sivka's saddle and poured a little into the cupped palm of his hand. 'This horse is not mine,' he said, 'for I have given him to my wife, freely and of my own will. I travel in the Summer Country on my own feet. I swear to the truth of this in the old way, by Earth and Air and Fire and Water.'

He pursed his lips and blew across the water in his palm, then poured it carefully so that it soaked into the bare earth but did not extinguish the tiny crackling flames running over the heap of twigs, and finally returned the square of damp soil to where he had cut it free, so that the tiny fire burning there was snuffed at last.

'And I swear it by cold iron and by my own warm blood.' With the edge of his dagger he sliced a little notch, no more severe than a shaving-cut, across the tip of his left thumb just below the nail, the place where such a cut would be least inconvenient, and caught up a drop of the welling blood on the dagger's point. Ivan held the long blade upright for a second or two so that the little ruby bead stayed on the steel, then reversed the weapon and thrust it down, through the centre of the newly restored piece of turf and beyond into earth that had never been disturbed, making all whole once more. 'Let any argue now,' he said, cleaning the *kindjal* on the grass before sheathing it so that he could properly concentrate on sucking his bloody thumb.

'Cleverly done, Prince Ivan.' The deep voice, grey and sharp and harsh as knapped flint, seemed to come from everywhere and nowhere, all at once: from the sky, from the forest, from the earth, even from the air around them. 'But then my mother said that you were clever; almost clever enough to be a wolf, but not quite . . .'

'The inquisitors want to witness this,' said Hermann von Salza.

'Why should they not?' replied Baba Yaga. 'There must be little enough excitement in their lives.'

'They want to witness the summoning,' said von Salza again, 'but first they want to purify the room.' He looked nervous, an expression unusual on the aquiline features of a Grand Master. 'You told me once, before all this began, that the spells you employed were not . . .'

'Devil's work?' Baba Yaga finished for him. 'No, *Herr Hochmeister*, they are not. Let your inquisitors purify and cleanse as much as they please. This spell will not offend your god. Indeed, it has no relevance to any god that you – or they – have ever heard of.'

They were standing together in the doorway of the library of *Schloss* Thorn, and Hermann von Salza was trying to ignore the newly scrubbed places on the floor where two of his best men-at-arms had died. Died, moreover, with their hearts torn from their armoured chests, at the hands of the same shrivelled old hag who now stood at his elbow. Neither he nor any of the Holy Inquisition were accustomed to asking favours of witches; the Inquisition was, if anything, even less given to that habit than himself. That was why, even though he had not exactly demanded permission for the witnesses to be given access, he had also fallen somewhat short of politely requesting that they should be there.

There was a cage in the middle of the room, set on a little pedestal of bricks between those two excessively clean patches of tiling. Its walls and floor and roof were barred, the bars of dull grey iron, and a heavy metal mesh filled the spaces in between. The bars, and the mesh, and the thumb-thick iron hasp on the door that made up one whole side all had the implacable look of something built to restrain whatever should be put inside until released, and from the look of its construction, that 'whatever' was something much stronger than the small size of the cage might have suggested.

Other than that, there was nothing of much significance in the room. A dozen candles had been arranged in a circle equidistant from the cage, but instead of being black, or carved with designs of ominous significance, or made of some obscene substance like the rendered fat of corpses, these were the ordinary white-golden beeswax candles used to light the *Hochschloss*. They were, if anything, expensive enough that the Grand Master wondered who had allowed Baba Yaga to get her hand on such things, when tallow dips were almost certainly sufficient for her needs.

There were several things inside the cage itself, arranged on a wooden platter that was little more than a plank. One was a solitary coin, its colour and lustre suggesting gold at first, though it might just as easily have been well-polished bronze. Beside that was a horn cup half-filled with some clear liquid, and on the other side, a plain wooden dish with some chips of wood piled up on it; both cup and dish were ugly, functional things, used by the sergeants in their own refectory and seldom if ever seen in the High Castle.

Von Salza was less than impressed. For the summoning of something like a Firebird, which he knew from its reputation if nothing else was a creature of bright magnificence, he had expected more spendid accoutrements than these. It was all rather cheap and seedy. He glanced sideways at Baba Yaga and reflected that the seediness of the spell was well matched by the seediness of the old witch who cast it. His thin, patrician nostrils twitched in disgust as a whiff of her proximity drifted past them. She was no cleaner now than she had been before, when he could smell her from the opposite side of the room. The only real difference was that he had taken to breathing through his mouth when in her company, and doing his best to ignore the outraged messages transmitted from his nose. There had been one good effect from Baba Yaga's sojourn in Castle Thorn: all the knights, even those who considered that bathing was either dangerous or tantamount to the sin of luxury, had taken to washing themselves more often, if for no better reason than as a reaction to the filthiness personified by the witch. Except for the tower where Baba Yaga had her quarters, the whole castle smelt better than it had done for a long while.

Von Salza was glad of it at any rate, no matter what the reason. He and perhaps a dozen other knights and sergeants who had served in Outremer, where water was more precious and more hoarded than any gold or jewels, had always bathed frequently enough to provoke comment. Some of them were simply enjoying the fact that for the first time since they had taken up the crusader's cross and joined the Order, there was water in abundance – sometimes, in autumn, water to excess both in the air and underfoot. Others, von Salza among them, held to a view that some Papal edict or other had probably declared heretical: that if God had created man in his own image, then it behoved man to show respect for God by maintaining that image in a reasonably clean condition, just as much as they would wash or repaint a holy statue when its appearance became shabby.

The Grand Master glanced at Baba Yaga once again, and wondered idly just whose shape she was supposed to represent. Baba Yaga, most probably; herself alone, without reference to any higher Power. The sin of pride, of course, and deserving of condemnation for it – except that to do so would be a waste of breath, and pride was one of the least sins on the calendar of iniquities that she had committed. Von Salza did not know how much of what she had said to him had been true, and how much

196

merely evil boasting that soiled the air which carried it. He did not want to know. Already in his mind were several plans for her disposal, once her usefulness to the Order was at an end. Even without Father-Inquisitor Arnald's threats hanging over them, von Salza found himself wondering if, had he known then what he knew now about this objectionable ally, he would ever have commanded Dieter Balke to bring such a creature back from Russia. Balke's own grim methods, violent and brutal though they were, had a cleanness about them that was entirely lacking in whatever Baba Yaga said, or did, or was. *Landmeister* Balke was at least a human being; Baba Yaga scarcely qualified for that title.

Von Salza sent a sergeant to fetch Father Giacchetti and the two inquisitors, noting ruefully the relief with which the man-at-arms took his dismissal. After what had happened here already, it was scarcely surprising that he would jump at any chance to leave the room; and there was always the stench of unwashed witch to be considered.

There were more books than before on what von Salza had come to regard as Baba Yaga's private shelf. Like one of those ghastly inbred tribes the Teutonic Knights had discovered – and exterminated – in the deep forests of the Prussian hinterland, all the books seemed different and at the same time shared a grotesque, deformed family resemblance. Even the deformations were similar: like the first grimoire he had ever seen in Baba Yaga's possession, each book was charred and its cover hacked and blackened as though struck repeatedly with a red-hot pickaxe. The Grand Master knew now that these were the marks left by the Firebird's claws, but comparing the damage to something more easily imagined made it slightly, very slightly, less frightening.

Except that it diminished nothing. This was the first result of his plan to expand the domains of the Teutonic Order, and the Holy Roman Empire, and Christendom: that a stinking hag should be enabled to lay her hands on books of black sorcery. Von Salza shivered, and blessed himself just as Father Arnald of the Inquisition stepped into the library.

'Well may you cross yourself, *Herr Hochmeister*,' he said. 'Attending such a filthy deed of darkness as this one is no task for the faint of heart.'

At one and the same time Arnald had managed to suggest that

197

he, the Grand Master of the Order, was lacking in faith, lacking in morals and above all, lacking in courage. Von Salza shot a brief glare towards the Dominican friar, then breathed out very gently through his nose and let the matter pass. There were other things happening here with more demand on his attention than the sharp words of a nervous priest.

When Father Giacchetti and Brother Johann came into the library, von Salza glanced at them casually; then turned to stare much harder at the older man, shocked at the change in Giacchetti's appearance. When the Apostolic Notary and his companions had first arrived at *Schloss* Thorn, all who saw him had been impressed by the way the rigours of the journey had made no impression on so frail and elderly a man. Then he had worn his more than eighty years lightly, but now they hung about him with all the weight of a shroud. It was the cold, of course; mixed with a certain amount of stubbornness, stupidity and, yes, pride – though the Father would never have believed that his behaviour was anything but pious and humble. The severity of the Prussian winter endured from within the dank and chilly walls of a castle was far worse than that of a Roman winter seen from inside the Lateran Palace, but despite that, the old fool had insisted on maintaining his own regime of Benedictine austerity.

The Grand Master should have been warned by Giacchetti's reaction to the comforts of his own private chambers in the *Hochschloss*. There was enough evidence of von Salza's flexible attitude towards the Order's vow of poverty, if one knew where to look and what one was looking at, a flexibility that went beyond mere efforts to make knightly duty in a fortress in Prussia feel less like time spent in Purgatory. Instead of taking him to task about his fine robes, ornaments of silver and gold, and all the various other indications of private wealth and Imperial favour, Father Giacchetti had chosen to condemn as sinful luxury the fact that rushes in the fortress were not being scattered loose across the floor, but were woven together and laid down as mats. Von Salza had been half-amused by that, and half-annoyed at such evidence of narrow-minded stupidity. He had been more amused when *Hauskomtur* Kuno von Buxhövden had informed him that Giacchetti had criticized his private chamber for being a knight's apartment rather than a simple monastic cell – as if there would be such an indefensible thing in a *castle*, for the love of Mary! The old monk had also complained about its bed, the necessary warm bedding laid on it, and even the charcoal brazier in the corner, all for being more comfortable than a true man of God might need.

In Italy, maybe; not in Prussia with mid-winter coming on. If that was not pride, Kuno said, then he, von Buxhövden, had never had a recognition of the deadly sins beaten into him as a child. The *Hauskomtur* had gone on to confirm that Giacchetti had flung the offending articles out of the room, refused in outrage von Buxhövden's offer to fetch him a simple pallet, then wrapped himself in his travelling-cloak and his habit and gone to sleep on the floor. Von Salza considered privately that suicide, even protracted and probably unintentional suicide, was a more reprehensible sin that the enjoyment of any amount of luxury, and had been about to remonstrate with the old monk from his own full rank as *Hochmeister* of a military order. Then he had changed his mind, deciding within a few seconds of von Buxhövden's arrival that he would let the Papal envoy do whatever he pleased, and take the consequences of that sin of omission on his own head. If Giacchetti's foolishness resulted ultimately in his own death, then there were already ways in which such a death might be put to good use, and – Dieter Balke being in Russia and unavailable to do a deed that would have concerned him as little as crushing a fly – all without the guilt of actual murder staining anyone's hands.

For an instance, there was now a need to put the fear of God and the Grand Master back into a certain inquisitor. Sooner or later, Father Arnald would have to be dealt with, whether that dealing involved his return to Rome or a one-way descent to the bottom of a dark pool that von Salza knew of in the forest. If the Teutonic Order had apparently proven itself to be just as ruthless as the Holy Office of the Inquisition, disposing of the least important member of the Papal delegation by way of an example to the others, then Arnald might prove much more amenable to a reasoned argument. Of course, if argument failed, he would certainly still prove amenable to a dagger between the ribs, and von Salza reserved that necessary business for himself rather than Balke. Business before pleasure, as Treasurer von Düsberg was fond of saying.

The three principal *Ordensoffiziere* of Castle Thorn came into the library a few moments later, accompanied by five knights that von Salza recognized as being among the few brethren with anything better than average singing voices. 'The Father-Inquisitor requested assistance in the necessary psalms of this rite of purification, *Herr Hochmeister*,' said Wilhelm von Jülich the steward as Hermann von Salza put his eyebrows up, not much liking any involvement whatsoever between his knights and the doings of the Inquisition. 'The *Herr Hauskomtur* von Buxhövden gave permission by his own authority—'

'But that can be overruled at your command,' said von Buxhövden. 'Only give the word.'

'Not without better reason,' said von Salza. 'If all they do is sing, well and good. Anything else, and they go out of here at once. *Verstanden*?'

The officers drew themselves up and gave him a quick salute. '*Na klar!*' they chorused, the uniformity of the response drawing a quick look of query from Father-Inquisitor Arnald. Hermann von Salza returned the look, and added an inclination of his head far more gracious than anything this Papal hangman could expect to match. Being raised a nobleman from a long line of noblemen was an advantage that the Grand Master was well aware of, just as he was aware that the lack of it was a factor in the strange savagery of men like Dieter Balke. Lacking the 'von' prefix of even petty nobility, such warriors often chose to make up for their lack of breeding and blood by engendering notoriety and an entirely different sort of blood instead. At least Balke was a knight, and occasionally remembered it; Arnald was only a Dominican priest and a lackey with an over-inflated idea of his own importance, without even *Ritterlichkeit*, chivalry, to moderate the extremes of his activities. It made him an easy man to hate.

The rite of purification began with a prayer and continued with psalms. The Grand Master and his officers, after a brief discussion, did not trouble to join in and stood instead with arms folded, bowing their heads politely at appropriate moments. In the view of Father-Inquisitor Arnald, they were already damned and burnt, and adding apparent hypocrisy to the list of their crimes would have been a waste of time and effort.

Von Salza watched, saying nothing but remembering the words of a certain Saracen in Outremer. '*Sieur Gran'maître*,' the man

200

had said, speaking Norman French more easily than von Salza himself, 'if your chirurgeons spent as much time in cleansing their instruments as your priests spend in cleansing the souls of their patients, then fewer of your brave *chevaliers* would perish from the attempt to heal their wounds.'

That worthy Saracen had been no fanatic, of which there were an excessive number on both sides in the Holy Land. He had simply been a physician expressing professional annoyance at the foolishness of waste. He had the advantage of a faith which considered that prayers and surgery could take place together, rather than one taking precedence over the other on the assumption that the patient would most likely die no matter what was done. Better, said the Christian Church, for a knight to die of a scratch in a state of grace after some priest had spent vital minutes gabbling over him, than to survive to fight for Christ again through the use of infidel knowledge. Von Salza had shared the Saracen doctor's view. There were many such pragmatists in Palestine, and probably the most pragmatic of them all had been the excommunicated Holy Roman Emperor Friedrich himself. That was perhaps why he was less well-regarded then the more colourful and more pig-headed characters like Richard *Löwenherz* of England and the heroic leper King Baldwin of Jerusalem – even though most sensible men regarded Baldwin's near-suicidal bravery as merely a well-concealed attempt to be free at last of his foul ailment. That so unpopular an Emperor should succeed in recovering Jerusalem and the Holy Places by negotiation, where dashing courage had failed, stuck in the throats of many besides the Templars. Not, however, Hermann von Salza's. He approved entirely, and thus it had fallen to the brethren of the Teutonic Order to provide the Emperor's guard of honour, and his only knightly escort, at the Holy Sepulchure. Friedrich had not forgotten, and when he felt inclined, von Salza still wore the mark of his Emperor's commendation, the thin gold cross of the Kingdom of Jerusalem overlaid and so edged in black, *fimbriated* in the heraldic language of blazoning, by the hammer-headed cross of the Order.

Father Arnald made the sign of the cross with a silver aspergillum, sprinkling holy water to the cardinal points of the compass, and began a lengthy benediction that was almost an exorcism and, for good measure, directed almost straight at the

Grand Master. Von Salza blessed himself absently and found himself wondering if before this business was completed, he might have to call on the Emperor's memory for favour and protection once again.

Prayers and palms, *Te Deum* and *Non Nobis*, musky smoke from the censer swung by Brother Johann and the cool spatter of sanctified water from the aspersorium under Father Arnald's arm, bell and book and candle. If it had been Giacchetti's and Arnald's intention to be visually impressive as well as spiritually cleansing, they had succeeded. There were many signings with the cross, in the air with fingers and incense smoke and across the floor with holy water, and as much calling for aid to the appropriate saints and archangels.

Even though Hermann von Salza crossed himself at the proper responses, his gesture was automatic and prompted by the half-seen movement of other hands, so that he was invariably some fraction of a second late. The reason was not disrespect: he was watching Baba Yaga, prepared to prevent any interruption by force if necessary. The mocking glitter in the old witch's curd-rimmed eyes had warned him from the first instant, and he was relieved when the last prayer was intoned and the last psalm sung without any incident being provoked with the inquisitors. Father Giacchetti stepped forward and leaned a handsome Italianate crucifix in a prominent place against the wall, said a *Pater Noster* in the hurried, slipshod Latin of a priest for whom the great prayer had become just one more part of any service in which it appeared, and gestured a dismissal to the impromptu choir of knights. Von Salza was quietly gratified that, though they first bowed to the Papal envoys, all five then turned to him and slammed a perfect salute before taking their leave. It proved . . . something.

Then Baba Yaga stood up. Squirming off the corner seat where she had perched with her bony legs drawn up well clear of the splashes of holy water, she advanced on the crucifix and stalked all around it, subjecting the silverwork and its anguished subject to a close scrutiny. 'Why,' she said at last, 'do any of you believe that a Russian Firebird would be disturbed by the presence of such an image? The supposed execution of the presumed son of the Jewish god.' There were gasps, even an oath or two, and much crossing of breasts. She swung on Father Arnald, one thin arm stabbing out at his face like a spear so that the Dominican flinched backwards, grasping the heavy pectoral cross he wore around his neck and raising it like a shield between them. 'And yet you and your so-Holy Inquisition,' she shrilled, 'burn the people who worship that same god, and you dare to call your executions "Acts of Faith". You make use of fire to honour this image, and then you expect that the same image will frighten Fire. Know this, inquisitor: there was fire before your god made the world, and there will be fire to eat the world when your god is long forgotten. So tell me, what use is *this* when all is said and done?' and she slapped at the crucifix with her open hand so that it scraped against the wall.

Father Arnald showed more courage than Hermann von Salza would have given him credit for, when he stepped past the witch to set the holy image straight. Perhaps the inquisitor knew, as von Salza had already guessed, that her supposed raging was no more than the same ugly teasing that she had already tried on him; or perhaps he was just a braver man than his position required. Certainly he had come to Castle Thorn prepared to accuse and condemn, if such was necessary, with no more force to back his words than an old monk and a pretty boy. That much at least suggested he was unafraid of words.

'That you have to ask the question, hag,' said Arnald softly, with such dignity that for a moment the Grand Master almost liked him, 'tells me that any answer I might give is far beyond your comprehension. But rest assured, we of the Holy Apostolic Office will endeavour to enlighten you. If you play with fire, you will surely be burnt.'

Baba Yaga leered at him. 'Not by such as you,' she said, and showed him her back for whatever dagger he dared to stick in it. There was no chance of that, and von Salza did not even tense himself to prevent it. Arnald was a Dominican friar and an inquisitor. The one did no violence at all, and the other ordered it at second hand to be performed by others. Baba Yaga was safe enough, and knew it.

She set about lighting the circle of candles, then lit oils and scented gums in a metal dish. Their perfumes were almost nauseatingly sweet, so that when they mingled with the fragrance of holy incense and the smell of burning, the result became drifting skeins of smoke that pricked at the nostrils and set the eyes to watering. Baba Yaga inhaled the sickly heaviness as though there was some nourishment in it, and grinned so that the rust on her ragged teeth gleamed wetly in the candlelight. Then she spoke a phrase in words that seemed all consonants, without vowels to soften their jarring dissonance, and drew symbols in coloured powder on the floor that in their complexity rivalled the illuminations of an Irish missal. Finally she clapped her hands, cried a single harsh word to the empty air and waited. The candleflames fluttered, then the candles themselves sagged slightly as the temperature in the library soared past that of midsummer in Jerusalem. Harsh light and harsher shadows filled the room.

And suddenly the Firebird filled the iron cage.

The grey outline of the bars wavered and seemed to billow outward, as though they were restraining a haze of the bird's heat as much as they restrained its wings. Both of those constrictions seemed to anger it, because the Firebird stamped its monstrous glowing talons against the wooden platter and the floor of the cage – von Salza saw sparks go spitting from the iron bars and realized why they had been raised on bricks – and threw back its head in a high, shrill screech like that of a goshawk the Grand Master had once owned.

Then the hackles rose on his neck and he crossed himself again, this time with absolute sincerity, for there were words in that wild, savage voice, words that though they were neither in Russian nor High German, he could understand.

'Once more you have called me, witch,' cried the Firebird, 'and once more I have come here at your bidding!'

'Then take the offerings I have laid before you,' said Baba Yaga in a voice whose harshness was a sharp contrast to her normal ingratiating tones, 'and make your offering to me.'

The Firebird looked from side to side in the confines of its cage. The platter was charring black, its surface acrawl with embers like tiny glowing insects, and the ugly horn cup was smouldering and filling the air with stink. Cutting through that heavy organic smell was the sharper odour of alcohol coming to a rolling boil. Von Salza had smelt that particular stench before, during a fire among the storage in Castle Starkenberg, and had never forgotten what had caused it: the cup contained *Korn-schnaps*, the harsh grain spirit drunk by sentries to keep them warm in chilly weather, and he also knew it was unlikely to boil for very long. He was right.

The spirit exploded with a startling *whoof* and a yellow-cored blue flash that sprayed liquid flame all over the Firebird. It plainly took no hurt either from the explosion or the billow of flame that followed it, and that was hardly surprising, since von Salza was certain that its own plumage was already far hotter than the burning alcohol. Indeed, the only notice that it took of the incident was to dip its hatchet beak into the cup and drink what *Korn* remained, then crunch up the cup itself for good measure.

The wooden platter and the dish on it had long since passed their flashpoint, and both they and the pile of wood chippings, pine by the smell of their smoke, were all blazing merrily. The coin, whether gold or bronze, was no more than a blob of molten metal that ate its way into the surface of the platter for a few seconds until the Firebird leaned over to peck up first it and then the pine chips.

Hermann von Salza saw no evidence that it enjoyed the taste of either. What he saw and sensed instead was evidence that Baba Yaga was very wise to have the cage door shut and bolted, because the Firebird radiated rage and rumpled dignity along with the waves of heat that came rolling off it like a sun beating from desert sand. The witch was taking foolish economies with her spell: inadequate payment, cheap food and cheap drink, if he wasn't mistaken in what he had just seem. As a man who had employed mercenaries in his time, the Grand Master knew what sort of risk she was running, and had he liked her better or found her of more real use, he might have given her some sort of warning. Instead he kept quiet, reminded of yet another of Dieter Balke's wise little maxims: 'Let the one who makes the bed sleep in it'. If Baba Yaga's own carelessness gave him a way to be rid of her, then he would take the gift and be glad of it.

'What have you brought this time?' demanded Baba Yaga.

'A book,' said the Firebird. Its voice had lowered in pitch so that it was no longer painful to hear, but the wildness and the rage were still there, thrumming behind every word like a deadly undertow beneath the placid surface of a stream.

'Good,' said Baba Yaga. The harshness had drained from her

voice, and been replaced by a soft purr of greediness that was very close to lust. It was a foul sound. 'Give it to me.'

'I took it,' said the Firebird. 'It is mine to keep.'

As Hermann von Salza listened, still barely believing his own ears and with one hand tight on the cross around his neck, he felt more and more certain that Baba Yaga had made a mistake in daring to summon this creature. From the little he had gleaned from various books on the Art Magic, a summoning was not so much a polite request for audience as an order to attend upon the summoner, and the Firebird had an air of such furious pride that even one so ignorant in the Art as himself could see that orders were not kindly received. The witch had gravely compounded her error by trying to cheat it of what was its proper due, and he suspected that she had also forced it to steal on her behalf. That too had not been a good idea. Von Salza began sweating more than was justified even by the heat. There was a glitter in the Firebird's eyes that he had seen before, in the mad, murderous eyes of that goshawk of his just before it took off the top joint of a clumsy falconer's thumb. Except that this time, the glitter was magnified a thousand times.

'You took it only at my bidding!' snarled the witch. 'You keep only what I permit you to keep, and I do not permit you to keep this! Give the book to me!'

The Firebird opened its beak and hissed at her, a sound like the pouring of molten iron, and the candles guttered and died, melting into pools of wax as the library grew even hotter. But it spread its brilliant wings as far as the cage would permit, and the confines of its iron prison became still more cramped as the glowing hooks of its talons slowly became filled with the bulk of a metal-covered book as torn and gouged and blackened as the others. Von Salza squinted into the glare that surrounded the creature's body in an attempt to see better without going any closer. Whether the book had been there all the time, but unseen, or whether the Firebird had willed it into existence only when asked, he did not know.

'Here,' said the Firebird. 'Take it.'

Von Salza glanced towards the library door, making certain that the way to it was clear. He felt sure that demand, refusal, submission and this last and deadliest step, temptation, had all been played out before, and the mere fact that Baba Yaga was still

206

alive rather than a smear of fat and charcoal indicated that she had not yet fallen for the trap. But there was always a first – and in this case, last – time for anything.

The witch laughed, a wild cackling sound as frightening in its way as the long howl of a wolf heard on a lonely road far from home and safety. 'Soon, soon,' she said. 'But not yet. What news among the Rus? Are they still at enmity with each other? Do they threaten war?'

'Yes,' said the Firebird.

'When will there be war?'

'Soon.'

Again von Salza found it hard to trust the evidence of his own ears, but this time it was not because he was in awe of the sorcery before him. Baba Yaga was questioning the Firebird as she had promised to do, and it evidently had no choice except to answer; but whether through stupidity or active malice, the questions were so clumsily phrased that it was able to reply in no more than a single word, and had no intention of volunteering anything more without being asked. The Grand Master felt his own temper rising, and despite his own apprehension took a step forward, closer to her and closer to the Firebird.

Baba Yaga snapped her fingers. 'Until I summon you again, go!' she said, and the Firebird vanished abruptly, without ceremony, leaving only the echoes of an angry screech hanging in its wake. Pulling on a pair of heavy blacksmith's gloves, she scuttled to the slowly cooling cage, unlatched it, and pulled out the new grimoire. It was still too hot for her to open, and von Salza was glad of it, for there was an unpleasant aura about this book, more intense than any of the others. She set it down, then turned to glower at him. 'If you are unsatisfied with any aspect of my sorcery, *Herr Hochmeister*, then feel free to perform the summoning yourself.'

Von Salza drew in a long breath, intending to tell this filthy peasant hag just how unsatisfactory he found everything about her. The breath came out again in a long hiss through his teeth, clenched tight and bared in what not even the charitable could have called a smile. 'I might do just that,' he said. 'But with courtesy. And without the cage.'

Besides confirming everything he needed to know, the look of terror on her face was a reward in itself.

Father-Inquisitor Arnald walked through the eerie warm stillness in the library, watching Baba Yaga as she huddled over her latest trophy, then glanced at the Grand Master. 'It hates her,' he said. 'Even more than you hate me and all that I stand for.'

Von Salza swung around to give the inquisitor his full consideration. The words were not exactly an overture of friendship, but there was more fellow-feeling in Father Arnald's voice than he had heard since the Papal envoys first arrived in *Schloss* Thorn. He shook his head. 'Not hate,' he said. 'I thought it at first, but I was wrong. We are opposites, you and I. In what we think, in what we do; in our willingness or otherwise to question what we might be told to do by others. Opposites cannot truly hate each other, any more than the reflection in a mirror can be other than reversed. And as for the Firebird: if that was hatred, then I have never believed how strong the meaning of the word could be.'

Arnald was not outraged by what he had witnessed, nor by what von Salza had said to him. The inquisitor had probably long ago seen and heard enough to thicken his skin somewhat. Instead there was an air of astonishment about him, and more than a little fear. 'Get value from your servant while you can, Grand Master,' he said quietly. 'If that thing ever gets free of its cage, her usefulness is at an end. And may I give you something in the nature of a friendly warning?' Von Salza raised his eyebrows at the word 'friendly', but nodded all the same. 'When it eventually happens, I would recommend that you be somewhere else.'

He came drifting as silently as smoke from between the trees, a wolf with eyes as green and as cold and as hard as jade. His fur was grey, grey as iron or a Russian winter sky, and while he was not as big as Sivka – few creatures were – he was certainly bigger than any more common horse that either Ivan or Mar'ya Morevna had ever seen.

'Very clever indeed,' said the Grey Wolf. 'My mother may be wrong about you after all, because I could have been no more clever than that myself.'

There was something unsettling about the way something so large could move so quietly, and Ivan was grateful that they had sent Chyornyy back to his stable. The poor beast would have panicked at the advance of this grey apparition, and if he had not been warned in advance by the wolf's own mother, Ivan would have been terrified himself.

That was not to say he didn't feel a distinct qualm, because with a wolf so big, the canine fangs revealed by its tongue-lolling pink and white grin were half as big again as his own fingers, and the massive carnassial teeth behind them were ivory shears a palm's width across. 'You won't be needing that, Prince Ivan,' said the Grey Wolf, mild amusement in his voice.

Ivan looked down and discovered that his sabre was halfway from its scabbard. He hadn't thought about drawing it, hadn't consciously meant to draw it – but the fine curve of steel gleamed up at him for all that, an example of the triumph of trained instinct over intention and common sense. He slapped the silver-mounted blade back into its silver-mounted scabbard loudly enough for the click of hilt on locket to echo back from the woods around the clearing, and laughed softly, a quiet, scornful noise, for sharp as it was, the light *shashka* sabre would have been no more use against such a mass of bone and muscle than a broken toothpick. Not even all that silver would have been of any use had matters come to blows, and he was glad that they would not, because the Grey Wolf was no *oboroten'* werewolf. Instead, like his mother, if he chose to change his shape at all he would become more something like a were*man*.

There was a flicker in the sunlight, as though a cloud had passed swiftly across the sun, and a young man stood on the grass. He was tall and brown and splendidly muscled, and his eyes were still the eyes of a wolf. Except for the cloak of grey fur that hung from his shoulders to his heels, he was as naked as a new-drawn blade. That disadvantage of clothing seemed not to concern him in the slightest, for he made the same deep, arm-extended bow of respect to Ivan and Mar'ya Morevna that Ivan had made to the standing stone, and did it just as well. 'Serayy Volk Volkovich, at your service,' he said. The sunlight wavered again and the wolf came back. 'That service will be true, in whichever form I take.'

Barely distracted by the bow and by the brief moment of humanity that engendered it, Ivan looked at the Grey Wolf for a long while, very thoughtfully, as if he was trying to see beyond the changes of form, beyond the formal words – or more simply, as if he was still trying to take in the sheer size of the beast. 'So you are

209

the Grey Wolf, Wolf's son,' he said. 'Your mother made your introductions to us, in a manner of speaking. She said that we would meet, somewhere or other, and that you wanted to go into my service.'

'In exchange for my life, when I was a cub,' said the Grey Wolf. 'All true, that.'

'Of course,' said Ivan. 'But I could wish that when *Volkmatushka* had told me that, she had also mentioned that you had—'

'Grown?' suggested the Grey Wolf helpfully.

'She told us,' said Mar'ya Morevna, 'only that you were no longer a cub. She could have been a little more specific as to the details of that growth.'

'She could,' the Grey Wolf conceded, 'but it's much more entertaining to let people find out at least some things by themselves.'

'So this was in the nature of a joke?' said Mar'ya Morevna. 'Please notice that none of us are laughing. Not even you.'

'Not so much a joke,' said the Grey Wolf. 'Those tend to be crude things at best. Regard it as more of a diversion. But I am glad to have met you here, rather than further along the road.'

'Why so?' asked Ivan, even though he was already beginning to have a sneaking suspicion about what the Grey Wolf's answer would be.

The Grey Wolf looked from Ivan to Sivka, and then at the carving on the standing stone. 'From that careful oath-taking performance I witnessed from the woods,' he said, 'I presume that you know any man who rides his horse to the right will lose it. Did you ever give thought to what might happen to that horse?' He showed his teeth in a wicked grin, and they seemed if anything larger and more numerous than before. '*I* happen to it.'

Sivka took a couple of paces backwards, pawing at the ground with one ponderous fore-hoof, and even though a horse has no eyebrows to reinforce the expression, he managed a very creditable glower of warning at the Grey Wolf. 'You would try,' he rumbled ominously. 'But you would have to try very hard and very fast, because *I* might happen to *you*.'

'You can't be waiting all the time,' said Mar'ya Morevna. 'Not every time someone goes down the right-hand path, surely?'

'Often enough,' said the Grey Wolf. 'Or something like me: a bear, or one of the great cats.'

'What cats?'

'Come now, Ivan Tsarevich; you know about the lynxes that live in the Russian forests. Why should there not be lynxes in the woods of the Summer Country?'

'Lynxes as large as you?'

'Perhaps not quite as large as me,' said the Grey Wolf, 'but certainly large enough. They could easily make a meal out of a horse, if that was necessary.'

'But surely,' said Ivan, 'even if you had not overheard my oath, you would have known when we met later that Sivka was no longer my horse.'

The Grey Wolf shook his head. 'How would I know, not being a part of this land and its magics?' he said. 'A beast of the Summer Country would know it, but I am a Russian wolf and' – again there was that wicked, toothy, tongue-lolling grin – 'I'm a stranger here myself, just as much as you.'

'Hardly as much,' said Prince Ivan. 'What would a Russian wolf be doing in *Lyetnaya-Strana*; killing things for entertainment's sake, or at the instruction of a warning carved into an old stone?'

'Both, and neither,' said the Grey Wolf. 'As for what other reason I might have for being here, I could make some impudent remark like, you can't so easily have forgotten what the weather can be like in Russia at this time of year. But instead I will say only this: the doings of wolves are not necessarily the doings of men, and by the time you are old enough and wise enough in the Art Magic to understand all the many layers of the answer to your question, you will also be wise enough not to need to ask it.'

Ivan grinned wryly. 'Are you sure you couldn't be a little more ambiguous?' he said.

'We wolves taught cunning to the foxes,' said the Grey Wolf. 'We have subtlety of mind and cleverness with words. I could be so obscure, Prince Ivan, that you would not have the slightest notion of what I was talking about.'

'Like some lords who try their hand at politics,' said Mar'ya Morevna, smiling thinly, 'instead of leaving such matters to their High Stewards and First Ministers. Not that the stewards and ministers are any clearer, sometimes.'

'Hardly surprising,' said the Grey Wolf. 'After all, who do you think taught the art of politics to men in the first place?' In the sudden silence that followed, the Grey Wolf licked daintily at his paw then scratched one ear to show how unconcerned he was about the shock he had just caused.

'How?' said Mar'ya Morevna.

'Who?' said Prince Ivan.

'And when?' said Sivka.

The Grey Wolf ignored every question for a moment, scratching harder than ever. 'A flea in the ear,' he said when he was finished, 'can be a damned irritation.'

'So can creatures who don't answer what they're asked,' said Ivan. 'Especially when they want to enter service.'

The wolf thumped his tail against the ground and put his head on one side like a dog trying to make friends. Then he grinned again. 'Consider your own brothers-in-law, Prince Ivan. Are they sorcerers who take the shape of birds – or birds who take the shape of men?'

'They are all human,' said Ivan; but despite the confidence of his reply, he – even he, who had attended all their weddings – had to pause if only for the merest moment. The Grey Wolf, not missing that hesitation, nodded sagely.

'Of course they are,' he said.

'Then why ask, if you already know?'

'To prove a point. You assumed they were men who took on the shapes of Falcon, Eagle and Raven; but when I put a tiny hint of doubt into your mind, you had to think of proofs that would refute that doubt. People assume all the time. My mother told me – before the event – that when she first met your wife the Tsarevna Mar'ya Morevna, she would be presumed at first to be no more than one of your ex-lovers.'

Ivan glanced sideways at Mar'ya Morevna, who said nothing, but her sudden blush was sufficient proof that *Volk-matushka* had guessed right. This time the Grey Wolf did not grin, a demonstration of delicacy that Ivan suspected was most probably not much to do with good manners, but a great deal to do with the reputation of his dear wife's temper. She still had her bow in both hands, after all, and an arrow on the string, and whatever else the Grey Wolf had demonstrated himself to be in their brief acquaintance, stupid was not one of them.

'So,' said the Grey Wolf, with just a trace of smugness in his deep, growly voice. 'If even an enchanter of wide-famed skill and noted beauty can be deceived by what she expects to see' – his tail thumped again when Ivan grinned at such accurate if wickedly timed flattery – 'then how much more easily may ordinary folk be fooled. They expect to see what the stories say: men who become wolves when they must, at the full moon. They do not expect, and therefore do not see, wolves who can become human whenever the mood takes them. And then we tell them what to do, and how to run their lives, and how to run everyone else's life, and after that we all sit back and laugh.'

At the thought of it, the Grey Wolf laughed too, and the sound made Sivka snort and sidle nervously across the grass. Ivan saw the look on Mar'ya Morevna's face, and knew that she was feeling just the same fluttering of raised hackles as he. A day, an hour, five minutes ago, and he would have sworn on any stack of holy relics that even though a talking wolf grinned like an ordinary wolf, all teeth and tongue, because it spoke like a man it would perforce laugh that way too. He would have been wrong, and his swearing done for nothing, for the laughter of a wolf was wolf through and through with no suggestion of the human in it. The low, sonorous howl ran a handful of ice along his spine in something of the way an ordinary wolf-call would have done; but this soft sound lacked any trace of the usual anguished melancholy, and instead, deep and chuckling and laden with the mirth of a knowledge that had nothing to do with men, was somehow far, far worse.

'I like you, Ivan Tsarevich,' said the Grey Wolf. 'And I enjoy your company. Not, of course, in the way that wolves usually enjoy the company of men. Or horses, for that matter. And I still offer you my service. Do you accept it?'

Ivan looked at the Grey Wolf, and at his jade-green eyes. Not the colour of cat's eyes, these, that reflected light like jewels. The Grey Wolf's eyes had their own light, a phosphorescence ghostly pale in the sunlight of the Summer Country that poured down into the clearing, but all the warmth of the sun would never take the chill from the eyes of a wolf. Ivan knew the Grey Wolf was lying – or at least stretching the truth until it had lost all of its original shape. In another circumstance or another time when he had been less than careful, he, and Mar'ya Morevna, and Sivka, would all have been just so much meat for that voracious appetite. Just food; and to a Russian wolf, food was whatever could be eaten. To accept the offered service of such a creature was almost as unsettling as the prospect of refusing it. 'For how long?' he asked.

'A year and a day, was what your mother told us,' said Mar'ya Morevna.

The grey fur on the wolf's shoulders twitched in a style of shrug that he had plainly borrowed from his mother. 'I think not so long,' he said. 'But certainly until this matter of the Firebird and the German knights is settled one way or another.'

'Saint Basil strike me!' Mar'ya Morevna swore, then quickly made the sign of the life-giving cross in case the saint should take her at her word. She turned to Ivan, and made a little gesture of apology. 'You were concerned that we knew nothing about the Teutonic Knights, and you were right!'

That admission was of small comfort to Ivan Aleksandrovich. Being concerned about the doings of the *Nyemetsi* was all very well, but he had not let it go any further than concern. And this was the result.

'The Firebird I know about already, more or less,' he said to the Grey Wolf. 'But what connection does it have to the German knights?'

The Grey Wolf's grin became so long and wide that it ran back beneath his ears, giving Ivan and Mar'ya Morevna a view of more teeth than any three wolves had a right to own. 'Of course, you wouldn't know about it,' he said, almost leering in delight. 'It's supposed to be a secret. And so it seems it is. At least from other people. I might have thought my dear mother would have mentioned the matter when she met you, but it appears not. How much do you know?'

'Less than you, apparently,' said Ivan. 'Perhaps it was another of those matters we would find more entertaining to learn about by ourselves. I give you back another question: how is it that you are so well informed?'

'I don't spend all my time in the Summer Country, Prince Ivan. Or in the shape of a wolf. But we wolves have sharp ears, whatever form we take. We hear things. And besides' – the Grey Wolf sniggered softly, a throaty and far from pleasant sound – 'even though it's been said before and will doubtless be said again, you are what you eat.'

Ivan flinched slightly, and didn't bother to hide it. 'You say "what".' He managed after a few seconds to regain his composure, trying hard to be cool and distant and Princely. 'Why not "who"?'

'Because "who" is for others of one's own folk,' said the Grey Wolf just as coolly. 'And regardless of my dear mother's fondness for the shape, we of the wolves were never even slightly human.'

Ivan stared at the Grey Wolf. 'I can believe that,' he said.

The Grey Wolf was unperturbed by his gaze, and was plainly not feigning that unconcern for his benefit. Ivan finally shrugged inside his head and pushed his shock back into whatever compartment it had sprung from. As well be shocked at a horse for eating grass; although it was not in a horse's nature to gloat over the hay put into its manger. And that raised the awkward question of whether even the Grey Wolf had been gloating, or just acting according to his own nature – which was by no means that of a dog by the fire. But he had not forgotten that snigger, or how little such a sound had to do with the simple requirement of finding food. The Grey Wolf might be terrible, but far less so as servant than as master.

'Though it be for no duration set by word or written contract, Serayy Volk Volkovich,' he said, 'I accept your service.' The Grey Wolf did not turn to human shape but, by extending one forepaw on the ground and touching his long muzzle to it, his bow was undeniably correct. 'Now,' said Prince Ivan, 'answer our questions, and my wife's as well as my own.'

The Grey Wolf looked from one to the other and then back again. 'How much do you need to be told?'

'I think,' said Mar'ya Morevna, 'we need to be told a great deal more than hints and suggestions and oblique remarks.'

'Then best we talk as we travel. The right-hand path, was it not? After such an elaborate performance to preserve your horse's life, it would be a waste to go by any other route. Certainly he'll find it safe enough, now that you've met me. And even better, Ivan Tsarevich, for the same reason you no longer need to walk. Ride on me, the Grey Wolf, as part of my service to you. I'm strong enough to bear you wherever in the Summer Country you might need to go.'

Ivan looked at the shaggy pelt, and at the Grey Wolf's posture, which even standing still was nothing like that of a horse. He couldn't begin to imagine what a running gait would feel like, and quite apart from anything else he would be riding bareback. 'Never mind how strong you might be,' he said. 'I haven't ridden bareback since—'

'Since the last time,' said the Grey Wolf. 'And since we don't have a spare saddle, and since I wouldn't tolerate one even if we had, then bareback it will be again. You can put that riding-whip away as well. You won't need it.'

'I wouldn't have hit you with it, in any case,' said Ivan.

'This is a true thing,' said Sivka.

The Grey Wolf looked from Ivan to the double lash of the Cossack whip, and then – scornfully, Ivan thought – at the big black horse. 'Of course he wouldn't, even if he had to,' the Grey Wolf said. 'Unless he forgot, and did. Just as I wouldn't tear his hand off, even if he hit me. Unless of course *I* forgot, and did. Your choice, Prince Ivan.'

'Ah,' said Ivan. 'Well, since you put the matter like that . . .' He took the whip from where it hung at his wrist, wrapped the lash around the handle, and gave the whole thing to Mar'ya Morevna, who tucked it in one boot.

'Yes indeed,' said the Grey Wolf. 'I thought you were clever. Now I see that you're wise, too. But then, most people come around to my way of thinking, sooner or later. Sooner is always best.'

Lacking a stirrup to lever himself with one foot, or even a saddle's pommel to drag himself up by, Ivan sank his fingers into the deep fur of the Grey Wolf's shoulders and vaulted across his broad back. The wolf grunted and looked back at him, making pretence of sagging under his weight. Then he straightened up and shook himself. 'Hold on with your knees as usual,' the Grey Wolf said. 'But keep your fingers from tweaking the ruff at my neck and your heels well clear of my sides. Remember, dear Prince, that I am not a horse, and have no need to be given instructions.'

Ivan knew that much already. The Grey Wolf might well have been as big as any ordinary horse, but a wolf body was built and muscled quite differently. The broad, furry shoulders tapered far too suddenly into lean flanks, and the ribcage around which Ivan's

216

legs were clamped was far narrower than a horse's barrel chest, so that he had the constant and far from reassuring feeling that his knees were much too close together. Without reins his hands felt strangely empty, and what with the instability of his seat and one thing and another, his fingers itched to sink into the deep fur of the ruff and hold on tight. He envied the ease with which Mar'ya Morevna swung herself into Sivka's saddle; he was already missing the familiar pressure of stirrup against boot and cantle against spine.

'Sit still,' said the Grey Wolf, 'stop wriggling and don't pinch. Unless you deliberately jump from my back, I won't let you fall.'

As they moved off through the forest, the Grey Wolf began to explain what he had learned about the elaborate plot to cause a war between the Princes and Tsars of the Rus. He told them about the Teutonic Knights, about the Firebird – and about Baba Yaga. That startled Ivan more than all the rest, especially as the details came to light.

'She may be a witch,' he said at last, 'and an evil old hag at that. But surely she's a Russian witch!'

'And so should have been loyal to the Rus?' said the Grey Wolf, amused at the notion. 'Ivan Tsarevich, you've survived meeting one Baba Yaga already, the one with the horse-herd, whose house lay beyond the burning river. How many more must you meet before you realize at last that a Baba Yaga is loyal only to herself? This one is not concerned in the slightest about what the Teutonic Knights intend to do in Russia, or to Russia. What does concern her is much more personal. Revenge. On you. For the death of her daughter.'

'Her *daughter*? If the witch who fell into the river of flame was her daughter, then this one must be as old as—'

'As old as sin,' said Sivka. 'And a most appropriate age it is, too.'

'*Boga radi!*' said Ivan. 'If this had involved only the Princes, it would have been easy. But a foreign power, using Russian magic . . .'

'It makes matters excessively complicated.' Mar'ya Morevna stared thoughtfully at Sivka's ears, as though trying to read some sense from the pattern of their twitching.

'Not a foreign power entirely,' said the Grey Wolf. 'The

Teutonic Order is more a state within a state. The knights owe allegiances to all manner of people: the Roman Pope, who is lord of their church; the German Emperor, who is lord of their country; but most of all, to their Grand Master, who is the lord of their . . . family, I suppose. And you are most fortunate in that, for if you count only the knights as a threat, then their numbers are small.'

'How small?' said Mar'ya Morevna. Ivan recognized that tone of voice: she spoke not as a sorcerer, nor as a Tsarevna, but as a commander of armies and, moreover, one trained in the tactics of the Greeks of Byzantium.

'Two thousand, no more,' said the Grey Wolf. 'And not in one place, but scattered throughout their castles between here and the Frank country.'

'They call themselves crusaders still,' said Mar'ya Morevna grimly. 'I wonder why. The title was appropriate when they fought for the Holy Places, and was still so when they fought against the heathen tribes of Prussia. It seems less proper when they fight against us. Are we not Christian, just like them?'

'They say not,' said the Grey Wolf. 'They say that because you follow the Greek teachings and not the Roman, you are false Christians and thus far worse than the pagans whose sole sin is ignorance. If this small venture is successful, others will follow, claiming that God gave them the victory.'

'Against Himself?' Ivan was bewildered, and more than a little angry, in the way that pointless theology always made him feel. 'Will no-one think it strange?'

'Hardly any,' said Mar'ya Morevna, 'and least of all those who stand to gain from it. Enough would listen in any case. There are men like that among the Rus. Men who want only the fighting, the plunder and the glory, and who care nothing for the cause. Besides, Prussia was a trackless waste of swamp and scrub—'

'And forest far thicker even than this,' said the Grey Wolf helpfully. 'No cities, no merchants: no-one to plunder, and only each other to witness the glory. Though I have never understood the glory of drowning in mud. It makes the meat even harder to get at than their iron suits do; and those just make it taste of rust.'

Mar'ya Morevna shot the Grey Wolf a look that suggested to Ivan she was still capable of being shocked by the beast's casual

218

ruthlessness, and then nodded. 'Quite . . .' she said. 'So no wonder they have begun to cast their eyes on the Rus lands. After Prussia, we must look a treasure trove indeed. Even after the looting is done, and if they haven't burnt too much, there will be so much less for them to do before they can bring in their own vassals.'

'And start levying their own taxes, from their vassals and from what remains of ours. They have to be stopped.' He shook his head as another thought intruded. 'And so must the Princes: otherwise they are going to do exactly what the German warlord wants, this *voevoda* or Grand Master or whatever he calls himself, and tear each other apart so that all his knights need to do is mop up what remains.'

'And the best way to do that,' said Mar'ya Morevna, 'is to find a Firebird with one tail-feather missing, and persuade it to tell the assembled Princes that all the thefts and other acts of hostility were not the act of a malicious neighbour.'

'But—' Ivan twisted around on the Grey Wolf's back, lost and regained his balance, and began to speak, only to be hushed by his wife.

'The feather alone proves nothing. We need the Firebird and, more, we need its goodwill so that what it tells them is the truth. Without such a witness, we would be wasting our breath. Since I am one such Prince, and since you, Vanyushka, are the son of another, I greatly doubt that a man like Yuriy of Kiev would take our unsupported word as Gospel.'

'In that case, O-Tsarevich-who-was-my-master-and-who-will-be-soon-again,' said Sivka, running all the words together into a single honorific title, 'regardless of the strange way that time runs in the Summer Country, I think it would be best if we made haste to find the Firebird with the missing feather.'

Chapter Eight

Dieter Balke grunted slightly with effort as he raised the slab of ice again and chocked it in place with a length of timber. *A baulk of wood*, he thought, and grinned coldly. Not that grinning in any other way was possible, for even though he was sheltered from the view of casual passers-by on the bridge overhead, he was by no means sheltered from the wind. It had begun to freeze the slab in place among the rest of the river-crust again, despite all the work that Balke put in to keep it easy to open, but fortunately not so much that it had been difficult to break free. As it swung back like the trapdoor which in a way it was, the waters of the River Dnepr gleamed up at him, black and cold and endlessly hungry for whatever tidbits he might feed it.

Once the ice had been secured, it was only a few messy minutes' work before he was ready to remove the chock and let the slab drop back into place. Balke shoved with both hands and heard a splash in the dark water, looked in, and swore. After a hurried *Ave* in penance for the oath, he leaned in to poke with the end of his trusty beef-rib at where one recalcitrant foot had caught on the lower edge of the hole, resisting all the efforts of the current to tug it out of sight beneath the ice. Once the foot came free and its late owner had drifted away to join the others somewhere downstream, Balke sent all he could scrape up of the stained snow and, more regretfully, the beef-bone after them before dropping the lid of ice back into place. He dropped it rather than lowering it carefully as he had done before, and for the same reason. The rapid descent let it slap against the surface of the river, so that water jetted up through all the cracks, smoothing them and, within minutes in this weather, sealing them tight. He would not need this means of disposal again, for his departure from Kiev was a matter of some urgency. Balke made the sign of the cross towards the river, and then again over his own chest, and spoke the words of a shortened Funeral Mass that he employed on such occasions. It was not hypocrisy, but charity and concern for the

220

souls of his victims. Dieter Balke had no hesitation in killing, if that killing was necessary, however light the pretext, but as a warrior-monk he made sure to exercise both sides of his rôle.

It had served him well, that beef-bone, not least as an excellent and tasty meal by courtesy of Great Prince Yuriy's name-day celebration, even though that celebration had already come to a jarring and premature end, at least within the walls of the Prince's kremlin palace. It still continued just as merrily outside, among the common people, for Yuriy's subjects were not about to let a little thing like the unexpected delivery of a severed head – so long as it was nobody they knew – interfere with the one day in the year when they could eat and drink and by so doing regain just a little of what they had paid out in taxes.

He had guessed rightly about the spies from Novgorod and Vladimir. Both men, when he met them, had requested in the polite, well-armed way which accepts no refusal that he set aside his knife and whatever other weapons he was carrying before they came too close. Neither had said anything at all about the beef-bone, though one of them had grunted quite loudly when Balke hit him with it underneath the ear.

Afterwards, the still-rowdy celebration had justified the way he staggered down towards the river, each time supporting his limp victim as though the man was no more than dead drunk. Revellers were unconscious and heading that way all over Kiev, so that a pair of drunks with only one of them still more or less sober enough to help the other was not something likely to cause comment.

What would most certainly have caused comment was what happened to each spy when they reached the riverside, for the sight of Dieter Balke hard at work removing someone's head with a knife would have sobered up Silenus. That was why he took so much care to remain under cover, despite personal discomfort. It would have been most regrettable to have been forced to kill some innocent person just for leaning over the bridge to throw up, simply to prevent them from mentioning what they had seen before or afterwards. And then there were the heads themselves. For the stratagem of provocation to be effective, they had to be more or less intact and in a good state of preservation. That meant waiting, suffering from the cold that no longer troubled them,

221

until they had drained somewhat, and then gathering together enough clean snow to pack around them before taking both back to his lodgings in a merchant's-quarter tavern.

The Gate that he had constructed was already aligned to outlets in the appropriate cities, and Balke wasted no time in despatching his icy packages to the disguised brethren who awaited them. It was a pity there had been neither time nor opportunity to set up as many Gates as he had wanted to – near Khorlov, for instance – but since those already prepared had been opened without the knowledge, much less the permission, of the Grand Master, Balke had decided not to push his luck too far. If when told about them, von Salza ordered that they be closed and destroyed, it would be done; and for such a task, half of the Rus lands was more than enough territory to cover, never mind the whole of them.

It was fairly certain that Hermann von Salza suspected something of what was going on, although typically he had said nothing about it yet. The way in which his *Landmeister* could travel easily between certain places, and yet was faced with the usual difficulties when making for other destinations, was not likely to have gone unnoticed. The congratulations or condemnations were probably being held in abeyance, to be laid before Balke depending on whether he succeeded or failed. Whichever happened, he had privately decided that it would be better if he offered to make formal confession of his new skills. In that way, whatever the Grand Master determined was best for the Order would be protected by the Seal of the Confessional. If the art of creating Gates was to be made a matter of public notice, it would be von Salza who would do it, even though the secret had been discovered by Dieter Balke acting, as usual, on his own initiative. It had taken him a long time to extract all the details from the Prusiskai shaman, including the interesting knowledge that a Rus sorcerer had also taken the Gate magic away with him but had never dared to use it. So the shaman said, but he had died shortly after Balke had been forced to press him stringently for confirmation of the statement. Certainly there had been no sign of Gates in Russia, except for those he had prepared himself, but one could never be too careful.

Balke checked the first head's wrappings, then set it down in the centre of the Gating circle and primed the spell with two quick strokes of a brush, altering a character on the circle's perimeter. That simple action opened a prepared Gate in the Novgorod lodgings of a spice-merchant who was more than he seemed. The package faded, going from solidity to transparence while a man might draw three breaths, and for an instant the sockets of a crystal skull looked at its slayer with dead eyes like teardrops. Then eyes and skull and snow and leather wrappings all winked out of existence and the circle was empty again.

Balke reached for the second head and hesitated with his arm outstretched, frowning at his own extended fingers. They were trembling. He grunted in disgust and clenched a fist once or twice to drive the tremors away; but when he put this next head into the Gate, he made certain that its face was turned away from him before he primed the spell.

And that was when the letter arrived, literally out of thin air three feet above the Gate. The *Landmeister* started at the small pop of displaced air it made, but still reacted fast enough to catch the sealed and folded parchment before it dropped to the floor. Balke tore it open and scanned the few scrawled lines it contained, then swore viciously to relieve his feelings. The Gate had provided something more disturbing than just a dead man's stare.

After making the proper penitential prayers for the swearing, Balke read the letter again. It came from Gottfried Kuchmann, the knight sent specifically to keep an eye on the only Rus prince Baba Yaga had named, and the one for whom she reserved her most vitriolic hatred. Kuchmann's letter dutifully reported all that he had seen and overheard: how Ivan of Khorlov and his wife had left their kremlin in great haste, looking for some creature called a Firebird; how it had been done; and where they had gone. *Fra* Gottfried did not suggest a reason why, but after wearisome hours listening to Baba Yaga's schemes of vengeance, Dieter Balke suspected that he knew. He could also see what might happen if their search was successful. Not only the old hag's plotting, but the far more elaborate and important designs of the Teutonic Order, could all be brought to nothing unless action was taken to prevent it, and that quickly.

There was no swift way in which he could warn either Grand Master von Salza, or even Baba Yaga herself, of this new development, because there was no Gate actually within the walls of *Schloss* Thorn. For caution's sake, Balke had constructed the Thorn Gate in a stand of birch trees well out in the forest, where its presence was hard to find and easy to deny. It was an hour's ride from the castle, but almost four times that if a man walked on his own legs as Balke would have to do. From the tone of Kuchmann's letter, the time was best not wasted. Balke grinned savagely. He would have to find and kill the Tsarevich personally, and Baba Yaga's thirst for revenge could go be damned.

He looked at his hands, feeling the clamminess of sweat on them, and spread their fingers wide. Then his mouth stretched in a wide, happy smile. They might have been sweating, but they no longer shook. Balke opened his merchant's satchel and from its depths pulled out a rumpled, dog-eared sheaf of notes, scribbled on odd bits of parchment or vellum tied together with a leather thong run through the corner. He consulted first one page and then another, made changes to the Gating circle with quick, confident sweeps of his brush, and watched a faint heat-haze distortion rise from its centre as the Gate opened again.

Balke reached once more into the satchel, and drew out his beloved Turkish mace. A horseman's weapon, its haft, engraved with half-heartedly defaced quotations from the *Q'ran*, was as long as his own arm and its ponderous striking head, enclosed for safety in a leather scabbard like a falcon's hood, was almost as big as his two clenched fists. He had heard all the mocking comments before, many times, both kindly and coarse, and his sole response had been to observe that a phallus with thumb-long spikes on it was not much of a substitute for anything.

Dieter Balke rested the great mace on his shoulder, and stepped through the Gate into the Summer Country.

'But I told you before, summoning is not the sort of spell to use if you want the Firebird to be on good terms with you. Which we do.'

'True; but at least summoning is quicker than this.'

'Maybe so, but I would prefer that the Firebird helped us of its own free will, rather than because we were using the same crude compulsion as Baba Yaga . . .'

Wrangling amiably, and assisted by occasional side-comments from their respective mounts, Prince Ivan and Mar'ya Morevna rode through the forest glades of the Summer Country. The air had that stillness and close warmth of a sunny late afternoon, and where the golden light of the westering sun could not reach the forest floor, it set the foliage ablaze with shades of luminescent green.

'Perhaps he would prefer to hurry,' said the Grey Wolf sardonically, 'so that all of you can get back to the winter blizzards waiting for you in Russia. I can oblige, if you want.'

Mar'ya Morevna laughed. 'I don't want,' she said, 'so you keep out of this.'

'Ah,' said the Grey Wolf. 'A private fight. I see.'

The forest had been opening out around them, and now the ground fell away to the west down the slope of a small escarpment, flowing out into sweeping meadows like the wide Ukrainian grasslands beside the River Don where Sivka had grown up. The meadows – they were too well-cultivated to be called steppes – were dotted with little stands of trees, pretty ones like beech and linden, that had evidently been planted for no other reason than because they looked nice. As the sun slipped lower in the blue sky, white and golden clouds began to rack themselves up in the western horizon as though the impending sunset had been choreographed for magnificence. Set snugly in the curve of a river not very far away, the red walls of a kremlin began to glow warmly as they reflected the evening light. Newly lit lanterns twinkled in the shadows cast by its towers, and over the distance the sound of a church bell rang sweet and clear.

Ivan glanced back at Mar'ya Morevna, smiling gently and shook his head in disbelief. 'This,' he said, 'is becoming ridiculous. An itinerant ballad-singer would be ashamed to dare describe it.' He swung his leg over the Grey Wolf's shoulder and slid down to the ground, folded his arms and leaned back against the furry ribs to watch what looked fair set to be the sort of sunset that only existed in the noble old *byliniy* epics. Certainly he had never expected to see one with his own eyes.

A kestrel-hawk cried *kee-kee-kee* high in the air above the ridge as it broke from its hovering station and came slanting down to see whether the riders had disturbed anything small and tasty. The bird's shadow flicked across the meadow, briefly darkening the grass and the scatter of small yellow flowers that grew among it, then halted, a little cruciform blot of blackness, as the kestrel reached a warm updraught rolling off the face of the scarp and hung high above their heads on tapered wings that barely fluttered to support it on the rising air.

Ivan looked up at the bird, smiled again, and thumped the Grey Wolf on the shoulder in a friendly fashion that was very definitely the backslap exchanged by *bogatyr'* warriors and nothing at all like a man patting a dog. The wolf grunted, then lay down with shaggy head resting on huge paws and made a reasonable pretence of going to sleep. Ivan walked over the springy grass and gave Mar'ya Morevna his hand to help her down from Sivka's high saddle; not that she needed the assistance, but the courtesy was what mattered. She leaned her head against his shoulder and they stood watching the sunset side by side.

Sivka, a realist like most horses and not over-impressed by any sunset when there was grass as good as this waiting to be eaten, promptly lowered his head and began grazing. Then he snorted, put his ears back and stamped.

The kestrel had not shifted from its place three hundred feet straight up, but its shadow was moving. So were the shadows of the scattered trees at the edge of the forest, sliding off across the grass in long stripes of darkness and extending down the slope towards the setting sun. Ivan stared at them for a moment before his brain realized the wrongness of what his eyes were telling it. Shadows in the evening pointing *towards* the sun? That suggested a source of light as bright as that same sun at noon, and the suggestion was entirely correct.

Even though it was high overhead, the Firebird's rapidly beating wings made a rhythmic whirring hiss like those of a wood-pigeon as it flew swiftly across the deepening blue vault of the sky. Looking up at it, Ivan and Mar'ya Morevna had to squint their eyes to mere slits if they wanted to see more than a single intolerably bright bead of light, and for this own part, Ivan was half expecting that the Firebird would leave a trail across the heavens like that of a falling star. The only trail it left was a glow of unnatural violet and orange inside their eyes, a track on their eyelids that burned bright for many minutes afterwards whenever they blinked. The shadows of kestrel and trees and even individual blades of grass slewed as it passed, until by the time the Firebird's brightness had been swallowed by the greater glare of the setting sun, everything was once more as it should have been.

'No, not summoning, I think,' said Mar'ya Morevna. 'When I speak to something like that, I would prefer to have it reasonably well-disposed towards me.'

The Grey Wolf woke from his doze with a snap. Halfway to his feet before he was fully awake, he looked hurriedly from side to side to see what he had missed. 'Up there,' said Ivan helpfully, and pointed towards the sky. The Grey Wolf looked, bristling and showing a hint of ivory under lips beginning to curl back from his huge teeth; then he saw what Prince Ivan was indicating, and immediately relaxed again.

'A Firebird,' he said, and returned to snoozing with a determination worthy of a cat on a cushion.

'Not *the* Firebird, then?' said Ivan, trying not to sound too disappointed. The Grey Wolf opened one eye, looked at him for a count of three, then closed it again and produced a snore.

'Hardly,' said Mar'ya Morevna. 'You've travelled to the country where the Firebirds live. What makes you think that the first one you see will be the one you want?'

'Luck?'

'Hah. Funny man.'

'Let's see if you find this as funny: where are we intending to sleep tonight?'

With the sun dropping behind ever thicker layers of cloud so that darkness spread like ink from beneath the shadows of the forest, Ivan's question was not funny at all. He guessed that he was not the only person thinking of the enormous lynx-cats that the Grey Wolf had mentioned, and for all its beauty in broad daylight, he was unwilling to find out if *Lyetnaya-Strana* was as pleasant for unprotected travellers once night had fallen.

'What about that kremlin yonder?' said Sivka. Ivan looked at the big black horse and grinned; Sivka was by no means finished with eating – what horse ever was – but out in the open after dark there were more important things even than food. Safety, for one.

'Do any of you know good stories?' asked the Grey Wolf.

Ivan shrugged, and Mar'ya Morevna looked blank. 'A few,' the Tsarevich said. 'But mostly gossip.' Then he began to grin.

'Like the Firebirds. Is a piece of juicy scandal really enough to get us a bed for the night?'

'A man riding a wolf and a woman on a talking horse?' said the Grey Wolf, and would have raised his eyebrows had he possessed a pair more separate than the patches of pigmented fur on his forehead. 'Bed and board, I should imagine, and as much wine as you could want, if the scandal's juiciness is rich enough.'

'Even though it bears no relevance to anyone the folk in the kremlin might know?'

'Who cares about relevance,' said Sivka, 'if the story is funny and dirty enough. You should listen to your own grooms and stable-people sometime, little mast—er, once-my-master-but-no-longer.' The Grey Wolf grinned toothily at Sivka's hasty correction, but said nothing. 'It doesn't matter who the story is about so long as it makes them laugh.'

'About me?' said Ivan.

'Ah now, Tsarevich,' said the Grey Wolf, 'would you ask a spy to betray his sources?'

'All the time,' said Ivan.

'Then I suggest you put a stop to it,' said the Grey Wolf, 'or soon nobody will tell you anything.'

'Did I ask for your opinion?'

'No,' said the Grey Wolf, then, generously, 'but you can have it gratis.'

'If you two have quite finished,' said Mar'ya Morevna in a tone of studied patience strained to its limit, 'I should like to see whether or not the good people of the kremlin will let us in or not.' She put foot to stirrup and rose into Sivka's saddle, then looked at Ivan and the Grey Wolf. 'You two can stay here and argue precedence all night, but Sivka and I are leaving.' She jabbed her heels briskly into the black horse's flanks and cantered away.

Ivan stared after her for long enough that the heavy thud of hoofs on well-cropped turf had faded almost to silence, then said, 'I wasn't discussing precedence. Were you?'

'Not that I noticed. But then, the Princess Mar'ya Morevna is a most perceptive lady, and she may well know more about the inside of my mind than I do myself.'

Prince Ivan grinned at the Grey Wolf and laid one hand between the shaggy shoulders to better swing himself astride.

'That,' he said, 'would not surprise me in the slightest. Well, come on; are they going to beat you to the kremlin and the warmest place beside the fire?'

'Not while my four feet can run across the wide white world,' said the Grey Wolf, and took off in pursuit more swiftly than an arrow from a Tatar's bow. Even though those feet of his were padded paws rather than shod hoofs, the Grey Wolf's claws dug into the ground and propelled him so fast that Ivan's hat flew off. Regardless of instruction, he sank his fingers into the wolf's ruff and held on tight with all the strength that he could muster. They passed Sivka and Mar'ya Morevna a few seconds later, and skidded to a halt beside the red kremlin's gate with enough time in hand for Ivan to regain his breath and restore some order to his wind-tousled hair, so that he looked slightly respectable by the time the guards came running out to see what all the fuss was about.

But there was never any sign of his hat again, either then or later.

'*Don't declare war until we get back*, he said,' muttered Tsar Aleksandr of Khorlov. 'A pity my son hadn't thought to give the same advice to' – the Tsar flicked through the sheets of seal-heavy vellum strewn across his desk, – 'Prince Yuriy of Kiev, the two Princes of Novgorod, and both Yaroslav and Aleksandr Nevskiy of Vladimir. Formal defiance from all of them.'

'It would appear, Majesty,' said Dmitriy Vasil'yevich Strel'tsin, 'that a great many differences have been set aside on Khorlov's behalf.'

'So it seems.' Tsar Aleksandr straightened the sheets and fingered a weighty ribbon seal as though the image pressed into the wax held some answer to his dilemma. 'How many days have they been gone now?'

'The Tsarevich and the *gospozha* Tsarevna? Eighteen days, Majesty.'

'And still no reply?' Aleksandr Andreyevich had asked the question not half an hour before, and both men knew it, but the High Steward bowed his grey head as though this was the first time of asking.

'None, Majesty.'

'Defiance, yes,' said the Tsar, half to himself. 'That I could understand, if they have been given the heads of their spies to consider as I have been given mine. But this; to offer battle, never mind the madness of even considering mounting a campaign in the deeps of winter . . . What can they be thinking of?'

'I can only presume, Majesty,' said Dmitriy Vasil'yevich, 'but since Khorlov is not only the smallest of all these domains, but also the one most lacking in powerful allies, it may be that the Great Princes have resorted to their old stratagem of using us as a common enemy for all the rest to concentrate against. And since campaigning in winter is unheard of, except for the accursed Tatars – the levies would almost certainly refuse any summons – the battles will be small but savage, fought by picked household troops.'

That was the custom among the Rus: whenever possible, the season for war was restricted to high summer, after the spring planting but before the harvest. With their forces bolstered by peasant levies, a realm's army could be increased to two or maybe three thousand men, but it was a foolish Prince indeed who for the sake of fielding a great host risked losing all the vassals who would bring his harvest in. His *boyar* noblemen and *bogatyr'* champions would regard such a ruler as unworthy of their fealty, and might even overthrow him and set up someone with a more practical grasp of reality in his place. It had happened before, and would doubtless happen again. War was not something undertaken casually, despite what all the letters on Tsar Aleksandr's desk might have suggested.

'How many men does Guard-Captain Akimov have under his command?' he asked.

'Two hundred horse and foot in the kremlin garrison, Majesty,' said Strel'tsin, 'with a further fifty in the Guard.'

'And the others?'

'At last report—'

'Before someone hacked the heads off our spies and sent them back to us!'

'Yes, Majesty. At last report the Great Princes had a similar number. Even Prince Yuriy has only three hundred soldiers altogether, and he would never dare to strip his kremlin garrison so bare as to bring all of them here. I would estimate that of the

230

hosts of Kiev, Vladimir and Novgorod, each realm can spare no more than a hundred men to send against us.'

'Estimates and presumptions.' Tsar Aleksandr looked at his chief advisor and oldest friend, and gradually a wintry smile spread across his face. 'Dry statistics. But no real concern that I can see. Does nothing ruffle that composure of yours, Dmitriy Vasil'yevich?'

'Inaccuracies, Majesty,' said Strel'tsin, quite straight-faced. 'Also guesses without a basis in fact, and accounting errors not in the Tsardom's favour.'

The Tsar barked a short laugh. 'And what would you presume that we should do now, with an estimated total of three hundred soldiers trudging through the snow towards this kremlin?'

'Prepare for a siege, but offer to talk first.'

'Will they talk?'

'Majesty, the Princes of the Rus are not Frankish knights, to rush headlong to their destruction simply because they could not be troubled to find out why. They will talk. It is what comes after the talking is done that we should be prepared for.'

'If Vanya does not return with the Firebird before then,' said Tsar Aleksandr sombrely, 'there will be little point in his returning at all. Twenty days, you said?'

'Eighteen, Majesty. But the *gospozha* Tsarevna's Captain of Guards should be here before the twentieth day, and he too is travelling with a hundred men. I might venture to suggest, Majesty, that one hundred men from the army of Mar'ya Morevna is worth a great deal for their reputation alone. It might even serve to give some of the more aggressive Princes pause for thought.'

Tsar Aleksandr Andreyevich rose from his seat and looked at his High Steward for a moment, then he walked past him to gaze down from the window of the kremlin towards the empty snowfield beyond its walls. In a week, there would be three hundred professional soldiers encamped there, with five pugnacious Princes at their head and little intention of returning home again without something to show for their long march. 'I think, Dmitriy Vasil'yevich, that we will need a more solid defence than mere reputation. We need proof of what has happened here. We need my son. And we need the Firebird.'

*

Seen from under the shadow of its gate, the red kremlin was nothing like so imposing a fortress as Khorlov. Ivan dismounted from the Grey Wolf and looked up at the walls, shaking his head slightly. They were low, the battlements that topped them seemed more for decoration than for any martial purpose, and they were pierced through by ornate windows of a size that would admit not only a besieger but whatever horse he happened to be riding at the time. If anything, the kremlin seemed more like a country mansion tricked out with a fancifully military appearance than a stern citadel built to keep an enemy at bay.

Even the guards had been in no great hurry, despite the commotion of hoofs and wolf-paws outside the gate that they were presumably supposed to be protecting. They came out at a run, sure enough, but Ivan didn't need to be a military genius to see that they were motivated more by curiosity than by anything remotely fierce. Only two of the five were carrying weapons, and those were *bardech* axes of such elaborate design that Ivan was hard put to work out where the ornamentation left off and the cutting edge began. He got his next surprise when one of the soldiers saluted the Grey Wolf and addressed him as *gospodin*, enquiring after his health and in every way indicating that the two were acquaintances at least and very possibly old friends.

'You didn't tell me you had been here before, "*gospodin*",' he said between his teeth while maintaining a smile for the sentries' benefit.

'You didn't ask me,' said the Grey Wolf, unconcerned, 'and I didn't think it was important.'

'Are you two arguing again?' said Mar'ya Morevna as she reined Sivka to a halt behind them, 'or is it a discussion this time?'

'Just a difference of unsolicited opinion, Mar'yushka,' said Ivan, and found himself wanting to smile at the foolishness of it all. He hadn't been so expertly made game of since his sisters married and left home, and the Grey Wolf could have given all of them lessons in the art. 'It seems that my new servant won't provide answers unless I ask him a question first.'

'Except of course when I think my views on a subject are relevant,' said the Grey Wolf.

'Of course,' said Mar'ya Morevna, dismounting neatly and

accepting the courteous salutes of the guards with a little nod of her head. 'Well, announce us, someone.'

The Grey Wolf took on that duty with undisguised relish. 'From my master Ivan Aleksandrovich, *Tsarevich Khorlovskiy*, and his wife the Tsarevna Mar'ya Morevna to the *Grafinya* Countess Vasilisa Kurbit'yevna in whose hunting-park they travel, greeting! My master the Tsarevich demands guest-right and—'

'And no, I demand nothing of the sort.' Ivan laid a hand on the Grey Wolf's long muzzle, regardless of how close his fingers were to those enormous teeth, then made a very small bow towards the guards. 'Prince Ivan and his wife *request* guest-right of the lady of this kremlin, if it pleases her. Manners, Volk Volkovich, are something that wolves plainly haven't learned.'

'Say "don't often need" and you'd be closer to the truth.'

'Say "have no time for" and you'd be striking the target fair and square,' said Sivka's huge voice. That at least provoked more than polite reaction from the guards. If they were familiar with a talking wolf who stood as big as a horse, a talking horse who stood bigger still was something new. Ivan, Mar'ya Morevna, Sivka and the Grey Wolf were all bidden enter the red kremlin, or the red hunting lodge as it now seemed to be, while one of the guards straightened his livery coat and then went dashing off into the principal building.

When he returned, his mistress the *grafinya* was right behind him, and when they saw her, Ivan and Mar'ya Morevna exchanged what could have only been called a significant glance. Vasilisa Kurbit'yevna was little and birdlike and twittery, and while she showed no surprise that they should have come from beyond the Summer Country and was evidently eager for whatever news and gossip they might have, both of them had met such persons often enough at court to know that they would get no information in exchange.

That was not strictly accurate – though the usefulness of the information was another matter entirely – for the twittering Countess was not alone in her kremlin-shaped hunting lodge. There was a small dinner-party already in full swing when they were ushered into the building's Great Hall, and if that hall was smaller than some they had seen, it more than compensated for any lack of size with the splendour of its decoration. *Grafinya*

Vasilisa or her architect had apparently visited Greek Byzantium at some stage, although by what route Ivan could not guess, and had been much taken with the vaulted ceilings of the St Sofia, and had recreated them in miniature.

During the meal, a simple country repast of six courses and six wines, Ivan and Mar'ya Morevna took turns at entertaining the company with gossip and witty conversation. It was unfortunate that the other guests were much of a kind with their hostess, and that they had started their drinking much earlier in the day, for otherwise the exclamations and squeals of delight at each story would have been most gratifying. As it was, Prince Ivan soon concluded that he could have gained much the same response by reciting the books of the Old Testament, just so long as he accompanied each word with salacious eyebrow-play. At last he gave up and turned his full attention to the quite excellent cooking. The day's hunting had been successful, for there was a great deal of game in the form of braised rabbit with sour cream, vinegared wild boar with enough garlic in its sauce to lift his hat off if he hadn't lost it already, and an assortment of birds cooked in an assortment of ways.

Ivan listened with one ear as Mar'ya Morevna tried to turn the giggling and tipsy conversation around to something worth hearing. Firebirds were mentioned several times, as were perches of gold and iron for them to sit on, but he could also hear a consistent refusal to loan such things to strangers. The only reason given was a vague declaration that to do so was 'not quite proper', and Ivan knew well enough that where etiquette was concerned, people could be as inflexible as over religion. Mar'ya Morevna knew it too, and stopped asking before her persistence became an irritation. She looked at Ivan, rolled her eyes expressively and returned to pointless gossip for the rest of the evening.

They spent the night between cool linen sheets in a bed not quite as large as a principality, and woke refreshed early the next morning. 'No point in asking about the perch again,' said Mar'ya Morevna as she looked out of their bedroom window, 'even though it's right there for the taking.'

Ivan looked over her shoulder and muttered something under his breath. The perch, in the shape of a capital letter *T* of wrought iron and filigree gold, was set into brackets whose thickness

234

suggested something about the weight of both the perch itself and the Firebird which was meant to come and sit on it. There was a long handle to one side, presumably so that when the perch was occupied it could be brought into the hall so that the Firebird could relate its news of what was happening across the Summer Country. The presence of the handle suggested something else as well, a question that had been niggling at the back of Ivan's mind ever since his hand had closed on that bright, burning tail-feather.

'They aren't hot all the time,' he said. Mar'ya Morevna looked at him. 'Firebirds. You thought they could moderate their heat, though we've never seen proof of it. Well, there's your proof.' He pointed at the handle, two curves of iron inlaid with gold that came around to meet a plain wooden grip in the middle. 'The gold hasn't melted out, and the wood isn't charred.'

'Useful to know,' said Mar'ya Morevna, 'in the event we ever get the chance to use one of those perches ourselves.'

'They kept saying no all evening?'

'You heard most of it, and what you didn't hear was just the same. We're travellers from Moist-Mother-Earth to the Summer Country; interesting curiosities, sources of news and stories, but strangers. We can't be loaned a perch-of-honour in case we, how did the Countess put it, "fail by ignorance rather than malice to treat the Firebird with respect". I gather that means if the thing is offended, it stays away from where the offence was given. It's a matter of honour. As I understood it last night, they can't be compelled and so a visit from a Firebird confers prestige.'

'As if a Tsar should stop to take wine in a merchant's house?'

'Something like. But if that merchant were to repaint his house and call in all his friends to greet the Tsar, and then the Tsar rode by without stopping, think how he'd look. No matter how magnificent the perch or falcon-block you set out for the Firebirds, if they don't use it, your reputation suffers. And it suffers even more if they used to come calling, and then stop because you've done something to annoy them.'

'Like pulling feathers out of their tails?'

Mar'ya Morevna shrugged. 'Maybe. Even though we're going to give the feather back. Oh well. Foreign parts, foreign notions.'

Ivan pulled his shirt over his head and tucked it into his breeches, then looked for the one boot that always took refuge underneath the bed. 'So we're wasting our breath?' he said in a muffled voice.

'Perhaps. And perhaps not. Vasilisa Kurbit'yevna told me that not everyone has such rigid views. She just couldn't remember anyone with flexible ones by the time I thought to ask.'

'I'm surprised,' said Ivan unsympathetically, 'that she could even remember her own name, never mind anyone else's. For such a small person she was managing to pour away a lot of wine.'

'That's what drinking parties are about,' said Mar'ya Morevna. 'Or hadn't you noticed?' She glanced out of the window again, up towards the sky, and her face turned serious. 'And never mind wasting breath. We can't spare the time for another wasted night like the last one. Remember what I told you about the dangers of staying too long in the Summer Country. I'm allowing us two more days, and that's all.'

'You said something about the waxing and waning of the moon,' said Ivan. 'That's more like thirty days, surely?'

'Time runs faster here.' She began sorting her own garments from the mess of tangled bedclothes. 'Two days. Then we have to leave, whether we have the perch and the Firebird or not.'

They left the hunting lodge a little later in the morning, after offering courteous thanks and farewells to the Countess Vasilisa Kurbit'yevna. Those farewells were particularly courteous by being delivered in soft voices, for the birdlike little Countess had the rumpled look of a sparrow mauled by a cat, and from the knotting of her delicate brows and the dainty way she pressed her hand to her temples, her head appeared to be giving her considerable trouble.

Ivan looked back briefly from the crest of the ridge overlooking the red hunting lodge, and smiled sourly at the sight of a distant figure striding down out of the woods with a long bundle of something resting on one shoulder. 'Another hunter, I suppose,' he said. 'Bringing meat, looking for money. Well, I wish him better luck than we had at getting what he wants from that drunken little sparrow. Damned stupid perches. You'd think we wanted to steal one.'

The Grey Wolf paused and looked back over his shoulder. 'Then do it,' he said. 'Next time you see one of these perches, don't ask. Steal it. The answer to your problem is as simple as that.'

Ivan stared back at the Grey Wolf and straightened his back from the comfortable slouch he had adopted while he rode. 'I am a Tsar's son,' he said, very much on his dignity – perhaps too much so, since the Grey Wolf's suggestion was something that had already crossed his mind. 'I do not steal.'

The Grey Wolf sighed. Had he been an ordinary wolf, that would have been no more than an expulsion of breath. As it was, the sound was expressive of many things. 'All right,' he said equably, 'then borrow one. You can always put it back after you've found out what you need to know. If you don't intend to keep what you've taken, nobody can call it stealing.' Ivan snorted, and said nothing.

Their destination this time was something other than a hunting lodge, and for that much, the chance of someone sober enough to give his request the consideration it so urgently needed, Ivan was grateful. The Countess had directed them to the kremlin of Tsar Vyslav Andronovich, and whether Vyslav Andronovich was the ruler of the whole *Lyetnaya-Strana* or, like Ivan's father, held his domain as only a part of it, had not been made clear. It hardly mattered now. Whether he was a great ruler or a petty one, everything hinged on how he would respond to the request for a Firebird perch put to him courteously but directly, as from one Prince to another.

Except that the Tsar wasn't there. Vyslav Andronovich was spending the night in *his* hunting lodge, and none of the kremlin officials could say when he would return.

With only a day left before Mar'ya Morevna insisted that they left the Summer Country, theft – or as the Grey Wolf had put it, borrowing – became suddenly far more than just a quickly silenced option. It became the only practical way to achieve what had brought them here. Prince Ivan knew that he could have requested use of a Firebird's perch from one of the palace officials. He also suspected that if his request was refused, the Tsar would likely maintain that refusal when he finally returned to the kremlin. It took a while before his conscience was beaten into submission, but at last Ivan concluded that dishonourable success was better than honourable failure. Soft boots and his darkest coat became the order of the day.

Or more correctly, the order of the night.

Ivan leaned down to where Mar'ya Morevna was sleeping and kissed her lightly on the forehead, then slipped out of the handsome suite of rooms that Tsar Vyslav Andronovich's High Steward had granted as guest-right. As the door closed he looked back at her face in the lamplight, wondering anxiously if this was really the proper thing to do; then squared his shoulders and, right or wrong, did it.

Vyslav Andronovich's fortress was laid out in a way familiar enough to one who had grown up in such a place: main gate here, secondary gates there and there, towers at intervals along the walls, and the kremlin palace itself facing the square. Ivan had spent what remained of the daylight strolling idly about, fixing locations in his mind – and one location in particular. *Pochyotnyy nasest*, the perch-of-honour all dark burnished iron and glinting yellow gold, was set on a stone pedestal to one side of the kremlin square, high enough that when one of the fire-elementals gave out its news it could be heard clearly; but the perch was still not so high that it was beyond the reach of a man of average height.

Ivan had said nothing of his intention to Mar'ya Morevna, knowing full well that she would have presented him with a dozen sound reasons why he should keep his hands to himself, as she often did in other circumstances. Ivan preferred to present her with the perch. It would leave the pedestal, of course, but not Tsar Vyslav's kremlin, and if all went swift and smoothly he could return it before anyone noticed it had gone. After that, with the Firebird's cooperation assured, it would be a simple enough matter for the blacksmiths and goldsmiths of Khorlov to make it a suitably honourable perching-block for when it appeared before his father and the other Princes.

The streets were very dark after full night had fallen, illuminated only fitfully by the firefly gleam of lanterns hung above house-doors. Since the householders and not the city fathers had put up those lamps, no two were of the same design, and no two cast the same amount of light. Once his eyes became accustomed to the gloom Ivan could see well enough not to trip over things, but the thought of having to run from a hue and cry through such darkness was a great deterrent to being caught.

The few people he met after night had fallen, including the

kremlin guards, nodded greeting to him with such friendliness and trust that Ivan felt a little knot of guilt form in his belly. As the guilt increased inside him and began eroding the armour of self-assurance he had built up, he quickened his steps across the square, glanced once at the kremlin palace and once at the shadowed walls, then grabbed the gold-worked crossbar of the perch and tried to lift the whole thing from its iron brackets. It refused to move.

And when he tried to shift his grip, Ivan's hand refused to open.

He wrenched once, throwing his full weight behind the effort hard enough to send a jab of protest through the joints of wrist, elbow and shoulder, and then the knot of guilt became a leaden ball of cold fear hanging in his guts.

It was still there, and he was still there, after ten minutes that had lasted a lifetime. Then there was a rattle of hoofbeats and a group of people on horseback came cantering into the square. Dressed in the greens and browns of hunting costume, they chattered together and were as cheerful as anyone else he had seen in the kremlin of Tsar Vyslav Andronovich. The cheerfulness lasted until they saw him, and then shattered like a sheet of glass. They reined in their horses and stopped in their tracks, not believing what they saw, and this time there was no friendly nod of greeting. Even in the pale glimmer of a starry sky, Ivan could see the expressions of shock and betrayal on their faces, and shame turned him scarlet to the roots of his hair. If any of them had said something angry it would have been easier to bear, but even when two mailed soldiers came forward to release him – his fingers unlocked from around the chilly metal perch in the instant that they took him by the arms – not a word was spoken.

If he had been flung into a cell, that too would have made it easier, but instead, though their firm grip on his biceps never slackened, they guided him back into the kremlin palace and upstairs to the guesting-rooms, and there they knocked on the door.

Mar'ya Morevna answered the polite rapping, and the way she stared at Ivan when the guards escorted him inside was dreadful. Without a word being spoken, she knew what he had tried and failed to do. He heard the door click shut, and then the rattle of a key as it was locked from the outside. Mar'ya Morevna reached out and took both his hands in hers. 'You were acting for the best, Vanya,' she said. 'But you should have waited. At the very least you should have asked me if this was a wise thing to do. Instead you did it anyway.'

She sat down on the bed, gazing up at him, and held his hands close against her face. 'I am a warrior and a commander of armies. I do what must be done. But you . . . you were never so ruthless before. Where has the honour of the Tsar's son gone?'

And that was worst of all.

Tsar Vyslav Andronovich was waiting for Prince Ivan in the Council Chamber of his kremlin at first light next morning. Mar'ya Morevna was there, seated to one side with the Grey Wolf lying at her feet and Sivka, haltered, was behind her chair. There were six soldiers armed with halberds around them, no over-ornamented useless weapons this time, just simple ashwood tipped with steel. The low sunlight shining through the chamber windows glittered from the interlace of bright scratches where their blades had been sharpened. Ivan looked along the Council Chamber, and saw the gold-worked iron perch that was the contention in this case sitting squarely in the middle of the floor in front of Vyslav Andronovich's throne. The Tsar was there, reading a scroll that he allowed to snap shut as Ivan was escorted into the room, and despite a shame-faced inclination to keep his gaze lowered, Ivan could not help but stare.

Vyslav Andronovich was the first person he had encountered in the Summer Country who truly looked as though he belonged in a world other than that of Russia. The Tsar was a giant. Ivan was a handspan under six feet in height, and sturdily built; Tsar Vyslav Andronovich looked to be almost half as tall again, and massive. Some accident had broken his long, straight nose and it had set crooked; the same accident had left a webwork of white scars over his high cheekbones. If he had been an ordinary man of ordinary height, he would have been simply ugly in the attractive way some ugly people are, for beneath the scars and the smashed nose his face was kindly and his mouth wide, full-lipped and prone to smile. Instead, having concluded that nothing could be done about his appearance, he had enhanced it with a head shaven in the Turkish manner and a great black spade-shaped beard, so that instead of being ugly, he was awesome. And the mouth beneath the sweep of his moustache was thin, compressed and most definitely not smiling now.

The two men-at-arms who served as his escort touched Ivan's shoulders as a signal he should stop where he was, in front of the perch and the great chair of state. Ivan would not have believed that he could feel any worse than at the moment of his arrest, but every time he was treated with more respect than a criminal deserved, his shame grew deeper still.

Vyslav Andronovich consulted the scroll again, then stared in silence at Prince Ivan for some minutes. All the muscles of his face seemed frozen in position, so that it was no longer possible even to hazard a guess at what he might be thinking, but Ivan felt sure that there were questions being asked behind those cool eyes as to why a young man who called himself a Prince and had been granted the guest-right due to such, should then be captured thieving from the public square. He was right.

'You style yourself Ivan Aleksandrovich, *Tsarevich Khorlovskiy*, from the lands of the Rus that lie beyond the standing stone and beyond the Summer Gate,' said the Tsar at last. His voice was all of a piece with the rest of him, not harsh, but deep and mellow as a note played on a cathedral organ so that Ivan was reminded, briefly and without relevance, of Sivka. *Tell the truth, little master*, said the horse's voice inside his head. Ivan ground his teeth on all the convincing excuses that sprang to mind, and finally nodded acknowledgement.

'Majesty, my father is the Tsar in Khorlov's kremlin,' he said, and waited as the reply was written down, then very quietly added, 'and he did not command me to do any of this.'

'No matter who commanded you,' said Vyslav Andronovich. 'A Tsar's son who steals from his host is no prince, and deserves no more consideration than a common thief. Tell me: why should you be treated other than as what you are?'

'Because I was not stealing, Majesty,' said Ivan. 'I was only borrowing. Borrowing can't be stealing, if the intent to keep the property is not there. I would have put the perch back after I was done with it.'

' "I", and "I", and "I", but never "we".' The Tsar twisted his heavy moustaches between fingers and thumbs, training the resultant points out across his face. 'You cover your companions well, Ivan Aleksandrovich, so that one might almost think them ignorant of this. But from what sage authority did you hear the interesting legal quibble between borrowing and theft?'

After a few seconds of silence, Tsar Vyslav Andronovich stroked his moustache again and smiled sadly. 'You need not say so aloud,' he said. 'But you were quoting that learned counsel your new servant, the Grey Wolf.' Ivan stiffened, stared straight ahead and said nothing. 'You should remember this, young sir. The man who believes everything the Grey Wolf tells him is the man most likely to be found half-eaten in the woods.'

Ivan heard a snarl, a scuffle of paws on the wooden floor, a thud and then a stifled yelp and knew well enough that the Grey Wolf had tried to take exception to the Tsar's words, and had been disciplined for it with the butt-end of a spear. 'Majesty,' he said, 'whatever you may think of him, my servant the Grey Wolf is not on trial. I would ask you of your courtesy, please restrain your guards.'

'Let it be done,' said Vyslav Andronovich, and made some gesture of instruction to the armed men in the Council Chamber. 'Now,' he said, 'I am wonderfully ignorant of the ways in which other times and places regulate their lives, but in the Summer Country at least, anyone who borrows an object without first asking for permission from that object's owner is stealing it. In fact, and in law. Did you ask for such permission?'

'Of course, Majesty.'

'Where?'

'At the hunting lodge of Countess Vasilisa Kurbit'yevna, Majesty.'

'But you did not ask for permission here?'

'You were away from the kremlin, Majesty, and—'

'And my High Steward was not good enough.'

'He was . . . Excuse me, Majesty, but he was just another intermediary, and I have had enough of intermediaries, no matter how trusted and efficient they may be. In this present matter, they have always refused me.'

'But you hoped that I might not?'

'A man can only hope, Majesty.'

'So why did you not wait to ask me? Why did you throw away your honour and take matters into your own hands?'

Ivan stared at Vyslav Andronovich and saw what he hoped was a glimmer of sympathy in the Tsar's dark eyes. 'Majesty, waiting needs time, and time is something I cannot spare! The matter of the Firebird concerns my father's life and the safety of his realm—'

'And goes beyond your honour as a *bogatyr*', and as a prince, and as your father's son?'

Ivan drew a long breath to calm himself, then nodded. 'Yes, Majesty. It does.'

'Then I think, Prince Ivan, that you should tell me all about it. Bring your lady wife up here, and – yes, and your other companions as well. If a man is going to hear truth, he can never hear it from too many sources.'

After ten minutes of discussion as intense as the crossfire of arrows, Tsar Vyslav Andronovich looked from Ivan to Mar'ya Morevna, and then at the unhuman faces of Sivka and the Grey Wolf. 'I give no reason why,' he said, 'but I believe your story. If you had asked *me* for the brief use of a Firebird's perch-of-honour, I would have loaned it to you without scruple or condition.'

Ivan gazed at the Tsar, wondering privately whether he would really have been so amenable to no more than a vague request for help. Until now, neither he nor Mar'ya Morevna had been in the habit of pouring out their woes in the hope of sympathy, and it still felt slightly improper. The troubles of Khorlov were none of the Summer Country's business, except where the Firebird was involved; and that was a matter which involved only the Firebird, rather than Princes and Tsars and Ministers, however sympathetic. 'And if I ask now?' he said.

'It seems a little late for such courtesy, Prince Ivan,' said Vyslav Andronovich. 'After all, no matter that your motive was of the best, you have done me a wrong.'

'So what can I do to set it right?' said Ivan, knowing that the conversation had taken on the grim inevitability of actors in a play.

'You were willing to steal one thing for yourself,' said Vyslav Andronovich. 'If you want it so very badly, then make yourself willing to steal something else. A crime, shall we say, to cancel a crime.'

'Be careful, Vanyushka,' said Mar'ya Morevna, laying her hand on his sleeve as though to hold him back from a dangerous decision. 'All the lords of the Summer Country disapprove of theft just as much as this Tsar—'

'Scarcely, *gospozha* Tsarevna,' said Vyslav Andronovich. 'I disapprove of it far more when I am the victim than when I stand to benefit.' The Grey Wolf growled low and deep in his chest, and one of Sivka's hoofs scraped across the floor to leave a gouge that would be there when the kremlin crumbled. The Tsar looked down at the mark and smiled faintly. 'You have staunch supporters,' he said, 'but so that the decision can be yours alone, I think my guards will escort them all to their original places. I would not want your choice influenced by your friends, Prince Ivan. Of course,' he said once they were alone again, 'it may make things easier to know that you are not so much stealing someone else's property, as recovering a gift which I gave away by mistake. In a fit of excessive generosity. Most excessive generosity, and a most unfortunate mistake.'

'So explain the error and just ask for it, or them, or whatever, to be returned.'

'Would your father the Tsar do such a thing, Prince Ivan?'

Ivan shrugged. 'Perhaps. Or perhaps not. The question has never arisen. But despite that, you still want me to reach a quick decision?'

'Quick,' said Vyslav Andronovich, 'and correct.'

'Correct for you, Majesty, or for me?'

'Just correct is good enough.'

Saying 'yes' would be so easy, and the Tsar, who knew better than most, had assured him that everything would be all right afterwards; no blame, no accusations, and all the help he might need. But no matter what Vyslav Andronovich might say, there was still the way that the guards had looked at him when they found him in the square and pried his fingers away from the Firebird's perch. Against that, there was the sound of Mar'ya Morevna's voice and the way she had held his hands and assured him that what he had done was right. He could deny it, make it just one more thing done for the sake of convenience, put a knife in her trust and twist the blade. But some things were worse than winning. They were worse even than dying. Some things could not be lived with.

Prince Ivan looked at Tsar Vyslav Andronovich. 'Then the answer I find most correct,' he said, 'is *no*.'

The Tsar gazed thoughtfully at him. 'You are young, and rash. That much has been proved already. I will give you one minute to reconsider—'

'No, Majesty,' said Ivan. His voice was cool and neutral, neither mannerly or rude. 'I don't need a minute. Or an hour, or a day. Or however long my life in the Summer Country might be. I was wrong. What I did was wrong. But two wrongs never make a right. I said no. I mean no. Now make an end.'

'As you wish,' said Vyslav Andronovich, and with a nod towards his guards, clapped his hands together.

Chapter Nine

Shadows danced through the cold and pillared darkness of the *Unterschloss*, and the flames of torch and candle fluttered in the air stirred by the movement of huge iron gates as they were swung shut. A great echoing clang rolled up from the crypt beneath the fortress chapel, and it was as if that noise formally signalled an end to the funeral proceedings, for the two files of sergeants who had acted as an escort to the bier were already relaxing even before they were dismissed.

Albrecht von Düsberg took a heavy black key from the crowded ring hanging from his belt and twirled it in the lock, then pushed at the cold metal of the doors to make certain that they were secure. It had been explained to him by the *Hauskomtur* that the checking of the crypt door was a traditional part of any interment in Castle Thorn, whether of knight or unfortunate guest, but in von Düsberg's view, it was one of the more pointless things to do. Nobody outside the burial chamber would want to enter it before they absolutely had to, and certainly nobody inside would be coming out without assistance. But Kuno von Buxhövden had insisted, so Albrecht went through each and every step of the procedure and kept his opinions to himself. He was glad to be out of the crypt; it was dank, chilly, and faintly foul-smelling, since even though the cold that breathed from the rock walls ground into the marrow of a man's bones, it still wasn't really cold enough. There was a miasma of corruption hanging inside that was a better *memento mori* than any number of carven skeletons.

'Surely by now Father Giacchetti sleeps with the saints,' said Brother Johann Thalen, and crossed himself for what had to be the hundredth time. He had been repeating the sign with a sort of feverish intensity since Giacchetti died, as though it was a shield against the intrusive realities of life and death. Von Düsberg glanced at him, and thought such a sudden display of delicacy was an ironic attitude for *ein Schönling* who kept company with an inquisitor. With a recent private conversation with the Grand

Master still very much in his mind, he began to wonder if the boy had actually started to think for himself at last. Father-Inquisitor Arnald had seemed less troubled by the death of the Apostolic Notary, and the Grand Master considered it likely that he would shortly be presented with a Papal letter of authority stating that in the event of Father Giacchetti's sudden, unexpected and unfortunate death, Father Arnald would succeed him. Whether that letter had been written in Rome and signed by the Holy Father was another matter. Brother Johann was skilled with a pen, had the calligrapher's great advantage of young eyes, and the even greater advantage that as an inquisitor's secretary, nobody would dare to question the authenticity of whatever papers he carried. Albrecht smiled grimly and said nothing.

Hermann von Salza, however, was not so reticent. 'Certainly our late brother of the Benedictines won't lack for good companions,' said the Grand Master. 'There are many brave knights laid to rest down here.' Then he grinned, and with his features underlit by the candle in his hand, the effect was unnerving even to von Düsberg, who had been half-expecting something of the sort. 'Very few saints, though, and I doubt that they would want Father Giacchetti in their company in any case, unless somewhere in the calendar there's a patron for stupid old men.'

'*Herr Hochmeister?*' Brother Johann didn't understand; or didn't want to understand. 'How could he be stupid? He was a good and holy man, and he died of the cold in this dreadful place, and of the infirmities of his own venerable age.'

Von Salza held the candle higher and stared for several seconds at the yellow spearpoint of its flame. 'Did he?' he said, and blew the candle out. 'I thought he died because he couldn't heed a warning.'

Father Arnald had been pacing to and fro, waiting for the final business of the funeral to be concluded so that, presumably, he could present von Salza with the letter. The inquisitor was walking slowly, head lowered in apparent thought or prayer, through a pool of the wan light that filtered down the stairs from the chapel above. Only Albrecht von Düsberg was placed well enough to see how, at von Salza's words, he stopped in his tracks and his head came up with all the colour drained out of his face. 'Explain that,' he said. 'Explain it at once.'

247

'Right here and now, in front of everyone?' said von Salza in well-simulated surprise. 'I'd have thought such things were better discussed in private. *Fra Tressler*, have one of the tower rooms heated so that—'

'Stay right here, all of you!' rasped Father Arnald in a harsh voice, even though von Düsberg and the other *Ordensoffiziere* hadn't moved and indeed had no intention of doing so. The Father-Inquisitor stalked across the crypt until he stood face to face with Hermann von Salza. The friar was breathing heavily and his fists were clenched, while the Grand Master looked calm and at ease with the world. 'There are things that need to be said between us, *Herr Hochmeister*, and this is as good a place as any.'

'Is it?' Von Salza folded his arms and made to lean back against the wall, then looked from the damp stone to the white silk of his mantle and thought better of it. Albrecht von Düsberg concealed a smile. 'You'll have to speak for yourself, in that case. I have no great fondness for standing around in an open grave.'

'A grave that holds a man you put in it,' said Arnald.

'Now I think that *you* had better explain, Father-Inquisitor. No knight would be so free in making such allegation unless he was willing to defend it with his sword. Since you, however, are protected by your cloth . . .' The insinuation was obvious.

'Protected? As Father Giacchetti was protected? Then the protection of my cloth counts for very little!'

Kuno von Buxhövden took a step forward and laid one big hand sympathetically on the inquisitor's shoulder. 'Please, Father, come away from this place. It's not helping. Even a man of the cloth can become over-wrought by grief for one of his brethren. There's no crime in it. And don't worry about the rest; you obviously don't realize the gravity of what you're saying.'

Father Arnald glared at him and flung off the *Hauskomtur*'s hand so violently that von Buxhövden swayed back in anticipation of a blow. 'Do I not, then? So why will nobody tell me what veiled warning Giacchetti ignored – warnings like those I've heard a dozen times since I came to this castle.'

'Veiled warning?' Von Buxhövden's honest face was puzzled. 'There was nothing veiled about it.'

'At long last! Praise be to God, a man who isn't afraid to utter honest threats!'

Von Salza and his Treasurer, the only two men privy to this particular secret, watched as the *Hauskomtur* backed away. His puzzlement had given way to nervousness. 'You aren't well, Father-Inquisitor,' he said. 'Not well at all.'

'Father Arnald,' said the Grand Master, 'perhaps it's just as well that you insisted there be witnesses present when we spoke. Brother Johann?'

'*Herr Hochmeister?*'

'Have you ever heard any of my knights or officers utter a threat aginst Father Giacchetti?'

'No, *Herr Hochmeister.*'

'Then write, boy. Write that down, the way that you've been writing everything else.'

'Yes, write,' said Father Arnald. 'Write how they killed Giacchetti, as a warning to me!'

'Write that accusation down as well, Brother Johann,' said von Düsberg quickly. He had been expecting the charge to be made eventually, but not so soon, and not so conveniently before witnesses. 'Kuno, Wilhelm, make your marks as validation of it. Your seals can be appended later.'

The Grand Master watched as the *Hauskomtur* and his steward fumbled briefly with the secretary's pen, then stared at Father Arnald for a moment. 'Kill that old man as a warning?' he said at last. 'Don't flatter yourself. Think it, if it gratifies your vanity; but we are the Teutonic Order, not the Order of Assassins. Our killing is done in the open, and if someone is enough our enemy to warrant being warned of it, then he already warrants killing. But you, Father-Inquisitor, are very much alive. What does that suggest?'

Arnald's mouth worked, but no words came out.

'Father Giacchetti killed himself, in spite of *Hauskomtur* von Buxhövden's many warnings to him. I'm sorry if I insult his memory, Brother Johann, but he was worthy to join the company of saints only if sainthood can be equated with stubbornness and stupidity. If a man chooses to glorify God by mortifying his flesh, well and good. Fasting and silence strengthens the spirit without weakening the body, and a Crusader must always be strong in body to fight for the faith. We of the Order have lived in Prussia for long enough that we might be expected to know something of

249

the climate. Father Giacchetti thought otherwise, and acted as though he was still in Rome. He was told a wearisome number of times that there was no sin in dressing warmly, in sleeping in a bed, in having a brazier in his room. He ignored all of that, and we all know the consequence, may he rest in peace.'

Von Salza crossed himself, then glowered at Father-Inquisitor Arnald. 'It was only through the good graces of my officers that he was not buried without rites, as a suicide deserves! And you choose that funeral as the time to accuse me of his murder. With what proof? By what *right*, other than your own self-importance? Because of it, you wanted an escort of my knights to bring you safely back to Rome. I refused. Now I withdraw that refusal, Father Arnald of the Holy Inquisition, because I want to make quite certain that you – and what has just been written down – both reach the Pope intact. What happens afterwards is his concern.'

The Grand Master drew himself up very straight, and made the sign of the cross again, this time right in front of the inquisitor's confused and angry eyes. 'Perhaps von Buxhövden is right, and you aren't well. If so, you have my pity.'

'I don't want your pity!'

'All the more reason to grant it, then. And you also have my leave to go.' Hermann von Salza moved his hand slightly, and the two files of sergeants who had flanked Father Giacchetti's coffin moved to flank the inquisitor instead. 'Take him away.'

The Tsar's guards came to attention at that handclap and saluted him, then all of them – even those who stood behind the throne – marched from the Council Chamber. Vyslav Andronovich watched them go, then summoned a servant with a chair. The same man brought Ivan his dirk and sabre and helped him fasten each sheathed blade to his belt. The return of his weapons made Ivan feel better, but more even than that, he appreciated the gesture of trust. Another chair was brought for Mar'ya Morevna, and then the Tsar sat back in his throne and stroked once more at his moustache.

'This is more comfortable,' he said. 'But I dislike having unanswered questions hanging over a discussion.'

'So *no* was the right answer after all,' said Ivan. 'I had begun to wonder.'

Tsar Vyslav Andronovich smiled slightly, revealing square, strong white teeth amid that thicket of black beard. 'No need to wonder. The test was a crude one, but necessary. I had to be sure of your motives. Noble reasons for a theft are easy to claim, but hard to maintain. Two wrongs do not make a right, you said. A thief would not think that way. I ask pardon of you both, and offer you some food and drink as a small recompense.'

He clapped his hands once more and gave rapid instructions to the servants who came hurrying in. Within a few minutes, two small tables – each one already set with silver and crystal – were whisked in and set down before Ivan and Mar'ya Morevna. She fell to with a will, but Ivan contented himself with merely eyeing the food on the plates before reaching for an ice-encrusted vodka flask instead.

'If our explanation satisfies you, Majesty,' he said, pouring three fingers' depth of the icy spirit into a small glass, 'then might we ask again for the loan of the Firebird's perch?'

Vyslav Andronovich sipped daintily at his own cup, a handsome thing of onyx and silver, and looked at him over the rim. 'I can do better than that. I'll *give* you a perch-of-honour, so that the Firebird can ride with you when you return to the wide white world. If your intent is still to prevent an impending war, well and good, but if you need to put a stop to one already being waged' – the cool, disinterested way in which he spoke of the unspeakable made Ivan shiver – 'then delay should be avoided at all costs.'

'In that case, Majesty,' he said after putting his vodka back *zalpom*, at a single gulp, 'how can we make certain that the Firebird who next visits your kremlin is the one we need?'

The Tsar's moustache moved as his mouth formed a thin smile. 'The lady your wife knows. Don't you, *sudarynya*?'

'Do I?' said Mar'ya Morevna. For just a moment she looked rather less confident than the Tsar's words made her appear, and then she nodded. 'Set the usual forms of invitation before the perch: fragrant wood, fine vodka, a gold coin – and the tail-feather.'

'Just so,' said Vyslav Andronovich. 'The tail-feather most of all.'

'But no spells?' said Ivan. 'Nothing to command it to come here? You said yourself, Majesty, delays should be avoided.'

'There will be no delays. And besides, making this particular Firebird angry with you is something to be avoided even more.' The Tsar laughed. 'By the sound of what you've told me, it's probably not in the best of humour at the moment, and trying to give it still more orders won't do anything to improve its temper. Do your people have the proverb about how to catch wasps?'

Ivan poured himself more vodka and thought for a moment. 'Is that the one about using honey, not vinegar?'

'Exactly. I could quote you pieces of wisdom in that vein for an hour, until you fled screaming.'

'No need, Majesty. When I was younger, my tutor was also my father's High Steward and First Minister.'

The Tsar grunted in sympathy. 'Then you know exactly what I mean. But the honey, in this instance at least, is the feather. The Firebird will want it back.'

'And what will its reaction be to the man who pulled that feather out in the first place?'

Vyslav Andronovich glanced at him, drew breath to say something encouraging, and then shrugged instead. 'If I knew, I would tell you. But . . . well, you're returning property to its rightful owner without any attached conditions – which I would strongly advise, if you were considering anything else – and you intend asking help from an invited guest rather than demanding service of an indentured servant. Those will all stand in your favour.'

'I see. Thank you.' Even when Mar'ya Morevna gave his hand a reassuring squeeze, Ivan didn't feel very happy at the prospect of meeting the Firebird again if it was already 'out of humour', as the Tsar so coyly put it. He had seen at first hand just what it could do. The second glass of vodka went the same way as the first.

'Don't worry, Vanyushechka.' Mar'ya Morevna grinned at him with a cheery confidence that had to be real, because he knew she wasn't that good an actress. 'At least when you ask for something, you do it more politely than Baba Yaga.'

'Yes, Baba Yaga,' said Sivka, who had been listening in silence except for the occasional flick of an ear. 'Of all the things that could be summoned to do her bidding, why something so splendid as a Firebird? When I was a grubby colt behind the other Baba Yaga's stable, I never saw anything but dirt and foulness.'

The Grey Wolf raised his head from his paws and grinned with all his teeth. 'That,' he said softly, 'is the point. This witch is arrogant. She wanted the satisfaction of the vile when they bend the beautiful to their will. And it gave her more than that. Her own hand was hidden.' He looked at Ivan and Mar'ya Morevna, and all but wagged his tail. 'If I were other than a wolf, and carried gold, I would wager it that neither of you thought of Baba Yaga until I mentioned her by name.'

'The Baba Yaga that *I* knew was dead,' said Ivan. 'I saw her fall into the burning river with my own eyes; and the notion of a hag like that having any living relatives never even crossed my mind.'

'It seems, Prince Ivan,' said Tsar Vyslav Andronovich, 'that even ancient hags have mothers. And I suspect that though this Baba Yaga of yours has never loved anything but herself, she would want to have revenge on you just for its own sake. Her daughter's death is just a convenient excuse, and whatever rewards she has gained from these, these—'

'Teutonic Knights, Majesty.'

'Thank you. So long as there was a chance to hurt her enemies – you, Tsarevich, and everything you hold dear – I'm sure she would pay *them*.'

'She's been stealing, or having the Firebird steal, books of magic and the like,' said Mar'ya Morevna. 'That would also divert suspicion from their involvement, since from the little I know of the military orders, they don't approve of sorcery.'

'You mean, my dear lady,' said Tsar Vyslav Andronovich with a vast and gentle cynicism, 'that their public voice claims not to. The private attitude of their high and mighty will be quite different.'

Ivan snapped a last shot of vodka down his throat and stood up. 'We should begin, Majesty. If it won't stick to my hand again, I'll take the Firebird's perch back out to the square and—'

'No need for that. This won't be like the normal way that the Firebirds fly from one place to another in the Summer Country. For one thing, I don't think flying is involved at all. Prepare the perch-of-honour to welcome it right here and, whether you believe this or not, it will just' – the Tsar waved both hands in an expansive, descriptive gesture – 'appear in the middle of the room.'

Glancing quickly at Mar'ya Morevna, Ivan smiled. 'Just

appear?' he said softly, half to himself. The blisters on his hand were not yet fully healed. 'Yes, Majesty, I think I can believe it.'

'Once the gifts are prepared, I'll have the doors closed and guarded. In the bad times, before my father's father's time, my Council Chamber was the strong place of this kremlin; a redoubt where the Tsar and his family could retreat and hold out against their enemies until rescuers arrived. There hasn't been war or raiding in the Summer Country for half a hundred years, so I use it more as a room for private discussions.'

Mar'ya Morevna had studied the door earlier. It was triple-ply oak, with every second layer of planks running at right angles to the one above so that they could not be split along the grain. Lock and hinges were of black steel, with large, imposing rivets, and the bolt on the inside was a bar of forged iron thicker than her wrist. She approved of such security, but at the same time it was scarcely courteous either to the Tsar or his subjects to automatically assume such steps were necessary. 'I can see how privacy could be assured,' she said, 'but is there so much need for it?'

'That depends,' said Vyslav Andronovich, 'on how sensitive you regard your own affairs.'

'In Russia, very. Here . . . hardly at all. A token couple of guards outside the door will be more than enough.'

'So be it.' The Tsar clapped his hands again. When the servants came in to clear away the small tables, two others were with them. One carried a gold plate piled high with chips of fresh-cut cedar and sandalwood so fragrant that Ivan could smell it directly the servant brought it into the room. The other carried a flask of vodka like the one he had been punishing in one hand, and a fine silver beaker in the other. The beaker was set down in front of the perch and then, even though from its size it was properly meant for ale, it was filled to brimming with more than two pints of the best 'Tsar's vodka', *pshenichnaya*, distilled from wheat, thick with a cold far below that at which water froze, and innocently clear. The metal of the beaker immediately began to frost white, so that its embossed design resembled something carved from a block of snow. Misty vapour rolled down its sides and drifted on the floor.

'Thirsty creatures, Firebirds,' said Ivan to nobody in particular, 'and cheaper to keep for a week than a fortnight.'

Vyslav Andronovich himself provided the gold coin, an odd,

old, heavy thing that he chose with care from among the selection presented to him by the servant who had carried in the plate.

'A medallion?' asked Mar'ya Morevna, looking at its lumpy outline curiously. The Tsar held it up between finger and thumb.

'No,' he said. 'A coin from the old Greek times, a gold *stater* of Aleksandr *Bol'shoy*, who thought he had conquered the world. It seems appropriate to use it against these German knights who seem to have such similar notions.'

'Mother Russia isn't the whole world.'

'Tell that to the peasants,' said Ivan. 'It's all they have.'

Mar'ya Morevna raised her eyebrows and turned to look at him, seeming not too annoyed at being corrected. 'Spoken like your father. You may well prove a Princely ruler after all. Blood will out.'

Ivan leaned over to pat her gently on the cheek. 'I'd much rather it stayed where it is, thanks.'

The Firebird's feather was in one of the saddlebags stacked neatly to one side of the Council Chamber, carefully laid between two flat pieces of wood to keep its quill and barbs from being damaged, and then bound in strips of leather. When Ivan opened it, there was only the slightest delicate singe-mark in the face of the wood, a perfect pokerwork representation of the feather. Even though it had long cooled from its original furnace-throated glow, like the stolen grimoire *Enciervanul Doamnisoar* it had never grown completely cold, and the confinement of what little heat remained had turned the feather warm again. Prince Ivan hefted it thoughtfully in his hand, feeling that same strange not-quite-there sensation as before. Both his father and Dmitriy Vasil'yevich Strel'tsin had told him – frequently, oh so very frequently – about how much there was in the world that he didn't yet know but had to learn before he could be a good Tsar to his and to Mar'ya Morevna's people. And then he encountered something like this. No matter how much one learned, there was always more.

Once all was prepared and everything in its place, the Tsar said, all they had to do was wait. So they waited. Conversation was shallow, bright and pointless, because every few minutes either Prince Ivan's or Mar'ya Morevna's eyes would slide sideways to stare at the iron-and-gold cruciform frame of the perch, and they

255

would lose the thread of whatever they were saying. Ivan wished he had kept a tighter hold on the vodka-flask and not let the servants make away with it so easily. The fierce spirit wouldn't have helped matters, indeed he doubted if even the huge measure set out for the Firebird would make him drunk right now, but at least it would give him something to do with his hands besides a desire to nibble at his nails.

Then Mar'ya Morevna sat up very straight, her head on one side as though she was listening to something, and raised her hand for silence. All three of them heard the sound at the same time, but only Ivan recognized it. The last time he had heard that thin hissing, like a forge-bellows or the pouring of molten metal, the circumstances had been such as to make him remember.

A blast of wind hammered at the air of the Council Chamber, driving heat and glare before it like leaves in an autumn gale, and the source of that wind expanded out of the heart of darkness lying behind the light to become a pair of monstrous, glowing wings. Sivka squealed and reared up, raking at the gust of hot air with his great hoofs, while the Grey Wolf chose the part of more discretion and lay as flat as he was able. The Firebird hovered before them for a moment, like a kestrel made all of gold and flame, then settled onto the arms of the perch with a rasping clank of claws on iron and folded its wings with all the leisured haughtiness of a Prince arranging his robes to best advantage around his throne. Sparks flew, but they were only such sparks as might be struck from flint by steel, and though the room had grown much warmer than before, it was not entirely uncomfortable.

All the discomfort, for Ivan at least, was centred around the look in the Firebird's eyes. Despite all the armour he had been wearing during their last encounter, it knew him. He was prepared as best he could be for almost anything except what happened, because it just sat there as quietly as a falcon on its perching-block, watching them, doing and saying nothing. The heat it radiated – though much less than the furnace-blast that Ivan remembered all too well – worked quickly, melting the ornamental frost coating the beaker of vodka and bringing the alcohol in it to a bubbling, blue-flaming boil. The Firebird thrust its beak into the inferno and drank daintily, throwing its head back with each sip so that an arc of spitting sapphire droplets sprayed across the floor. It was as well, thought Ivan, that the Council Chamber was tiled rather than timbered; but then if Tsar Vyslav Andronovich was in the habit of entertaining *zhar'yanoi* fire-creatures, which from his knowledge of their habits seemed likely, he would have had the tiles installed as a matter of course.

When its vodka was finished, and the Firebird actually picked up the beaker in its beak and tilted it so that the last few drops could trickle blazing down its throat, it set about the pieces of wood and soon filled the air with a scent like burning incense. After that it preened for a moment, snapped up and swallowed the gold Greek *stater* almost as an afterthought, then spread its wings and tail out like something on a banner and bowed low to the Tsar.

'Hail, Vyslav Andronovich!' it said. 'And greeting to your guests.'

Though he had been listening for it, Prince Ivan heard no threat in the Firebird's voice. It was a harsh sound, almost metallic but not especially unpleasant, and he guessed that the creature was waiting for the Tsar's advice before reacting to their presence one way or the other. Everything about it seemed restrained by comparison with what he had last seen: less hot, less bright, less shrill and above all less savage. It was almost as if the Firebird's humour had been restored after its *zakuska* snack, enough vodka to put three strong men under the table and the presence of at least one friend.

'Hail, Firebird!' said Vyslav Andronovich, 'and be welcomed as another guest.'

The Firebird looked at them again; or rather, it spared just a glance for Mar'ya Morevna, then put its head first on one side and then the other as it studied Ivan up and down. 'Guest?' it said shrewdly. 'Or performer of favours?'

'That depends entirely on you, *gospodin* Firebird,' said Ivan, hoping desperately that he had given the title its correct gender. 'I ask only that you listen to my – to our request.'

'Listening can't hurt,' prompted the Tsar, and the Firebird's head snapped around to shoot him the same spiky stare down the curved blade of its beak as had pinned Ivan in place that last time.

'No. But other things can.' The stare transferred itself to Prince Ivan and, if anything, intensified until he felt as if he was being glared at by matching black gemstones with hot coals at their centres. 'My feather, Tsarevich?'

Rather than setting it in front of the perch with all the other gifts, Ivan had kept the long, glowing plume cradled in his hand. Now he looked down at it and flinched just a little, realizing that returning it was to be a physical gesture rather than, as he had supposed, the feather simply vanishing away and reappearing in its proper place.

'Where, ah, where do I . . . put it?' he said.

The Firebird snapped its beak in irritation, but when it also gave him a long, slow blink Ivan felt his suppressed worries – all right, he thought, call it terror and be honest with yourself as well as everyone else in the Summer Country – fade away. That protracted blink had been a sign of amusement, and deliberately human enough for him to understand. 'You really wouldn't like it if I told you what that question brought to mind,' it said. 'But lay it in front of me. I have to eat it before another will grow.'

That made a sort of sense. Ivan walked closer, still on his guard, and leaned over to set the feather gently on the plate that had contained the wood-chippings. As he straightened, the Firebird's head shot out on its long neck almost too fast for his eyes to follow. Ivan responded more to movement sensed than seen, flinging himself sideways as he might have ducked a sword-stroke. He wasn't quick enough.

'That's what it feels like, more or less,' said the Firebird, rather muffled because the hank of Ivan's hair that it had just wrenched out by the roots was still in its beak and beginning to singe most nastily. It spat the hair out, stamped its feet once or twice so that more sparks went skipping over the floor, and then settled the plumage ruffled by its lunge. 'Now you know it, now we're even, now we can talk.'

Ivan Aleksandrovich sat up from where his dive and roll had sent him and managed by great strength of character and a lot of common sense not to shoot the bird the sort of glare that it deserved. Except, of course, that it was right, and didn't deserve anything of the sort. He had been squarely paid, as the Firebird and the raw patch on his scalp both told him, but first landing hard on the tiled floor and then rolling over on the even harder pommel of his sabre had put interest on the payment. He investigated the plucked spot with one finger, winced, and said several of the words with which Russian is abundantly supplied. It didn't ease the sting, but it relieved his feelings.

Their discussion with the Firebird made him feel still better. Ivan had never dared to hope that it would be so amenable to their requests, but a lot of that had to do with its own barely suppressed fury at having been made such use of. He had a definite feeling that it would have agreed to anything just so long as it could break free of Baba Yaga's malign influence, and that being presented to the Princes of the Rus as this year's reason why they shouldn't fight was a small price to pay.

There was another price as well, and the Firebird wanted to collect that one in person. 'Are you proficient in the sorceries of Gate and circle?' it said.

'No,' said Mar'ya Morevna, and Ivan knew from that flat reply that she was not just being honest in the way of the Summer Country. A lack of skill in anything irked her, and most noticeably if it involved a branch of the Art Magic when she was adept at so many others. The Firebird, however, merely stared at her from its hot, dark eyes, until finally she said, 'But I have the spells for constructing a Gate with me.'

'Then prepare one. I will show you the proper symbols for source and destination.' The great beak snapped twice, angrily. 'They have become part of my mind, this past while.'

With the manuscript of copied spells already in her hand, Mar'ya Morevna hesitated again. '*Gospodin* Firebird, I've seen you come into this room without a Gate to guide you,' she said. 'The Gatespells are dangerous, and—'

'Not to such as I. Proceed.'

'But why resort to one at all?'

The Firebird raised its crest and ruffled all its feathers, then preened them back into place with vicious jerks and claws and beak. 'There is a matter of honour that must be attended to,' it said after a few moments.

'Baba Yaga?'

'Who else has kept me enslaved to her bidding?' The harsh voice grew shrill as the Firebird's temper began to slip. 'Who forced me to come and go at her command from the confines of a cage, and even in my despite scamped on the very substance of the summoning?'

259

It bated, hawklike, smiting the air with its spread wings until they left tendrils of flame and sparks in their wake with each new stroke. Everyone in the Council Chamber, whether man or woman, horse or wolf, flinched from the fiery rush of wind and protected their faces until the Firebird settled back onto the perch.

'You will open me a Gate to the castle of the Teutonic Knights,' said the Firebird as calmly as if its spasm of rage had never happened, 'and the reason for it is this. Were I to go to that castle now, by my own will, I would still be subject to the wishes of the witch. But if you send me, to go, to do a certain deed, and to return, then your desires, though they be my desires, would have precedence over hers.'

'Now I understand,' said Mar'ya Morevna. 'But would you willingly put yourself under my command?'

'There is a thing called trust,' said the Firebird simply. Mar'ya Morevna and Prince Ivan both bowed at the compliment. 'And I have been unwillingly commanded for long enough.'

When it was drawn at last, the circle reminded Ivan of the convoluted pattern that had been constructed in the snowy courtyard of Mar'ya Morevna's kremlin, to bring them East of the Sun and West of the Moon. But there were differences; he was not schooled enough in sorcery to spot them yet, but he knew that they were there in the same way as a man might know the direction of the sun even with his eyes closed. Ivan stalked around the Gating circle, eyeing it as he might a viper in the grass, and he took as good care to stay well clear of its perimeter.

'These symbols go here,' said the Firebird, peering first at Mar'ya Morevna's spells and then at the circle on the floor, directing her brush with gestures of beak and claw. 'And these, over there.'

As the symbols which might have been letters or as easily ideograms or numbers were painted in, the aspect of the circle changed. Ivan needed no training in the Art Magic to understand this: it was the difference between the sheathed sword and the naked blade.

'If you want my opinion.' The Grey Wolf was at his elbow, bristling. 'I would not share the entire kremlin with that thing.'

'And here we are, in the same room.'

'If I was certain this was your idea, dear Prince Ivan,' said the Grey Wolf, showing his teeth, 'I would probably bite you.'

'I suppose the correct response is to say I'd let you,' said Ivan, 'but I'm sure you'll understand if I don't—'

The crash as the door of the Council Chamber flew open cut his words off short. One of the guards that Tsar Vyslav Andronovich had stationed outside it came in, but nobody took the man to task for his rude entrance, because he came in backwards and already dead.

With the heavy door wide open, all the sounds that it had muffled could be clearly heard: the shuffle of feet shifting position, the quick rasp of breathing, and every once in a while the sharp clang of steel on steel. Then there was a single dreadful *crunch* and the second guard followed the first through the doorway. His body slid across the floor with the force of whatever had struck it, and a horrible foreshortening effect gave the illusion that his head had been driven partway down into his own chest.

Then a third man stepped inside, slammed the door and bolted it, and when they saw the mace cradled like a child in the crook of his left arm, nobody thought that the guard's manner of death was an illusion any more.

'Dieter Balke, *Landmeister* of Livonia,' said the man, giving a little jerky bow. Except for Balke's claimed title, the language he spoke was Russian, but his accent was German. This Dieter Balke could be nothing but a Teutonic Knight, and from the sound of it a high-ranked and therefore dangerously skilful one. He surveyed the chamber, betraying no surprise at anything he saw, then turned to face Ivan. 'You,' Balke said, pointing with the spiked head of the mace, 'are Prince Ivan Khorlovskiy. Yes?'

Ivan's *shashka* sabre came out of its scabbard and up to a guard position, but even that razory curve of steel looked insignificant by comparison with the ponderous mace that Balke was carrying as easily as if it had been a riding-whip. If ever there was a time when he might have wanted to deny his real name, this was it. How and why Balke had come to search for them in the Summer Country, Ivan didn't know; but he was willing to wager the Gate spells came into it somewhere. Mar'ya Morevna's father Koldun had found that sorcery in Prussia, and the Teutonic Knights owned the entire province by now. What method the *Landmeister* had used to track them to Vyslav Andronovich's kremlin was another matter. Ivan had a feeling that he had seen Balke before, because the big knight looked horribly familiar. His mind's eye could see that distant figure on the hill, walking purposefully down towards Vasilisa Kurbit'yevna's hunting lodge.

'How did you know where we were, *Nyemetskiy rytsar*?' he asked, lowering the point of his sabre a little and taking care to sound almost casual about the question.

'You ask that, who left a trail that a blind man could follow!' said Balke, and laughed. 'The Teutonic Knights have friends in unexpected places.'

'Even here?' asked Ivan. Balke grinned at him and closed those big white teeth of his on any other information about such sources of friendship. 'Who knows the Teutonic Knights in the Summer Country?'

'Is that what you call it? What with all the work to get my other questions answered, that was one I never thought to ask.'

Before Ivan could draw breath to say anything else, Balke had poised his mace easily in both hands and was walking forward with the quick stride of someone with a job to do and no more time to waste about it. 'Enough talk. Time to die.'

Ivan dropped his guard; trying to block such a mass of metal was asking for a snapped blade, and glissading the mace-strokes wouldn't work either, because of the spikes that would surely snag somewhere. There would be a broken sword again. The only safe thing to do until he had sized up his opponent was to dodge—

'Vanya! *Vanya!* The Gate! For God's sake, the Gate!'

—And the area for dodging in had suddenly shrunk by half. The presence of the Gating circle forced him sideways instead of back, nothing like as far from Balke's mace, or even from the circle, as he had wanted. But that curtailed space worked both ways. If he had little room in which to move, then so had Balke; and there was a good deal more of the knight, height and weight and balance, all of it affected by the momentum of that ponderous iron club he carried.

When the mace-head screeched across the floor in a shower of sparks and splintered tiles less than a finger's thickness from his ankles, Ivan realized with a jolt that Balke had long since come to terms with his size. The man moved as lightly as a fencer. Only a frantic jump straight up and as much backwards as he dared had saved one or maybe both of his feet from being mashed. Ivan

262

ripped out his long Circassian dagger and crouched low behind the blades of sword and dirk, trying to remember what Guard-Captain Akimov had taught him to do.

Tire him out. That was what Akimov would recommend. *Let him move around, let him drag his great lump of ironwork after you, let him—*

But don't let him get so close!

Ivan ducked and dodged in a frantic wrench that couldn't be dignified by calling it a sidestep, and the chair over which he tripped exploded into matchwood so hard and fast that he felt the sting of splinters in his cheek and jaw. The spiked mace whirred as it swung through the air again in a great wide swashing blow, invitation to come in under its arc and use a dagger. Ivan didn't attempt it; not yet, anyway. Balke was probably hoping he might try such a tactic, because the end of the mace-haft, metal like the rest of it, came to an ugly conical point almost certainly for use against someone who came too close.

Ivan moved sideways instead, risking a quick glance over his shoulder to make sure he wasn't going to be trapped by wall or corner. Nobody would help him, because nobody could: there was barely enough fighting space for the two of them as it was, and they were carrying the only weapons in the room. However much Mar'ya Morevna and the Tsar might want to interfere, they were wise enough to know that, unarmed, it would be a literally fatal error.

Cramped as he was between walls and furniture and the whispering threat of the open Gate, Ivan couldn't change position enough to force Balke to follow him. Instead of moving about and tiring himself, the German knight planted the ball of one foot squarely into the gouge he had driven through the tiles. Well-braced by that rough, sound footing, he merely swivelled almost on the spot to keep Ivan always in front, where the mace poised low in both big hands could reach him.

Ivan glowered, wishing that the *Landmeister* had chosen anywhere else to stand. Mar'ya Morevna had primed the Gate to Castle Thorn just an instant before Balke came bursting in, and now, with the German knight and his lethal mace in the way, there was no chance for her to get close enough to disable the spell. Ivan could actually hear it, a sinister hissing sound like sand poured across parchment. One step too far, and he would be wrenched from where he faced just one adversary and flung into a fortress filled with them.

'Stand still, damn you,' snarled Dieter Balke, sounding less cool and collected than he had been. Ivan narrowed his eyes a little at that. If the man was getting impatient because he had been expecting this fight to finish quickly, then maybe, just maybe, it was because he knew he couldn't wield so monstrous a weapon as that mace for very long. He risked a tentative jab with the sabre's point to test Balke's speed again, and as he felt the tingling thump of impact in his wrist, tried to convince himself that the *Landmeister*'s swing was fractionally slower than it had been.

Balke laughed, and poised his mace again. 'You're slow, *Rus'kiy*,' he said. 'Slow in your movement and slow in your mind. Still wondering how I found you?' He jerked his head towards where the Firebird sat on its perch like a heraldic eagle. 'You asked one little bird for information. I asked another. It took time but your little sparrow Countess sang a pretty song of who you were and where you went.' The man grinned again, a thinner, wider stretching of lips. 'Eventually.'

Ivan went white, and all the blood that drained from his face seemed to boil up behind his eyes so that Balke's outline wavered beneath a hot red fog. He had guessed already, but being told by Balke's gloating voice was far, far worse. Past caring that the German was trying to provoke him into doing something stupid, he lunged at the *Landmeister* so hard and fast that even though the mace came up to meet him, it was just a little bit too slow.

The striking-head missed him completely, if that properly described how one of the spikes ripped through his coat and gouged his back beneath one shoulder-blade, but the iron shaft hit his ribs on the right side hard enough to lift him off his feet. Ivan thought he heard bone break, and his sabre flew from fingers that refused to hold it any more.

At the same time he felt the jolt all down his left arm as the long straight blade of the Circassian dagger went into Balke up to the hilt.

The knight roared something that might once have had words in it, and tried to shorten his grip on the mace trapped between

264

Ivan's arm and body so that either the spiked head or the spiked pommel would be of some use.

Ivan clamped the iron haft against his side, squeezing tight then tighter still around until his ribs creaked in protest, but letting the mace go would be much, much worse. His left hand punched Balke in the belly again, and again, and again, and the dirk went thudding into meat each time. Then he fell down, and the mace came with him. He felt the spikes tear at his back again, but there was no force behind them any more. The *Landmeister* of Livonia had a more urgent need for both his hands: trying to stop his guts from slipping out.

Dieter Balke staggered sideways with blood and fouler matter spurting down his legs. There was a moist, rending noise, and glistening loops of tissue burst explosively outward past the frantic scrabble of his fingers to slop down around his feet. Balke skidded, stumbled, tripped – and then fell sideways into the hissing warp of the open Gate. There was a single horrid scream, the only sound that had come out of him since he first felt Ivan's dagger, but it cut off as abruptly as the slamming of a door.

'*Bozhe moy!* What a way to die!' Mar'ya Morevna crossed herself, and after a moment so did Tsar Vyslav Andronovich. Prince Ivan got to his feet and stared for a few seconds at the empty Gating circle, both arms hanging limply by his sides while blood dripped and puddled from the dagger-point. Finally, left-handed, not caring one way or the other, he made the sign himself.

'No worse than what he did to the little Countess,' said Ivan. He looked at the Circassian blade, dully noticing where its fine edge had nicked on bone. 'At least steel is clean.'

'Steel?' said Mar'ya Morevna. Her face was still pallid with shock. 'Your dagger didn't kill him. The Gate did.'

Ivan glanced at his wife, and then at the shimmering, hissing circle. 'I don't understand.'

'I prepared it for the Firebird. Most specifically for the Firebird. Nothing else.' For a few minutes Ivan cradled his aching ribs and stared at nothing so that thoughts could tumble through his mind without distraction from anything but pain. Then he stared at the Gate and was glad he felt too weary to be sick. 'Wrong size,' said Mar'ya Morevna in a soft, remorseless voice. 'Wrong shape. Wrong species . . .'

'Whereas I am correct in all of those respects,' said the Firebird, 'and there is unfinished business requiring my attention.' It spread it wings and glided the Gate, crossed the perimeter of the circle and winked out like a snuffed candle – then was back an eyeblink later in what looked like a continuation of that same glide. One wing dipped into a smooth banking turn, and in no more than twenty seconds it was back on the iron-and-gold perch, preening its feathers and looking as if it had never moved at all.

Ivan had not even had time to reach the chair towards which Mar'ya Morevna was guiding him. He sat down very carefully, favouring his right side, and watched as his wife destroyed the Gate and returned her file of spells to the safety of a closed saddlebag. Only then did Tsar Vyslav Andronovich walk to the door that Balke had bolted and swing it open, admitting a crowd of concerned kremlin servants, guards, ministers and at least two physicians. Ivan relaxed and let them go to work.

There had been no reason to ask the Firebird if its matter of honour had been concluded. There had been a faint, foul smell of scorched fat hanging about it when it came back through the Gate, and a greasiness on its sickle talons that coiled away in wisps of smoke even as it preened. He winced and gasped as the surgeons probed gently at the purple bruises forming on his side. No; there was no reason to ask at all. And no desire to, either.

Hermann von Salza strode through the corridors of Castle Thorn so fast that Albrecht von Düsberg had to break into an occasional trot in order to keep up with him. For a long time the Grand Master was so lost in his own thoughts that he didn't notice the Treasurer's discomfort. His mind was in a turmoil. Father Arnald had played perfectly into his hands, and now the worry was, how perfectly? It would not have surprised him to discover that the wily inquisitor had some other trick concealed up the capacious sleeve of his Dominican habit, but it was likely the sort of trick that would require his own presence in Rome to counter. There was so much about the workings of the Church that came with such a caveat: attend in person, or be ignored.

Ignored . . .

He stopped at once and waited for von Düsberg to come panting along the corridor. *The man really is too fat*, he thought. *If armour grows any heavier, then wearing it will kill him.* 'Your pardon, *Fra Tressler*,' he said aloud, 'but I was thinking of other things.' Von Salza smiled to himself. That was true enough. *I still am. But I won't say anything aloud, my good Treasurer, to spare your feelings.* 'You did very well, Albrecht. I hadn't expected an inquisitor of all people to give us such a useful confession.'

'Thank you, *Herr Hochmeister*,' said von Düsberg, straightening his clothes and knightly mantle as he regained his breath. 'Is it truly useful? I mean, what will happen to him when he reaches Rome?'

'Not enough. Prayers, penances, an admonition from a Bishop – or from the entire College of Cardinals, who knows? No more than that; the man is a Father-Inquisitor, after all, and they can do no wrong. But rest assured, he won't trouble us again.' Von Salza started to walk again, keeping himself to a more sedate pace for Albrecht's sake.

'Can you be sure?'

'Better than that; I have *made* sure. There is a letter in the various reports that are accompanying Father Arnald back to Rome, and the knights who escort him will carry further copies.'

'About the secretary?'

'More or less. Mostly less. Unlike the Holy Office, I make no unfounded accusations: those require proof, and I have none, since the obtaining of it would be a matter less than proper for a knight of this Order.' Hermann von Salza knew himself to be a tolerant and worldly man, more so indeed than a Grand Master should be, but he permitted himself a little smile at the prospect of assigning someone notoriously strait-laced like Kuno von Buxhövden to kick open doors after dark. *Less than proper?* he thought. *It would probably be fatal, and not for Kuno.*

'And too much trouble?'

'Peace, Albrecht. Such cynicism does not become you.' Von Salza took the last three steps at a stride and made for the library.

Von Düsberg shrugged and followed again, looking disappointed. 'Then if you can't prove anything, what good is this letter?'

'Read for yourself.' Von Salza paused with his hand on the library door and drew a tightly folded sheet of parchment from his belt. 'This is the rough draft. What His Holiness will see is rather more flowery, and rather less obvious. But the facts remain much as you see them.'

Albrecht waited until they were inside the library and the door had been closed behind him before he opened the sheet and studied it. The warning about it being rough was well-made because, although the Grand Master wrote a good book-hand, it was liberally spattered with blots, crossings-out and emendations. ' *"My knights,"* ' he read, ' *"are hard, rough men with no time for the soft language of court, and they relate what they see to what they know."* '

'And Father Arnald's travelling-companion and secretary is a handsome young man,' said von Salza. 'Extremely handsome, and disturbingly young. To the coarse eye, of which there are sadly too many in the world, he has so obviously the appearance of fulfilling other functions—'

' *"That I grow concerned not merely for the good repute of the Holy Inquisition and the Dominican Order, but even for that of the Church at large. If what my knights and sergeants have said is true, then something must be done about it, and seen to be done, and if untrue, then the good Father Arnald must be commanded to avoid provoking such speculation in the future."* '

'The fact,' said the Grand Master, 'that he's also arrogant and puffed with self-importance only serves to make those he encounters think badly of him, regardless of how matters truly stand.'

'This is a bitter pill for anyone to swallow, *Herr Hochmeister*,' said Albrecht, folding up the parchment and giving it back.

'These will sweeten it.' Von Salza gestured towards the shelf where the books of magic had been racked like a conqueror's trophies. 'Even if they're destined only for a locked closet somewhere in the Apostolic Chancellory.'

Neither of them had heard the door open, but they both heard it close, slammed shut with considerable force. Baba Yaga leaned against its timbers and scowled at the Grand Master. 'You dare to send my books to Rome?' she said.

Von Salza raised his eyebrows. The witch's insolence never ceased to amaze and sometimes amuse him, but today he found it just an irritation, like one of her lice. 'Your books? I said before, no such arrangement was made with me.'

268

'Then I'll take it up with *Landmeister* Balke,' Baba Yaga snapped, 'and until he returns, these books stay—'

There was a sound like the crack of a huge whip, and for a moment von Salza suspected Baba Yaga of working some crafty sorcery to help her spirit away her books; but she looked as startled as the two knights, and the grimoires were still on their shelf. Something touched his face with cobweb delicacy, and he automatically wiped at the irritation. Albrecht von Düsberg made a tiny, choked whimpering noise and stared at him in horror.

Von Salza's hand felt sticky. He glanced at it and felt as though he had been kicked in the stomach. There was blood smeared from palm to fingertips. He looked about wildly and saw everything in the library misted with a fine beading of blood: books and chairs, floor and walls, Albrecht's and his own white robes. The smell of it began to fill the air. But where. . . ?

'Oh, dear God, look at the *wall* . . .' moaned von Düsberg, and started to be sick.

Hermann von Salza had his long sword halfway from its scabbard by the time he swung around, and the blade rattled against its scabbard as a monstrous shudder lurched through him. Dieter Balke stared at him and at his sword out of one eye, from halfway up the wall. The other eye, the rest of his head and most of his body save for the tips of three fingers, were all inside the bricks. And he was alive.

A fat tear squeezed from Balke's eye and down the wall, making a streak through the film of blood that covered it. Half of his mouth was still free, the rest trapped. 'Help me.' The words dripped and slobbered. Nauseated, von Salza stared up, unwilling to use the sword that was the only help he could give, but unable to sheathe it while the, the *thing* still lived to see him do it. 'For the love of God, please help m—'

The wall quivered like something seen through a haze of heat, and all the cohesion of its structure that the Gate spell had disrupted was abruptly, completely restored. It became solid again, without man-shaped, man-filled cavities, and the joints of the bricks wept blood. Three fingertips dropped away and pattered on the floor, but the half-face adhered briefly; then it slithered down, leaving a trail of bloody fluid as though it was some monstrous, ghastly slug.

269

Revolted, von Salza shut his eyes, then wished that he had thought to block his ears from the sound it made as it finally struck the floor. He turned away from what had been the *Landmeister* of Livonia and stared at Baba Yaga. If she said anything, he had decided he would kill her, but even the witch was struck silent by what they had witnessed. Von Düsberg had fainted.

'It seems,' said the Grand Master, breathing hard to suppress his heaving stomach and deliberately choosing a subject that had nothing to with what lay behind him, 'that you will have to take the matter of the books up with me after all. And I say you will not have them.'

Baba Yaga's lips curled back from her ragged teeth. Balke's death was already forgotten, unimportant next to her own desire. 'Is that your last word, *Herr Hochmeister*?' she hissed.

Von Salza raised his sword and rested its blade on his shoulder, diplomacy and even caution swallowed up by grief and anger. 'It is.'

The witch shrugged. She turned as if to go, reached out to the door – and shot the bolt an instant before she rounded on von Salza with her hand outstretched and the fingers spread like hooks. 'Then I'll have your heart instead!' The Grand Master made to swing his sword and take that hand off at the wrist, but a huge pain exploded inside his chest and the weapon clashed harmlessly away as he clutched at a chair for support. Baba Yaga croaked a chuckle. 'I knew this spell was fast enough,' she said. 'You didn't, because last time you didn't see me use it that way. But it can be slower still, Grand Master von Salza. Shall I show you just how slow it can be?'

She moved one joint of one finger, and von Salza felt the wrenching of that movement as though the finger's nail was buried in his heart. Sweat burst out all over his body, and he ground his teeth together until the hinges of his jaw crackled with the strain, determined not to give Baba Yaga the satisfaction of hearing him scream.

'No point in that,' she said, walking close enough to him that the charnel reek of her breath penetrated even the agony. 'They always scream eventually. Ask your inquisitor, or better, ask his pretty little friend.' Her finger moved again, ripping him inside—

And then the pain stopped, and von Salza almost collapsed.

He tried to draw himself upright before it began again, but the look in Baba Yaga's eyes had changed. No longer narrowed with hatred and the joy of killing, no longer leering at his face the better to enjoy his agony, they were staring over his shoulder, bulging further from their sockets than he would have dreamed possible. Von Salza had watched men at the stake after the fires were lit, and seen them dragged greased and screaming to a blunted spear-shaft sunk into the ground, and not even they had looked so terrified.

The specks of black and glowing purple cleared from inside his eyes, so that all at once he could see how some huge light behind him had thrown his shadow across the floor and wall, stark and black, as though it had been cut from silk. The clamour of his own outraged heart faded from his ears, and Hermann von Salza heard a voice, a hiss like flame granted the power of speech. It was behind, above, all around him. Like the light, it was everywhere.

'No cage this time, Baba Yaga. Say farewell.'

The Grand Master had seen the Firebird in its cage, and had been amazed, even in its confinement, at its size. Now he realized just what a size that truly was. He could feel no heat, only a swirling in the air as huge wings spread out to either side, spanning the library from wall to wall. They beat just once, then closed as the Firebird stooped.

Von Salza knew that he should look away: everything from horror to nausea to simple decency told him so. But he watched, fascinated, as unable to close his eyes or turn his head as the merest rabbit cornered by a stoat.

Baba Yaga died.

Not slowly, for von Salza watching. Not quickly, for Baba Yaga in the Firebird's claws. But quietly at least, save for the thunder of the flames.

She died in silence, even though her mouth gaped wide and wider still, for the howling column of fire that gathered her into its embrace had eaten out her lungs before the shriek was formed. She went black as her skin and flesh and fat were roasted into charcoal, and she went white as the burnt meat whirled up in greasy smoke from calcined bones, and she went grey as all that remained became a wisp of ash and stink and dry, dry dust.

The Firebird hung on empty air as what was left of Baba Yaga

271

drizzled from its clenched talons, then turned its head towards the shelf of grimoires and screeched in triumph. The sound went through von Salza's ears to his brain, defying him to make some attempt to stop it. Instead he backed away until a chair struck him behind his knees and he sat down heavily. The Grand Master knew that he would stay there until the Firebird had gone, and that he was not going to try to stop it. He could feel the pain in his heart with every beat, and he felt very tired, and he knew that he did not want to die as Baba Yaga had just died.

The Firebird opened its wings still wider, mantling like a falcon over its stricken prey, and though just the number of things on that shelf should have made the task impossible, it gathered up every one of them. Then it looked at von Salza one last time with its curved beak gaping in a hiss of laughter, and was gone.

The sound of his pulse in the ears was the sound of the clock of his life, and it was running down. Hermann von Salza, Grand Master of the Teutonic Order, sat hunched like an old, old man with his hands pressed tightly to his chest, not caring that those hands were trembling. The half of Dieter Balke's face that could still be recognized stared up at him from a puddle of bloody slime on the floor, and because of the way loose skin had been dragged out of place as that half-face came sliding down the wall, its expression was a sneer.

Have you lost your zeal and stomach for the Crusade, Herr Hochmeister? it seemed to say, in the harsh, brutal words that only Dieter Balke would dare to use to his Grand Master. *Has the sight of dying and the threat of your own death suddenly become so foreign? Can this be the same Hermann von Salza who tied Saracen prisoners to live pigs and burnt them two by two at the Moslem hours of prayer, so that we broke the siege of Kerak in a week and the Templars stood amazed? Have I died for nothing. . . ?*

'No.' Von Salza's voice was no more than a whisper, but his fingers flexed on the arms of the chair until the knuckles turned white, and he heaved himself back onto his feet with a surge of effort that made him stagger. 'By God and Mary, *no!*'

Fists had been pounding on the door for a long time now, ignored and all but unnoticed. Von Salza took three reeling steps and wrenched back the bolt so abruptly that Kuno von Buxhövden all but fell inside. The *Hauskomtur* had a drawn sword in his hand, but it sagged until the point clinked on the floor as he took in the carnage in the library.

'These are my orders,' said Hermann von Salza, paying it no more heed than if the place had simply been untidy. 'An escort of two knights and ten sergeants will take the inquisitors to Rome. A sergeant will help *Fra Tressler* von Düsberg to the infirmary. The rest will come with me.'

Von Buxhövden gaped; the Grand Master's commands were never so simple and direct. Then reflex took over. '*Zu befehl, Herr Hochmeister!* At your command!' He summoned up enough composure to sheathe his sword, then diffidently cleared his throat. 'Er . . . Where are we going?'

Von Salza smirked at him, a smile as bright and fragile and as near to shattering as porcelain. 'To Russia, Kuno, or to Hell. As you can see from the mess' – he glanced at it and laughed a tinkling little laugh as though the porcelain had broken at last – 'my attempts to be subtle didn't work. We'll have to use our swords . . .'

Chapter Ten

With the memory of Dieter Balke's unfinished squawk of horror still refusing to get out of his head, Ivan Aleksandrovich had refused under any circumstance – or force or persuasion either, he had stubbornly elaborated – to be returned to Khorlov through anything resembling a Gating circle. Mar'ya Morevna hadn't wasted her breath in trying to change his mind. She knew her husband's moods by now, though keeping up with them had sometimes been a problem, and this obstinate streak was as inflexible as a bar of steel. She had spent most of the day talking to the Firebird instead.

Ivan didn't really care one way or the other, just so long as Gates weren't involved. He had enough to think about in any case, for the kremlin doctors who had patched up his ribs – unbroken, they had said, only through some sort of minor miracle – had advised him that he would be in a certain amount of discomfort for the next few days. The men had meant only to reassure him, but Ivan was already familiar with the school of kindly understatement as practised by doctors, and knew from experience what that discomfort would feel like. He had been correct; the bruised bones and muscles in his side hurt him when he moved, and when he was still; also when he stood, sat, lay down, ate, drank or went to the privy. He could have tolerated all of that, had it not also hurt him with a most particular small twinge every time he breathed and – typically – didn't trouble him in the slightest when he didn't.

'If it was something else that I could actually stop doing,' he complained to the Grey Wolf while they sat together in the sunshine, 'then I think it might just be bearable.'

'You could stop breathing,' said the Grey Wolf unhelpfully. 'You very nearly did. I saw how that knight swung his mace at you, and he wasn't meaning just to knock the dust out of your clothes.'

Ivan grimaced: he had been hoping for sympathy. Mar'ya Morevna had said much the same thing, and she had also refused to work a Healing on his ribs. The reasons were sound enough:

274

that a sorcery worked in the Summer Country on someone not *of* the Summer Country might unravel like bad weaving when he returned to his own place; that the sort of enchantment he had in mind worked poorly on bruises and best when closing cuts and punctures, 'like a needle and thread, but quicker', as she had put it; and that because of the soundness of her reasons, he should wait till they went home.

With so much of it around, it was a pity that such sound reasoning didn't do much to ease aches and pains.

'And bring that thing home with you,' she had said almost as an afterthought, with a speculative look in her eye that suggested what Ivan privately called *Oh God not another good idea*. Dieter Balke's mace had been resting on his shoulder at the time. He had picked it up just after the fight had ended – and carrying it about with him hurt, of course, like everything else right now – but he had intended to bring it back home anyway, as some sort of souvenir. Not to use, however; Ivan had a perfectly good mace of his own hanging up with all his other war-gear in the Armoury Tower, a light, handy, well-balanced weapon without the foul associations that made Balke's feel as though it was coated in rancid fat.

Vyslav Andronovich had also expressed a pointed wish that he take the ugly thing away, and Ivan had a feeling that the Tsar would be glad to see the mace, the Firebird, the Grey Wolf and all the rest of them get out of his kremlin. There was no surprise about that: reports were still coming in of the trouble they had indirectly caused by being the reason for Dieter Balke entering the Summer Country, and the ruin of Vasilisa Kurbit'yevna's hunting lodge had been only the worst of it.

It all suggested to Ivan that there might indeed be such a thing as luck, despite Mar'ya Morevna's profession otherwise. *Landmeister* Balke had shown a talent for destruction matched only by the Tatars, and by rights his mace should have knocked Ivan's head off in the first exchange of blows. 'Being saved for something', had been Sivka's view, between mouthfuls of oats. Whether that something was better, worse or just more interesting, Prince Ivan was in no hurry to learn.

The Grey Wolf sat up, his big triangular ears pricked towards some sound that Ivan had missed. 'I think we're leaving,' he said.

275

'How do you know?'

'Instinct.' White fangs gleamed in a lupine grin. 'Also hearing the Tsarevna declare that this time not even you can complain about the route she and the Firebird will be taking back to Khorlov.'

'Oh indeed. Let me be the judge of that.' Ivan put his head back and let the sunshine of the Summer Country warm his face. If the Grey Wolf was right, it might be his last chance until summer returned to the wide white world of home. The Rus endured their winter rather than enjoyed it, but the brooding presence of winter made summer, when it came, all the brighter, warmer, merrier. That pleasure, small and gentle as it might be, was missing in a place where there was no winter at all and the three remaining seasons blurred together into one. When he had first ridden into *Lyetnaya-Strana*, Ivan had been only half-joking when he had wanted to stay. Now he knew that he was not joking at all in wanting to leave.

Mar'ya Morevna emerged into the sunlight with the Firebird's perch in one hand, and the Firebird on the other wrist like some impossibly huge falcon. From the ease with which she was carrying them, neither the bird nor its perch-of-honour were as heavy as they looked. 'Whenever you're ready,' she said. 'Vyslav Andronovich has had the pattern prepared and the mirrors set up in the kremlin square.'

'That spell? But it won't take us back to Khorlov.'

'The alternative was a Gating-circle, Vanya. We can be in Khorlov in less than a day. And anyway, there are things that need to be done in our own kremlin; Chyornyy and armour to collect, books' – she smiled wickedly – 'to be put into the library for copying before I give them back, things like that. Come on, we should make our farewells.'

Ivan got to his feet, slowly and cautiously but with a wince and a sharp intake of breath for all that. He looked at the Grey Wolf, who hadn't moved, and said, 'Shall I release you from my service now?'

The Grey Wolf flattened his ears just a little. 'Why? What service have I done you, besides a little carrying from place to place?' Ivan grinned; the Grey Wolf had shown poor manners for a servant, but the wit of a dangerous good friend had been as sharp as his own teeth.

276

'Then you'll come with us, after all?'

'There was never any doubt. Now I've heard about this business and how it started.' The Grey Wolf glanced at the Firebird, who feigned not to notice. 'I don't want to be told about the ending of it second-hand . . .'

Tsar Aleksandr looked at the assembled Princes and sighed. They had been here in the small hall of his kremlin for almost a week now, and what had begun as discussion had escalated to argument within the first two days. Only the presence of Mar'ya Morevna's Captain-of-Guards and a good hundred of her best troops was a moderating influence, and the Tsar wondered grimly how much longer that could last before someone agreed to differ long enough for a combining of forces. That afterwards they would fall on each other would be meagre consolation, and just what some enemy had long been hoping for.

He turned away from the beginning of yet another squabble and stared out of the window, suppressing the feeling that it would be better for all concerned if he walked out of the room and locked the door behind him until they had fought the matter to a conclusion. It would certainly simplify matters. The Tsar sighed again, his breath freezing as it touched the small panes of glass, so that he had to scrape the rime away with a thumbnail and the edge of his hand. The world outside was stark white from horizon to horizon beneath a cold blue sky and a pale winter sun, and the encampment beyond Khorlov's walls looked more like a besieging army every time Aleksandr saw it. Men-at-arms from three hostile Principalities were out there; the *bogatyrs* were of course within the walls. As the sound of accusing voices welled up again behind him, the reality of what was still only an appearance came home full force. Those tents had been shifted since they had first been set up six days ago, so that now they truly *were* a siege-camp.

The first flash of rage died down, and its place was taken by a cold, dignified anger. There was evidence out there right before his eyes of collusion between at least two of the Princes, and the best way to nip that in the bud was to draw it to everyone's attention in public debate. Tsar Aleksandr peered through the thick, bubbled glass in hope of seeing some foolishly-raised banner, rubbed at the pane again, then gave up and opened the window. At the same time he was listening for whoever's voice was first to falter when they saw what he was doing. He did not expect every voice to stop at once.

'Father?' said a voice he hadn't heard in nearly three weeks, 'we're back.'

Ivan and Mar'ya Morevna were standing by the door. That in itself was not enough to have silenced the bickering Princes, but the company that they were keeping had proven much more effective. A horse could never have climbed up the stairs to reach this room, but it was quite plain that a wolf the size of a horse was a great deal more nimble. The Grey Wolf might have been enough in himself to place a damper on any Princely quarrel; the Firebird hovering by Ivan's shoulder on the thermals of its own heat would have driven them in panic from the room, had the blazing spread of its wings not filled the doorway from one side to the other.

Aleksandr Andreyevich looked with astonishment at his son and daughter-in-law and concluded that the hug they both deserved would be out of place right now. Both of them were in armour, but the Tsar could see that they were wearing not only iron but dignity as a shield against the scorn of the other Princes. Not, flanked by the Firebird and the Grey Wolf, that anyone was daring to be scornful; but that dignity should be respected all the same. 'Sirs,' he said, keeping his voice calm with an effort, 'this is my son Ivan Tsarevich, and the Firebird of which I told you.' Then, unable to resist the chance to sink a dainty pin in several noble hides, 'His wife the Tsarevna Mar'ya Morevna you must know already, if only by the reputation of her armies . . .'

After their shock wore off and the Firebird's perch was set formally in the centre of the table so that it had a chance to speak, the Princes surpassed all previous levels of noise that five noble gentlemen could make without actually shouting at the tops of their voices. As the Firebird told them of its involvement in what had been happening, their responses swung like a pendulum between outrage and sympathy. Tsar Aleksandr noted with silent annoyance that when he had told them almost the same things, such sympathy had been noticeably lacking.

'Can anyone,' said Pavel Mikhaylovich of Novgorod, avoiding his brother's gaze and so managing to sound even more full of his own importance than usual, 'be so stupid as to attack us in the depths of winter?'

'You were all quite prepared to attack each other,' said Mar'ya Morevna pointedly, producing an awkward little silence, for which the Tsar wanted to kiss her. 'But stupidity has nothing to do with this. The Grand Master's hand has been forced, but he knows how we make war and that we don't dare raise the peasant levies at this time of year. It makes parity of numbers much easier to achieve.'

'*Gospozha* Tsarevna.' Great Prince Yaroslav rose fractionally from his seat and gave her the ghost of a bow. His son Aleksandr Nevskiy didn't trouble even with that, sitting with his arms folded and a look of slight discontent or perhaps constipation on his face. 'There are a hundred men from each of our three realms encamped beyond the walls of this kremlin, gathered against . . .' Mar'ya Morevna and Prince Ivan both gave him a hard stare at that, and the Grey Wolf rumbled a growl low in his barrel chest. Yaroslav had the good grace to stumble over his words and hurriedly alter what he had been about to say. '. . . Er, that is, one hundred each. Yes. Er, how many do the *Nyemetsi* have?'

'About four hundred sergeants, certainly no more than that, and perhaps thirty knights,' said the Firebird.

'That means we outnumber them by three hundred men,' began Mar'ya Morevna, but stopped abruptly when Ivan tugged her sleeve.

'Sixty,' he said.

'What?'

'We outnumber the Knights by only sixty men, if that.' He glanced quickly at the Princes. 'When the worthy Great Prince Yaroslav said "each", he meant "each city".'

Guard-Captain Fedorov had brought one hundred soldiers from Mar'ya Morevna's kremlin; Khorlov could spare the same number, stiffened perhaps with a sprinkling of Akimov's guards, and Yuriy of Kiev had his full hundred soldiers; but Boris and Pavel Mikhaylovich had only their hundred between them, as had Yaroslav of Vladimir and his son. Aleksandr Yaroslavich Nevskiy met Ivan's look with a glare of his own, as if warning him against use of the word *subordinate*, and Tsar Aleksandr glowered at the man's insolence. Nevskiy lived in Vladimir and under his father's roof, and Great Prince Yaroslav showed no inclination to abdicate in his son's favour. In the Tsar's view, that made him as subordinate as anything the word might mean.

'Four hundred men-at-arms and thirty knights,' said Yuriy Vladimirovich. 'They took . . . was it Prussia or Livonia? with only half that number.'

'Kulm, Kürland and Livonia,' said Mar'ya Morevna bleakly. 'Not Prussia. And the Livonians were not expecting them.'

'Neither were we, until your little bird sang to us,' said Aleksandr Nevskiy, and if he had taken a week over it, he could not have made a worse choice of phrase. The Firebird had told the assembly everything that had happened, and all but the dullest of them had seen how the death of that other little bird Vasilisa Kurbit'yevna was still a raw place in Prince Ivan's mind. They all saw how his hands closed as though they were wrapped around the Prince's neck; but then he relaxed again as he realized that would do no good, and a great deal of harm.

Tsar Aleksandr breathed a small sigh of relief at his son's restraint. It was mingled with a regret that Ivan hadn't let himself do something painful but less permanent to Nevskiy, something to take the smug look off his face and the curl out of his beard. The Tsar knew that if any of his three daughters had been there, they would have resorted without further ado to the punishment they had visited on Ivan so many times before, dragging Aleksandr Nevskiy out to the kremlin's moat and flinging him in. Even if they had to break the ice to do it. He hid a smile at the thought. At this time of year, that wouldn't so much take the curl from Nevskiy's beard as fix it permanently.

There were times when the Tsar had to track ideas through the undergrowth of words in a council meeting as though they were elusive small animals. And there were times when they sprang full-grown into his head; one did so now. There *was* a way to offset the Knights' near-equality of men, and without emptying Khorlov's garrison. Not that he would have dreamed of doing that anyway; professed unity against the invaders was one thing, but he still didn't trust the other Princes. Allies had taken advantage of such situations before, and they would do it again. But not to him.

'Dmitriy Vasil'yevich,' he said to the High Steward, 'write me a letter. Defy these Teutonic Knights in language they will understand. Flay them with words. Then offer them battle in . . .' The Tsar hesitated, calculating quickly, and shrugged. 'A time and place we will decide later. Leave that blank for now.' There was no question that the Grand Master of the Knights would get his letter in good time to act on it; the Firebird would take pleasure in making sure of that. He glanced at Mar'ya Morevna for assistance; it had been a long time since he had learned how to choose one battlefield over another because of favourable ground, and almost as long since he had last used the skill himself. Mar'ya Morevna, only the other hand, was famed for it.

'The plain of the River Nemen west of Grod'no,' she said after a few moments' thought. 'Fourteen days from now.'

'These Rus,' said Albrecht von Düsberg. 'How do they fight?'

The Grand Master looked up from a tactical diagram he had drawn in the snow with a twig. 'Horse and foot,' he said laconically. 'Like us, but without any weight of armoured knights.'

'Kuno said they fight like the Mongols.'

'Oh, did he? Then you'll know what to expect.'

'But I've never fought the Mongols.'

'You've fought the Saracens,' said von Salza. 'I saw you. And horse-archers are much the same wherever you go. It's just that there tend to be more of them when you deal with the Mongols.' He gestured at the tangle of lines in the snow, warming to his subject. 'But these Rus haven't faced heavy cavalry before, or they would never have chosen to meet us on this ground. Forested hills here and here, to conceal our preparations. The rest of it flat, open – even the river's frozen so hard that we need have no fear of the ice giving way beneath us. We'll stand fast on the hills, among the trees so that their light horse can't come at us, and hold there until horse and foot advance together. They'll be bunched together to mass their forces, and that's when a single charge at the proper point of weakness will crack them like a nut. Once the line is broken, we pursue and slay at leisure.' Von Salza smiled. 'They've demonstrated their heresy already, by offering resistance. We won't need to take prisoners.'

Von Düsberg nodded sagely and wandered away, bundled like everyone else against the cold. The Grand Master watched him go, then breathed a sigh of relief and cast about for his twig. His advance scouts had brought him reports and drawings of the River Nemen, and now he scraped another couple of lines into the snow and tried again to work out the best place for his crossbow-men; having to deal with von Düsberg's interest at the same time had not helped his concentration. However, since he knew both the publicly accepted and the private reasons for it, the Grand Master did not have the heart to shoo his Treasurer away. What most of the other knights and sergeants thought was that von Düsberg knew nothing but numbers and the counting of them, and on the eve of his first major battle was trying to find out what would happen. That was not strictly true, since Albrecht had seen service in the Holy Land.

The anonymous comment from someone that the Treasurer was scared and trying to hide it with a smokescreen of babble, was a little more accurate, but not where the coming battle was concerned. Von Düsberg's chattering and the Grand Master's curtness performed the same function, but what they were concealing was nothing so simple as fear. They shared the secret of how Dieter Balke had died, and if it came out that the Rus had killed the best and strongest of his knights, von Salza knew that the invasion would fall apart. Kuno von Buxhövden had guessed a little of it, but he would say nothing; and besides, he had not been there. He had not *seen*.

Von Salza's plan was of necessity very simple. Knowing that the Rus were undamaged by the hoped-for internal war and almost certainly aware by now of what was threatening them – and that they would be prepared to meet that threat by spring – he had been forced to act much sooner than he had intended. The inclement winter weather was far too unreliable for a protracted campaign, and because he had moved in a hurry to avoid the risk of the Rus turning out their peasant levies, his forces were limited to those available in *Schloss* Thorn, a paltry thirty knights and four hundred sergeants.

Knowing that Dieter Balke had taken Livonia with a respective twenty and two hundred cheered him slightly, but Balke was dead now. And anyway, he had been felling trees and building timber *Balkenburgen* – the pun had amused von Salza at the time – as defensive strongholds all along his route and had never been confronted with the need for a set-piece battle, no matter how small. Lacking the leisure to build even such small, primitive fortresses, what the Grand Master had wanted to do was capture at least one and maybe two towns, and hold their kremlin citadels until reinforcements could be brought up in the Spring from other castles of the Order. That was how it was done in the Holy Land, and it worked – at least, so long as the towns could be captured and their populations quickly subdued or slaughtered without too much opposition. The Rus opposition, however, was already here, or would be by the morning, and this damned country was too wide open to sidestep them by a forced countermarch.

In the best traditions of chivalry they had contrived to send him formal defiance and a challenge to meet in battle on the banks of the Nemen, but directly he saw the scroll, prepared in both Russian and Latin, he realized that it was also intended as a warning. That the Firebird had been its means of delivery was only one part of that, for the seal-impressions and accompanying marks or signs-manual were those of every Prince and Tsar who had been subjected to Balke's and Baba Yaga's interference. Only the scout-supplied knowledge that, despite all those names, their army was as tiny as his own kept the Grand Master from becoming worried. Compulsion worked both ways; he had been forced to move quickly after Balke's plan had fallen to pieces – just like Dieter himself, thought von Salza with brutal, compassion-blunting humour – but by doing so he had compelled the Rus to a swift response with only the household troops they maintained during the winter. According to his scouts, the numbers of each small army were nearly equal, and since they had encountered no advance guard of Russians beyond their army, it was probable that the enemy had not yet posted their own watch. Von Salza drew in the snow again, smiling to himself at the advantages of advance warning. Efficient scouts, knowing what was over the next hill: that was the key to war, just as much as the men and the weapons.

A wolf howled somewhere up in the wooded hills, making horses stamp and whinny throughout the Teutonic Order's camp, and Hermann von Salza glanced up sourly from his map-making. If there had been time and safety in which to do it, he would have organized another sort of hunt than the brief daily forays which augmented their rations with fresh meat. He didn't like wolves:

the brutes seemed to sense battle, just like the vultures in Outremer, but at least the carrion birds didn't gloat about it. Von Salza listened, frowning, sure he had heard this wolf before because the howl was noticeably deeper than normal and the animal probably bigger in proportion. A pack leader, most likely. He entertained brief notions of a new wolf-fur lining for his cloak, but knew he would forgo the luxury if the damned creature would just stop following his army . . .

'. . . And they have crossbows,' the Grey Wolf concluded. He glanced back towards the snow-covered ridge along which his tracks were still plainly visible. 'Perhaps a hundred, maybe a few less. I didn't wait to count each one.'

'That shows clearly enough what they think of us,' said Great Prince Yuriy of Kiev. The observation drew blank looks from those who didn't understand, and world-weary, cynical smiles from those who did. 'Their last Pope,' he explained for the benefit mostly of the brothers Mikhaylovich, 'declared in full council session that because of the severe wounds it caused, the use of the crossbow against Christians was henceforth banned. But it was still considered most suitable for killing pagans and the heretical.'

'So they consider us infidel, then,' said Mar'ya Morevna. 'I'm glad of it.'

'Glad?' Aleksandr Nevskiy laughed, an unpleasant, deliberately grating sound that had nothing to do with humour. 'Then for all your reputation as a commander of armies, *gospozha* Tsarevna, it's plain you haven't seen a crossbow being used.'

'Have I not?' said Mar'ya Morevna in tones of such innocent surprise that it drew smiles from the other Princes and left Nevskiy floundering. 'So tell me, what makes it so different from our own bows?'

'The penetration, for a start!'

Mar'ya Morevna glanced quickly at Prince Ivan in case he disapproved, received the imperceptible nod and smile that let her go ahead with whatever discomfiture she had planned, then leaned back in her camp chair, lowered her eyelids and shot that hooded, loaded look at Aleksandr Nevskiy. 'I'm happily married,' she purred. 'You don't need to tell me anything about penetration.' This time there was such a crash of laughter from the others that it drew curious glances from the common soldiers nearest their commanders' tents. Nevskiy wattled purple with fury and embarrassment.

'Madam, that was—'

'Unladylike?' said Ivan coolly. 'Well, Aleksandr Yaroslavich, perhaps it was. My wife best knows her own mind on such matters. If when commanding soldiers and thinking like a soldier she feels it appropriate to talk like a soldier, then that is her privilege. You, however, do not talk like a gentleman, and for that you have no excuse.'

Aleksandr Nevskiy grabbed for his sword, but stopped abruptly when the Grey Wolf snarled eloquently at him. The sound was like a sheet of metal being torn in half, and Nevskiy took just one look at the expanse of ivory displayed for his exclusive benefit and slapped his half-drawn blade pettishly back into its scabbard. 'Do you always let animals do your fighting, Ivan Tsarevich?' he said, producing a fairly creditable snarl himself.

'Birds, beasts, men, women. Those who think well enough of me will always defend me. How many will defend you?'

'Enough of this!' Mar'ya Morevna slapped her hand so hard on the map-laden trestle table around which they all sat that it wobbled and all but collapsed. 'I confess, it's just as well we have the Teutonic Order to contend with, or we'd all be at one another's throats. And I meant what I said about the crossbows. I'm glad the *Nyemetsi* are using them and not ordinary bows. Crude jokes aside, the weapon's only real advantage is penetration. At battle range, it can put a bolt through the heaviest mail yet wrought; for the first time, a vassal can strike down his armoured master from a safe distance. That's the only reason for the Papal ruling, because I've seen what a thoroughly approved and acceptable mace can do, and the wounds it makes are worse than any crossbow.'

'But that means it can penetrate our armour too!' said Pavel of Novgorod.

'Our own arrows can do that already,' said Mar'ya Morevna, 'if they're shot straight and true from a good horn-and-sinew bow, and I doubt that a sergeant's hauberk is anything like as good as that of a knight. We can pierce their mail as easily as our own, and more often than they expect. Tell me, Vanya, how many arrows can you loose in, let's say, one minute?'

285

Ivan pulled a parchment-fletched arrow from the crammed quiver on his right hip and balanced the missile on his finger before returning it. 'Carefully aimed, oh, about six. If aiming doesn't matter, then twelve or more.'

'Quite so. And, Highnesses, we all have archers among our forces who can easily better that. In the same minute, because of its great power and the effort thus needed to draw it, a crossbow shoots once or maybe twice. And I doubt, under such a storm of arrows as we can lay on them, that they'll be shooting either fast or straight.'

'But that doesn't do anything against their knights,' persisted Pavel Mikhaylovich. 'We still can't pierce their mail. They'll ride right through us!'

'Not if we shoot their horses.' Ivan glanced at Sivka and Chyornyy tethered nearby. Both of them had put their ears back, and Sivka in particular was giving him a white-eyed sidelong glare. A bottle of ink, red ink, chose that moment to slide from the unsteady table. It fell to the ground and spattered scarlet blotches all across the snow.

Ivan watched the splashes soak in, red on white. 'A reminder of tomorrow,' he said softly. 'Whatever our differences, be careful, all of you.'

The morning dawned clear and still and very cold, so that although there were no clouds in the hard blue sky, there was a fog of breath hanging above each Prince's small host as they moved into position.

Ivan Aleksandrovich, sitting halfway up the southern slope, leaned forward to pat Sivka on the neck and took a sighting between the horse's ears down towards the River Nemen. Or rather, where the river would have been had its crust of ice not been covered with packed snow so that it was impossible to decide where the bank ended and the water began. It meant that it would be impossible to tell when the Teutonic Knights actually crossed the border, for what that was worth. Aleksandr Nevskiy had been hot for exact times, exact places, all the paraphernalia of history; but then, he had a vested interest, since his father's archivist had accompanied the army and would be chronicling the victory.

Ivan hoped it would be a victory. He had no doubt, however,

that only Prince Nevskiy would be named more than once. The rest of them, Yuriy, the Mikhaylovichi, Mar'ya Morevna and himself, would be spear-carriers, names mentioned only to show what notable personages were inspired to follow Aleksandr Nevskiy's leadership in the defence of Mother Russia. For a man so friendly with the Tatars, that was ironic. Ivan was mildly vexed at all the glory-hunting, and that was all; in fact, given Nevskiy's personality, as quick a source of annoyance as a wasp caught inside armour, it was remarkable. A level of mild dislike followed him everywhere he went – though the chronicler seemed impervious to it, which said something about how much he was being paid – so that for Ivan to remain unworried about what was being written down and who was being left out seemed almost unhealthy.

It had more to do with preoccupation. This was Prince Ivan's first battle, and though he would have been glad to know it would also be his last, there was a double meaning about the phrase that made him shy away from considering it. He had fought one of the Teutonic Knights already, and if *Landmeister* Balke was an example, they would be hard to beat despite Mar'ya Morevna's reassurances. All Ivan wanted from a history of the Battle on the Nemen was that he and his wife lived long and happy lives after it was won.

He shuffled his shoulders inside their layers of Indian cotton padding, leather, mail, and the various plates riveted to the hauberk over chest and shoulders. It was his own armour and it fitted, unlike the last time he had worn mail, and his ribs no longer hurt, except for a complaining twinge if he moved the sorcery-healed muscles too suddenly. It all made for a certain amount of comfort, if he could only set aside the cold, and the remarkable nastiness of field rations that he could still taste at the back of his throat, and the prospect of someone beyond the river who was going to shoot or throw or swing something with sharp edges at him. That individual attention was actually more bearable than an impersonal bow loosed at a venture; it was easier to do something about the man who faced you, even when it was over a distance, than one who just shot into the thick of a crowd.

Ivan would be doing that before long, unless Mar'ya Morevna stopped him. There had already been a lecture on personal safety in battle, which mostly had to do with keeping out of it and letting the professionals like Guard-Captain Akimov get on with what they knew best, and a rider that the succession in Khorlov had not yet been secured by the provision of an heir. Now *that* had sounded so much like one of Dmitriy Vasil'yevich's homilies that Ivan had almost ignored it. But not quite. Despite the thinness of their own tent, and the proximity of far too many others, he and Mar'ya Morevna had made love very gently, quietly and tenderly far into the night. If a child was quickened by it, or by the warm nights they had spent together in the Summer Country, so much the better; and if not, well, it was a better way to spend the night before a battle than in fretting about what the morning would bring.

Or in dictating how the battle yet unfought had been won, and who had been most instrumental in the victory, as he had heard Aleksandr Nevskiy doing. Ivan grinned sourly. Except for a few little details like his own importance, he was quite willing to have Nevskiy's prophecy come true.

Then he stiffened in his saddle as the low sun struck a glint from something metal in the wooded hills beyond the river. Even though there was more than a *versta* of open snowfield between that ominous small twinkle and himself, Ivan fumbled for the helmet at his saddlebow.

Sivka blew out plumes of steamy vapour from his nostrils like a dragon, and stamped once. 'Here they come,' he said.

They were the first distinct words spoken aloud since he had ridden up here. Oh, there was a background mutter floating up from the ranks of infantry, sharpened now and then by a sergeant's grated opinion of just how crookedly their lines were dressed, and the brittle chatter of high-born horsemen was a counterpoint to the clink of harness, but those had been noises, not voices. The hill had been quiet, a place where a man could think. Not any more. Ivan slapped the top of his helmet to settle it onto the padded mail hood he wore beneath, then buckled the chin-strap and snapped down nasal and cheek flaps. His vision dropped at once to almost straight in front and his hearing became distorted by the echoes of his own breath, but there was something very reassuring about a layer of steel between himself and harm. He turned Sivka's head towards the army, and cantered down to join Mar'ya Morevna.

The baggage train went rumbling past him, heading towards the river. Each massively constructed wagon carried a cargo of pointed stakes, cut earlier that morning from the pine trees cresting the ridge. Those stakes would be driven into the ground between each wagon once they reached their appointed site on the Rus side of the river, and the wagons themselves, weighted with logs and their double sides deployed into loopholed wooden shields, would be chained together in a circle. Nothing more or less than a portable kremlin, the whole thing was called a *gulyagorod*, a 'walking city', and it had been proven in battle against the Tatars. Whether it would withstand a charge of mounted knights was a question yet unanswered, but from what Ivan had heard at last night's final council of war, anything was better than being caught by them in the open.

'God and all the Saints damn them to Hell,' said Hermann von Salza. He spoke without heat, the words almost a formal request rather than a curse, seeming to voice his anger more because it was expected of him than because he truly felt it.

'They have a *Wagenburg*,' muttered Kuno von Buxhövden. He sounded almost plaintive, like an overgrown child shown good reason why he can't play with a favourite toy. 'That puts paid to any sort of charge.'

'Why so?' Von Salza, already straight-legged in the long-stirruped knightly saddle, put both hands on the pommel and craned himself a little higher against the weight of his mail. 'Look, man, and see for yourself. They're planting stakes between the wagons. That means a fixed *'Burg*, not a mobile one, while we, Kuno, we remain as mobile as our horses will allow. And if we can entice them out . . .' He slapped his destrier's shoulder, and the horse flinched snorting from the impact of the mailed mitten. 'Then we grind them through the ice beneath our hoofs, and let the river wash the mess away.'

Albrecht von Düsberg trotted towards them. The Treasurer was wearing full harness, even to the full helm – which neither von Salza nor *Hauskomtur* von Buxhövden had troubled to put on just yet – in the presumed hope that it would restore something of his old valiant appearance as a Crusader in Palestine. Had his weight been now what it had been then, that hope might have been justified. As it was, he just looked like a fat man in tight armour, and von Salza was privately glad that this battle was being fought in winter. Too much heat, too much dust, too much strain, and von Düsberg would be dead before he ever saw an enemy or raised his sword for the good of God and the Teutonic Order.

He removed his helm with its dramatic transverse crest of black feathers, and von Salza frowned slightly. Even now von Düsberg was panting and red-faced, his chin – or the uppermost of them – compressed by the edge of his mail coif in a manner that looked far from comfortable. If an hour's march on horseback to the field made him like this, what in God's name would he look like at the end of the day?

'The sergeants are mustered, *Herr Hochmeister*,' he said once he had recovered enough breath to make the announcement in a single sentence. 'They await the order to advance.'

Von Salza looked once more towards the *Wagenburg*, now edged with sparks as the infantry who manned it took up their positions. Then he shook the reins and walked his horse forward to the edge of the trees and looked down at his own foot-soldiers. Half of the crossbows were there, flanked and screened by spearmen. They were to have remained in place, acting as bait for the Rus cavalry until the Rus commander's patience wore thin and he committed his infantry to the assault, but thanks to their accursed fort of carts, the position was reversed. Now von Salza would have to advance and press the *Wagenburg*, otherwise the Rus would just sit secure behind their wooden walls until, as was inevitable in battle, someone made a mistake.

The rest of the Order's men-at-arms were still under cover in the woods further up the slope, from where they would advance at a run once the Rus foot had been engaged. All of the cavalry, both knights and mounted sergeants, were up here. The sergeants would act as a mobile reserve, sent to cover weak places in the Order's line or probe at the Rus, but the knights would be held back – whether they liked it or not, von Salza reminded himself – until the proper opening appeared, and then, only then, would they burst from the forest in an irresistible flood and sweep the enemy from the field.

Hermann von Salza, Grand Master of the Teutonic Knights, looked up towards the sky. '*Im namens Vater und Sohn und*

290

Heiliger Geist,' he said, and crossed himself, then looked at his *Hauskomtur* and his Treasurer as they did likewise. 'Sound the trumpets. We go.'

'There!' cried Mar'ya Morevna, pointing with her whole arm. 'Coming out of the woods! Spearmen!'

Everyone paused for the merest instant to look across the Nemen, where shadowy blocks of grey-clad men topped with twinkling steel marched from the shadow of the pine trees and down the slope towards the river. Then all those people not already in assigned battle positions abandoned whatever they had been doing and ran in a sort of controlled chaos to their places. Ivan sat quite still on Sivka's back and tried to look calm and noble, until he realized both that nobody else had noticed and that they weren't wasting time with such posturing.

'It's all right, Vanyushka,' said Mar'ya Morevna with a tight grin that betrayed the lack of colour in her lips, 'they'll get the pose right when they do the painting.' She vaulted into Chyornyy's saddle and tugged her bow from its case. 'Just make sure it's not a carving for your tombstone.'

Prince Ivan gave her an odd look, wondering if the thought that had been going through his mind had been so obvious to everyone else. 'You watch what you're doing as well,' he said, jerking his chin at the bow. 'I thought you were commanding, not fighting.'

'I am. But I don't want to waste the time in getting this thing ready if I need it in a rush.' She stood up high in her stirrups and peered at the approaching German men-at-arms. 'If the sky stays as clear as this, the glare is going to be far from pleasant,' she said casually. 'It's a pity there won't be heat as well as light, to make the *Nyemetsi* sweat a little. Oh well. There are other ways to make them sweat than sunshine.' She plumped back into the saddle and turned for a brief consultation with Prince Yuriy of Kiev, then laughed. It sounded hoarse, as though her throat was already too dry.

'No, not yet,' she said. 'They're safe enough in the *gulyagorod*; safer than the cavalry would be, out in the open, until after—'

'What's that?' Directly Ivan asked the question, he knew its answer. The advancing Teutonic sergeants were chanting a psalm, the deep-throated roar of their voices drifting eerily across the silent snow. 'Dear God,' he said, and crossed himself, 'they really are regarding us as heathens, aren't they?'

'They follow their orders,' said Prince Yuriy, 'just as our soldiers do. And if being told the enemies are heathens, or heretics, or Jews, makes the killing come a little easier, their commanders will have done that too. *Gospozha* Tsarevna, the cavalry. . . ?'

'I said not yet. I'm waiting.'

'Waiting for what?'

'For them to engage, and . . .' As the formation started out across the frozen River Nemen, the singing stopped as if the soldiers had paused to draw a breath. Their spears shifted apart, there was a movement in the ranks behind them, and then the silence was burst apart by a great *whack*, as though a wet hide had been slapped against the ground. There was a convulsion among the wagons, and men spilled out of them as crossbow bolts ploughed through wood and mail and flesh. '. . . And waiting for that,' Mar'ya Morevna finished. 'There's range for one more volley. Now we know what they do, when the singing stops again, the cavalry goes out.'

Yuriy Vladimirovich stared at her with a mixture of respect and open revulsion. 'You're a cold one, Mar'ya Morevna. I'm glad you're on our side.'

Mar'ya Morevna smiled at him, no more than a stretching of lips over teeth. In the distance, the psalm fell away again to silence. 'Remember that, Prince Yuriy,' she said quietly, 'and send the horsemen out – now!'

The *whack* of another crossbow volley was almost lost in the rising rumble as two hundred horses went from a standstill to a flat-out gallop. Their riders plied *nagayka* whips with a will, knowing that they had only a minute to cover the distance between shelter and shooting range before the crossbows were reloaded.

The high shields raised around the wagon-fort blocking their view of the ground beyond it, and unable to see the cavalry pouring from their snow-covered defile, the ranks of sergeants shuffled together as they closed around the crossbow-men. The thunder of the psalm began again, but as they resumed their advance, a glitter rippled all down the front of the formation as those big spears they carried swept down to the horizontal. They met the *gulyagorod*'s wooden wall with a rustling crash that sounded like a wave striking a shingle beach, and like a wave they lapped around it, not quite enough of them to close the circle.

The horsemen of the Rus swept down on them, curving around the rear of the stabbing, shouting, killing, dying foot-soldiers, and launched a blizzard of arrows at anything in the tau-crossed grey surcoat of a Teutonic sergeant. Crossbows shot back and emptied saddles, but by fives and tens rather than the deadly concerted volleys of before. Mar'ya Morevna had been right; it needed a special sort of man to load and aim and loose his single missile when there were twenty or thirty or a hundred others all coming back at him. Those special men died faster than the more ordinary ones who dived for cover, because by standing up to shoot they exposed unarmoured legs and arms and faces to the whirring steel-tipped hornets. While a man might look on one arrow in the thigh as no more than a wound, when ten of them criss-crossed then one was bound to open up the artery and drain him dry.

Sivka jerked his head and jigged sideways, muttering, and Ivan was suddenly aware that the Grey Wolf had slipped up silently beside him and was watching with what looked like disapproval. It puzzled him. 'I thought wolves enjoyed battles . . .' he began to say in his most unfeeling voice, then let the rest of the sentence die unspoken. Sounding unfeeling was easy; being so was hard.

'For the sake of the food they leave behind?' the Grey Wolf finished for him. 'Of course we are. But we don't enjoy them when we're far too close. If I wasn't in your service, Prince Ivan, I'd—'

'Bite me?'

'Not straight away,' said the Grey Wolf. 'I would have enough manners to wait.' So that was what unfeeling sounded like when it was sincerely meant, thought Ivan. 'I was going to say, I'd be over the hills and far away until things were more quiet. Like the Firebird.'

'The Firebird hasn't gone,' said Mar'ya Morevna. 'It's waiting, just as I am.'

'Again?' said Ivan.

'Again. Battles are mostly about waiting, Vanya. Before they start; after you give an order but before you've seen if it's been heard or carried out correctly; before you've seen if it's worked.

And waiting for the noises to stop afterwards. That's the hardest waiting of all.'

'But they're being butchered!' shrilled Albrecht von Düsberg for the third time, bouncing in his saddle in a mingled ecstasy of horror and excitement.

'Albrecht,' said *Hauskomtur* von Buxhövden, 'shut up.'

The Grand Master glanced at them both, watched von Düsberg glare and ride off in fury to join the knights, then nodded silent approval to von Buxhövden. This was the waiting time, the hardest part of any battle: an unseen, unheard duel of wills between the two commanders. The winner would be the one who could longer bear the sight of his own troops being slaughtered, for then he could watch what his opponent had chosen to do and counter that move with devastating force. The Treasurer had never commanded more than a small company of knights in all his time with the Order. He had never been in a situation where lives had to be deliberately thrown away so that others could be saved, but such situations occurred in every battle, whether they had been planned for or happened by some grim mischance.

Behind him, further up and further in among the shadows of the trees where they could neither see nor be seen, his cavalry were dismounted and standing by their horses. There had been protests from the knights, but von Salza had been adamant. He knew, from having watched it go wrong more than once in Outremer, that the only knight who could not go barging off when the excitement became too much for his precious pride was a knight out of his charger's saddle.

Forty knights and fifty sergeants; not much of a reserve with which to win a battle, unless that reserve was committed at the proper time. He watched coldly as more Rus spearmen advanced on the beleaguered *Wagenburg*, and responded by releasing his own remaining men-at-arms. There were more protests from his knights when the order went back that the sergeants, and *only* the sergeants, were to mount and hold themselves in readiness.

Von Salza waited, while the infantry battle seethed like a pot stirred by the circling Rus horsemen, and he waited while his mounted sergeants went plunging down the snow-covered slope and into the flanks of the enemy, for all the world like knights, and he watched as every last man that the Rus had sent to his side of the river began falling back. They were retiring in good order and close formation, just the way he wanted.

'I win,' said Hermann von Salza, and released his knights at last.

Prince Ivan saw the line of horsemen emerge from the forest and pause, dressing their ranks and drawing closer together. Though the Rus made little use of fully armoured knights, he knew what they were doing. A charge needed cohesion, above all else: it was the difference between throwing a handful of iron links into someone's face and striking them with the entire chain. These distant, unreal figures, white-robed knights astride white-trappered horses manoeuvring on white snow, were forging that chain even as he watched. There was a flicker of black against all that white as the big shields were fronted and the hammer-headed crosses came on view.

The line began to move, passing from a walk to a run – destriers did not trot, since a man in armour was unable to rise with the gait – to a canter. By the time they levelled out onto the flat river-plain, they were galloping. There was another flicker, hazy and hard to see, as the long lances dropped into rest, and the drumming rumble of the charge began to reverberate between the hills.

There was still a small force of cavalry behind the Princes' tents, bodyguards rather than a military reserve. Unable to bear what he was watching any longer, Ivan raised his right arm and saw their captain signal his response. That was enough. Without waiting for someone like Mar'ya Morevna or Yuriy or anyone else with the authority to make their orders stick, he slashed his arm down and charged out of the defile with the reserve behind him.

Ivan heard Mar'ya Morevna's voice behind him. At first it was the expected cry to stop; but immediately afterwards, in an exasperated tone he knew all too well, it issued orders to someone for his protection. Who, he didn't know. He felt terrified and knew that what he was doing was stupid in the extreme, but at the same time it was swallowed up in the exhilaration of the headlong gallop and the knowledge that he was doing *something*. Light horse in fewer numbers had broken a charge before, when the charge was committed to its target and the light horse was unexpected. It could happen again.

Except that to break a charge, they had to be there. Ivan lowered his head and clamped his knees and began to pull away from the horsemen at his heels until they closed the distance. The ring of wagons went past – *flick* – still boiling with men striving to kill each other. Fleeing Rus spearmen went past him – *flick-flick-flick* – as he and his little company sped down the slope and onto the river ice, hoofs hammering, heart hammering, breath hammering. And now he could actually hear the oncoming knights even over the beat of Sivka's hoofs, a thunderous sound that rolled in the air and shuddered in the ice beneath him. They came across his front with a roar like the ending of the world; he loosed the single arrow he already had on string and saw it fly with those of his companions into the flanks of knightly horses, and then they went crashing into the flank of the knightly line.

It broke the charge.

The long file of knights, crouched over their lances, concentrating on whatever target filled the eyeslits of their helmets, were folded up like a reed pushed firmly against the wall. Their own speed and weight did most of the damage, one man spilling two and even three of his neighbours, man and horse together. Those not thrown from their saddles were thrown from the line of their charge, becoming individuals once more and not the awesome, unstoppable force of less than a minute before. Out of that confusion of bloody snow and kicking horses, maybe twenty knights remained. And they went hunting their tormentors.

Ivan reined Sivka in so hard and fast that the big black horse reared back almost to his haunches, and he suspected it was just as well his noble steed needed every breath for galloping, or such clumsy horsemanship would get a severe piece of his mind.

The nearest Teutonic Knight was even less sympathetic. His horse had skidded on the ice and almost fallen, as so many others had done, but whether from the severity of his hand on the reins of because he had managed to stop the beast before its hoofs went right out from under it, he was still upright. There was already blood on the black-crossed white trapper over the animal's flanks, and it was freshened as the portly knight rammed home his spurs and wrenched his sword out of its scabbard.

Prince Ivan grabbed for the mace hanging from his saddle and pulled it free, not taking time to get his wrist through its loop. If the weapon fell, it fell, but if it wasn't ready to be used, *he* might fall instead. He knew which he preferred.

The knight surged forward at him, all white robes and black crosses and blank iron face beneath that black transverse crest, and Ivan put his shield high to take the sword, swinging his mace into the space beneath. The shield boomed and twisted on his arm; the mace-haft stung his fingers as its head slammed against the hardness of mail and the fat and yielding flesh beneath. There was a confusion of limbs as the knight's head and arms went back and his legs came up, and then he was out of the saddle and rolling on the ground.

Ivan bore left and kept on going. To slacken his pace so near the enemy foot-soldiers was to invite one at least to try his skill with a crossbow bolt, and another squad of knights was already bearing down on him. The long lances dipped and steadied, and he could hear the rumble of the hoofs increase its pace as spurs went home.

'Back!' cried Sivka, turning on the spot in a way that would have required a complicated use of knee and rein had Ivan tried to make his mount perform the same gyration. He did not, however, try to stop him. The horse might not have been a great battle tactician, but he knew when flight made better sense than doing what he was told. He chanced a look behind as Sivka accelerated again. The seven knights were still hot after him, leaning forward down the shafts of their lances as if competing to be first to skewer him. Ivan jammed the mace through his belt, slung his shield behind his shoulder to where it bounced wildly but stayed out of his way, and pulled bow out of case and arrow from quiver. The bow thumped, and one knight was immediately deterred from further pursuit when his horse went out from under him with an arrow in its chest.

Sivka flinched, leapt, squirmed, all at once and mostly in mid-air, so that Ivan almost followed his victim to the ground. He saw why an instant later, as with still just one foot in the stirrup he passed the fat knight he had unhorsed with his mace. The man was back on his feet, staggering with the momentum of the sword-swing that had just failed to take off both of Sivka's front legs.

And then the knight was down again, this time to stay. Three of the seven knights who had been chasing Ivan went down with him in a tangle of yelling men and squealing horses, and a fourth, clearing the crash with a great bound as though over a fence, came down with both fore-hoofs close together on the sprawling German's helm. It went almost completely flat, and the eye-slits vented a gush that stained the snow for yards.

Ivan's mouth twisted in disgust, tempered with unashamed relief that it had not been him. So much for all the stories that horses would not trample people on the ground. If they had to put their feet down and you were underneath, that was just too bad, and once more right of weight would triumph over right of way. He wondered what the black crest fixed crosswise had signified, then dismissed the question in favour of Sivka's raking hand-gallop towards the *gulyagorod*, and wondering what the Hell would happen next.

It happened all too soon, in the shape of a single Teutonic Knight who still had his long lance. The knight came at Ivan no faster than a canter at first, as if he wasn't quite sure what to do. Ivan reached down for another arrow to encourage him to go away, and encountered empty space. The quiver was gone, and a look back told him where. It had come adrift back there where Sivka had evaded the dead knight's sword, and Ivan had been so busy trying not to come adrift himself that he had never felt it go. No-one else was nearby to come to the rescue with a fortuitous arrow out of the blue, and this new knight, definitely not dead, lowered his lance, raised his shield and touched spurs to his horse. Instantly responsive, the destrier's haunches convulsed under the long black-crossed trapper, and it exploded from that leisurely closing canter into a full charge within three strides. The knight gathered his mount between rein and spur and lunged behind the thrusting lance. There was no chance to dodge.

The point took Ivan's shield full in the centre, and it seemed to be the shield rather than the spear that punched him backwards over Sivka's withers. The Teutonic Knight thundered past in a spatter of churned snow, far too close; he had tried to trample as he went by. Ivan rolled over, scrambled onto knees and fists, then sagged helplessly. The swirling, star-filled world inside his head let him rise no further. Beyond the dancing specks of fire that filled his eyes, he could see a blurred knight on a blurred horse come around in a long half-circle, and a blurred bright lance-point lowered to aim straight at his face.

Then something large and loud happened in the world of blurs; a howl and a scream, the sound of breaking wood, receding hoofbeats and a metallic rending noise. After that the blurred world went away for a few seconds, and Ivan opened his eyes to find that he was face-down in wonderful, cold, immobile snow and everything had steadied again. 'They do this sort of thing for fun . . .' he mumbled in disbelief, and scrambled clumsily up again.

The knight lay on his back some thirty feet away, with the broken stump of his lance driven into the ground a little further off. Of his destrier there was no sign, though Sivka was coming closer now that Ivan was back on his feet. The Grey Wolf was beside the knight's body, which explained the black stallion's reluctance to come any nearer without his little master awake to protect him, and from what Ivan could see of the body, the horse was right.

Certainly *he* wasn't going any closer to it than this.

The Grey Wolf ambled up, licking blood off his muzzle. Then he hacked a cough, a sound such as any dog might make with something in its throat, but what the Grey Wolf spat onto the trampled snow were five small rings of mail. Ivan looked at them. Still linked, still shiny, but by the way their edges gleamed, pulled by main force from the dead knight's hauberk. Either that, or bitten.

'Mar'ya Morevna sent me to keep you safe,' said the Grey Wolf, speaking as though his teeth were sore. 'She didn't mention that I had to keep up with you first. Come on, damn you, mount up!' Ivan could see why the Grey Wolf was in a hurry. The Teutonic Knights and sergeants were re-forming their ranks with a practised ease that sent shivers running down his spine. Except for the corpses strewn across the river and on either side of the plain, it was as if nothing had ever happened to disturb their dreadful composure.

The Grey Wolf loped off towards the Russian side of the River Nemen, then turned and looked back at Ivan. 'She wants everybody off the ice,' he said, 'and if you want my opinion—'

'—I wouldn't wait to see why,' Ivan finished, swinging into Sivka's saddle. *Radi Boga!* For God's sake, if it's not the knights, then what? 'I don't need your opinion this time, Volk Volkovich. Because I share it!'

It was as if Mar'ya Morevna had been watching them. Ivan, Sivka and the Grey Wolf were not quite the last off the river, they shared the honour with a half-dozen of Prince Yaroslav's men, but they were still on the bank and nothing like far enough away when all Hell broke loose.

Or all Heaven, because it was as if the sun had come adrift and fallen onto the river. Ivan's shadow crossed the bank and up the ridge and into the woods beyond, and it was sharp-edged black the whole way. He turned, shielding his eyes against the intolerable glare, and watched as steam went up from the Nemen with a whistling roar that shocked the ears. The ice on the river didn't melt; it exploded into huge chunks that reared like a giant's building-blocks and then came crashing back to break off others like them. Everything on the river went into it instead, their tiny cries lost in the bellow of steam and the creaking, screeching sound as the slabs of ice grated together while the river's current, freed from the iron grasp of winter for a while, tumbled away downstream in a ponderous whirling dance that led towards the Baltic.

The Firebird rose like a phoenix from the ruins, curving on wide wings high into the steam-shrouded air, while the heat that washed off it brought a brief, false spring to the valley of the Nemen. Its light grew brighter and then brighter still until there was nothing in the world but flare and shadow.

And then it was gone.

What few knights and sergeants remained were those who had not yet reached the edge of the river, and a commander who was too shocked and sickened to think of going anywhere at all. The sickness and the shock wore off, but it did not bring back the host of men who had gone out to war and not come back again. When Prince Ivan and Mar'ya Morevna carefully crossed the river, well upstream, they dismissed the guards surrounding the Grand Master and stared at him for several minutes, wondering about the pale, handsome face above the clothing with such blatant signs of wealth, and the cross, and the cruelty. There seemed to be nothing they could say, and finally Ivan turned his horse to go. It was von Salza who finally broke the silence.

'You have not killed me,' he said, his Russian clumsy but clear enough, 'and that is a good and Christian act.'

300

'So despite the singing of psalms, and the use of crossbows prohibited against Christians by your Pope, and all the trappings of a Crusade against the infidel, we're Christian after all,' said Ivan. 'Just because we haven't decided to kill you out of hand, as you deserve. How many French or German lords would be so lenient? Perhaps we should take your head off just to be sure.'

Von Salza's face went almost as white as his clothing. 'Neither you nor your witch-wife dare to kill me!' he snarled. 'Know this, both of you: I still command a thousand knights and sergeants. We took Livonia with less.'

'The soft words, and then the threat,' said Mar'ya Morevna. 'Nothing changes.' She tapped her *nagayka* riding-whip gently against her leg and looked von Salza up and down. 'What we dare and what we do are no concern of yours, *Nyemets*. If we had decided you were better dead, you would not be drawing enough breath to defy us.'

'And this is not Livonia,' said Prince Ivan. 'We are not the Prusiskai barbarians. Your thousand knights and sergeants could not be assembled from the other castles of your Order before the spring, and by then we would be ready to meet them with ten thousand.'

He shifted in his saddle, leaning forward in the same gesture of scrutiny that his father had employed a thousand, thousand times, and from the cool eyes shadowed by the iron rim of his helmet to the cool steel of the mace he carried crosswise like a sceptre, he looked the Prince that birth and rank – and duty, honour, obligation and marriage – had made him. 'Best you remember what I say, Grand Master of the Teutonic Order,' said *Velikiy Knyaz' Tsarevich* Ivan Aleksandrovich Khorlovskiy. 'If you come back, we will be waiting. We will always be waiting. And next time, you will die a worse death than the knight you sent to kill us.'

'Indeed.' Von Salza glared at Ivan, fighting down black fury. In another place and time, he would have released Dieter Balke to take revenge for the slight in whatever way that strange and terrible man deemed proper. Except that Balke was dead, and now he knew who had killed him. There was a new, hate-filled respect in the way he eyed the Rus prince.

'It is only because I am as you name me, a Christian knight and a leader of Christian knights' – he signed them both with the reversed crucifix of the Romans – 'that I do not prove the lack of difference between one Eastern barbarian and another. But I am also an Archduke of the Holy Roman Empire, and I take oath by it. From where the sun now stands, I swear that your land – and all the lands of the Rus – will be at peace and untroubled by the knights of the Order from this day forward. For my lifetime. I can say no more than that.'

Ivan glanced at Mar'ya Morevna. 'Do you believe him?' he said, with an edge to his voice that suggested he had already made up his own mind on the subject.

She shook her head. 'Words, words,' she said. 'Easily spoken, easily forgotten. Nor would I trust him to regard such an oath as binding. He took pains not to swear by his cross.' Von Salza gave her a look that made Ivan glad the man had been disarmed, but Mar'ya Morevna seemed not to notice. Instead she pointed her *nagayka* whip at the Grand Master and narrowed her eyes. Her lips moved silently.

Then the double lashes of the whip cracked as she snapped it downward, and for an instant Ivan could see a cloud of blue-white sparks swirling like gnats on the cold air. They struck Hermann von Salza squarely in the face so that he reeled in his saddle, then flared brightly and vanished.

'But I believe him now,' said Mar'ya Morevna. Her voice was bleak. 'You called me a witch, Grand Master, and that was scarcely polite. I am a sorcerer. And this is a whip. A means of inflicting pain. You and your knights had best not return to Russia. Otherwise . . .' She ran the lashes of the *nagayka* between her fingers so that more sparks dripped from them, sizzling like liquid fire. Von Salza gasped and shuddered, clutching at his head with both hands as though those drips of fire were searing the brain within his skull. 'I want peace in the land before my children are born, and if I have to hurt you before you hurt them, so be it.'

Prince Ivan's head snapped around, and he stared at his wife with a huge smile threatening the stern gravity of his expression. Then he raised his hand to sign the Grand Master with a blessing of the life-giving cross. He did it in the Russian style; then repeated the gesture backwards, in the manner of the Roman Church. 'Live long, if you live in peace,' he said. 'And may your God go with you.'

At a gesture from Ivan, the guards returned and escorted Hermann von Salza away to where the remnant of his army were already trudging back towards the border. Mar'ya Morevna watched him go, carefully plaiting the lashes of her whip around its handle before thrusting it through her belt. Ivan, however, was watching her.

'You didn't tell me anything about children,' he said.

Mar'ya Morevna smiled at him. 'I wasn't certain myself until today, even though being sick five mornings in a row should have suggested something besides bad rations. And as for telling you, this morning you had enough to think about.'

'How do you know?' This time Mar'ya Morevna laughed out loud. 'I mean, are you sure?'

'Vanya, most women are sure. I'm a sorcerer. I'm *certain*.'

'But when. . . ?'

She leaned from her saddle and patted Ivan's arm, grinning wickedly. 'With you, my loved, it's hard to be sure. But I think it was that first night in the Summer Country.'

Ivan shook his head, still only half-believing what he had heard; then he stared at Mar'ya Morevna. 'For Heaven's sake, you've just been in a *battle*! You must be exhausted! Shouldn't you lie down for a rest?'

'Ivan,' Mar'ya Morevna started to say, 'it's going to be months before I need—' Then she smiled and shrugged. Not even the fairest Princess in all the Russias could object to being pampered, just a little . . .

Posleslovi
(A final word)

Despite Prince Ivan's blessing, Hermann von Salza did not live long. He died three years later, but during those years he kept his word, to the letter, to the death, and perhaps just a little beyond. The people of the Rus had what they wished: peace and plenty for the most part, although for those who wanted more, that was granted too.

History tells even to this day of Aleksandr Nevskiy, and how he defeated the Teutonic Knights in a battle on the ice. Of what other lords and princes might have fought beside him, there is no mention. It was Aleksandr Nevskiy's own chronicler who first set down the tale, and he recorded no other names.

Hermann von Salza went into the grave in the year 1239, and the peace he promised died with him; for in Spring of the next year, the Tatars of the Golden Horde rode back into Russia . . .

Bibliography

AFANAS'EV, A. N. (trans. Guterman, N.), *Russian Fairy Tales/Narodnye russkiye skazki* (Pantheon 1945/Random House 1973).

AL-AZRED, A., *Kitab al-Azif/The Necronomicon* (restricted-print facsimile no. 290 of 348, Owlswick Press 1973).

BROWN, R. A., *Castles, A History and Guide* (Blandford Press 1980).

CHAMBERLAIN, L., *The Food and Cooking of Russia* (Allen Lane 1982/Penguin 1983, 1988).

CHILD, H., *Heraldic Design* (Bell & Hyman 1979).

COE, M. D., *Swords and Hilt Weapons* (Weidenfeld & Nicolson 1989).

De BAILLIE du CHAT, K., *Medieval Costume* (Raymond's Quiet Press 1978).

De ROSA, P., *Vicars of Christ – The Dark Side of the Papacy* (Bantam 1988/Corgi 1990).

DOWNING, C., *Russian Tales and Legends* (Oxford University Press 1956).

FENNEL, J., *The Crisis of Medieval Russia 1200–1304* (Longman 1988).

FRAZER, J. G., *The Golden Bough* (Macmillan 1978).

FUNCKEN, L. & F., *The Age of Chivalry parts 1 & 2* (Ward Lock 1980).

GOLDSTEIN, D., *A Taste of Russia* (Robert Hale 1985/Sphere 1987).

GOLYNETS, S. V. (trans. Kochov, G. A.), *Ivan Bilibin* (Aurora/Pan 1981).

GRAVETT, C., *German Medieval Armies* (Osprey 1985).

GRIMAL, P. (ed.), *Larousse World Mythology* (Hamlyn 1965, 1989).

GUIRAND, F. (ed.), *New Larousse Encyclopedia of Mythology* (Hamlyn 1968, 1974).

HEATH, I., *The Crusades* (Patrick Stephens 1980).

KEEN, M., *Chivalry* (Yale University Press 1984, 1987).

LONGWORTH, P., *The Cossacks* (Constable 1969/Sphere 1971).

NEUBECKER, O., *Heraldry: Sources, Symbols and Meaning* (Macdonald/Black Cat 1988).

NICOLLE, D., *The Crusades* (Osprey 1988).

OBOLENSKY, D. & STONE, N., *The Russian Chronicles* (Random Century 1990).

PAYNE-GALLWEY, R., *The Crossbow* (The Holland Press 1990).

PRAWER, J., *The World of the Crusaders* (Quadrangle 1972).

RIASANOVSKY, N. V., *A History of Russia* (Oxford University Press 1969).

RILEY-SMITH, J., *The Crusades: A Short History* (Athlone Press 1987, 1990).

RILEY-SMITH, J., *The Atlas of the Crusades* (Times Books 1991).

RUDORFF, R., *Knights and the Age of Chivalry* (Viking 1974).

RUNCIMAN, S., *A History of the Crusades, Volume III* (Cambridge University Press 1954/Penguin 1978).

TENBROCK, R.-H. (trans. Dine, P. J.), *Eine Geschichte Deutschlands/A History of Germany* (Max Hueber Verlag and Ferdinand Schöningh 1968/Longman 1969).

TOMASĚVÍC, N.B. & VARTABEDIJAN, M., *Russia* (Bracken Books 1989).

TREECE, H., *The Crusades* (Bodley Head 1962/Souvenir Press 1978).

UDEN, G. and BAYNES, P., *A Dictionary of Chivalry* (Thomas Y. Crowell Company 1968).

Von FRANZ, M.L., *Shadow and Evil in Fairytales* (Spring Publications Inc. 1983).

WARNER, E., *Heroes, Monsters and Otherworlds from Russian Mythology* (Peter Lowe 1985).

WHEELER, P., *Russian Wonder Tales* (The Century Co. 1912; P. Wheeler 1940/1946; Thomas Yoseleff 1957).

WISE, T., *The Knights of Christ* (Osprey 1984).

ZVORYKIN, B. V. (ed. Onassis, J.), *The Firebird and other Russian Fairy Tales* (Viking 1978).